Anna Maria D[...] [...] [t]o a family of Italia[n] [...] [vill]ages of the Abruzzo[...] [...] the humanities, she [...] [...] [wh]ere she worked as a cadet journalist by day and a violinist in the local symphony orchestra by night. In 1978 she returned to Australia where her writing on film and her column in the *Sydney Morning Herald*'s *Good Weekend* magazine became well known. She has written several opera libretti including *Bride of Fortune* (Perth Festival 1991), and is currently writing fiction full-time. She lives in the inner-west of Sydney with her husband, a violinist, their two school-aged daughters and their baby son.

SONGS

of the

SUITCASE

ANNA MARIA DELL'OSO

flamingo

An imprint of HarperCollins*Publishers*

Excerpt from the poem *Il Grande Passo della Mia Vita*
(The Great Step of My Life) by Lidia Valerio Dell'oso, 1996.
Excerpt from *Filipino Women: Challenges & Responses*,
Ethnic Affairs Commission of NSW, 1992.
Excerpt from *Benzo Junkie* by Beatrice Faust, Penguin, 1993.

Flamingo

An imprint of HarperCollins*Publishers*, Australia

First published in Australia in 1998
Reprinted in 1999, 2001
by HarperCollins*Publishers* Pty Limited
ABN 36 009 913 517
A member of the HarperCollins*Publishers* (Australia) Pty Limited Group
http://www.harpercollins.com.au

HarperCollins*Publishers*
25 Ryde Road, Pymble, Sydney, NSW 2073, Australia
31 View Road, Glenfield, Auckland 10, New Zealand
77–85 Fulham Palace Road, London, W6 8JB, United Kingdom
Hazelton Lanes, 55 Avenue Road, Suite 2900, Toronto, Ontario M5R 3L2
and 1995 Markham Road, Scarborough, Ontario M1B 5M8, Canada
10 East 53rd Street, New York NY 10022, USA

National Library of Australia Cataloguing-in-Publication data:

Dell'oso, Anna Maria.
    Songs of the suitcase.
    ISBN 0 7322 6456 1
    I.Title
A823.3

Accordion supplied by Christiaan Dolislager of Accordions 'n Folk,
Petersham, Sydney
Cover photo by Brett Odgers
Printed and bound in Australia by Griffin Press on 79gsm Bulky Paperback White

8 7 6 5 4 3   01 02 03 04

Contents

Acknowledgments

The author would like to thank the following people and institutions: the Literature Board of the Australia Council, Peter Bishop and the Varuna Writers' Centre in Katoomba, Gordon Darling, Jill Hickson, Joe Eisenberg, Janis Wilton, Belinda Cotton, Laura Mecca and the Italian Historical Society of Victoria, Ugo Ceresoli, Louise Bayutti, Teresa and Livio Benedetti, Anne-Marie Elias, Dr Diana Cavuoto-Glenn, Paul Thompson, Glenn Hunter, Sue and Sam Saffir, Lidia and Donato Dell'oso, Michelle Marshall, Lisa Bryant and Deborah Saffir.

And most of all David Saffir.

These stories have appeared in different forms in the following publications: *Love by Arrangement* in *Loves* edited by Jean Bedford, Angus & Robertson, 1995; *Song of The Suitcase* in *Family Pictures* edited by Beth Yahp, Angus & Robertson, 1994; *Harvest Day* in *Motherlove* edited by Debra Adelaide, Random House, 1996; *Unravelling* in *Cutting the Cord* edited by Debra Adelaide, Random House, 1998; *Homeland* in *Homeland* edited by George Papaellinas, Allen & Unwin, 1991; *Zia Pina* in *Growing Up Italian in Australia*, State Library of NSW, 1993; *Harbour* in *Harbour* edited by George Papaellinas, Picador, 1993; *The King of The Accordion* was first published in 1995 as part of the King of The Accordion Travelling Exhibition by the New England Regional Arts Museum, commissioned by Joseph Eisenberg and sponsored by the Gordon Darling Foundation. *Unravelling* is dedicated to the memory of Stephen Lardner and Lachlan Marshall Lardner.

For David, Rebecca, Tamara and Benjamin

Part One

Ballads

Love by Arrangement

I am a researcher into arranged love, a kind of private love detective specialising in the marital relations of minorities. I dig around at the bottom of family-contracted marriages, trying to find stories, secrets, motivations, outcomes – the manoeuvres of hate and of love. I take marriages home and prise them apart and try (perhaps unwisely) to shake the religion and culture from them and see what's left – a love match in disguise, a fortunate but dull compatibility, a resigned formal partnership (that can quickly flare into violence) where the wife does this and the husband does that and they meet through the children and the culture. Strangely enough, after a while, the sorrows of enforced marriage look similar to those of self-chosen marriage – the generations of women who go to their graves never having enjoyed sex, the jealousy between husbands and wives, the blood and bruises of a husband's beatings, the suicide and murder-suicide, the possession and abduction of children. There are brutal Western romances and passionate arranged matches, yet whether a couple finds love or finds hate, it is crucial who makes the arrangements in the house of love.

I save cuttings from newspapers like, '*A father plotted to have his seventeen-year-old daughter murdered after she had "disgraced" her family by dating an Australian boy in defiance of an impending arranged marriage, a Melbourne court heard yesterday*' and '*Suitable match for my daughter, age twenty-one years four months, 1.63 m, slim and beautiful, in travel and tourism, caste no bar*' or '*An educated Hindu Bengali family, well-settled in Australia, seek a suitable, homely and well-educated girl for their twenty-four-year-old 179 cm Electrical Engineer son.*'

By day I trudge around mosques and churches; I drink glasses of Coca-Cola and cups of coffee (Turkish, Greek, Lebanese, Italian, American and Nescafé) with women in faraway suburbs. I knock on the doors of fringe religious houses (or cults, as the tabloids call them) in streets where the lawn-mowing neighbours stop to look up at me and when I leave a breeze of Luxaflex blinds follows me down the road. I take trains to places I have to look up in the *Melways* and the *Gregory's*; I don't drive my car because I want to eavesdrop on the conversations of headscarfed Muslim schoolgirls. I make phone calls to people who are not sure they want to talk to me; I have to get past husbands with a polite 'Is Leonie there ... Can I speak to Fatima? Is Nada home ... Maria ... Christoula?'.

I store conversations in shoeboxes marked *Cross-Cultural (Filipino)*, *Cross-Cultural (Islamic)*, *Proxy Marriage, 1950s (Greek and Italian)*, *Family Arranged Marriage (Indian, Arabic, Assorted Southern European)* *International Mass Marriage: Unification Church*, *Immigration and Welfare Marriage: Students*. The voices are mostly from ethnic and refugee communities or religious fundamentalists or cult movement women – quiet seekers of utopian answers to a messy world – and a range of working suburban women, the train-catchers, mortgage-repayers, kid-raisers and supermarket *schleppers* invisible to feminists redefining gender and documenting the end of marriage and the death of the nuclear family. Though I once got a letter from a self-described 'university educated, white Protestant middle-class Anglo-Saxon Australian woman' who said her family forced her into an arranged marriage. She wrote:

'I succumbed to the pressure (from my parents). No doubt, as much as anything, I married (the man) to escape the rigours of a demanding, exacting mother whom I could never please, never satisfy. By following her choice, I knew I did not marry for love, but I was sufficiently old-fashioned and dutiful to believe that if respect was maintained love could grow.

But of course, the marriage failed ... Having the responsibility of a baby did not help, he became worse ... I was denied the use of transport, of a phone or contact with family and friends ... He threatened to shoot me.

I spoke to my mother about my fears. Her advice: "You are his wife. It is his prerogative to shoot you if he wishes.'"

It can be exhausting and harrowing to gather so many different testimonies to arrangements in the house of love. I switch on television soapies, supposedly to mainline some no-think junk but really to plug back into my own Western Hollywood culture of helpless sex – that hormone dictatorship of love with which I am so comfortable and familiar. 'Days of Our Lives' is my favourite because virtually every scene is about The Couple and their conflict between romantic fantasy and an inconvenient fate. Fantasy always wins. 'Days' is like bad Chekhov: pairs of lovers frustrate each other over a hundred episodes while no one cares that the plot is being cut down into crappy secret societies and amnesiac twins.

Eventually I slink off to work alone from my home office, well away from the newly delineated sex-roles and the kids of my own marriage (a cross-cultural love match which was something of a revolution in one generation, as my own parents married by proxy shortly after the World War II and met each other for the first time as adults in Australia). Into the night I sit with a pair of earphones plugged into a Sanyo talkbook:

'My mother-in-law was forced to marry someone but close to the wedding day she ran away because she loved my father-in-law. There was a terrible scandal but they managed to marry anyway. Even as an old man he'd say, "rub my back, Zahra" and they'd go into the bathroom and have a bath together ... It embarrassed me when they did things like that but they were great together. He used to sing her love songs. "You play this when I die, Zahra," he'd say to her, "Because I want them all to know how much I love you ..."'

I pause, rewind, I change tapes, I fast-forward: what was that again?

'...I had a contract upon marriage of fifty thousand Lebanese lira and it was agreed I would get forty thousand if the marriage did not work. Ten thousand was given to me in advance to spend on whatever I wanted: furniture, gold, clothes. I put three thousand Australian dollars as deposit on a single-fronted home in Mortdale ... I remember when he wrote to me, my friends at work – they were Greek, Chinese and Australian – said I was crazy to go to Lebanon and accept "someone you don't know". But he was my cousin, he was part of my family. You know, one of my sisters fell in love and got married, an ideal marriage, a love match. But she divorced after her first baby. They split up when their baby was only three months old ... postnatal depression, financial problems ... they were both nineteen ... they couldn't handle it ...'

In our 'Days of Our Lives' culture, arranged marriages are pushed to the fringe of our consciousness, where they are regarded as bizarre or medieval. But they also fascinate us, probably because they threaten the popular view of relations between the sexes – the idea that marriage is a purely personal matter that mostly revolves around a helpless and obsessive sexual attraction. The arranged marriage can brutally reveal the truth about the economic, psycho-social and sexual relationships between men and women – a truth that gets in the way of eyes meeting across a crowded room.

It was a steamy afternoon. I was buried in photographs and micro-cassette tapes. '... *so we married in New York, in Madison Square Garden, and when we saw each other, I realised I was with a person I didn't know ...*' I was replaying '*person I didn't know*' when a shadow fell across my computer screen. I swivelled around. In the doorway was a slight woman with cropped black hair wearing Blundstone boots and a black skirt. She handed me a takeaway cappuccino and a bag from which peeked a fat croissant.

'Thought you might be hungry,' she said. I uncapped the coffee lid and took a swig. 'Thanks,' I replied. 'So what can I do for you?'

'No names,' she said. 'Just think of me as a client.'

'Okay,' I shrugged. 'How can I help you?'

In the light I could see she was, as they say in welfare circles, of Non-English Speaking Background (NESB) –

Eurasian, young, maybe in her mid-twenties. She handed me two photographs. The first was a coloured snapshot from the late 1960s of a middle-aged southern European man with his arm around a tiny laughing Asian girl, maybe Filipino, Vietnamese or Thai, it was hard to tell. The other was a scratched sepia-tinted studio shot from the 1920s. A heavy-lidded dark-eyed bride in an ankle-length silk wedding dress stood with her hand on the shoulder of a moustached older man. It was from the days when husbands and wives from Mediterranean villages did not pose against each other's shoulders in the Hollywood 'sweethearts' position. In this earthy time and place, photography was a grave and expensive ceremonial recording. It did not try to hide that the patriarch came first. He sat on a wicker chair with his legs slightly loose and his suit sleeves comfortable. She stood demure and straight beside him.

'Your grandmother?' I asked.

'Let's just call her an ancestress of mine.'

'An arranged marriage?'

The Client smiles. 'Aren't all marriages arranged? Isn't that what makes them marriages – the arrangements?'

I shrug my shoulders. This is my problem. What is an arranged marriage anyway? Is living together in an inner-city terrace before deciding to get married any less arranged by local custom than a father approached by a suitor who is secretly favoured by the marriageable girl? Is an arranged marriage mostly courtship rituals?

Is subtle matchmaking by your friends or a commercial agency an arranged marriage?

'So you want me to find out her story? Who she married, why, what kind of life she had?'

'I know her story. Greek island girl, poor, sixteen, married off to a forty-year-old alcoholic widower. It was a bad match but all she could get because she had epileptic fits as a child and people said she had "bad blood".'

The girl glanced at the picture of the late 1960s couple. 'I know their story too. Four months of love letters from Kalgoorlie to the Philippines. He sent her an engagement ring in the mail. She left him when I was three and we spent years moving from place to place hiding from him.'

'So you're well informed about marriage,' I said.

'Maybe. But I need a different sort of information about them.'

'Such as?' I asked, although I knew. It was the same thing everybody wanted to know.

'I've had some thoughts about it.' The Client handed me a piece of paper. It was crumpled but the writing was neat and thoughtful:

'Can you love someone you have never met? Can you make married love by arrangement, taking into account morality, religion, propriety, good sense, the transfer of money and land, the new world for the Third World, and the happiness of families? Can you have sex with this stranger and make room in the bed for them all – your parents, his parents, the Imam, the Priests, the Reverend Moon, the Department of Immigration, his mates, your poor family in debt at home in the Philippines or the gossips in a brick-veneer sixteenth century village in the Australian suburbs who sniff out every change to your "reputation"?

'You can. Of course you can. So many have.'

I folded it up and handed it back to the Client. I stared at the snapshot of her parents. 'What else have you got?' I asked.

The Client handed me a package. It was a mail order catalogue of Asian women from Jasmine of International Professional Marriage Consultants. The covering note said: '*Thank you for your enquiry. I now enclose a small number of photographs and details of some of our ladies. If there is someone you like, please phone me immediately so I can help you to meet her. If not, please also phone and I will send more photographs and details.*'

I flicked through the pictures: they were passport-sized head-and-shoulder portraits of Asian women in sweet schoolteacher dresses, each with an identifying number stamped like a tattoo on her chest.

I matched 'SSI 32' with her profile statement. 'I'm Indonesian, so that gives me a head start,' she jokes. 'Seriously I am thirty-two, five-foot-four tall and nicely average in build. Friends say I have a lovely smile and I'm

11

very friendly with others. I do have a little girl, now twenty months old, so you would have to accept and love her as I do ...'

ABP 35 caught my eye. She had a vulnerable look that made me wonder whether she had made it safely into Western first-world marriage. Older than most of the others, ABP 35 wore a frilly blouse with a string of pearls around her neck. Leaning stiffly against a tree, her eyes and her smile seemed to go in different directions, as if she was perpetually watching her back. 'I am Filipino, thirty-six this year, five-foot-four in height,' she writes bluntly. 'I love being at home, watching some television, gardening, listening to music, cooking good meals and keeping everywhere really clean and tidy. I come from the country, so someone who lives in a small town or in the country would suit me best.'

I'd read an Ethnic Affairs Commission report on Filipino women in Australia which revealed that '*those (women in mixed marriages) living in rural areas most often live in mining towns.*' I had a vision of ABP 35 married to a middle-aged stranger with little education and a dislike of aggressive bitchy Australian women, (like his ex-wife), ethnics and Aboriginals. I wondered if ABP 35's dream of 'the countryside' included red dust and corrugated iron under a temperature of forty degrees and the slamming down of housekeeping money by a husband who wouldn't take kindly to half of it going to her family back home. '*To date,*' said the 1992 report, '*eleven Filipino women have reportedly died violently in Australia. In most of these eleven killings, the Australian husband has been convicted or charged with the murder of his Filipino wife ... In November 1991, the Thai community in Sydney was shocked by the first publicly known killing of a Thai woman by her Australian husband. The victim had only been in Australia for a year.*'

For a moment I had an unprofessional longing to ferret out ABP 35's name and phone number, to ring and ask her, 'Are you all right, are you coping, is it okay, are you still alive?'

There are people who say, reasonably enough, that an arranged marriage is preferable to romantic love because it takes into account many other factors than a transient sexual and emotional infatuation – the 'falling in love' so important to Western culture.

But in practice, this careful selection of compatibilities and sensibilities is a luxury in a world where 'the increasing commodification of women' can basically come down to the choice of taking your chances as an exported bride or working in the commercial sex industry. That's when the mail order arranged marriage exposes the exploitative relationship between first-world and third-world countries. Marriage is still very much a means to economic survival. Men and women don't have equal powers or rights, particularly among the less educated peoples of countries torn apart by poverty or war. A girl is married off – or she herself may bravely seek an arranged and/or cross-cultural marriage – for the economic, social and personal benefit of her family. There is very little regard to her real chances of happiness or to her human rights.

I filed the mail order brides away. It was the collection of smiles that unnerved me – Revlon lips parted hesitantly to any stranger to thumb over and scrutinise, compare, reject or masturbate to.

'Have you read the latest copy of *Lilith*?,' I said to the Client. 'It's like *Quintanales* said: "To find us squabbling over who may or may not be called a feminist, who may or may not join or take part in this or that, is a privilege, as most women in the world eat shit."'

'And my foremothers were probably first among them.'

'But you think there's something else involved, right?'

'Look,' she said. Her hands were shaking her car keys. 'I just want to know one thing.'

Here it comes, I thought. No matter what we know or learn to understand, analyse, justify and forgive of the truth, it seems we all hope we are the product of at least one moment of joy – that we came into being when a man and a woman joyfully tumbled on a bed and whipped up the orgasm that shot us into the world. If it wasn't like that, we feel ashamed and cheated.

The Client was no exception. 'I just want to know,' she said, throwing me the file as she left, 'did my beginnings ever have anything to do with love?'

Later I lay out the mail order brides' photographs in a row on my filing cabinet. Next to them I place my mother and father's portraits, separately taken to send to each other before they decided to marry as relative strangers. There is a kind of love that is made by photographs and distance. A decision to look for a husband or a wife is made. A photograph is sent out across the seas.

The women in my family have strange wedding photographs. Brides of fortune and of war, they were nearly always alone at the altar or the registry office, promising themselves to unknown or barely-known men in America, Canada, Argentina and Australia. They found suitors by family reputation, connection, arrangement and negotiation and they agreed to marry them through a long series of engagement letters, which they took on board ship with them, bound up in ribbon and wrapped in their dowry sheets and linens.

Sometimes the brides are posed against framed photographs of the men they married by proxy. He can't be there in person but the bride's in-laws have garlanded flowers around the groom's face. This has an iconic effect, making him look like one of those pictures of the martyred dead that mourners take to political funerals. The artificial flowers around his head highlight the fragility of it all.

Sometimes the brides are lined up outside the village church with all their family and friends. These new paper wives look marooned among the people they know they will never see again – the gamble of love and husband and a future in '*l'America*' had to be paid for with the blocking of every escape route back to the house of the father and the unpicking of every thread of the communal life that supported them. Some of these proxy brides, knowing it was a paper marriage, hadn't gone to the expense of the elaborate bridal gown that was promised them since birth but dressed rather in pre-War suits. Only a lace veil revealed them as brides.

Some struggle with this defeat and triumph – their great day as *La Sposa* with nothing, not even a bridegroom. Maria Giovanna – Z'a Mari (Zia Maria) – was married off because her oldest brother wished to get married himself and his fiancée (powerful with her considerable dowry) didn't like the idea of the unmarried sister remaining in what should be the wife's domain. The fiancée said it was because of the burden of another dependent, although this would have been unlikely as Z'a Mari worked in the fields like a man. Still, I could sympathise with the smart bride. Marriage was a make-or-break lifetime business for a woman and to leave an unmarried sister in the home – and her childhood home at that – would be bad domestic politics. It would be like a new chief executive officer failing to sack the old middle management and install his own loyal team.

So a marriage was quickly arranged for the stolid girl. Carrying a bunch of white paper roses, she made her way up the hill to La Chiesa della Madonna di Loreto, where the women of the village were married, whether their husbands were there or not. Years later, my mother, remembering her own lonely journey to the church on the top of the hill, wrote a poem that could have been spoken by any of those brides of fortune.

On that cold starry morning,
I regretted having signed those papers.
For the last time
I climb down the hills of my village
Like a child.
The square is filled with murmuring people.
The car arrives, a kiss, a hug,
And I shed a few tears, as do my friends and
    relatives.
I sit down, my thoughts in turmoil.
I can feel my courage leave me.
From the window of the car,
I see the last houses of the village
Blur past me under the stars.
We cross the river and I no longer see anyone.
Farewell my home, my village, goodbye.
I can only hope I will return to you in better
    times.
Mother of God, I don't know where I'm going
Nor what kind of people I will meet there.

I always hated that print of Z'a Mari walking painfully along the steep incline, a photo she unaccountably kept gilt-framed on her commode. 'You look like a dag in that dress,' I once said to her as a rude teenager. The old lady shrugged her shoulders. '*Eh, va bene, okai*,' she retorted, tweaking at my miniskirt. 'You look like a prostitute in yours.'

'Why didn't you wear white?' I said.

'Why don't you get married?' she countered.

'He doesn't look like Frank,' I said. Frank (Fortunato) was Z'a Mari's husband, dead for several years.

Z'a Mari shrugged her shoulders.

'Fortunato wasn't there,' Z'a Mari said. 'He was in Australia. How could a girl go halfway round the world unmarried? *Sole le puttane fanno così*. What if he decided he didn't want you any more? No, no. I didn't let anyone make me a fool. I married him by proxy. Aldo stood in for him because my father was dead. Fortunato came from Lanciano; it was my father who knew his uncle, old Zi' Gennaro di Svizzero.'

'You're kidding,' I said, repelled. 'You mean you married a guy you didn't know? Just from a photograph?'

'No! *Ma sei stupida*?' said Z'a Mari angrily. 'Everyone knew his family: good people, hard workers. I was no beauty. I had no education. I was only a *contadina*, good *solo per zappare la terra*. What did I want? *Un signore, il principe di Monaco*? I didn't see him because of the war. Then after the war he was in Australia, working *a la*

Quinsalan', cutting the sugar cane. He send me a photo, very nice, taken *a la Luna Park* in Melbourne with your father. They worked *a la Holden* then, *a la Williamstown*, you know.'

I knew the picture Z'a Mari was putting together for me wasn't right, that it was heavy with things unsaid, resentment, threat, blood, soil, some kind of love that wasn't love – the hard black love of the family women I knew. I didn't question her further because I didn't want to be like them, the crones with the kerchiefs, the knee-high Coles support stockings and gold teeth. Nor did I want to be like my mother, obsessed with what people thought – *gli altri, la bella figura* – and anxious about my every move.

I determined not only to fall in love but to allow myself to be sentimental and over-dramatic into the bargain. Why not? I saw it as a luxury of material wealth, like second bathrooms and dishwashers. Romantic love was a cultural product that I aspired to have, like books, music, education and equality between the sexes. I hoped that the more in love I was, the more I could escape the hard earth of my blood and bones.

What these black gnarled old women knew about love, I didn't want to know.

The more stories and tapes I send the Client, the more introspective she gets. 'It seems there are two schools of thought about love,' she writes to me. 'The first says that love by definition cannot be contained by marriage or such commitments – indeed that marriage is the hand that squeezes at the throat of love. As Emma Goldman writes: "*Marriage and love have nothing in common; they are as far apart as the poles and are in fact antagonistic to each other.*" The second says that at some point love must lean against reality – that love is forced out of its narcissism by marriage or the marriage-like commitment and so, in conflict, grows to reveal itself as love. Which do you believe is right?'

I fax back that I don't know, but maybe the truth is part of both – love is wild and it is cultivated. At the end of the day, it probably doesn't matter which kind of love you pick. It only matters that you get the conditions for it right.

I rock down the railway line to visit a mosque in a suburb that I can't name for fear of offending the religious women who have agreed to see me.

Every community has its troubles. Yesterday I got a phone call saying I might be able to speak to an eighteen-year-old Arabic girl who had been abandoned at the airport with a one-way ticket home by her Australian-born arranged husband, who was having an affair with someone else. Another girl, a Greek convert to Islam, was rejected by her reluctant arranged husband on a pretext so he could claim the twenty-five thousand dollar dowry his family settled on her. On a lighter note, I'm following the delicate and intricate courtship of an Arabic-Australian girl by a suitor tipped to win her and her family's favour. If so, I might be invited to a forty thousand dollar wedding.

I look out at the station platform. Feminists from the professional classes say that marriage no longer exists. Dale Spender wrote that wives, in the form we most commonly know, are really things of the past. Yet from where I am sitting, wedged between baby strollers and Big Fresh bags, it seems that reports of the death of marriage (and de-facto marriage is, by definition, marriage) have been greatly exaggerated. I suspect that marriage and family exists all right for the ethnic girls laughing and poking and hitting each other in the rush to get a seat. If they are growing up anything like I did then marriage exists as a bloodline into the family, which is the bloodline of culture and identity and not just a simple matter of the 'oppressive patriarchal institution' that drives my Anglo feminist friends to psychotherapy, or to long stints away from their repressive bourgeois nuclear relatives.

It might disappoint those excellent women who become 'feminist teachers working on behalf of ethnic minority girls, teaching them the errors of their cultural backgrounds and the winning ways of the mainstream' to know how stubborn these 'minority women and girls from Non-English Speaking Backgrounds' are about their

21

'oppressive patriarchal cultures', their outmoded peasant attachment to family and clan, their 'internalised sexisms' and their obstinate belief in their abilities to wash the grains of love out of the gold-rush miner's pan of marriage – and that includes traditional and family-arranged marriage.

In wanting to be married and to have families, we wog girls so inclined want to plug into all the blood-flow of the cultural connections, all the riches of partnership. Romantic choice in marriage is the revolution. It might mean going outside culture and custom, venturing into the wilds of cross-cultural marriage. In wanting love, we want what the rich, the well-connected and the beautiful have always had as they broke the rules throughout the centuries in adulteries, affairs, re-marriages and same-sex liaisons. In a wealthy industrialised Australia, with its laws protecting the rights of women, we women of NESB can take what our foremothers could have only grasped through power, wealth, social position and sexual allure: we want the luxury of unpunishable and frankly sexual love, and we want it set into the wedding ring. A feminism that sees such marriage as irrelevant and family connection as anachronistic is not interested in the real lives of most of the world's women but in abstract theoretical scholarship and the power aspirations of an elite.

I get off the train, holding the door open for a Muslim mother of three so that she can push her pram through and hold her toddlers as they jump the large and dangerous gap between the Tangara train and the platform. 'Mind the gap', as the station signs say. Mind the gap.

Dolls are a girl's puppet theatre of love. In 1964 the prima donna of the playground was Malibu Barbie. Under the kitchen table, I got my cheap Japanese imitation Barbie ready for a date with Ken – mini sun dress, hat, wicker basket and tartan blanket. I had to imagine Ken and speak all his lines because at that stage I didn't have a Ken doll. Below the table was the sand, the sun and Barbie doing the Twist; above me, the smell of coffee and *savoiardi* and women's voices murmuring like the far off sound of the sea.

'For more than a year I was lucky. But every month he was upset. Was there something wrong with me? With him? He was worried that he had waited too long to be married, that he was too old. He took me to doctors and I pretended to be upset that I had not conceived. But all the time, I was smiling inside: thank God, thank God, thank God ...

'I got pregnant straight away. I was sick for months. I didn't know what to expect, I had no sisters here, no mother. Just after I got home from hospital with my son, I'd look at the Australian girls kissing their boyfriends on trams, holding hands all lovey-dovey, giggling and being silly and I wanted to vomit. I wanted to slap them. "You wait, you stupid bitches," I wanted to say to them. "You just wait and see what's in store for you at the end of those caresses!"'

My mother's friends pushed aside their cups. There was the rustle of paper; photographs were passed around to exclamation and scrutiny. 'It's a love match,' said the women. 'They are so happy. She gave him a watch, a ring. He bought her a three-bedroom house and a washing machine. They're so happy. So much in love. *Come Romeo e Giulietta.*'

Under the table, Barbie kissed an invisible Ken on the tartan blanket.

I used to go without permission to Susie Chen's house. We both lived in dark little semi-detached houses at the ungentrified ends of streets behind K Junction. Susie and her big sister Rose lived with their Chinese cleaning lady mother, who, like my parents, didn't come home from work till after five. That meant more than two hours of unsupervised play at each other's forbidden houses.

Because of our Barboids, Susie Chen and I never made it into the game of boyfriends-and-girlfriends that was played between the girls with Malibu Barbies and the boys who attacked them with wild disgust. So we were locked out of the kissy-kissy stuff behind the K Primary School peppercorn tree; we never got to stand under its branches to say those naked shocking words: I love you. From far away we could only hear snatches of sexy, ring, bridesmaid and giggly little girls poems like *Roses are red, Violets are blue, Kiss me baby, 'cause I'm hot for you* ...

From her mother's drawer, Susie Chen pulled out a silk-covered album. To my surprise she put it to one side, that wasn't what she was looking for. No, Susie Chen was scrabbling with practised fingers under the drawer liner of old newspaper till she pulled out an unframed photograph, thick and trimmed with a sort of lettuce-leaf edging. She handed it to me. It was a portrait of a young Chinese woman in a long white European wedding gown tightly laced at the waist. With her huge floaty Edwardian hat, she looked as slim and tiny as a doll. The bride stood with her hand on the shoulder of a much older-looking Chinese man, who sat comfortably on a tapestry chair.

'It's Great-grandmother,' whispered Susie. 'She came out from China to marry this man.'

'Is he your great-grandfather?'

'Yes,' said Susie. 'She ran away from him to live with another man, and they found her and beat her and killed her.'

Another child would not have believed her – okay, they might have *beaten* her but they wouldn't have *killed* her, no way. But only the previous Saturday, I had been through the Victoria Markets holding my grandmother's hand as we pushed our way through the crowds. My eyes darted from the cheeses to the salamis to the bolts of cloth. Suddenly I felt a blow on my face. 'Don't stare at those men,' hissed my grandmother, 'keep your eyes to yourself *or I'll kill you*.'

Love was not a joke. Susie Chen and I were friends because we came from unforgiving cultures where girls were set on their guard against men from a very young age and the unspoken boundaries of honour were patrolled by vigilant and sometimes harsh and bitter women.

We stared at the porcelain face and the beautiful clothes of the unblinking Chinese woman. Her hair was smooth and I had a longing to brush it, to button and unbutton her lace gown, to slip her shoes on and off her feet.

I fly interstate and drive into a far suburbia where the trio of McDonald's, KFC and Pizza Hut repeats endlessly into the horizon. The mosque is at the top of a hill, behind a highway and an overpass. The community room is sparsely furnished with two wooden desks, two telephones and shelves of religious writings on the Koran. Black-robed women flit past, crying out to their pre-school children who are playing in the yard outside. Being mindful of accuracy in the light of Salman Rushdie's exile and Taslima Sarin's flight to Paris, I take out both a tape recorder and a large notebook. The cheerful Shi'ite girl laughs. 'No, no, please don't worry,' she says, offering me a chair, a Nescafé and a Scotch

Finger biscuit. 'We can't make a *fatwa* against you! You have to be a Muslim before we can do that!'

We all laugh. As mothers and wives, and even as NESBs, there is an affinity. I like their passion, their sense of honour. Yet I can also feel rising in me a flight of panicked birds, my Western fear of the East. 'Why do you enter the temple of the Infidel,' whisper the nuns of my Catholic Sunday School, 'when thou shalt have no other gods but Me?'

The translator, Fatima, comes in swathed against the heat in a Turkish chador. She is friendly but her words can't help unnerving a middle-class agnostic Western feminist. 'The wife,' she says, 'must obey the husband in everything unless it means going against Islam ... The man and the woman should at least see each other before the families arrange the marriage. Yes, we believe in sexual chemistry – in the possibility that you *could* love that person. But it is much more important that the man has that feeling, as a man's sexual drive is nine times greater than a woman's ... A woman's love is whimsical, a man's love more enduring ... Girls are encouraged to marry young at fifteen or sixteen to prevent sex out of marriage, which is forbidden by law ...'

Yet growing through the law are the tips of wild leaves, strange flowers, unnameable grasses. 'For myself, I like to work only with women,' says Fatima. 'I find culturally that the men I meet here have a problem with listening to what women say ... Please, this is very controversial in our community so be careful what you say. But some people are coming to think that maybe temporary marriage – what we call *Muttah* – could be an option for our young people who are born here and have to cope with the Australian ways. Instead of sex out of marriage, they could negotiate a contract for a month, three months, a year of marriage. So they could enjoy each other in a proper marriage and continue their studies. Both parties would agree to follow whatever is set out in the marriage contract – sex or no sex or whatever. It is better than just sleeping around ...'

I talk to her of a scandal in Melbourne involving an arranged marriage and the attempted murder of a Muslim girl by her parents. Fatima's voice shakes. 'We feel so much outrage when we hear these things. They hurt the whole Muslim community. This family has hurt all Muslims by doing these outrageous things. You feel such pain within yourself when you hear this happening. These are customs of the cultures of these people. They are only the practices of races and tribes. *It has nothing to do with Islam.*'

I make my way home, feeling as though I have been thrown across centuries, lands and cultures. I am suffering cultural shock similar to what it might mean to arrive chaste with Islam and a chador, protected and supported by your father, brothers and uncles, to a place of riotously coloured long-haired women in shorts and make-up. So this is how it must feel to run smack into the

Pill, rock videos and lesbians tongue-kissing in Franklins. Through the looking glass of culture, I can feel the offence and defence – the fear of having to walk your children through a war-zone where the combatants of sex and love run amok.

This decadent West and fundamentalist East in my head replay the early relationship between my parents and myself – the ancient ways of *honore* against the Rolling Stones. It brings up *padre*, *padrone*, rebellion against patriarchy, and the comment of an Italian priest who once said to me 'so often the image of a happy ethnic family is held by violence'. But right now I don't want to be reminded of the days in the late sixties when teachers had to plead with my father to allow me to go on school excursions. This is ancient history, sometimes I'm not even sure it happened.

I flop out and switch on 'Days of Our Lives'.

On the fax sheet were a pair of names and an address in the northern beaches. 'Go and see them,' said a note across the top, 'if you want to understand courtship practices and ideals different to your own. This couple should interest you, if only because they so gracefully negotiate cultures, religions and centuries – Arabic and European, post-industrial and feudal, Islam, Christianity and Buddhism, and even computers and spirituality. The disenchantment with the romantic fashions of the West, the consideration of a loving and cultured family, the maturity and gravity of the young people involved, all will show you that love is as much cultural as it is fated or biological. Why should the construction of a complex and enduring love be left to unconscious drives, hormonal desires, flimsy narcissistic infatuations and chance, which can so often be sterile and unobliging? To those who have grown up in our culture, the old ways, when artfully practised with inspiration and wisdom, have something to offer in arranging the conditions for love.'

'But let me tell you now,' laughs Bahram when I talk to him over the phone, 'this was not an arranged marriage.' Sipping Coca-Cola in their apartment, I see what he means. He and Mina are that most blessed of couples, the husband and wife destined to be lovers. It's just that their relatives happened to think of it first.

Bahram was the expatriate son, jaded with the West, returning to Iran for a visit after fourteen years in Australia and Europe. For many years a practising Buddhist, (by contrast, one of his brothers is a Shi'ite Muslim fundamentalist), Bahram is a restlessly philosophical man who has studied engineering, literature, psychology and philosophy in France and Italy and now works as a consultant in the computer industry. In his thirties, he found himself on the shelf as a Western love victim, one of those 'men who love too much' with several long turbulent relationships that ended badly.

'I naturally seemed to attract the most disastrous women in my life. My challenge was to discover why I was doing that, why I wasn't valuing myself. I came to realise that finding a partner wasn't about seeing someone you like physically and letting the hormones do the work. That's not a *decision* from my point of view. I didn't want to get together with anyone again unless their character was suitable. Because when the level of hormonal attraction dies down, what are you left with? Are you left with someone who is a lovely person? Are you left with someone you can talk to?

'I carry a lot of cultural history. I am Iranian, I was born into an Islamic family and even though I am non-practising as a Muslim, that culture and influence is part of my being. I realised it could be easier to live with someone who understands that part of me. But I also saw that it wasn't enough simply to marry an Iranian woman. It was more important to choose someone with an open mind. So I had a long discussion with a close friend, who just happens to be my mother. She suggested several women as examples in a general way, concentrating on their characters, saying only "wouldn't it be nice to live with someone like this or someone like that?"'

There was no pressure ... simply a persistent suggestion to meet Mina. 'Just give it a chance,' said his mother. 'Oh you must meet her,' said an uncle. 'Everyone is talking about how happy and energetic she is.' Bahram's mother threw a lavish party to which many of Teheran's wealthy bright young people were invited and the star of which was Mina. An uncle then arranged for Bahram to work in the computer business where Mina was a supervisor, so they could get to know each other as computer compatibles. This was a master-stroke as both Bahram and Mina are technology obsessives.

Bahram succumbed as happily to these strategies as an Yvonne Allen client to an agency-booked Dinner For Six. He and Mina married within weeks and moved back to a small apartment in Sydney. Mina is studying English at TAFE and works with Bahram in their computer business. She seems a happy bride – 'I've never had any doubts about my marriage.' But she struggles with being an immigrant, living away from friends and family. Strangely enough, it was Bahram's mother who gave her the courage to come to Australia. 'Before I left, she told me that Bahram had made the best decision as our characters are nicely matched for each other.'

'So,' I say, 'it was basically like an old-fashioned Aussie matchmaking. Mum knows a nice girl and sets you up at the BBQ.'

'But my mother had never met Mina,' says Bahram.

'We didn't know each other at all,' says Mina.

'She knew only of her family background,' says Bahram.

'We knew the general "feel" of his family,' says Mina.

I leave full of admiration for Bahram's mother.

Sometimes minority religious practices reveal more about mainstream Western marriage than flicking through copies of *Vogue Brides* magazine. In the early afternoon, I knock on the door of a Federation house in the suburbs. Elizabeth, a follower of the Reverend Sun Myung Moon, leads me inside with her baby on her hip.

Elizabeth is an Anglo-Irish fifth generation Australian from a wealthy and artistic Perth Catholic family. She is something of a nineteenth century beauty – fine-boned and pale as paper. She also has a PhD in geology and in her university days was a fine amateur cellist, giving chamber music recitals with her professional musician sisters in Perth. Now she lives estranged from her birth family in this scrupulously neat Unification Church house, shared with smiling Korean Moonie visitors.

It's through Elizabeth that I'm introduced to a small group of middle-class women of various ages and in different stages of marriages that were ritually arranged through the Unification Church. There is Danielle, a Frenchwoman in her early forties, a mature and serene mother of three school-aged children. There is the shy Marjorie, a young newly-wed from New Zealand who is getting close to forty weeks pregnant, and there is Rachel, a lively and talkative American with two daughters, a toddler and a pre-schooler.

These women's Moonie husbands are all Australians (except for Elizabeth's who is German) and the couples were all apparently strangers (at least virtual strangers) to each other, brought together through the divine intervention of the Reverend Sun Myung Moon assisted only by a pile of colour photographs by his side.

As experienced wives and mothers, Danielle and Rachel can afford to talk frankly about arranged love, sex and childbirth. Marjorie is more reticent as she had the devastating experience of being rejected by her first partner from a Reverend Moon matching ceremony. (The man, an American, refused the match and left the movement.) Danielle, a former Catholic introduced to the Moonies by a boyfriend when she was nineteen, looks back on her stable fourteen-year arranged marriage to admit that she and her husband 'only fell in love after our first daughter was born'. Married in one of the Reverend Moon's mass ceremonies in New York's Madison Square Garden, Danielle and her husband waited two years before they lived together – a kind of courtship in reverse.

The American, Rachel, was a wounded flower child of the seventies, a college drop-out embittered by the divorce of her affluent New York Jewish parents. She drifted stoned through the last of the hippy communes of the Haight-Ashbury district in San Francisco and travelled onwards, to Mexico, Guatemala and Canada. At twenty she met a black student at Stanford University, to whom she had a baby that she put up for adoption. At twenty-two, she met a mesmerising older Ukrainian man in a spiritualist book store in Vancouver and impulsively agreed to a Green Card marriage to him in exchange for financial support in going back to college.

It was to be the first of a pair of arranged marriages. After a dazzlingly traditional Ukrainian ceremony – 'with a choir and gold crowns and in front of the entire local Ukrainian community' – Rachel left her husband at the airport during their honeymoon in Acapulco. He felt she owed him a sexual relationship. That wasn't how Rachel understood the deal. So she fled back to the United States, where she found peace working on a fishing boat called the *Full Circle*.

Shortly after, she joined the Unification Church and eventually the Reverend Moon matched the witty rebel (whom he has written about as a 'laughing-eyes girl … (with) a complicated heart and mind … easy for others to misunderstand …') to Mike, one of his Australian yachting crew. 'I didn't like him at all at first sight,' says Rachel. 'I was hoping like mad to be matched to an African because I had a "thing" about black guys. But anyhow Mike and I prayed together for two days and after that it was hard to keep our hands off each other.' Since their 1987 marriage, their relationship continues to be volatile (she hints at physical fights and divorce). But her spiritual beliefs seem to give Rachel the missing structure and control in her tempestuous nature – she says she and Mike are working things out for better and not for worse.

A woman's right to choose. A few years ago, Elizabeth's family abducted her and put her through nine days of de-programming. They brought over two

American 'exit counsellors' to 'try to break my faith', as she says. Like nearly everyone outside the Moonies, her parents found their daughter's choices shocking. Why would a bright, tertiary-educated Western woman from a wealthy background – a young woman with a doctorate degree and the means to be financially independent in a post-feminist era of undreamed-of choice – enter a marriage arranged by a distant Korean elderly man? For Elizabeth, it is a question of faith. 'We believe the Reverend Moon is the Messiah. He has very deep spiritual insight and picks up things that normal people wouldn't see. He can see things in your ancestry and in your spouse's ancestry that will make you able to perfect each other's characters.'

Maybe a mistrust of love, a wounding by family and a distaste for the cult of individualism make some people burn-out on choice. The Moonie women talk as if their *right to choose* is offered as a ritual sacrifice to Universal Love. The Reverend Moon has a vision of the creation of 'International Peace' and 'World Families' by cross-cultural marriage. He likes to match Asians to Africans and South Africans to Pacific Islanders to hasten the melting pot of peace on earth. This might mean that your personal marriage – your great love that's so individual, so random and so prey to dissolution in the West – becomes not just your idiosyncratic choice, your little boat rocking in the sea of relationship, but part of a collective act for world peace.

Maybe it's also a reaction to the fact that in our society it is possible to be an eternal youth – 'this isn't really it' – until old age smashes the illusions of endless choice – 'oh my God, I forgot to have a baby/write a novel/win an Academy Award!' Some people have a feeling that love will only come to them through limitation, through a kind of death of the endless possibilities. Then it's a relief when the Reverend Moon acts as the Lord of Karma, saying 'okay, enough procrastination and preparation, this is it ...'

Though later I am told that, as a younger man, Reverend Moon rebelled against his family to arrange his own match to a pretty Korean girl young enough to be his daughter.

Raja is another who swims in the opposite direction to her culture in the ocean of love. A convert to Shi'ite Muslim fundamentalism, Raja is a mystery to her parents and to people on the street who abuse her for her traditional Middle Eastern Islamic dress. For a start, she is an Englishwoman. Her name used to be Carol and she was born in Manchester, emigrating to Australia with her family when she was three years old.

But Raja enjoys confounding stereotypes. As a freckled, blue-eyed Westie Muslim in an Iranian chador, she speaks with an acquired broken English accent and smokes a cigarette while she talks passionately of Islam and love. For it was love that brought her to Islam and to her private fundamentalist revolution against her family culture of suburban working-class romance. Although there is nothing more romantic than her own cross-cultural marriage and conversion to Islam, the thing she wants least for her son and two daughters is the radicalism she displayed in marrying their father. She is fundamentalist through the best of motives. Not everyone can cope with the dark side of western sexuality and she shares the same kind of fear that recent immigrants have of this culture as too threatening and too fast – the 'going with' guys that lead you to 'fall' (falling in love and falling pregnant) and then the years of marriage-affairs-divorce, the single parenthood, postnatal depression, alcohol and drugs. She sees this as a culture of loaded choices, betrayals, longings that go nowhere leaving love always out of your grasp ... so that in the end an uncomplicated passionate nature becomes the defensive, pain-filled woman she saw her mother become.

When Raja was Carol, she grew up influenced by a converted fire-and-brimstone Christian fundamentalist 'who was always talking about the Day of Judgement', and an alcoholic mother. By the end of high school, Carol was determined to 'find a guy who was different' to the teenage hormonal sex-love mayhem that was going on around her – the flirting in class, the screwing in cars, the drinking, the parties, the fights and jealousies, the long-haired apprentices cruising the discos with their mates and a pouchful of joints and a six-pack of beer. While her girlfriends were getting laid or semi-raped or wondering 'will I, won't I, is he the one?', Carol was at home with her Pen Pal Club. For years this hobby of writing away to get 'lists of people overseas' was like a thread of travel and literary adventure, spinning Carol out of the western suburbs and into the world.

Carol was so naïve she didn't know that Ahmad, her Arabic pen pal, was a Muslim, only that he talked about God a lot and signed his letters 'In the name of God … and peace be with you'. After leaving school, Carol decided to visit him. On the surface this seemed innocent enough but the people around them in both Arabic and Australian cultures knew that such a visit by an unmarried and unchaperoned girl of seventeen to an Islamic man's home and family was more than a casual tourist call. Only the fact that Carol had so many strikes against her as a Westerner and a Christian rendered her an unlikely contender as a fiancée for Ahmad, whose parents had arranged for him to marry a local girl, a marriage he kept delaying.

Her parents objected. '"Muslim!" my dad said. "You keep away from them, they're bad news," and my mother said "*Please* love, *please* don't go over there and get married."'

Her arrival in the Middle East was confusing and exhausting, standing alone at the airport with people staring at her, waiting and waiting. She had no idea what to do if Ahmad did not meet her. 'Then his sister spotted me. He hadn't recognised me because he was expecting a typical Western girl in shorts or jeans. I was wearing a nice long pink dress, very modest.' For the rest of the day, the Australian girl was welcomed and paraded in front of relatives speaking between them English, Arabic, French and Farsi. Finally, at midnight, her head reeling from the sounds and sights and the food she had never seen or tasted before, Carol was shown to her bedroom in the attic of Ahmad's mother's house. She fell into a restless sleep, knowing she was way out of her natal geography in this high bedroom in the land of the Arabian nights, her pink dress on a chair.

She awoke at dawn. Someone was singing outside and it went through her skin and bones. It was the Muslim call to prayer. 'When I heard the Muezzin,' she says, 'it was like all my life I had just been crawling out of the rubble to be here.'

Somewhere in the black night pierced with the stars of Persia, Egypt and the Lebanon, Carol had dreamed herself into Raja. Within four days, the Australian girl and her Arabic pen pal had decided to marry.

I don't know Raja well; she will always be a stranger, a pale-skinned blonde (from what I can see of a wisp of hair) rustling black-gowned and veiled in a garden, smoking cigarette after cigarette and looking dreamily back into the past. She tells me what she feels she can afford to give away of her story, keeping back the doubts and all the grit of love that are none of my business or anybody else's. But it seems to me that a love story like the one she is telling me is truly a leap of faith. Was it as much a falling in love with Islam and Arabic culture as with a man, with Ahmad, her husband? On the surface it seems as impetuous and romantic as 'some enchanted evening, you will see a stranger', only she hadn't *seen* him, she had *corresponded* with him. In a courtship where the rules are new and the potential for danger is great, the common ground, the unspoken contract, was drawn up swiftly between them. They had talked about marriage in their fourth letter to each other and they fearlessly used those grave binding words: husband, wife.

I hand in whatever tapes and reports I think might be useful to the Client. Over the next few days the fax machine squeals madly and pages of comments curl all over my office floor.

> 'Once upon a time in a terrace house in Newtown,' she writes, 'a princess called Juliet, a thirty-something lawyer, has been "going out" with her boyfriend for twelve years, meaning she's his kind-of de-facto wife without actually living with him. She's been overseas with him, she's shared houses with him, she's travelled through India and Europe with him, she's cooked him meals when he's been sick, she's picked up his dry-cleaning,

she's bought an investment block of units with him, she drives his leased Camry and has had an abortion to him. In twelve years never once have those words "husband, wife" been spoken between them.

'As the princess gets close to forty, she begins to wonder whether her body would be able to swell out round and heavy with something other than pre-menstrual tension. Baby, pregnant, children, house – they're the grave binding words that they can't utter. The words have barbed wire around them and a skull-and-crossbones: beware nuclear family, contaminated waste. They seep poison into their silences. "Who decided we can't talk about these things?" she writes in her diary. She underlines baby, pregnant, children, house, husband, wife. "I am being controlled," she writes. "I am being fucking controlled!"

'"Love," said the nurse gently, handing a cup of tea to Juliet after her second abortion. "Love is only real if it allows you to be what you must be. If it is killing you, obsessing you, taking up all your energy to maintain, then it is not love but illusion. No matter what you feel about it."

'"But I love him," sobs the princess. "I'm not attracted to other men. (They're wimps,

they're boring.) He's the only one that I can
ever love. I LOVE HIM."

'"Some people prefer to live with illusion,"
says the nurse. "That's always possible. But pay
the price."

'"What price?" says Juliet bristling. "What
kind of judgmental crap is that? What's 'the
price'?"

'"Your Highness, it is my duty to remind
you that in European fairytales the price of
persisting in an attitude of illusion or delusion
is nearly always the loss of the magical child."'

I laugh. The Client has a brutal bullshit detector and
being young she has no generosity toward humankind at
all. But I know what she means. It's usually those
girlfriends of mine who have suffered the most in love
but don't quite realise it, who get intensely interested in
my interview tapes of arranged marriages. 'I'd love to be a
fly on the wall,' sighed one, who had just divorced her
second husband and was now waiting for her married
lover to get through his separation counselling and
divorce *his* second wife.

'It's so ridiculous,' said another, dropping in on me
one afternoon, eyeing my notes while pretending not to.
This woman struggled to raise two asthmatic children
alone while her partner of fifteen years lived in a separate
house down the street because he couldn't handle the

kids waking and crying and he needed his own space. 'How can you love someone your parents choose for you?' she says shaking her head in pity. 'How can you spend the rest of your life with some bloke the Reverend Moon picks out of a line-up? How do they have a sex life? How do they have children to each other?'

'I don't know,' I said. 'This Moonie girl says she didn't even know how to pronounce his name on their wedding day. Now they've got three kids and their own business and they call each other "honey" and "darling".'

'It's stupid,' she said, turning away angrily.

'Things could change,' I confess to the Client, 'but I know in my heart that I'm made for long hauls, that I've got a stubborn black endurance for love from centuries of women's whispers, childbirth, suffering and subversion. The endurance – the dragged-through-trials-blood-and-children kind of love – that never fitted in with postmodern cool wariness or the New Age if-you-love-let-it-go stuff. The kind of love I had never went with the flow. It never did its own thing. I had no grace in love. Till I got wise, the seriousness, the weddedness of the way I loved made me ripe only for torture, for being the sulky girlfriend of womanising drinkers and Peter Pans.

'Why do we do this? Because there is nowhere for our passion to go. Look, I wanted more than anything to be a flirty flip-out in love. I pretended to be cool. I pretended I didn't mind. But underneath I was too earthy, too real.

Too many foremothers raped on their wedding night. I've always suspected that at some point love turns into blood and bone. That's the kind of love it's got to be if it's useful. Because I am finding out that love is not ornamental. It's got to be able to grow things in it and from it. Don't listen to words; words don't count. Too many women fall in love with a man's words and fly around in the air beneath his wings and all that, only to be brought down to earth by a smack in the mouth.'

'It's funny too,' the Client faxes back to me, 'how we always ask the wrong people about love and marriage. Take Elizabeth Taylor, for instance. Because she's been married eight or nine or whatever times, the magazines made out she was an expert in love. But Elizabeth Taylor didn't know zip about love. Your Auntie Ruby and the average resident of a women's refuge knows more about love than Elizabeth Taylor.

'In fact she was really bad at love, that's what reassured people: at least I'm not that fucked up, at least I'm not that superficial. Still we don't want to know how to love because we've got a feeling it's quite hard and looks a bit "boring" on the outside and it will ask from us something that we don't want to give. What we really want to know is how the powerful, the famous and the beautiful raid love and burgle passion and get away with it. Why is there this conspiracy of silence about well-practiced love? Why is it that those who have a genius for relationships are ignored and even demeaned?'

'Listen,' I said. 'There's this Cambodian lady I know who got separated from her husband when the Khmer Rouge threw them out of Phnom Penh into the countryside. She had married her husband the traditional way, arranged by the families. They had four children (and the oldest girl will probably be the Labor member for Cabramatta in about ten years). In the Pol Pot years, the wife and children ended up in a province near the Thai border. The wife was told her husband was dead. The Khmer Rouge wanted stray suspect widows like her to marry, it was part of their killing fields communism. Like most of the population, they were starving, sick and near death. One child had already died in the wife's arms. Still the wife avoided remarriage. Can you imagine the risk she took to do that, in a situation where you dare not pick a grain of rice for a dying daughter?

'Was that love? Or was it only propriety, a grim hanging on to honour? If so, it would have been a suicidal luxury. Her husband was dead. It wasn't like their marriage had been a love match in the first place, they weren't Romeo and Juliet. No one could have blamed the wife for doing the pragmatic thing when their lives were being lived at the end of a bayonet and rifle. Why did she do it? Is this what you would call love? Or would love, the way we think of love, would that kind of love have just gotten in the way?

'Then the Vietnamese came in and this family fled through the jungle into Thailand, with mines going off all around them and three armies – Thai, Vietnamese and Khmer Rouge – all hostile to them. While in the jungle, the wife and kids meet another party that includes her husband. It's a miracle, a Hollywood movie. Then, toward nightfall the next day, the family in front of them is blown away by a plane flying low. They have to leave the two surviving stranger children bleeding to death at the crater's edge, clinging to the sarong of the dead mother they can't even see any more, she's just blood, dirt and shrapnel. Finally they make it to Camp. The wife is forty-five years old and about nine months later she has a baby in the Camp hospital.

'If you gathered the lovers of history around the campfire and invited each couple to tell their stories, how do you think Elizabeth Taylor and Richard Burton's would come up against this tale of two middle-aged Cambodians who run a hot bread shop in the back streets of Cabramatta?

'Listen, just find any wog in black who is still happy to wear her wedding ring. Go and ask her about love and tenacity and the Lord of Karma.'

'Did you love Nonno?' I ask my grandmother. She is watching the soaps as she does every day: 'Days of Our Lives' followed by 'The Young and The Restless' and 'Perfect Match'.

'No,' she says. I take this in calmly. I'm glad, I think to myself. No bullshit. My grandfather died years ago and my grandmother is not a sentimental woman. Only when she has the time to channel-surf in a granny flat out the back of my parents' place does she luxuriate in star-crossed lovers and Californian kisses.

'It was not right to be in love,' she says. 'People would gossip about you. You had no chance to fall in love. The village, *gli altri*, watched you and you watched yourself. You were never alone with a man who wasn't your brother or your father. If, by bad luck or your ignorance, you were seduced – or even just touched or kissed – and people talked about you, you had to marry that man, if he could be married. If not, you were ruined and the reputation of your family was gone. No, I didn't love him.' For a moment her eyes glittered with an old rage. 'But I would have killed any *strega puttana* who so much as looked at him.'

Did my beginnings ever have anything to do with love?

I arrange to meet the Client at a nearby church. The ministry of the Reverend B is on the main street of a grey middle-western suburb, up from the railway station and past Chinese, Italian, Lebanese, Thai and Vietnamese cafés. When I walk past the hall, the Reverend's helpers are clearing up the lunch they serve at their soup kitchen drop-in centre.

With his church planted at one of the crossroads of multicultural Australia, the Reverend B is a legitimator of relationships reviled by family and custom – those wild loves that break out of and break up cultural and religious rules to show us that we are of the same species, that this woman can mate with this man and it will be okay. This is the church that couples run to when no one else wants to honour the fact that love has somehow – and improbably and unsuitably and who knows, maybe not even permanently – sprung up between them.

So the Reverend B's church is a sanctuary for love. Here he has married Chinese to Aboriginal, Ethiopian to Swede, Sri Lankan Tamil to Lebanese Maronite, Serbian to Croatian, Muslim to Catholic. Because of all the tapes I have fast-forwarding and backtracking through my head, I find it soothing to sit here at the church hall dining table, looking over my notes, sipping a cup of tea served by the Reverend B's daughter.

Love. No questions asked except the sacred ones of honour and justice. What a relief.

Inside the church, the Client is waiting. I hand over folders, tapes, photographs – assorted evidence of arrangements in her house of love. I know they don't add up to an answer, just a set of family and cultural stories she'll have to accept. 'From my decadent and limited Western cultural perspective,' I report to her, 'the arranged marriage has the potential to be truly disastrous, a savage fate symbolised by Indian brides murdered by their husbands for their dowries. Yet I know perfectly well that in a love match, disaster can always be arranged by your own temperament, by the culture within, and not only the specific qualities of the men and the moralities of your clan.

'But for me it's not the point whether a love match fails where an arranged match succeeds. The right to have disastrous loves, the right to seize dangerous love, forbidden love or to make a purely sexual choice, is something the liberated woman has over her patriarchally bound sister. To be able to forage for happiness outside the village and hearth, to live as virgin female (virgin as in the wild undomesticated nature, true to the natural state) is quite a different existence to the socialised and contracted woman, even though, at any given moment, one might be happier, more protected, more valued than the other.'

The Client takes up the files. 'I see,' she says wryly. 'So the most I can hope for is that I will be richer in my sorrows than my grandmothers.'

The Reverend B comes to sit on a pew. 'I have seen hopeless men marrying really smart women. I have seen people marry and get into trouble and I've seen them dust themselves off and start over and over again. I often encourage the couple to give their warring relatives a video print of the ceremony they wouldn't attend. Just to give the relationship the honour it deserves. The only thing I am sure of is that God doesn't want people to live together in misery.'

Did my beginnings ever have anything to do with love?

I am looking for a tape in an unlabelled box on a shelf somewhere at the back of my office. There is a story on it about a remote southern Italian village and a church that no one goes to any more.

La Chiesa della Madonna di Loreto is in the main street, which is only a dusty cobbled path, centuries old, that winds to the top of the hill before it drops steeply again toward the olives and vineyards of the valleys. A few small old-model Fiats negotiate the road but it's really only stocky mountain legs that get anywhere around here.

The church is closed. It looks like just another ancient building crammed between a general store and a haberdasher's in the medieval village. People no longer come because the Mass is now celebrated down the hill at Santa Maria Maggiore, a large modern church with new stained-glass and walls painted with faux marbling to imitate the churches of Rome, so real, so grand.

Yet the dark old church in the old street is still sacred. It's still on consecrated ground. Now and again, the priests will be asked to open it to foreigners who want to marry there. They come with unpronounceable surnames – McKenzie, Cohen, Kozlowski, Brookes – but they inevitably bring papers and photographs of other names and other faces of three, four, five generations ago – Aguccio, Vaccari, Dell'angelo, Di Biasi. The villagers shake the foreigners' hands, invite them in, pour them *bicchieri d'aranciata* and do their best to recall, though privately they murmur '*Eh, va bene,* aren't we all related to Adam and Eve?'. Finally, on a Saturday afternoon in the

European springtime, the couple from Chicago or New Jersey or Melbourne will come blinking out of the darkness to stand on the old church steps in the sun. They will drink a ritual glass of sweet wine. The photographer snaps his Nikon, the confetti and rice flies, the bells ring.

Half drunk and swathed in tulle, the couple totter down the same steep road that brought them there.

Song of The Suitcase

Families are people who carry the same baggage over generations and continents.

My family came out of an immigrant's suitcase which was hauled on to the wharf at Fremantle, Western Australia, in 1951. The handle of that first suitcase from which we were dragged out and raised up was held by my father, a single man, alone.

Nowadays, on the *terrazza* of his marble-balustraded *castello* in the Melbourne suburbs – after a glass or two of his rough-as-guts homemade red wine which you must pretend to love or you won't get a word out of him – my father will tell you stories of his first day in Australia, how he dragged that suitcase in forty-one degree heat, how he sweated rivers in his best woollen suit which he'd had specially made in Naples for his disembarkation in Australia.

Fremantle was a frontier town; I imagine it like a scene from a John Wayne movie – my father, the outsider in his uncomfortable suit, gets dumped off the stage coach on to the rattlesnake desert.

He and his mate, the *paesano* from Casalbordino, had heard of a boarding house run by Italians. They had its name on a scrap of paper, ready to show to people who could point them in the right direction because the two *paesani* couldn't speak a word of *l'inglese*. They waited by the side of the road for what seemed a long time. The odd car and the occasional bus rattled past but none stopped, no one offered them a lift, no one gave them a second glance. What was worse, no one explained what 'Hail Bus Here' meant.

The sun went down. The desert night settled around the two strangely dressed dagos straight off the *Oceania*. The far-off lights of the town must have twinkled at them like an ironic smile. They ended up kicking, dragging, pushing and punching their suitcases all the way into Fremantle.

It was in Melbourne that my natal family – *Mamma e Papà, sorella e fratello* – was finally shaken out of all the luggage that followed, those suitcases, trunks, airmail letters, packages of cloth, gold jewellery and pre-war photographs wrapped in tissue paper.

We cleared a space in a dark old house in Collingwood and set up a life – a job in the Melbourne breweries, a night shift at the sweets factory, a Simpson's wringer washing machine, two dozen nappies and a crate of tomatoes from a *paesano*'s orchard at Greensborough. A green-enamelled Kooka gas stove and three kids – only three kids, you know, because to have more kids you needed *le nonne* (the grandmothers) and our grandmothers were not part of our luggage in this country, they weren't part of the deal.

To compensate, other things came with us – family traits stowed away in the holds of our characters, bits and pieces packed by ancestral hands long ago to emerge like apples or stones or bitter herbs.

My mother brought the photo album and its stories, along with the two or three most precious books from her schooldays. From her shipping trunk straight off the *Oceania*, she lifted out her unacknowledged love of words. Unable to study herself, words and learning were all bound up with the character of her brother, my estranged uncle, Zio Gennaro, the black sheep of her family. The eldest son of modest, hardworking *contadini*, Gennaro had polio as a child and was crippled in one leg (family guilt made the story change over and over: 'he poured a pan of boiling water on it', writes one of my aunts from Milan; 'he fell from a high wall and broke his leg and it never healed properly', writes another from Aquila). Unable to take up his birthright and work in the fields, Gennaro was sent by my grandparents to the seminary to be trained for the priesthood.

There he stole himself an education. In the seminary library, he dreamt of writing books and so he left and eventually married – against all advice – a rich distant cousin from the north and tried to settle down with her and his baby son in a provincial town by the Adriatic sea. When the marriage failed, he broke off so violently from my grandfather that he had to meet his mother secretly by moonlight in the fields. He finally migrated to Switzerland, where he taught and wrote in exile, bitterly cut off from a family that was not permitted to speak to him until my grandfather was dead.

I met him in Switzerland when he was an old man living alone in Basel with a typewriter and a pension. Limping painfully to the drinks cabinet, he poured my husband and me a drink of whisky. 'You see this leg?' he said. 'Fate marked me with this leg! This leg took me away from the land, from my family, from my home! This leg has been my greatest fortune!' He sculled the whisky and banged it on the table.

The little sister left behind with whispers and slammed doors in the night blamed Gennaro's education for his differences. She believed the people who said that his storytelling – which he had chosen above the land or the altar – had caused nothing but problems.

So my mother didn't trust words, even though she had her brother's ability to tell stories. It took her more than forty years to trust this part of herself. In her twenties she told us stories as if they were nothing – *favoletti,* she would say derisively as we laughed ourselves silly and begged and pleaded for another scatalogical tale

about priests and pots of gold coins, about eldest and
middle sons with too much *furberia,* about stupid-smart
donkeys and not-too-bright peasants.

'*Favoletti, stupitagini, fantasie! Non si può mangare i
favoletti!*'

Yet no matter how much she sneered at words, it
made no difference. Well before she left Italy on the
Oceania, the possibility of another Gennaro had already
been packed into her baggage.

The daughter in exile, the betrayer of the photo
albums and of the dialect of centuries – I was already
there sitting at her feet, laughing myself silly at the stories
of a man whose face never appeared in the photo albums.
Without my mother seeing – or maybe she did, from the
corners of her half-closed eyes – I stole Gennaro's words,
I pocketed and carried them around with me.

I wanted to find my Zio Gennaro; I wanted to ask
him, 'How did you find your path, how did you swim
against all these people in the photo album, how did you
throw off all the baggage, all the blankets, the
embroidered tablecloths, the linen dowries – and the soil,
the clumps of Abruzzese mountain dirt around your feet?
What have you got to give me from your suitcase? Give
me something!'

For a long time I thought I would find Gennaro's
address in the back of my mother's wardrobe. When she
was out, I scrabbled around in her things, searching for
clues. When I played at being an orphan, when I imagined I

was going to run away into the horizon and travel over the top of the world, it was Zio Gennaro I was going to meet.

In the cunning way a family has of growing wherever it lands, the relationship my grandfather had broken and flung out of the house all those years ago was picked up, dusted off and carried around like marbles in the knapsack of his five-year-old grand-daughter.

Superstition, portents, dreams and rituals were a part of the family baggage that transported well. It always amazed me how vigorously hocus-pocus grew at our place.

'What colour do you like best?' said my mother to me when I was seven years old.

'Red,' I replied.

My mother frowned and shook her head.

'Selfish,' she said. '*Il rosso* is the colour of egoism, of selfishness.'

I kicked the kitchen steps, devastated.

'That's not true,' I said. 'That's just superstition.'

'No,' said my mother. 'That's your character. You can't do anything about your character. *Nel carattere è la vita!*'

I had tears in my eyes and such a hate that I could have killed her with my own hands.

'So what stupid colour do you like?' I burst out. 'What's your favourite colour, then?'

My mother smiled faintly.

'*Il rosso.*'

In the difficult years when I wasn't seeing anybody from home, I'd pick up the phone in the middle of the night and it would be *la famiglia* talking to me in whispers. In those heavy days between exile and a wary homecoming, the family voices were cut across by a static that forced me to hang up, feeling sick, poisoned, cursed.

Yet the phone kept ringing. It rang at all hours and it had to be answered. So I began to study astrology from esoteric books imported from Europe and California, as a way of staying awake through the bouts of my middle-of-the-night phone-call sickness – Why aren't you married yet? Why don't you settle down? What do you want to do on your own that you can't do with us? Why don't you stop what you're doing and be what you're stopping and drop what you're being and why, why, why?

I'd look out the window and the night would be full of stars.

I sat down at my desk with my ephemeris, my blank charts, rulers and calculators, the complicated books of transits, aspects, houses and the formulae for the calculations. I drew up the family maps as far back as I could go. 1913, Zio Giovanni, Sun in Capricorn, Moon probably in Scorpio. 1918, Zia Marcella, Sun in Scorpio, Moon most likely in Aquarius. 1914, Papà, Sun in Capricorn, Moon in Scorpio. 1932, Mamma, Sun in Scorpio, Moon in Gemini.

Finally, they were laid out in front of me – the X-rays of generations of blood and fate drawn in coloured inks and calligraphic pens, the hieroglyphic symbols as old as Egypt and China. Venus was exalted in Cancer yet time after time I found it alone and unaspected, telling me of the hidden nature of my family's love ... Here was something – the Mercury in Gemini spinning around the Gemini Suns of unfulfilled intellectuals, unwillingly bound to the land. There was the Moon, sadly in its fall in Capricorn for so many of the family's Scorpionic women – there they all are, my grandmothers and great-aunts, the *mater dolorosae* and snake-haired Medusas expressing breasts full of bitter milk.

I began to collect maps of all kinds that I overlaid against the stars – medical histories (diabetes, heart failure, overwork), childbirth (grim survivors mostly, but with some pelvic disproportion, possibly through malnourishment), lactation (a long flowing line of peasant wet-nurses broken only by baby health centre sisters and their bottle-feeding routines in the 1950s). I matched my ultrasounds with my sister's, I compared antenatal cards, iron counts and old Health Department baby books. Figures, notes, film, Saturn in the Twelfth House – I set it all out in front of me, matching prints and holding negatives to the light. In the end, whenever the phone rang in those dawn hours, I would take out my maps, fix a point in the heavens and try to trace the call.

'Every mother carries her daughter in herself and every daughter her mother, and every woman extends backwards into her mother and forward into her

daughter,' wrote Jung. When my first daughter was born –
the first daughter of a first daughter of a first daughter,
arriving under the chain of Scorpio Suns extending from
her great-grandfather, grandmother, uncle and father –
she emerged just as I had from my mother. Both of us
were pulled out by forceps; my daughter's two perfect
bruises on her temples overlapped the lost traces of mine.

Yet her safe birth was not a harbour. Within a day, the
white coats were around my bedside, telling me my baby
would be placed in intensive care while tests were run on
her condition. Maybe she had a problem, maybe she didn't.
We would have to wait a few days and see what emerged.

I have never known anguish like those few days of
hospital lifts going up and down between my ward and
the intensive care nursery where my girl lay screaming as
the nurses searched for a vein in which to place an IV
drip. In the dawn hours – 1 a.m., 3 a.m., 5 a.m. – I'd wake
up in my ward to the telephone, summoning me to feed.
I'd throw a dressing gown over my shoulders and pad
softly through the bowels of the hospital, through swing
doors and lights and far-off nursing stations. I would
hasten, then walk briskly, then run with heart pounding
toward my crying baby.

Just before the intensive care nursery was a ward of
kidney patients, geriatric patients and emergency beds.
The babies could not be reached without passing through
here. My running would slow to a walk as I slipped,
unnoticed, through this vast room of pained unconscious

people, old men and women sleeping with mouths open, the drip bladders emptying silently into veins.

I felt I was walking past life and death with my daughter stolen to the underworld. I was prepared to offer myself, willing to make any contract I could. Just give me my baby alive, let me have back my child alive, even in pieces, even sick or broken or crippled, I'll take any part of her you give me.

In the early hours of the third night, I dreamt a dream that was in fact a set of instructions from myself. The deal was that I must watch for three signs. I had to do exactly what the dream said *and bring no questions*.

'The first sign will be an old woman who will insist on looking through all the rooms of my house, especially one curtained room to the side. That place I will not allow her to enter. Then a little girl with plaits, one longer than the other, will beg me to cut both to size but I must resist. As I dream, the dream-self will do everything according to the instructions.'

I awoke at 5 a.m. to the ringing of the telephone, knowing there was nothing wrong with my daughter. After such a dream I knew she would be healthy, plump and mine to carry out of the hospital.

At 10 a.m. that morning, the paediatrician, obstetrician, nurses and a social worker arrived and took out my daughter's drip. They apologised for all the fuss and handed her over to me. We dressed her in the yellow wool and white booties of her *nonna* Loretta Maria, we wrapped her in her paternal grandmother Shushanna's shawl and we walked out of the hospital, not to return till three years later for the birth of her sister, Emily. Another luck child with blue eyes, a second daughter of the first daughter of my mother.

'But Mum,' says my first baby, Rachael, now a schoolgirl, 'what about the third sign? There's supposed to be a third sign.'

'Brush your teeth,' I say. 'Get into bed, it's school tomorrow and you'll be late.'

When she's asleep, I tell her the rest. 'My darling dear, the third sign was waking up into our life together. The third sign was not in the dream, it was in the living.'

As for the contract with the underworld, every parent knows that the price of the children in the meadow is to live in fear that something out of life will snatch them away. The days of walking through the woods and picking flowers with nothing but your own hunger and your own gods to answer to are gone.

Years later, I tell my mother of the dream of the three signs. She's wide-eyed but not to be outdone.

'I didn't want to tell you this before, Ninetta,' she says, shaking her head. 'But all that time I was praying for the baby at *il precepio* at San' Antonio's. I promised to *Gesù Bambino* when you come back to Melbourne, you take the baby and you show her *il precepio* and you give Him some money, okay?'

St Anthony's Catholic Church in Hawthorn has an Italian-style Christmas crypt with fairy-lights through Bethlehem, fountains and taped Christmas carols. The kids – unbaptised, irreligious and ethnically half-Jewish anyway – the kids love it, it's like Disneyland.

We throw coins and notes into the offerings box. I ask my Jewish agnostic husband what he thinks of all this – the favours and supplications pinned to statues, the Santa Marias of the various villages, the boxes of splinters from the Cross, the replicas of the Shroud of Turin.

'Whatever it takes,' says my husband, hoisting our youngest on to his shoulders so she can throw another twenty cents to *Gesù Bambino*.

Whatever it takes.

The suitcase packed in the middle of the night is lean, hasty and ill-assorted. I've seen it scrape the sides of wardrobes, bump up and down stairs to be thrown into the backs of cars. I've packed it grimly myself and have seen it packed by others in my family. I've watched it followed by shouts and whispers and threats and the sound of frantic dialling. I've seen it flung dusty on to beds, stuffed full of emergency, defiance, fury and fear. The suitcase packed in the middle of the night has to get away fast, into taxis beeping on 3 a.m. streets, away to dawn bus terminals and last-flight airport conveyor belts, or to be lost in hospital corridors while orderlies wheel labouring women through lifts and drip-stands flit after their bodies like angels.

Only the essentials of character and place are thrown into the suitcase packed in the middle of the night – the last props of the old life, a few tools for the new.

At 3 a.m. on New Year's Eve in 1972, after a terrible and bitter fight with my parents, I lugged a suitcase down D Road, then a four-lane highway through a desolate new outer-eastern suburb of Melbourne.

D Road at 3 a.m. wasn't a place for a sixteen-year-old girl in a party dress with an oversized suitcase to be hitching a ride. New Year's Day – youth, parties, alcohol, drugs – or quiet loners driving out in the backblocks, watching, waiting, spotting a flash of bare shoulders, a girl alone on the highway.

But I didn't give a stuff. I was the defiant, streetwise, rebel teenager: the 'girl at risk' as they say at community youth centres. As I walked and dragged the suitcase, laughing and kicking it brashly down the traffic island in the dark, my anger, my disgust, my hurt, my sense of injustice – all I had of courage – began to dry up.

It was silent on the highway. There were not too many houses or street-lights around, just the headlights of an occasional car heading towards the city. The dark pockets of bushland seemed to be moving behind me. Suddenly my suitcase, my clothes and my skin were marked out, exposed.

A car was approaching in the nearest lane. I stopped walking. Shut up, keep going! I thought. But I was seizing up inside, I was losing my nerve. An empty neon-lit corner petrol station stood on the other side of the road. I hobbled across with my stuff and hid behind a petrol bowser as the car slowed down. It crawled past, slowly, slowly, the orbs of its headlights searching bright for me against the bowser.

The driver was hanging out the window. With a shock I saw that it was my father, that the whole family was bundled into the station wagon, keeping an eye out for me.

I crouched down. I waited till the car revved up, drove down the hill and out of sight down the highway toward the twinkling lights of the city.

I kicked, dragged, pushed and punched my suitcase all the way home.

In the middle of the starry Christmas night, it's often the childhood family that knocks on the door and moves in with me whether I like it or not, unloading all its primal baggage outside my children's nursery and at the foot of the marital bed. Dumped in a heap are the familiar suitcases and trunks full of diamonds and snakes, the reels of documentary films I project onto the dissembling and contaminated screen of my memory: 1956, Birth and First Year; 1960: The Summer Mother Went into Hospital; 1968: High School and Discovering Music in an Old Violin Case.

Let's take out 1960: The Summer Mother Went into Hospital.

It's a childhood afternoon, hot, golden and round. I am somewhere on the uppermost circle of the spinning earth. I am playing *La Principessa Di Lanciana Provincia di Chieti Abruzzo Italia* in my head as I walk:

'And now *mia bella Principessa*, I put a star on your forehead.'

'*Ma perché, Brutto Tutto?*'

'Shut up and go back to where you come from!'

'*Ignorante!* I won't have you speak to me like that, *brutta faccia tosta!*'

'*Allora addio – addio a questa terra di sangue e sofferto.*'

'What? Don't speak all this wog to me!'

'You shut up your face yourself, *Brutto Tutto!* Or I will put the basil of the priests on your cheeks and on your gown of the deepest *setta di cielo – e dopo ci vediamo – ci vediamo qui è wog e qui non è wog!*'

My father and I are walking hand in hand. We are in a leafy place of stone paths and flowers. There is a heaviness in the air through which shadowy women walk gravely past. I hope we are going to see my mother; I'd like to see my mother in our house again, shaking Persil into the washing machine, throwing tomatoes onto sizzling oil.

My father is hurrying us while pretending he's not and I don't like it. His haste is cutting up my game, ripping down the blue fabric of the sky and filling it with a cement day in Kew in 1960, the smell of petrol, the growl of a nearby lawnmower, traffic, roses and faraway cooking.

My baby brother smells. I think he's done something in his nappy.

Finally – after so much walking that I have to lie in the middle of the footpath and cry and be smacked – finally the three of us come to a place of glass doors, wooden floors, polished tables, mirrors and waxy flowers: lily of the valley. I suppose it is a hospital and we are going to see my mother. We walk through a corridor of squeaking shoes. Beyond the door, I can hear children, the clattering of pots and pans, the jangle of cutlery being thrown onto trays. I am in a convent, a Catholic institution for children in emergency and long-term care.

My mother is nowhere to be seen.

The grey-veiled creatures take me firmly in their experienced arms. 'Come along now, there's a good girl, no crying, you're too big to cry now, you're the big sister now, she'll settle in a day or two, Mr Belliosa Bellerosa Bellsiota, it takes a day or two, come on now, no more crying, Daddy's got to go, bye-bye Daddy, you're the big sister now …'

The nuns, kind but brisk, do their best. As they keep telling me through the weeks and months ahead, 'There's no point crying for Mummy.' She's in a hospital on the other side of town, fighting a serious illness, fighting for her life.

In the year of my mother's illness, my father 'coped', as the neighbours said when they saw him hanging out the nappies before work at 6 a.m. But he was under terrible pressure. He was alone with three children, as alone as a housewife with 'Days of Our Lives', as alone as a single mother with no money and no place to go.

We had no relatives to turn to. Our family began with Loretta Maria and Enzo Domenico, a husband and wife who didn't have anybody in Australia but the virtual stranger they had just married. Imagine, Italians without *la nonna, i cugini, le zie.* In times of trouble it was like we were orphans; it was an exile of God's devising on top of the political exile of losing *l'Italia.*

My father was supposed to be working back-to-back shifts at a maltings works in that sour-smelling, truck-roaring stretch of Collingwood breweries on Victoria Parade. 1960 was not a time of council-run family day care schemes, play-groups, paternity leave, industrially negotiated family and compassionate leave or work-based childcare. Your family matters were your problem.

Mediterranean tradition says the family – *la famiglia* with all its *imbroglio* and *obligazione* and *vendetta* and *dispetto* – is everything. *La famiglia* is the fine net of steel that supports and strangles. But where was our family when we needed them? This is what caused me to go into spasms when I had to wear the pinched shoes of the Italian village girl, those sandals of conformity handmade for cobbled streets but hopeless for stomping and kicking around in an industrial complex. 'Who cares what *they* think?' I ranted. '*They* aren't here! *They've* never helped us! *They've* never done a thing for you all your life except force you to pack a suitcase!'

My parents sat thunderstruck, furious.

But I was brutally right – politics and emigration had shrivelled up *la famiglia* into a set of photographs and thin airmail letters stuffed into the back of my mother's wardrobe. Our extended family was a Kodak film-roll family, reduced to nostalgic memory, a shared name and the sendings of blessed money to La Madonna di Villa Marino. Tears, pleas and prayers wouldn't flesh them out, wouldn't make them real. *La Famiglia* that was there for centuries was gone in one generation. No one could help us. We had a lone uncle, Zio Dionino, trying to settle in Darwin and the rest of the relatives were exiles in their own country, emigrating north to Milan where the factories were, where their hands would be clean because they wouldn't have to *zappare la terra*.

So in 1960 my father took his babies of four and two years of age to the Catholic Church to be fostered until the family, *la piccola famiglia* of Mum, Dad and us kids, could get back on its feet.

At the convent I remember a room full of stainless steel sinks, like a vast kitchen for cleaning up babies. The moon bobbed through the windows, as yellow as the Velvet soap that washed our bottoms as we splashed in our glinting baths. We were all set out to dry on thin white towels, a room full of clean, combed, scrubbed and fed foster children sitting in a row, waiting for our pyjamas, toothbrushes and Hail Marys.

On a visit to the convent one afternoon, my father got down on his knees to talk to me. He took out a large cotton man's handkerchief, washed and ironed.

'Ninetta,' he said softly in a broad Abruzzese dialect so I knew he didn't want the nuns to understand us. 'Ninetta, I want you to do something for your brother.' I concentrated hard because this was family talk, this was our stuff, speaking in Abruzzese. My father handed me the handkerchief. He had tied it in four corners – north, south, east and west.

'When they put your brother out in the sun, you put this hat on him, okay?'

'Why?'

'Because he's a baby. When they put him in the sun and leave him to sleep, he burns his head. I don't want him to burn his head, Ninetta. Please –' he held out the handkerchief to me. 'You take care of him.'

But what about me? My fury shook me to the ground. I took my father's handkerchief and threw it at him.

'*Dov'è Mamma?*'

'Try to be good, Ninetta.'

'*Mamma!*' I screamed. '*Voglio Mamma! Mamma!*'

My father left, wiping his face – tears of course, now that I look back on it.

A long time passes, a time of cold hands, running water, combs through my hair. The institution has a dining-room of little tables flung out like toys against the black-and-white linoleum.

Finally at day's end I am outside, watching the sun roll away from me, like a ball on the afternoon tide. I lean against the convent wall in a long cotton dress that doesn't belong to me. Below, on the spreading hillside, fresh-cut lawn and leaves curl in a pile. There is a chill in the air. The afternoon has the smell of late May and suburban lemons; institution Irish stew wafts from the kitchens far, far away.

Under my feet I can feel winter, I can feel the soil turning away to some dark place down there. I'm seeing all the evenings of my future – all of them out there in the years to come, bundled up inside me like a stack of cards – all the five o'clocks on the far horizons when I will be alone. It's not too bad. Part of that melancholy feeling tastes like cumquats, like lemons sprinkled with sugar.

Under the tree, still in his stroller, my fat-cheeked brother Gianni sleeps, a bottle by his side. The setting sun makes a halo on his head. I watch as his face and neck are slowly covered in gold. Soon he starts to wake, squirming to get his head away from the light.

I clutch his little handkerchief hat. I turn it around and around, feeling the four solid knots on each corner – north, south, east and west – roughly tied by my father's big hands.

North, south, east and west
Returning home is always best
Casa, palazzo e castello
La casa mia è la più bella

I put the hat on my baby brother's head. At dinner time, when the nuns wheel him back inside and take the hat off his head, they undo its knotted corners. I go crazy; they have to prise me off the stroller as I foam at the mouth with fury. In the dormitory, I kick and scream for a long time, till the windows are thick with night. Finally I collapse into my bed without supper or bath or anyone knowing what '*Papa l'ho fatto per mio fratello!*' meant.

So many families walk through a life. I am thinking it's not just the natal family that shapes your bones, although that mysterious constellation of *Papà, Mamma, sorelle e fratelli* seems to be like a fate working its way through a life. There in the weave it makes a point of strength and beauty, yet a little further on, it becomes transparent, tarnished and weak.

The Italian families on television and in the movies – the Mafia *paesani* in the Bronx, in New Jersey, in Chicago – they laughed and played *bocce* and made pasta and made love; they had codes of honour, they loved *bambini*, they had the big weddings, they had these big fights and they made up – *Hey, okay paesan? No problem!* – and they were warm, you know, tribal and loyal, folding in on each other like the squeezeboxes of piano accordions playing *E Compare, Let's Make Some Music!*

Yet I remember a house with two parents, harried, tired and alone, making bowls of *caffè latte* for breakfast and leaving semolina and bread-and-milk for us on the stove as they were both out of the house by 7 a.m., out to the factories with Gladstone bags, metal lunch tins and plastic sleeve protectors.

The world was made up of our family and what was 'out there'; there was *Mamma, Papà, fratello e sorella* and there was *l'inglese*. Our parents pinned keys to the insides of our pockets, telling us, 'Never, ever open the door; never, ever speak to anybody on the way home; never, ever bring around friends; never, ever tell anybody about family, not your father's name, how old you are, where you father works, nothing'. When they handed out permission forms at school, I filled them in myself, badly, with wrong ages, false addresses, names misspelt. Where they asked 'Father's Occupation', I made sure I always wrote 'Don't Know'.

Sure there were *amici*. They arrived for formal visits on Saturdays with their dressed-up children. We frantically tidied the house. I polished each piece of my mother's wedding china, especially the *tazze di caffè* which would soon be filled with strong coffee, accompanied by *savoiardi*. I don't remember *paesani* drinking wine with my old man and slapping down the cards till 2 a.m. But no, I lie – years of exile have made me maudlin, especially around midnight on Christmas Eve, when all the family arguments are replayed like *It's A Wonderful Life*. In the early years of my childhood house, there were *amici, paesani*, weddings, some light-heartedness, yes – my brother's *battesimo* was a wonderful party in our home, my mother handing out *aranciata* and homemade wine in the swishing fifties skirts she sewed herself, the Box Brownie camera snapping at people drinking and eating cake. My cheeks were pinched and kissed so much by *paesani* that the smell of brilliantine and short black coffee still makes me flinch.

Yet as the years passed, the people receded and *il dottore* made house calls more frequently. *La famiglia* turned in on itself, just like any other suburban family where the men were wage-slaves and the women wandered down the corridors of fried fish and mopped floors, afternoons of 'Days of Our Lives', drawn curtains and mysterious illnesses – dizziness, fear of open spaces, sharp jarring pains at lights, sounds, temperatures, all of which had to be adjusted minutely to be borne, and worse, the sensation of things crawling on the skin, of the ground moving, of walls falling in ...

We'd hastily prepare the bed, flinging across the heavy silk brocade for the visits of *il dottore*. He would leave prescriptions of Valium, Mogadon, Serenid, Noctamid. We'd run down to the chemist's and rush back, like Little Red Riding Hoods with a basket of cakes, anxious to make it better for all the mothers of the world lying pinned to their beds, wrestling with their wolves.

The girl who stops to pick flowers instead of staying on the path between the chemist and the sickroom can wander around the plazas and forget about the prescription in her pocket. Suddenly the world is full of trolleys jostling around the carousels of the malls.

I forgot about the errands I was supposed to be running for Loretta Maria. I spent days out of the house, hanging out with freelance mothers who didn't mind an extra daughter tagging along. There was Cassandra, my violin teacher, who taught me for no fee for years; Joanne, a Christian who fostered kids I'd babysit and teach music. Later there was Marjorie in New Zealand, a spiritual seeker with two daughters and a spare bed for a third, and Lorna, the country wife, who had so many stray foster daughters rounding up sheep from the back paddocks that she hardly noticed when I turned up with my swag at the back door.

I think about the immigrant mothers of the 1960s who still lie exhausted on their beds full of pain in rooms with drawn curtains, waiting for their daughters to bring back the healing medicines from the world. I think how impossible it is for the growing daughter to stay on that narrow path between 'us, our house, our world, our pain' – and what is 'out there', out in the whirling fair.

As a child I had my suspicions about the jars of pills I saw tucked into the factory bags of bone-tired women or sitting like icons on the bedside tables of the Turkish, Arabic and Greek friends, the textile factory co-workers of my mother's generation. Ativan, Nobrium, Rohypnol, Benzotran. Even the words made me lethargic.

Thirty years later I read in Beatrice Faust's *Benzo Junkie* a list of the symptoms of the benzodiazepines: '*sad face, averted gaze, agoraphobia, claustrophobia, bizarre and painful oversensitivity to stimuli: light, sound, smell, touch, temperature, taste, sensation on skin: chewing, worms, insects etc, sensation of ground moving, walls falling in …*'

Sometimes, despite everything you wish for, you lose your family, you know what I mean? Maybe your luggage gets separated from theirs or your stuff is chucked out from a balcony window at 2 a.m. Sometimes it's as simple as, like, maybe they're pissed off with you because you're cheating at Snakes and Ladders or you've insulted your dead Aunt Graziella's gnocchi recipe, so your photograph is swiped off the piano, crashing into shards that pierce everybody's heart like the mirror of the Snow Queen.

I was sixteen and things were getting impossible. The answer was 'no' every time I breathed. Say I had to get the bus into town, to Allans Music for a violin string or the Viotti concerto I was supposed to be doing for seventh grade AMEB – 'Yes, honestly, I'm going to buy a violin string – yes, a violin string, *violino*, you know – Tell her what a bloody violin string is! – Allans, ALLANS – it's not a boy – it's NOT A BOY, it's a bloody shop, a MUSIC SHOP!'

I disappeared into the garage-studio under the house that I made warm with a Vulcan heater, a wooden table and chair and alpaca jumpers. I set myself up with a music stand, HB pencils, manuscript paper and a growing stack of music – the Mendelssohn concerto, the Bruch concerto, Viotti, Bach, the Beethoven *Romanze in F*, the Carl Flesch scale book and the grindingly boring, dreadful, mindless and mechanistic exercises by Ševčik which I loved and practised for hours into the night.

Those numbing Ševčik exercises propelled me into exile. One summer I heard of a Czech violin professor who had once been a student of Ševčik's in the 1920s. Jan Sedivka was teaching in Hobart at the Tasmania Conservatorium; overnight I packed a Kmart suitcase of clothes, my English fiddle and all my music and manuscripts.

For the next year, while I practised Gaviniés *études* in a room in Sandy Bay, my photographs were being ripped out of the family albums at home.

No matter what I want to make of myself, my character unfolds just as it is, like a bolt of cloth flung on to a counter: *nel carattere è la vita!* Yet there were times when I resisted the cut of the family fabric, when I pushed off the hand of nature throwing me down to earth like a bolt of red, red silk.

I left Australia for New Zealand at nineteen for my second leg of exile. It was a time of getting rid – once and for all – of the family baggage.

I set up my typewriter in the room of a house by the Avon River in Christchurch, on the cold South Island below which 'the ice floes grind and mutter'. The city was like a kid's storybook, full of oak, willow and ash trees, English postboxes, trellis roses and buttery ice-cream. From my new room, I threw everything out – ethnicity, papers, clothes, outdated ambitions, ten years of Kreutzer and the C minor scale ... I looked around, feeling light and virtuous. What else could I chuck? Accent, that was next. I stood at the old bay window with Katherine Mansfield's journals and practised whispering *fush and chups*.

At last I had everything the way I wanted it. I sat under the camellias by the old porch at Bealey Avenue to watch my flatmates bicycling home from university in the twilight. I am nothing like my parents, I thought to myself. Nothing. I have nothing in common with them.

Behind me in the mirror, the antipodean sun blazed down on my new world. Two suitcases on the bed. A new land outside. Exile at nineteen. No job and as yet no real friends. A determination that I would make something happen for myself and create a life from the ground up.

Yeah, right. I had nothing in common with my parents.

The natal family has cast its spell of life and death and the body over me, for sure, but I can think of many angel families, the families of blessings and warm cloaks that seem to look out for you on the crossroads and highways. These families – small, fluid, often unacknowledged – cross the membranes between friendship and kin. They soften the decrees of fate and genetics, or simply take the weight of the family baggage off your back.

Maybe the truth is that I walked straight into my angel families with a compass and a map, that I chose them for refuge or built them out of a dream or a longing. I know that many times I foraged for them in dry land and so saved my own life through the kin I unearthed around a faraway kitchen table.

When I was a teenage violinist with a rigorous life of lessons, examinations, orchestras, chamber music, recitals and gigs, I did it all from the isolated outer suburbs without the obligatory middle-class parents chauffeuring me around (as I do for my daughters now).

I was proud to travel the roads alone, with a *Melways*, a backpack and, slung onto my shoulders, a sweet-toned five-hundred dollar English violin that I found in a shop in the city. This violin was like a first child to me. At nights I would look at it tenderly as I cleaned it with walnut oil and felt the centuries at its back, the trudging feet, the suitcases, the oceans. Picking it up once, the violist Christopher Martin commented that it was 'so pretty. A pretty fiddle, that'.

On the night buses from the suburbs to the Conservatorium of Music, the Dallas Brooks Hall, the College of the Arts and the chamber music salons of Kew and Hawthorn, any kid I met with a music stand and yellow *Schirmers* editions hanging out of an army disposal knapsack was kin to me.

Soon I was living in the houses of these musical relatives, as we practised our Sibelius *concerti* in the middle of the night, cooked fish curries and drank Johnny Walker around op-shop sixties coffee tables. For a long time I half-lived at Cassandra's; on summer evenings large crowds of us turned up with bathers, towels, instrument cases, stands and scores of Pergolesi, Vivaldi and Bach. In the late hours of the night, the doors were thrown open and twenty *ripieni* strings would cry out the big deep chords of *The Christmas Concerto*.

Once, in the early days of my time in New Zealand, when I was working in the Christchurch Symphony, I found myself between rental leases and house-sitting. I was desperate for somewhere to practise for the orchestra's Royal Command performance for Her Majesty's tour. I turned up to check out a student mansion, a notorious dive in Rhodes Street, burning up the driveway gravel on the back of a friend's motorbike, with my suitcase wedged pillion and my English violin strapped to my back. The small family of arts students and one bespectacled poet looked at me dubiously.

'Just let me move in,' I said. 'I've got to play for the bloody Queen tonight.'

Smirking, they carted my stuff into a converted larder off the kitchen. Over the next twenty years the arts students and the poet lent me money, threw me a surprise twenty-first birthday party, flew across the Tasman to shake me out of bad times, sent me airmail letters, poetry books, huge painted canvases and photos of newborn babies. Twenty years later, our children send each other picture books and hand-drawn birthday cards.

My English violin was finally stolen in a burglary at a house I was sharing in Sydney with a band called Buonasera Angel. The lead singer, a redhead named Gina Malley, still meets me for an occasional cappuccino wake over the thousands of dollars of equipment we lost.

Maybe after crying and laughing all afternoon, you hitch past the streets of the familiar city and end up walking through the dark woods. For seven years – or maybe the time it takes to play a couple of games of pinball – you stumble around in the great forests of exile or the vast deserts of middle age, doing Italian courses in Perugia, cooking ratatouille in New Zealand, maybe joining the Orange People, buying a Honda 500cc. Finally you stop at the first trickle of brackish water you can find, the first hovel, the first YWCA on the horizon. You dump your backpack on the step and open the door.

There around a table is your family, playing cards, eating pizza, drinking Lambrusco. They pour you a glass, rent you a room and hand over the 'Situations Vacant'.

I was a conscientious black sheep, dutifully fighting with the Scorpios in my family, putting in years of telephone *litigio* so fierce that my weary father had to sneak me letters, birthday cards and a silver Gemini pendant without the others knowing. He even had to meet me at midnight outside the silos of the breweries where he worked.

On one of the twelve nights of Christmas one year, it hit me – why was I doing this? Stuff it! Let it be some other family member's turn for a few decades!

Outside the David Jones windows, I watched toy soldiers pick up their bayonets and put them down again. Then I wandered into Australian Airlines and booked a ticket home. For a long time I sat in Hyde Park and stared at the date and time of flight 404: *I've booked a ticket home.*

I rang my sister from the airport. I hadn't seen her since she was sixteen. I watched her arrive with a drawn face at the luggage carousel, a tall purse-swinging Italian princess with her own Celica. She was furious with me; she opened the boot of the car and stood with her back to me and her arms folded as I struggled to throw my suitcases in. We drove the fifteen kilometres to our parents' house in silence. In the driveway, she switched off the ignition and turned angrily to me.

'Don't think you can just walk back in here after all these years as if nothing's happened!'

Inside, the lounge-room had been redecorated and all the old 1950s suitcase photos had been enlarged, repaired, re-framed and lined up on the piano, nestling against each other with vibrant pride. My mother bustled in from the kitchen with a tea towel in her hands, wiping the sweat from her brow. She gave me a wobbly high-cholesterol hug.

'*Magre, magre, magre,*' she said pinching my arm. 'Go in and eat something.'

She looked around at gawping family members who had quietly gathered from upstairs bedrooms and basements.

'*Eh, va bene,*' she said defiantly, waving us all into the kitchen. 'What's the point of cooking if no one eats?'

Sometimes your dream family moves in with you almost without you realising it. They get carried through your front door in a safety capsule and soon they snuggle under your doona, throw laundry around and cut up your wedding-gown for dress-ups. Even when they go to school or agricultural college or leave for Darwin to marry someone you wish they'd never met, they're still there with their chipped Greenpeace coffee mugs in your cupboards and their baby health centre immunisation cards continually falling out of old copies of *Family Circle*.

My daughters were watching 'Sesame Street' in their favourite position, squeezed together annoying each other in the same tub chair.

'I love you, Emily,' said Rachael absently, her eyes glued to the television set.

'I love you too,' said Emily, wriggling to get comfortable. She pushed her big sister's elbow out of her lap.

'I love you three,' said Rachael, putting her arm back.

'I love you four,' said Emily, throwing it off again.

'I love you *five*,' said Rachael.

'I love you *SIX*,' said Emily.

When I got back from bringing clothes in from the line, Rachael was about to jump on Emily's head.

I think they were up to 'I love you twenty-five'.

Sometimes, late at night, when I am carrying my sleeping daughters from my bed to theirs, all my life seems to roll into one, gathering like the tide of a sea of tactile relationship. The waves of the years, of skin, blood and bone break on to this midnight shore, bringing me my two peach-faced daughters, beached at my breasts and in my arms.

Beyond my daughters' sleeping faces I see on the horizon a caravan of marching feet and suitcases, taxis and ships, passports and photo albums, letters and phone calls, all carrying the remains of the past toward the future. On their father's side are the Sapirsteins, the Freitags, the Tiomkins, the Schilsteins and the Polish ghettoes, the death camps of Europe, a row of little children's faces on a 1920s photograph – this family of my husband's family, where all but one or two of the children were killed by the Nazis.

In documentary films, I stare at the mountains of discarded suitcases at the end of the railway line to Treblinka, I scan the rows and rows of children's shoes leaning against each other, empty of feet.

My husband takes our sleeping children from my arms and carries them to bed, pausing in the hall light to look intently at their faces.

Family – so many shifting allegiances, farewells, enforced marches, gulag chains, betrayals, sacrifices, gifts, curses, magic blessings – the star on the forehead, the secret apple of nurture. The families of a person's life are always on the move through the heart's different countries, eras, and territories.

I have a bad habit of helping myself, without asking, to the endless grab-bag of my family's fabric, remnants and off-cuts. I steal them and haul them back to my workroom at night, where I do a spray-job and a bit of beading on them, including what I'm doing right now, this tattle-tale telling, this hocus-pocus of trying to hem a bit of truth with a thread of lies, the punishment for which might well be another seven years of exile.

No matter; all night long I stuff my luggage full of everything I can get my hands on – half-complete stories that only make sense in Abruzzese, bunches of unsorted familial threads, rolls of unsubstantiated gossip, packages of quick-fix morality – nothing is wasted in the journey around inspiration and memory.

I pack my suitcases to the brim. Yet when I look inside, all I see is the endless ocean.

Harvest Day

One night years ago I fretted that my period was overdue several days. From my bed, through the open curtains, I saw the full moon grinning down at me. In the moonlight I began to cramp and suddenly I understood my woman's rhythms for the first time. *The Moon, my Mother.* Since then I have always looked to the moon to check on the timing of things down there. Our moon-shaped clocks are just the little fish from that great yellow sea.

The moon was new on the evening of the day the medical centre doctor told me I was six weeks pregnant. I saw the thin milk ring above the trees of the park near our house as I jogged through the wet summer grass. Round and round, ten laps or five kilometres, for a few nights I took my body through its paces as usual. I felt sick and confused but I didn't know yet how to yield to this force so I clung to the routines of the taut life that I had made. It was strange to think of my foetus child afloat on a huge amniotic sea, too new even to know it had begun upon that old and ruthless journey. Like some random second of a ticking clock, it was a measure of almost nothing and yet it moved fiercely towards the hour of its being.

By the ninth month, I was huge. I was a big fruit. I was squelching heavy, drooping, sleepless, immobile. I had put on seventeen kilos and I was just there waiting. On the deepest level I knew nothing of what was to happen. I just seemed to spill out circular, a boundless belly. In my mind however I knew everything, or so I thought. In the manner of the day, I had read all the books and attended two sets of classes, practising with dedication to confront the unknowable.

At 11.10 on a Sunday night, I was reading Sheila Kitzinger's *Giving Birth, How It Really Feels*, when my waters broke.

Dream-knitted night, web-black thick
the phone spasms
that other cord, the moon
huge, full, heavy
unfurled, a calendar, a command
her great roundness slipping
huge fruit
down, down

Nothing had prepared me for the great gushes of blood that accompanied each small, but as yet virtually imperceptible contraction. None of the books mentioned anything like it and I hadn't heard of it from any of the countless women I had talked to. I was frightened, especially for the baby – not a good start. As it turned out, it was nothing much at all. A tiny corner of the placenta had lifted off; there was no danger to me or the baby. However at the time no one was taking any chances – the labour ward sister said to come in at once.

The hospital was around the corner, in the street across the local park; I had planned to walk my way through it in the first stage of labour. I decided to give the bleeding ten minutes to abate. I was keen to stay home and go into the labour ward toward morning because I wasn't really yet in labour and wanted to sleep while I could. I was already tired and knew I wouldn't rest in hospital because I can't bear fluorescent lights. My husband and I walked out into the soft night, taking our dog who was highly skittish and nervous of the new smell of me. Fruit bats flapped through the trees. We made it once around the Moreton Bay figtrees when I realised it was not a good idea to hang about – I was flowing like a tap, not clear or pinkish waters but bright red.

Apart from anything else, I couldn't think what to do with myself at home because we had already used just about every towel and sheet we had.

The labour ward sister had said over the phone that, as we lived so close, we might arrange to go home again if everything was all right. Once in hospital however, I was gripped in the system's rules and procedures, not to mention the huge stomach belt-contraption that measures contractions. The baby's heart-beat was strong, my blood pressure was normal, the contractions were very weak, barely pre-labour strength. The medical staff were evasive about the bleeding, which made me anxious as I was neither a child nor a fool. Later I learnt that evasiveness is hospital routine if they can't get an official statement from your specialist. That is, they'd rather worry you to death than tell you honestly and promptly what the hell, if anything, is going on.

The only way I deduced that things were a little unusual but basically okay was because I was still feeling well and fit, despite the blood gushes, and the staff dispatched me to the antenatal ward for the night and left me alone till 7 a.m. By then I had been in real labour for two hours, since 5 a.m. ... but I hadn't slept a wink all night.

Obstetrics had calculated my time as three days before the full moon, a reasonable guess, I thought. I was so certain I would be delivered at the full moon that I had made appointments right until the last minute. No one believed me except my obstetrician, a woman with two children of her own.

I was delivered of my child at an hour or so before the daytime rise of the full October harvest moon. I felt pleased that it was the one thing that had turned out according to my hunches rather than my studied expectations, the one thing that was purely instinctual and not out of a book or calculated.

What I hadn't dreamed of was that it would take thirty-two hours (excluding a few hours of the mild warm-up stuff) to see this child born. In labour the babe had turned from the classic head-down-forwards into an odd position. Ironically my pelvis was large enough for it to muck about in this way. I was working hard but not getting very far – the midwives were sorry to tell me how little I was dilating. A night, a day, another night and a morning went past as I was squeezed and thrown by that big fist of pain. I saw myself as I truly was, a piece of flesh pummelled by the life force, a speck of life in the universe, unimportant other than as the carrier of the ceaseless chaos. I hung on to the breath, *a-pant-a-pant-a-pant, scream, a-pant-a-pant-a-pant, scream* ... That's all there is, everything else is illusion. Among the screaming and the heaving, the clutching for the gas, the pleas for the anaesthetist – *get him, get him now, go and get him, get him, get him NOW* – I caught the edges of my helpers' eyes and faces and wondered, Don't they know this? We live on a precipice – a knife's edge!

In the end, after two nights and another sunrise, after the walks, the different positions, the monitors, the drips, the showers, the gas, the epidurals that worked, the epidurals that didn't work, the offers of pethidine fiercely (and probably irrationally) rejected – *no fucking pethidine* – (and suddenly I understood why torture can be useless on some people. Because there will always be that thing never to be relinquished. The thing that can't be budged dwells in an Orwellian Room 102 of our psyche, next to the object in Room 101 which we absolutely cannot bear and will do anything to avoid. I couldn't believe I was prepared to conk out rather than have the one thing I couldn't accept. I was amazed how cruelly my brain worked. It said no – *no and the ultimate NO* – and my body just had to obey). In the end, all I had was my own breath.

On the bottom line I found just this: in and out, light and dark, yes and no, one and two, this and that, you and me, birth and death, inspire, expire. In my ears it sounded as though all the world was reduced to the in and out of breath, light and fast blows on top of the battering waves. Tiny snatches – *a-pant-a-pant-a-pant-a-pant* – from the great Breath: In and Out. My husband leaned down to breathe with me, my girlfriend breathed on the other side but it was my sister-in-law Danielle, who had given birth to a girl four months before me, to whom I clung. She seemed to know exactly what to do and say and was relentless, riding over the top of my abuse and despair, accepting everything but giving me her breath to breathe, never stopping, *a-pant-a-pant-a-pant-a-pant, In and Out*.

On the monitor the baby's heart beats, beats, beats.

O darling it's your harvest day,
love's harvest day
the threshers sweat, the scythes are coming
a-pant-a-pant-a-pant-a-pant
a-pant-a-pant-a-pant-a-pant
O darling, the scythes are coming
my God, oh God, oh God, my God
a-pant-a-pant-a-pant-a-pant
Oh God, my God, oh God, my God
o-when o-when o-when o-when
a-pant-a-pant-a-pant-a-pant
a-beat a-beat a-beat a-beat . . .
O-babe, o-babe, o-babe, o-babe
let me see you, let me see you
let me see your face, let me see it
O darling, o, o, o, o darling,
O darling come to us, come to us, come to us
O darling, it's your harvest day
love's harvest day
the threshers sweat, the scythes are coming

We're making acceptable progress, that's why I'm not sectioned thank God. Somehow we are moving along, just meeting the medical staff's deadlines, but it's slow and I'm exhausted from the even slower labour of the previous day. I'm in a bad way but I'm determined to avoid a caesarean if I can. I'm so proud of my baby because his/her heartbeat has never wavered, not once.

Or so I think. During the night while I doze with the first epidural, the baby's heart dips. My husband is asleep; my sister-in-law notices and calls the midwives. An oxygen mask is strapped to my face and I breathe, confused and unknowing. David later told me that I was told why but I can't believe it. I don't remember the heartbeat dipping. How could I forget something like that?

I roll over. The baby's heart beats, beats, beats.

I sleep for four hours. I sleep for a lifetime. I sleep the sleep of a hundred years. It's like drowning, my life dances before me in a kind of storybook sunset: little coloured bits of times and feelings jingling like a kid's rattle in the light behind my closed eyes.

The summer before we decided to make the second big decision of our life together and become a family, I had a dream. I am in a long queue outside the Exhibition Buildings in a Melbourne that is nothing like the real place. There are all kinds of people jostling outside, waiting to take a series of examinations. I wait in the milling crowd, rocking a pusher with a baby inside. A woman bends down and smiles. 'My God,' she says, 'but she's so pretty.' I stare down at the baby. It is the first time I have noticed that I have a baby. I look closely at her. Pretty? Yes, I think to myself with some surprise; yes, she really is quite beautiful.

The woman asks, 'And what's her name?'

I smile. It's obvious.

'Rachael.'

Early in the morning the epidural wears off, leaving me in the middle of brutal contractions. I am in a raging storm. With renewed vigour I concentrate. I am full of hope but after only an hour and a half, I am as exhausted as I ever was. I am told I have developed a slight fever and since by now I am hooked to surely almost every contraption modern medicine has made available to the labouring woman, I decide to go the whole hog and demand more epidural top-ups. What the hell … I've done my best and a bit more. Fifteen hours without pain relief – and without the best painkiller of all, the knowledge that you are getting close to giving birth – is enough for anybody surely. Surely?

Yet I'm feeling confused, ashamed and betrayed by my body. A sense of failure together with a touch of female bio-posturing rages through me – women have babies all the time, what's the matter with *you*? At the same time, I know I'm being unreasonable. It's not my fault, or anybody's fault, that the baby has turned into a posterior transverse position with her head flexed. At the same time I'm thinking, why me? At the same time I know the answer is why not me – and be grateful it's not a lot worse. At the same time I feel that having a baby has been the biggest mistake of my life. Stop the labour, I want to go home and try it again in a few months time – or maybe never! At the same time I'm fearful for the child and I don't care what the medical staff do to ensure both of us come out of this alive and well. At the same time I am enjoying the relief of this epidural more than anything I've ever experienced and I almost – yes, I'm going to say it – I almost don't care what it might do to me or the baby in twenty minutes or twenty days or twenty years so long as I can get away from the pain NOW.

The baby's heart beats, beats, beats. The big fist of pain throws me from one end of myself to the other.

Contraction by contraction, the invisible cord pulls us tighter – Moon, mother, daughter, baby. Thirty-two years apart, contraction by contraction, I am still linked to my mother. We are again sharing the childbirth bed as I am rocked in the same cradle of pain that saw me into the world. I have inherited the pattern of this labour from her, I've been handed the baton of this long, long race and now it is my turn to run with it.

My birth was my first original story from her, my first knowledge of women's business and my first gothic horror tale. Unlike all the other stories, it was not set in once-upon-a-time but a definite date in 1956 and had no ending: it grew along with me like a heartbeat to follow me into death. Every time I exasperated her – which was quite often as I was a 'difficult' child – the story would unfold, tailing off with the oldest of mothers' curses: 'may you have a daughter like you.'

To my astonishment, the epidural top-up does not 'take'. I am left stranded on my back, unable to move from the waist down, as the contractions break over a corner of my pelvis. This is worse than no pain relief at all. I can't move, I am trapped like an insect under a gigantic pin. The anaesthetist is at an emergency caesarean, he will be back in twenty minutes. In my world all that means is another fifteen contractions. It may as well be never.

If I could walk I would throw myself out the window.

A-pant-a-pant-a-pant-a-pant, a-beat-a-beat-a-beat-a-beat, o-when-o-when-o-when-o-when …

She is twenty-five years old, she speaks no English and she has been labouring alone in a bed at Queen Victoria Hospital for a day and a night. Her husband, the only other kin she has in this foreign country, is not allowed to be with her, even if it were the custom among her people, which it definitely is not. Even so, he would be willing to be there because he knows her aloneness, the lack of women at her side. Instead he waits on the other side of town sick with fear, not daring to miss a day at the factory.

Doctors and midwives walk in and out of her vision, murmuring to themselves. She is a New Australian, she doesn't understand anything they say. So they say very little. Flat on her back, she is trapped like an insect under a gigantic pin. Is she dying, is the baby dying, why is it taking so long, what will happen, what are they doing? In elaborate sign language, a midwife tells her that her baby will be born in a few hours. Hours. It may as well be never. If she could walk she would throw herself out the window. She doesn't know how long she has been screaming. A midwife comes in with a needle. 'When you wake up,' she says, 'you'll have your baby in your arms.'

With the help of forceps I come into the world greeted by the midwives and doctor whose name is on my birth certificate. My anaesthetised mother is unable to be present. My father was not allowed to be present.

In visiting hours that night, my father presses a slip of paper to the nursery window to be shown his firstborn. He sees a red-blue bruised bundle like a squashed plum. He is so shocked the nurses have to reassure him there is nothing the matter with me and that I'll look prettier in a few days.

If I were a student over again, I'd study to become an anaesthetist. It must be gratifying and good for the soul to ease pain for a living. How wonderful to see a labouring woman's eyes light up with love at your footfall. How blessed to be the most beloved person in the room. Not the husband, not the helpers, not the midwives nor the obstetrician gets the affection, the gratitude, the passionate look of welcoming joy as does the anaesthetist.

Yet modern chemistry is not giving me a free ride. There is no relief until the epidural is re-sited. By then, even the anaesthetist is reluctant to give me yet another top-up.

I insist.

In the long gullet of this labour, I have come to digest a contempt for the puny world of men. Even for the strongest of them, the marathon is only two hours, weightlifting but a few seconds of exertion. The average woman in her first labour will go six times the two hours of the marathon to give birth. There is no turning back, no dropping out of the race, not even the option of simply collapsing – once a woman steps into the great gullet, once she is squeezed in there by the big fist, something must be spat out, an outcome which is never any less than life or death. A woman labours until her child is born. The power, wherever it is coming from, is relentless – greater than life, greater than death. For a woman like me, a father's daughter, a daddy's girl who has spent a long time in the world of men, this comes as more of a shock than it should. My understanding of work, of the verb *to labour*, comes from the way men measure it – heaving weights, climbing Mount Everest, fighting wars, commanding companies or running a country.

Now I know the ordinary woman in labour does more than that. All those things of the world that I valued and feared, that I complained of, that I made such a big deal about, are nothing compared to what I am facing in labour. Nothing. For hundreds of years of our history, men have been able to con women into thinking they're weak, they're oppressed and have to be liberated because women's work is nothing, any fool can do it. What a hoax. All that baiting about why there are no women artists or composers, no women generals or women on the boards of companies, when the question should have been why there are no great women rapists, mass murderers, cut-throats and warmongers, no great male nurses, home-makers, child-rearers? Oh what lies and corruption it's all been. Now there is a generation of women who've done all that alleged tough men's business and will continue to do it: we've flown the planes, we've been on the boards, we've made money on the stock exchanges, we've been in the parliaments and now we know – bearing and raising children is harder.

Seven centimetres. The entrance to the world is almost open. Only a finger's breadth remains between the cave and the light. Such a little distance to be born, such an immense journey for mother and child. From inside the physical, animal work of the labour, I can now feel a stillness above the waves of pain. This child is coming from a long way away. It is being called, I know it is.

Seven centimetres. I have to hang on but I am afraid because I know I can't be safely given another epidural top-up. Now I know what it is to face the end of the tether and have to stretch it some more.

Later, much later, I will be glad I have known this. Now that I know my power I feel for a moment that I understand all women and I know all pain.

I used to have a lot of ideas about things I had never experienced and I suppose, for someone who is naturally inclined towards ideas and the life of the mind, I always will. Now I will at least try to distinguish between thinking about life and living it, between opinions and feelings. Ideas, opinions, theories, philosophies, beliefs are just that: ideas – interesting, illuminating things that can and must change like chameleons in contact with instinct, feeling, experience. Otherwise how can there ever be any compassion?

I used to have a lot of ideas about the bearing of pain. During this labour I experience it. Of course, I am bearing it for a purpose, a joyful greeting – there are two of us and I am at the harvest moon of my life. Yet in the midst of my labour I have a sharp sense of what it must be like at the other end of the continuum, to be dying alone under the withering moon in this pain.

Those people who oppose euthanasia should put their bodies where their convictions are. I have a fantasy that the objectors enter a chamber where they must endure the simulated pain of those who can't bear it any longer. The moralists who come out of that chamber with their beliefs intact might possibly have a right to them. All the others who capitulate will surely be glad of the opportunity to finally know that great chasm between morality and wisdom, between law and compassion.

During contractions, a midwife walks in clucking her tongue. 'Poor dear, you're doing it the hard way.'

I snatch a breath. 'Oh yeah,' I scream out, '*so what's the easy way?*'

The midwife is taken aback. Then a smile slowly spreads across her face.

'The next one.'

My obstetrician is sitting at the foot of my bed. The time has come. Either I am fully dilated and she delivers by forceps or she does a caesarean. She says she can't stand to see me like this any longer. Put this way, I don't feel too badly. I sense her valuing of what I have tried to do. I am not just a contracting uterus with a badly positioned baby. I can see she knows the meaning of this for a labouring woman, the weight of it.

The examination is swift but it's a long moment as I lie trying to prepare myself for the idea of surgery, the idea that I have worked through all these hours only to undergo an operation I could have had at the beginning (supposing that we had the benefit of hindsight which we didn't). All this effort wasted. What a blow. I try to swing my mind back to everything I have read about coping with caesareans. I try to be humble to this force and just accept what it decrees. I try to think of how safe and easy it will be for the baby, to be lifted out like a peach from a syrupy tin ... All the while my rebellious body and soul squirms *please, please, please ... just let me finish the job.*

The last thing I need now is for someone to say, 'Why don't you just get knocked out and get it over and done with?' It's the sort of thing I might have said before I experienced this labour and understood. Do you tell a swimmer in the middle of her stroke, 'Why bother?' Do you tell an artist as she paints, 'Why are you doing this?' Do you tell someone drowning, 'Hey, you look awful, do you want a Valium?' In the middle of this storm I don't want to hear any God-how-awfuls, should-have-dones, might-have-beens, don't-worries, forget-about-its, think-positives, next-week-you'll-be-partyings and other bullshit ... I don't want to be distracted and offered platitudes, I want one hundred per cent concentration on what is happening *now* ... I am at the wall, by the chasm, in the deep wave's crest – I am where I know control is an illusion, right up against the heartbeat of chaos and that this is *normal*, this is what our lives truly are, only in the daylight world most of us can't face it. Birth and death are normal, suffering is normal, uncertainty is normal, joy and despair are normal, coins are paid to the ferryman on both sides of the river – paid from what you value, not what you can afford – and that is absolutely normal. Each contraction now brings me to see – how is it I have lived thirty-two years and not known any of this?

I have a chorus by my bed of husband, sister-in-law and woman friend, all singing 'yes, yes, yes'. Around me I have a litany of labour. What could have been a trauma, just random pain squirming poor and cruel into the void, is lifted into the oldest of all songs of creation.

Being with someone, murmuring along with their heartbeat, breathing with them is a lost art. The true midwives of birth and death, those who keep vigil at the bedposts, are rare. They are people whose eyes are accustomed to darkness and light, who stand waiting by night and by dawn, holding cloaks and soft wrappings at the crossroads and gateways. They stand at the threshold, at the breaking of the paths, watching the lights, the rain and the winds, welcoming and farewelling our journeying souls. The value of such people is above rubies. No machines that go ping can stand in their place. Yet so often that is all we have. Thank God it doesn't happen to me.

I am ready. O, the opening to the world. Full moon, the great roundness, O. I hear the obstetrician saying to the midwife, 'We can do this.' Inside I am singing. Joy. I hold tightly to my husband's hand. I am being covered in green sheets. The midwife apologises for them but I don't care. To me it is as though I am being decked out to meet the beloved, the creature who has squirmed inside me, the being to whom I have been pledged for nine long months.

The room is filling with the moment. Everything seems to be leaning forward and swelling. My eyes keep flickering towards the crib and its soft wrappings. I have forgotten the machines, I no longer feel the straps, the drips, the rolls of tape on my thighs. To my mind at least, the instruments are quiet, as in some spacecraft where the crew is watching for the unknown creature that has been sensed approaching. Stars, waiting, rolling, falling, darkness ... far, far away the giant white bear lumbers on the ice ...

In a mirror, I see my child's wet crown. The mirror wobbles away like water and I hear a sound like ... I've never heard anything like it, perhaps a kind of gurgle, a rattle ... I am at a loss, I think maybe someone has fainted ... I look swiftly around but no one is missing ... then I understand – it is the sound of a baby being turned in the birth canal and gently prised out. I must hold my breath if I am to push but after so many hours of the labouring rhythm I can't seem to get out of *a-pant-a-pant-a-pant-a-pant*. It has become like a reflex. The midwife has to hold my jaws shut as I give three of the greatest pushes of my life.

There is our wet babe curled upon my stomach, a big heavy long-limbed child I instantly recognise as *the one inside*. Our eyes feast and range over every part of the baby, checking, marvelling, recognising. Seeing this bonny big baby I understand everything – the kicks under the right rib, the squirms, the perpetual nine-month tummy ache, the ravenous hunger. I am happy just to feel the wet skin against mine, to accustom myself to the once-me-but-not-me sensation of flesh, fingers, hair, toes. All around me, voices are laughing and praising, urging me to tell them the sex of the child but I am too mesmerised and confused to work out how to do it.

It is my husband who shouts, 'It's a girl!'

Of course. A girl. I feel I have always known her, always, always my girl. 'So it's you,' I say. 'So it's you, Rachael.'

My girl has two stains on her new face, two round marks where the forceps pulled her into the world. The tiny stains are beautiful in their precision – no more and no less than what was necessary. They are the work of a masterly hand, like embroidery or the setting of diamonds. The sight of them fills me with gratitude and awe. They make my daughter's face more striking than any on the Sistine Chapel ceiling.

I am not the only one to admire my female doctor's skill – the midwives are openly impressed, especially as I have got away with only a small tear. It might be unfair but I am certain only a woman could have been so careful. It's hard to describe the love you feel for the attendants of your children. It's not just gratitude to be relieved from pain or harm but the feeling, very rare in life, that you have been completely seen. The woman in labour and her midwife are an ancient couple; with the advent of the male obstetrician, this pair has been made into a syndrome, something of a well-known joke, but it does not change the fact that it is real and powerful. To bring a human being into the world involves more than veterinary science. I have so much love for the attendant women who have worked with my husband and me on our harvest day.

My daughter sleeps in her father's arms. They lie curled in a bed across the ward from me. Like my mother before me, I am too exhausted to hold my daughter, to explore, cuddle and feed. At least in this generation, I suckled her briefly before I collapsed. At least in this generation, I can see my baby nearby through my half-closed eyes, see her cradled in the arms of my other self and know that her first hours were flesh-to-flesh with someone who loves her as fiercely as I do.

Rachael.

Don't let anyone ever say that these first things, the way of entering the world, don't matter. They can be overcome, altered, repaired, healed, resented, suppressed, forgotten and denied but they matter. Rachael. Seeing her little face against her father's turns me back into the bruised newborn of my mother's and my lifelong myth. I feel myself in the efficient swaddling of the nursery, tagged and alone under the fluorescent light. Mamma sleeps down a long corridor, the corridor of fear and pain, the longest corridor in the world. We struggled and fought to reach each other over that distance for years. I don't think my mother has ever got over the way I was born. I never knew any better. Until now.

warm blue
you heave your first breaths to shore
beached in milk shallows,
shell-secret ears, seaweed fingers waving
drawn up by bone and water
your face is pinched
by puckers, the half-sobs that crawl and scuttle
across ever-shifting skin, as your limbs
churn the deep dance of the tides

air cuts your lungs
they fly, two birds in the desert sobbing
you startle after them,
splayed on the edge of this burning rim
thirst prises open your undersea eyes
spilling in the blue blue tumult,
and the heat of some thick mammalian tremor
rolls you upwards

unravelled
you knead flesh through flesh
across the stinging spaces
now the first of the billion breaths
inflate you

puffing you to the edge of daylight
as you climb arms akimbo
to the brown fruit moon
latch on to flesh
mouth downwards suckling
on to the far forgotten echoes
the white unbroken shore forever inside
lapping
out

Taking her home is terrifying. Numb with exhaustion, stupefied from sleepless nights, crazy with love and rigid with fear, I struggle from day to night to day to night. The weeks become a blur. I am tied to her by an invisible cord – I leak milk at her every squawk. Her unhappiness drives me to despair, her suckling empties and fills me like the tides. When she sleeps and her face 'smiles with the angels' as my mother says, I cry with happiness and I wonder if I am going mad. I wait and watch through the heaviness of time with my beloved tormentor, growing her under the sun and the moon, weighing her plumpness and measuring her curled limbs.

Words are useless in this realm. All my life I clutched at words, patted them, cultivated them, played with them, nodded seriously at the world of ideas and concepts. Now I have to release them, watch them disappear like a flock of birds into the air.

The world of the mother is silent, watchful, physical, here-and-now. Like art, it looks simple. From the outside it seems as though anyone could do it. Yet it's a calling both profound and consuming, with its rewards and its punishments, its beauty and its hell. It ages women, rents them apart, shakes marriages, confronts men with the spectre of their own tenderness, ageing and frailty. Every day in mansions and in one-roomed apartments, in starvation and in plenty, women are raising children. So what, says the world, so what? It's normal to fear for your milk, it's normal to be sleepless, it's normal to have dying babies in the third world, it's normal to have seventeen-year-old single mothers in boxy flats going around the bend, it's normal to rock a cradle, comfort, jiggle, sing, pat, kiss, bathe, tend, defend, worry and love so intensely your life can never be the same again even if you want it to be. Earthy life itself is a 'so-what?' matter amongst us, invisible, interior and valueless. The mother is left at a loss for words, mute in the babble of politics and professions, wars and wages going on outside. The mother's world is the so-called art of the small. But the thousand and one things outside are as nothing against the slightest movement in her universe of nurture. She practises that paradoxical art where a little at the right time is everything. The outside world doesn't deal in this currency.

I talk to my mother over the phone, amazed that she could have done this three times. I apologise for being a bad baby, for never sleeping through the night for five years, for screaming my head off for months on end, for foraging into cupboards, stairs, laundries, for being a real pain in the arse. My elderly mother's advice to me is, 'Things go forwards not backwards. Every day she's growing older. When she wakes in the night, feed her and think of all the pretty dresses you'll sew for her.'

No matter what my daughter does, to my mother it is never as bad as what I did as a baby. Nonna aligns with the baby, defending her crying and wakefulness against the naïve mother who has yet to pay her dues. It's aggravating for me but at last my mother is free to enjoy babies, to revel in their little ways. It is pleasurable to feel this grandchild add to healing over the scars of the frightening things my siblings and I unwittingly did to my new and isolated young parents.

Oh the nights of patting-and-rocking and rocking-and-patting. We come to know the sighs and breaths, the screams and whimpers, the pacings and jiggings of the night. We have stumbled onto the secret society of mothers and fathers walking prams in the star-cold parks and driving through deserted city streets. The nights are heavy with the entangled dreams of babies and parents who snatch unsynchronised moments of sleep in the foggy exhaustion.

I used to watch dying third-world babies on the television news and think how unbearable. I used to glance at courtroom sketches of men who had raped, murdered and tortured people and I would hate them to the point where I would have liked to hang them myself. I used to see the family photographs of abducted children desperately reproduced in newspapers and think, No, no, no, not again. I used to see all these things and think, well it's a corrupt world and when people wake up to themselves/Party X gets into government/social security improves/the recession ends/the suburbs get better services/criminals get rehabilitated and so on, these horrific things won't assault us.

Now I understand the young mother who told me about the time she was staring out the window of a bus with her eight-month-old baby boy on her lap. A derelict staggered onto the road screaming abuse and she was surprised to find herself crying for the man. In that moment she imagined him as somebody's child, somebody's tiny little loved or unloved baby. The pain was overwhelming. Becoming a mother means walking around seeing everybody with new eyes, even mass murderers, dictators and torturers. It is astonishing to realise that everyone in the world was once new, wet, helpless and hungry, with a mouth straining for milk.

Now I can't watch news reports of starving dispossessed peoples and immediately think about world politics because half the time I am sitting with my own child at the breast. Seeing another woman unable to give her baby sustenance is obscene. I now know the cost of

that and the feel of that in my body. It hits me physically.
I'm not *thinking* anything, I am in tears.

My husband looks at me worriedly. Apparently it's
the hormones. The books say it's the big change in
hormones from pregnancy to lactation.

Yeah, the hormones. Women get so emotional at this
time. After all, it is only a matter of life and death.

Penelope Leach, Breast Is Best, Nursing Mothers,
controlled crying, comp feeds, *The Australian Guide To
Good Toys* ... the feed-'em-formula-and-be-done-with-it
school, the mammary-mafia-breastmilk-till-they're-four
theory ... dum-dums versus thumb-thumbs ... cloth
versus Cosies ...

Ideas. Over the next few weeks, I face a lot of ideas,
theories, philosophies, beliefs. From this time on, ideas
crawl over me like ants on jam. Yet the old certainties,
the faith in the system that once supported me well
enough have gone. Instinct will be my only
discrimination against the barrage of theories and
possibilities and advice. Yet my instinct needs sharpening
on the blade of experience. I have to make mistakes. In
order to care for my child I will do things I never
believed in and never read about and don't understand.
If they work, they are right. If not we will try something
else and fast. We will lurch from moment to moment.
Such a way of living is humbling for someone who used
to want to know what was going to happen next, the self

who believed, however vaguely, in good ways and bad ways of going about things.

I have come to hang on to the words of an older mother of teenagers who shrugs and says to me, 'Don't worry about good and bad, only love and what is necessary'.

I have always appeared to be more emotionally forthcoming than my husband. I leapt where he feared to tread. He weighs his words, I scatter them. When we saw our house, I knew it was the right one straightaway. He wanted to think about it. I adopted each cat and dog of our menagerie on impulse. He had his reservations.

In the weeks before our child was born, my husband suffered a crisis of confidence. He lapsed into broody silences, he watched a lot of television, he wasn't interested in shopping for change tables or size 000 singlets. We had some tense conversations about his fears for himself as a father. I was placid, dreamy and confident, sure that once the baby was in my arms, it would all unfold as it should.

When our child was born, I was tense, anxious, fretful and overwhelmed by my responsibilities, fearing for myself as a mother. My husband was placid, dreamy, confident, twirling the babe in his arms, bathing, changing nappies, wheeling the pram, sure that it was all unfolding as it should.

So much for the old certainties. So much for our old predictable life.

Anything can happen. Life must be responded to as it unfolds. Preconceptions, plans, beliefs just get in the way. We are in the middle of growing a mystery and therefore no one has the answers. Yet we need to sort out the chaos. My child is forcing me to become less judgmental, more cautious in drawing conclusions. Over and over I have to admit 'that's the way it was today' and 'I don't know for sure but this seems more effective than that for now'. I am nurtured by the stories and acceptance of other parents and their tact. We are all in the same small boat on the same great sea.

It frightens me to think I might have lived the rest of my life without knowing this humbling, extraordinary secret world – this milky furious love.

Unravelling

The only things I choose to keep from among my brother's things is a letter he sent to my mother from the Himalaya in the late eighties. It was in the year I got married that he first tried to scale the East Face of Trango Tower, 'a 3000 foot tooth of granite that rises like a bad dream' in the Karakoram Mountain Range in north-western India. He and his team-mates almost got up this rock, also known as the Nameless Tower, from which they hoped to see around them the greats – Masherbrum, Gasherbrum IV and even the tip of K2. But they had to abandon the climb due to a blizzard at the last stage. Folded into the letter is a tear-sheet from *Southern Geographic* featuring a heart-stopping photo of him and his team bedding down in a porta-ledge tent ballooning off the side of the mountain at 6000 metres. It was the shot that launched his career in adventure photography.

I tuck the photograph into the letter. I fold and refold along the creases.

Hey Tony. You were so right sweetheart. It really was the safest place in the world for you, rocking in that cradle of air, with the mountain saying 'Yes', the mountain saying 'No'.

I was in hospital after giving birth to my third child when my brother and his son died in a car accident. They were killed instantly on the South Island of New Zealand when a white male driving drunkenly along the road to Arthur's Pass collected them head-on and split their white Toyota Camry in two.

Tony was on holiday with his Kiwi-born fiancée, Sophie, a geologist similarly obsessed with anything that went up into the roof of the world. They were getting married in March, an unexpectedly happy development which had so settled down the grievances between my brother and his Sydney-based ex-wife, Danielle, that she agreed to send over the two children, Zeke, four-and-a half, and Clementine, six, for a school holiday skiing week at Arthur's Pass.

So the four of them, Sophie and Tony in the front, Clementine and Zeke in the back, were driving from the snowfields on a flat road on a clear day at 4 p.m. when the drunken meteor hit. Burned up instantly in his exploding car, he disappeared like snow into the eye of the setting sun. We never even knew his name.

Left on the highway, like some horrifically mutated cell, was the new order of our lives.

On the left were Sophie and Clementine, alive.

On the right were Tony and Zeke, dead.

It was as logical and senseless and simple and stupid as that.

Fear, dark beating wings, nausea, nameless dread. We had not named our newborn before the accident and afterwards Ari and I were in no state to make up our minds. It had taken a full sixty days after the birth of each of our older girls to settle on and register their names. Sixty days the law gives you and it comforted me that we could take just as long with this last bonny girl, born in the dead of night, waxy and startled with a pouty red mouth like a French movie star. She didn't cry but looked at us as if she had made this crossing many times. With her wise blue eyes and white streaks of vernix, she could have blown in over the Tibetan passes from Shangri-La.

But as the hours slid into days, and my lying-in was uprooted by a fierce instinct to flee the hospital and go to New Zealand, I became increasingly reluctant to name this baby. On her wrist identification tag, she remained generically 'Baby', tucked safely under my name, *Santina L. Schilstein*, her date of birth forever tied to the day of her uncle and cousin's death, the time of her birth *3.32 a.m.*, her sex *Female* and her *weight at birth 3.850 kg*.

And I was glad. Because the naming of the infant is the first thing of this world that separates you and not-you. The name is a knife, searching for you, cutting you away from whatever you're attached to – flesh, fantasy, future. Saying the name, writing it, can shake you up, it can stir all the invisibles in the air. When we were kids my brother used to hoard his *National Geographics* in the cupboard under the stairs. Looking through them once, I saw photographs of West African tribeswomen in labour. To ease their pain, the article said, they were given a drink made up of the words of the Koran written in charcoal and washed in water. More shocking to me than the sight of grunting naked women was the idea that words could be taken in by the body and made flesh.

At first I really did believe my reluctance to name the baby was because I was searching for something especially meaningful; a link to us that glistened with symbol, not just an image or a musical sound or a play name from my own fantasy of childhood. But then there was the funeral, an avalanche that buried nearly all our joy. As the debris of grief rattled down around us, I became convinced it was dangerous to name her, I wanted only to zip her up inside *sweetie, poppet, lovey,* safe from the chaos around us.

Danielle had left on the next flight to New Zealand, a few hours after the police knocked on her door: the tigress mother fighting to reach her injured child – Clementine alone in the hospital of a foreign city, crying 'mummy mummy mummy' on an international call – and the savaged mother, dismembered by the saving of one child meaning the loss of the other.

As for the loss of Tony, the father who had held them at birth, as tangled in the life-cord of them as she, Danielle had no time or space within to pay her proper dues of grief to him. That would enrage her later, when on some days it would be as if the dead were all plucking at her sleeve, wanting their bowl of tears.

By the time we arrived in the ice-cold city, Danielle had spent four days sitting with the bodies of her son and ex-husband. Every day she visited the funeral home in the early morning and late afternoon, holding Zeke and Tony's hands. In between, her lover Paul drove her to Christchurch Hospital, where they sat with Clementine as the child wolfed down hospital hamburgers and bounced her toy zebra on the bed. Unlike Sophie, Clementine had walked out of the wreckage into the arms of ambulance officers, uninjured but for severe bruising from the pressure of the impact on her seatbelt as it held her. No one knew exactly how long she had sat among the dead and injured, clicked into that tenacious sash. Later we learned she had been conscious throughout the whole thing. She had no blackout, no protective shock with its sedating amnesia. She witnessed simply, eyes open to the full impact.

In the evenings when the child was settled to sleep, Danielle and Paul crept down the corridors to Sophie's ward. Danielle cut up Sophie's dinner and the three of them watched the sun set over the Cashmere hills.

We knew nobody in Christchurch. The funeral service was conducted by a stranger minister who spoke in such one-size-fits-all platitudes that finally Paul and Ari had to stand up and ask him to stop. We then performed the rest of the ceremony ourselves, instinctively, like people caught up in a surprise rushed labour by the roadside.

Back in Sydney, I'm hanging on so tight that I am numb and bruised all over. Day after day, I walk home from Danielle's, marching fast, eyes blurred through the winter streets of Newtown. Wheeling the baby and dragging the two weary and still jet-lagged older girls ('I'm tired, I don't want to walk, I don't like walking, why do we have to walk all the time?'), I march past The Old Fish Café, past Holy Sheet wafting lavender oil from its chrome burners, past the baby health centre in Lennox Street. Eyes downwards, I concentrate on getting the pram wheels over the remains of condoms and spew in the gutter, until I see the familiar graffiti on the churchyard walls. *Time Killers, Sick of The City, Hands Held Violently on to Words That Mean Nothing, Play With Time, Nameless Dread, Monoxide = Your Doom.* I speed up so that the girls, busy breaking twigs off the cotoneaster bushes, have to run beside me to keep up. 'We're tired, we don't want to walk, why do we have to walk all the time?' they say.

Finally I turn into the wrought iron gates of St Stephen's. I stop under the spreading figtree. Its winter's arms reach high over the world ghetto-blasting in King

Street outside. Beside it stands the old Anglican church with its spire in the clouds. Behind it is the 1849 graveyard with its cracked headstones and plinths. On paths covered in grass and shaded by mourning trees, the names of the dead lie scattered.

Surely, among so many, I'll find the name to call my baby into the world. My big girls, Nahema and Chamade, vanish down the paths to play. It is no more than a park to them, this Victorian burial ground, with its creaking bamboo grove and plane trees, its yews and cypress and she-oaks. All the way through the funeral, Clementine had played like this with her zebra and when the caskets were consigned to fire, she dabbed her mother's eyes with fistfuls of tissues and never once looked behind her.

I sit with the pram under the figtree. I am in an orchard where memory rots, spilling its names everywhere. To find the names, I have to get right down into the earth, on my hands and knees.

The name is the first thing that is unravelled. It attaches itself to us like a ghostly placenta when we're born and peels off us when we die. Then the name lies in a casket of silence as people step around it. No one says the name any longer because of the damage it might do, as if every letter is wired with explosives. To say the name is to stir the snake and find it's still alive, its eyes glittering, the body pulsing, squeezing and pressing out our good life tears.

Say it to us anyway, write it on stone, say it in the wind or even the checkout queue at the supermarket if need be, don't worry, say it to us, don't be afraid.

But I am afraid. My baby's face is a mystery, asleep. There is wind in the bamboo, damp in the oak leaves and from the hill Newtown falls in a huddle of winter cloud. I bend over a broken railing and kick off leaves and twigs.

> *Emily Mary Harrison,*
> *died 24 Feb, 1863,*
> *aged 8 months 9 days*
> *Martha Jane Harrison,*
> *died 3 Sept 1864,*
> *aged 3 months*
> *Elizabeth Anne Harrison,*
> *died 30 Oct 1864,*
> *aged 4 years*
> *The beloved children of*
> *Charles and Elizabeth Harrison*

I cry softly. For the time being they may as well be my children. Because in the cradle of the world there are more ancestors than those of your family tree. Pushed out from the earth, you are raised by more than your genetic parents, your chromosomal destiny or the borders of your DNA.

> *Thomas and Mary,*
> *Beloved Children of John and Amy Follan*
> *Who departed this life in infancy –*
> *Also their beloved daughter, Isabella,*
> *who died 12 February 1878*
> *Aged 3 years 3 months*

No, enough of this. I call to the girls; it's nearly time to go home, back to my distraught mother, the rooms full of clothes that must be sorted. But at the last minute the baby wakes so desperate for the breast that she latches on to her own tiny fist and suckles hard. As I feed her, I read the tombstone nearby.

> *Harriet,*
> *Beloved Daughter of William and Mary Reilly*
> *Died 19 June 1849,*
> *aged 5 years 9 months*
> *'The weight of this*
> *sad time we must obey;*
> *Speak what we feel,*
> *not what we ought to say …'*

The school holidays are still unwinding. We watch other people's children going to the movies, stuffing themselves with popcorn and ice-cream, going to the zoo, tennis camp, vacation care, buying the next size uniforms, getting fitted for shoes at David Jones.

Danielle takes to grinding her teeth in her sleep. Her dreaming has so much effort in it that her jaw is bruised as if she has been slugged in a ringside fight. Night after night, she wears herself down to gum and bone and eventually only a prescription of Valium can get her to stop.

Inside her, the savaged mother just wants to be left to wander the world as a bag lady, unravelling to the core. No chance. The tiger mother gets her up every morning to do what must be done for Clementine – medical attention, the transfer of inheritance into trust funds, the changing of wills, the form-filling fight for every cent of social security entitlement so that worldly matters can never run her survivor daughter down. In a letter of condolence, Zeke's daycare centre returns the next term's fees and security deposit, as does the administrator of our kids' primary school where Zeke has had his name on the waiting list. The tiger mother banks the cheques and with the funds she books a private trauma counsellor for her daughter.

The tiger mother in Danielle decides Clementine must go back to school with Nahema in the new term. The cousins are in the same composite class; Clementine a year ahead. Clementine's cuts and bruises have healed; as for other wounds, they belong like seeds or pathogens in the realm of the invisibles. No one yet knows how they will migrate or manifest, how fast they may grow or what they might do to her life.

On the first day of term we arrive at school as a family in one car, Paul and Ari as well. The parents of our school community are already there to offer expressions of sympathy; we hug in a tearful gathering ignored by our children. Instead the girls drag their bags out of Danielle and Paul's four-wheel drive and with no more than a 'bye Mum bye Dad bye Paul' they walk off into the school grounds.

All the children have grown taller; their hair is thicker or longer or shorter, their facial bones shifting and aligning toward their tomorrows. We can almost hear the ferocious energy of their growing up crackling through the grass towards us.

Later in the morning, Clementine and Nahema's class walk to the park at the harbour's edge. In light rain, underneath the Moreton Bay figtree, the children and teachers place flowers, drawings, poems, marbles and trinkets. Around the slippery dip that Zeke played on every day after school, Clementine and Nahema wind a grass-and-dandelion chain.

When the last of the mourners return to normal life, the bereft know they have entered the true high country of grief. There the geography of afterwards is a different country to before and its landscape has to be negotiated painfully, centimetre by centimetre.

Danielle drives all over the city to strange malls, inconvenient delicatessens, faraway fruit barns.

Anything to avoid Big Fresh where she shopped every Saturday morning with Zeke squirming rebelliously in her trolley. Anything not to enter Target where she bought him coloured pencils and dinosaur stamps. Anything to escape the coffee shop where Zeke chased Chamade among our trolleys stacked with the week's peanut butter and toilet paper. Anything not to see the ride outside the butcher's where she gave away dollar after dollar for Zeke's amusement. Anything not to pass by Fuji Photography where she left the film of Zeke and Clementine boarding their holiday flight to New Zealand.

But as the weeks pass the sacred sites remain implacable. They never shift their geography even one centimetre. One by one they wait for their borders to be crossed.

One day she calls me and together we approach the Marketown shopping centre. At the top of the escalator is Fuji Photography but we turn away instead into Big Fresh and soon we're swallowed into the gullet of the aisles, massaged by consumables, processed through fruit and vegetables, bakery, fishmonger, dairy, bulk foods and then the numbered canyons of tins, packets, jars and boxes. We shop spaced-out by the sheer nothingness of the one thousand and one things.

At the checkout a girl in a peaked cap and a button saying 'Hi I'm Despina' mumbles the usual 'hello how are you today?' without taking her eyes off the till. Then, just as she swipes the last of the toilet rolls, she stares at Danielle with real connection.

'Oh hello,' she says, her face breaking into a smile. 'So where's your little boy today?'

The litre of milk in Danielle's hands trembles. 'Thank you for asking,' Danielle says, 'but my son was killed in a car accident in the school holidays.'

The girl looks at Danielle in bewilderment, then bursts into tears of shock, whispering 'I'm sorry, I'm so sorry, I'm really really sorry.'

'No, please don't be sorry,' Danielle says, patting her hand. 'It's good you remembered him. I like it when people remember him.'

On our way home, there is a feeling of warmth settling on us, like feathers shaking down. Because a near stranger to Danielle's world has noticed Zeke's passing it is proof that his absence has in some way strangely unsettled the world. It's like taking away a number on the road to infinity – it affects the cosmos through its every calculation, orbit and trajectory. If a stranger notices and regrets Zeke's passing, then what must the grass be feeling, the playground swings, the sky, the moon?

At the traffic lights I notice Danielle has fallen asleep, her jaw slightly open, her features unravelling.

Chamade begins to wake at around 4 a.m., crawling into our bed wanting a 'breastfeed'. I had weaned her with great difficulty but obviously the birth of the baby and the death of the cousin she played with nearly every day has sent her scurrying back to mother's milk. She no longer knows how to suckle but pats and talks to my breasts as if they were those security blankets or teddy bears that some children drag around throughout childhood. But at least I can understand this. It's when Chamade talks of being awoken by 'angels' that I feel uncomfortable. The 'angels', she says, annoy her because they 'wake me up all the time' and 'make me very tired.'

There has always been a vulnerability about Chamade that makes me want to keep her away from high playground slides and rocky shores; if I could I would ban all these spindles from the kingdom. So I try to get her to turn her angels into fairies, to show me that we're still only in *Jolly Postman* storybook land. But Chamade is adamant. 'I said *angels* and they keep *waking me up* and *making me very TIRED.*'

I check on Nahema. She is undisturbed by angels. At six and a half, she curls up under the doona with a *Babysitters' Club* book and when I ask whether she wants to talk, she says 'no'. But in the mornings there are tummy aches, real gut-rippers that curl her over into her pillow, unable to go to school.

One morning Chamade tells me she doesn't want a birthday party because 'I'm not going to be four years old.'

'You want to stay a little baby forever do you?' I say, smiling.

'No,' she says. 'I'm not going to be four because I'll be deaded when I'm four.'

Her teachers at kindy set aside a special time to discuss with me how Chamade is coping. She is asking all her significant adults there how old they are, how old their parents are and how old their children are. It seems she is trying to work out the right age for people to die. She asks, 'when I'm twenty-two how old will you be? Will you be deaded then?... When I'm ninety-four, how old will you be? Will you be deaded then? ...' I feel a wild grief that Chamade is compelled to search through numbers and formulae, trying to calculate these unknowable distances between life and death. The director assures me that Chamade's interest in death is as normal as curiosity about sex; it's just that death has come so quickly to the fore because of family circumstances.

One day I hear Chamade talking to herself in the bedroom – a heated one-sided conversation. The upstairs window bangs and there is a crash of chairs and spilling drawers. Putting the baby into the basinet, I run upstairs to find Chamade chucking Lego blocks all over the room. 'I've got nothing to do!' she screams, kicking a box of dress-ups everywhere. 'Everything's boring and there's nothing to do!' She flops down into the mess, sinking among the hats and feathers and old batik sarongs.

'When Zeke is finished being deaded,' she says, 'can he *please* come over and play with me?'

The weeks vaporise in a kind of slow meltdown of minor domestic emergencies: breastfeeding, banking, changing, bill-paying, putting baby to sleep, hanging out laundry, breastfeeding, worrying about having to go out to buy food, breastfeeding, waiting for a plumber to come and fix the rogue washing machine again, breastfeeding. I find it hard to justify what I spend my time doing. It's not so much that you underestimate the tasks but the limitations of each stage you are forced to live in symbiotic rhythm with, the physical helplessness and short attention spans and psychological barriers of six weeks, eighteen months, twenty-four months, thirty-six months. Throw in the chemistry of the older siblings and it's like you're the conductor of some crazy out-of-control fugue of childhood growing.

Unravelling is like that. We sit with each other for hours on end talking. From day to day I can't remember what we've said or what effect it's had; it's not that I forget the tasks of grief but rather the limitations and gradations of each stage, each pitch, each slipping back, going forward, staying with it. The hours and hours we spend unravelling go by like our children's faces.

I tell Danielle that with this new baby I am remembering that sorcerer's apprentice feeling of conjuring up more than I can cope with, the endless buckets of tasks lining up at the door. But you get through it, she says, and talks of how the children determinedly become more and more themselves, how raising them is like any creative life work only in mega-huge unpredictable dimensions, labyrinthine complexities, making it up as you go along, solving everything on the run. Daily there are moments – sometimes in bunches, sometimes singly – when you are happy. You think it's because they are in the world and that you're growing them plump under sun and moon. Later, you realise it's also because your life is being well-devoured, that time is enjoying a good chew on your bones. When it's like that it's bloody good on the mountain. Then when the children get ahead of you, when they leave for some weird or unknown trail on some other peak, backpacking on without a backward glance, you realise this is the whole point of the climb – that they have grown so much into themselves that you are squeezed out of their individuality. At last you're shed like a skin and they are in the world, 'I am'.

Danielle cries and I watch as she crawls into her ledge of pain. Her bitten face reminds me of how Tony's climbing hands looked in photographs – bloodied, swollen and as roughed-up as the rockfaces they clung to. At extraordinarily high altitudes, he told me, cuts do not heal.

I drop back at this point. I can't go there. I can only imagine what it is to have climbed so far, to be used up good and proper, to have made your way along the cliff-face, following the umbilicus through breast, body, gut, mind, heart and into the dreaming part of you that will never fray, never snap, that endlessly lets out for kilometres down into the canyon, through the glacier and into whatever terrain it must.

Only to find your child has fallen off the world.

They have fallen off the world and nowhere do they stand to say, I am.

The white noise of the world is like cloud. Television, radio, Internet, newspapers – the higher we go into its vapour, the swifter the hyperventilation, the disorientation, the fall. I'd like the white noise of this world to shut up and give us a break but it never does, it's like lead in dirt or CFCs in the food chain.

I'm losing my nerve. No one can see that I'm petrified here, that I'm in a position where I just can't move. *Get a grip, girl.* I am ashamed because I am just a porter in this expedition, it's my business to carry the mundane burdens and keep my head down; it's not my place to push myself up to the pinnacle and throw myself into the eye of grief. I have no right, not while three small heads lie safe on the pillows at the end of the day. I am the kin behind the next of kin, the handmaiden of what must be done. And to be honest, I have no hesitation in shouldering this load which is large but not heavy. What takes me by surprise, what throws me, are the force of the winds, the sonic boom in the echo of this avalanche.

I've been like this before. I was postnatally depressed after Nahema was born but in some ways I've always been like this, the anxious type, a parent of the alone-in-a-hostile-universe school. I was never a sensible mother like Danielle, who knew when to allow slack and when to rein in hard; who knew the difference between a cold and meningitis, a temper tantrum and attention deficit disorder. Tiger mother Danielle who had both of her children when she was over the age of forty, after she had spent five years backpacking through the African continent and the Middle East. Lone wolf Danielle who had met Tony fleeing from would-be rapists in an alley in Istanbul. In Africa she had been bitten by a dog and had to have injections in dubious hospitals with untrustworthy infection-control protocols. Motherhood had made her more vulnerable – back in Australia she'd ask for repeat HIV and hepatitis tests just to reassure herself that she had really got away with it all those years ago. Otherwise, she let the children be. Even after she and Tony split, she didn't gatekeep the children. She knew the difference between leaving them with unknown babysitters and putting them on a flight to New Zealand to be with their father.

I find it hard to believe in the benevolence of anything. My hair is always ready to stand up on the back of my neck. Always the sensation of being up high, the wings of the predator circling above and below while I hang on against the vertigo.

I visit Jane, my general practitioner. I tell her I suspect I am falling outside the shaded areas again and as they say in the Department of Health Blue Book, '*if you fall outside the shaded areas then consult your doctor or clinic nurse.*'

When I do the standard self-assessment test, it shows I'm moderately clinically depressed. Though the term doesn't do justice to the power of the snakes in my belly, the way the world is full of electricity, invisible tripwire, fault lines, forces clashing, fates ready to swoop, a constant sense of danger, of time's beating wings making me feel maybe just a little bit too alive, too on the edge, too ready for fight or flight. It's not very nice to see fate's spindle while you're slicing bread for the school lunches.

No, I mean I don't actually *see* it, I'm not that far gone. But I *feel* it, I feel the spinning, weaving, knotting and meshing of invisible ties all around me and my children.

Tony, I'm still stuck here, suspended over air, unable to move, letting down the team, a burden to the climb. But I have no choice. I have no choice but to keep going, one foot in front of the other. If I could walk off and lie my head in the snow I would. But back in my tent there's a bunch of kids wanting vegemite-on-toast.

Nine weeks later the baby is still not registered and though no agent of the state knocks at our door in the middle of the night, Ari begins to press for a decision, to suggest names he favours over others.

All of them set off flares of alarm inside me. At

Nahema's school, they are doing a programme called Protective Behaviours. A female police officer advises parents never to write their names on schoolbags, lunch boxes or keyrings. Because those who can call out your child's name have the power to deceive them. The name allows the predator into the circle of intimacy. The name can drag them into the underworld even when pet puppies, sweets or violence will not move them one centimetre from the school gate.

But Ari's sympathy is strained. It's been over two months since the funeral and we have no credit left on our MasterCards. At least claim the birth expenses, he says exasperated, flinging the Medicare form on the table.

The queues at the Medicare office are long, the floor crowded with barefoot grunge boys and their bull terriers, black-gowned gothic girls and old ladies dragging vinyl shopping carts. I see a video glimpse of myself in the security camera – a housewife in Supre T-shirt behind a pram loaded up with shopping. Nahema drags Chamade away and my sweet baby begins to cry. I have to ignore her; there is no way I can change her on this filthy floor to be sniffed at by dogs or to have cigarettes accidentally ashed on her by those dear old tarts of Newtown.

At the counter in front of me is a barefoot goth couple with a tiny baby dressed only in a No Frills nappy, a tie-dyed skivvy and a silver-and-shell bracelet. I recognise the pair from hospital birth classes – at close to

forty weeks pregnant she'd worn her goth version of
baby-doll dress and tights with her nose, eyebrow and lip
rings, Blundstone boots and dreadlocks. He'd been body-
pierced, torn-singleted and silent. Both had just fiddled
with their dreads and looked bored through the puff-
pant exercises.

So this is their baby, the half-naked scrap gurgling on
the counter. It can't be more than four or five weeks old
but already its ears are pierced by tiny gold sleepers.

The goth parents try to cash their Medicare claim or
whatever it is, but a teller holds them up on a technicality.
So they start arguing with each other, 'stupid cow' and
'fuckin' shithead'. Working themselves into a rage, they
park the infant like a passbook on the few centimetres of
counter in front of the tellers. There it balances
precariously as they really go for each other. Finally with
a *fuck ya*-this and a *ya fuckin' cunt*-that, they walk away,
leaving the baby on a ledge with a drop of a metre or
more to the floor.

If it were any child of mine or Danielle's, it would be
giving out a fling of its Moro reflexes by now and be
dashed in an instant. Yet that damn punk baby lies still,
mesmerised by the suspended advertising that moves like
a giant mobile from the ceiling.

And I'm thinking Jesus what mugs we are, we
maternal idiots wandering around strapping, buckling,
harnessing, slinging, clicking. *Schlepping* around with our
kids all day long, feeding them vitamins and

homoeopathic drops, holding their hands on roads between parked cars, checking food additives and babysitters' references, turning down the thermostats of hot water systems, never taking our eyes off them around swimming pools, insisting on nutritious breakfasts and never packing chips or lollies for playlunch.

But when push comes to shove, we're not given a centimetre's grace by the gods. How can this accidental kid, uncared for and already half rejected by the state, *how can it be so alive and our beloved dead?*

Our beloved dead.

The infant closes its eyes, rocked in the arms of some angel of neglect. I walk towards it and honestly I'm not sure whether to push it or grab it. But the goth mother must have remembered she'd misplaced a baby somewhere because suddenly she's flying back into the queue, her arms flailing towards me, smacking me hard on the chest in a full-on blow that almost knocks me to the ground. 'You fuck off of her, ya fuckin' bitch.'

I gather up my reluctant girls, I grab and drag them by the arms so hard they cry and kick, 'why do we have to walk all the time?'

I get to the churchyard still clutching the Medicare form crumpled between my hand and the stroller bar. As the girls play among the graves, I stare at Section 6: Adding a Newborn Child.

Is your family registered for safety net purposes? Yes or No?

If yes, the child will be added to your family safety net.

If no, please ask for a family safety net registration form.

Out from her darkened bedroom, Maria Domenica starts to notice the baby, the warm smell of her and the way her eyes glint blue as heaven. For the first time she asks to hold her. So I lift the baby from the pram into my mother's arms. The first words she says to her are, 'Antonia Domenica or Antonia Angelica, or whatever you like, but you're an Antonia for sure.'

I look at her as if she's blown down my house and left me to the wolves. *Antonia*, the feminine of my dead brother's name. Is that all my sweet child is to her, a cenotaph?

On the day Danielle and I face the last of the clothes – a pile for St Vinnies, one thing of Zeke and Tony's each for us – Maria Domenica shuffles in on her arthritic legs and catches us throwing out the jumpers she knitted for her grandson. Maria Domenica was apprenticed at five years of age into the centuries-old convent schools of southern Italy where every stitch was for God. Her knitting, like everything her hands make, is magical and perfect.

She nods in grim approval, waiting till we're done. Then, with surprising strength, she snatches the bag and drags it to her bedroom. All afternoon she sits by the heater, her glasses on her nose, a cup of sugared black coffee and her heart pills on a tray, as she unpicks sleeves, collars, fronts and backs. She unravels each knitted piece till soon she has gathered around her little balls of an almost radioactive wool.

I push the pram through the rain, laden with Woolworths bags and a small saved parcel of those radioactive jumpers. If it was up to me, I'd keep walking to Circular Quay and straight into the bloody harbour but MasterCards have to be paid, potatoes bought for tea, library books returned. Nahema's hanging off one side whingeing 'I'm tired, I'm hungry, why do we have to walk all the time?', while Chamade screams at having to wear a raincoat, and in the pram the baby has a tomato-red crying fit. I push ahead up to St Stephen's, hauling this lot uphill like Sisyphius's rock.

Outside the churchyard, a derelict sprawls across our path. Sheltered from the rain by yew and cypress, he lies against the sandstone wall, mumbling to an audience of bottles wrapped in paper bags. The way he tucks his stinking blanket around him and closes his eyes sends me off into a spin. Wallowing in piss and shit, cracked and aged before his time, with not a person who gives a toss about him, I can't leave him be.

I push the pram till it's right under his nose. In my clenched fists the wheels of the Steelcraft are as hard as graffiti: *If this woman were a car, she'd run you over.*

Hey you. What gives you the fucking right?

What gives you the right to let go when some of us are bound here, trussed to our responsibilities, our earthly love and the living of those loves? Always at the pit of the stomach, the love squeezing and hurting, while you don't even shake a pathetic stick at fate.

I hold the handlebar so that there is barely a hair between my tyres and his flesh. After what seems a long time, I move the wheels away from the tramp's forehead.

I hear the kids start to cry.

Rain falls soft over the graves of St Stephen's.

Maria Domenica lies crumpled on her bed, like some discarded black apron. She pushes out her grief in low moans. 'It should have been me, I'm old, I'm sick, I'm going to die soon anyway. Why wasn't it me?' It's been days and months, this labour of grief, rocking the death of her only adult son. I am the bitch nurse hounding her about her heart medication, her eye cataract appointments. She abuses me, tells me to mind my own bloody business, to get back to my own neglected husband, my filthy house, my unfed children; she will decide what drugs she takes and when. 'Oh is that so? We'll see about that.' So with my own keys I enter Maria Domenica's house without warning or permission, I tidy away the barely touched Meals on Wheels dinners, I look in the fridge, I tell her off for living on a crusted-over can of baked beans that she hasn't even bothered to transfer to a Tupperware container. 'Do you think we want to talk to any more dead bodies this year? We've had enough of that already!' I fling open the blinds, search disgustedly through her small chemist's shop worth of out-of-date prescription drugs. 'Where are your potassiums?' I hold out a glass of water and watch while she swallows them one by one. 'That's better, good girl.'

Once upon a time Maria Domenica was as large as a mountain, with boulder breasts, granite thighs, blizzard eyes and eagle-nest hair. She was so large that when I stole her wedding dress for dress-ups, my five-year-old self got lost in its folds. I half-panicked for many long minutes searching for an opening; a neck, a back, anything. Finally I pushed my way to the light, and, shaking my head, I looked over the new folds of myself. I saw a glacier flowing from my arms, great rivers of white tulle from my neck, pearly suns rising over embroidered folds sinking into the distant dust of the afternoon bedroom. When did she become so small, so birdlike, as thin as apron-strings?

Danielle tells me she and Paul will marry in the New Year, that they will try for a baby together as soon as possible, that they'll lease cars, buy investment properties, start a business, travel Europe. Eight weeks after the funeral, Danielle and Paul move into a house down the road from where she once used to live with Tony. When Maria Domenica finds out she can't bring herself to speak to

Danielle. What a torture when change is betrayal, when presence is absence, when life is a urination on the ashes of the dead. Maria Domenica barely acknowledges Clementine's first post-survival birthday but instead blows up a holiday snap of Tony and Zeke into a silver-framed icon at the centre of a lace doily.

I let myself in one day to find her, a seventy-five-year-old heart patient on a dozen different medications a day, screaming at the daughter-in-law who is still under sedation to get her from one moment to the next.

My mother cries, 'If you hadn't pushed things so far with the kids and Paul and holidays then Tony wouldn't have had to leave for New Zealand, he would not have been on that road, in that place, at that time.'

'He did it to get away from you,' Danielle says, 'you never let us have a marriage, you were in our bed from day one and he didn't want you to screw up what was happening between him and Sophie. He climbed all those bloody mountains to get away from you!'

I don't say anything to either of them, I stay out of it completely. I certainly don't say what I think. Which is that none of that killed him, none of what we did or said or were. No ethical behaviour, no betrayal, no loyalty, no investment of time or heart or dreams, no possessiveness, vindictiveness, jealousy, admiration, no plans for the future or contemplation of the past, no bullshit whatsoever counted for zip. Why doesn't anyone around here want to face the fact that there is no reason? Say it after me, folks. There is no reason. There is no reason. There is no reason.

We are unravelling too fast. Increasing sudden outbreaks of life rain down hard on us. Sophie takes as a lover one of Tony's oldest friends and moves to Adelaide with him. Danielle puts her old house on the market so that she and Paul can afford a dilapidated weekender down the South Coast. Clementine writes Paul's surname on her new lunchbox; she talks of Paul's older children as 'my step-sister Adrienne, my step-brother Dylan.'

I hate the way Maria Domenica lets her grief slash at her love of Clementine. Even so I feel her anguish at how our family must be vanquished. Sometimes when I look at Clementine it seems her very face is emptying itself of Tony, his genetic tracings vanishing like footprints in a blizzard.

'When will I be normal again?' sighs the sleepless pregnant woman. At first you think the life exchange will stop with the cutting of the cord at birth. Then I will be normal again. And no sooner is it cut than the snake jumps up through the spurting nipples and rushes through the enlarged breasts. And when you wean, the snake leaps to the mind and body as your children run through school playgrounds. You go to the gym to get your body back, you start studying again or plotting career re-entries from your carefully-hidden borders of domestic life. Oh God, when will I be normal again?

'When will it stop hurting?' says the bereaved mother, looking for signs, portents, markers in the landscape. After Christmas, after the summer holidays, after Easter, after the first empty birthday, after the anniversary of the day. When will the pain of this contraction end?

When are you going to name that baby?

One day in King Street I see a little goth girl, no more than eight years old, prising a baby off her hip so she can busk with a troupe of gypsy-gothish women and African drummers. It's the baby from the Medicare queue. Dirty and half-naked, it sleeps in its sister's guitar case as she performs a kind of Middle Eastern belly dance. The mother is nowhere to be seen.

Rock-a-bye baby in a guitar case on a street where passers-by throw you their loose change.

Still you sleep, breathe, grow.

Lately as I walk to St Stephen's I get the feeling I am being followed. I enter the gates and sit as usual under the figtree. I watch the children disappear down the hillside among the tombstones huddled against each other. I lift my baby from the pram, bunny-rugged and peach-warm, and as I breastfeed her I read the names until I am in a suckling trance.

> *Emily Mary Harrison,*
> *aged 8 months 9 days,*

Godfrey Walcott Fosbery
aged 6 years 9 months,
Isabella Follan
aged 2 years 3 months

Name the baby. Not Ari's name, not the family names, not these dead Victorian names. Her name. Tell them her name.

What's wrong with hiding my baby under 'honey, darling, sweetheart, gorgeous'? I can't speak their real names, not even here. Don't be angry but I have to lie to you: *Chamade, Nahema*, it's all bullshit, aliases, *noms-de-plume, noms-de-guerre*, underground code-names. You will never know who they really are.

Just tell them her name.

Listen, on the day my first pregnancy was confirmed, I floated through David Jones, light-headed, confused, jubilant, on my way to the baby goods department. As I walked towards the escalator, two beautiful women in black crossed my path. They sprayed me in a haze of perfumes and handed me their essences on two cards. The first was Nahema, eastern honeyed rose with velvety fruit and wood, meaning *passionate temperament*. The second was Chamade, light with hyacinth, ylang-ylang, blackcurrant buds and vanilla, meaning *surrender to love*. So that's where I've hidden them, in those cut-glass bottles deep inside the House of Guerlain. I am only prepared to name their essences. Hiding my babies means necessity will have to work harder to find them.

If I refuse to reveal their true names, who is there to devour when the black wind sweeps down the mountain and the death dogs come snarling around our tents?

You have to name her some time.

Forget it. 'Honey, darling, gorgeous' is as far as you're going to get.

When the kids return, the Medicare form is still scrunched up in my bag, the baby still generically Baby, I haven't committed to a single word.

Like all resistance fighters, I know what it means to give up the names.

When the mothers of our kids' ballet class get together, the conversation cannot help but turn towards the accident. Not in Danielle's presence but when she's out in the dressing-room hurrying Clementine into her leotard. The women turn over this 'it happened to someone I know' reality. They swap cautionary tales of misadventures, imprudence, naïvety. I listen as they tell of lucky escapes, of snatching kids back from malevolent forces, of accidents and of medical bungling.

Ladies, the true accident has nothing to do with your vigilance. Your parenting radar just can't pick it coming, it's off the screen, outside the shaded areas. If you can establish why, no matter how tenuously, then it is not a true accident but necessity laying its cards on the table after a long game with you. Yeah, okay, cause and effect is a temporary comfort. It's what we're looking for with our out-of-body experiences, our instincts and auras and inner warnings, our platitudes about a child not being ours but coming through us, how we have to be grateful for any time we have with them, how it was probably meant to be.

It was not meant to be. It was random, stupid, unnecessary. It could have as easily not happened as happened. As far as some divine plan goes, it didn't matter a toss to the universe: Yes and No were equally possible. A mystery is not a mystery if you can explain it.

I pick up the baby to suckle her even though she hasn't cried. I close my eyes and focus on the sounds of the piano and the thump of children's feet on the polished floorboards.

Maybe if I can get away from all these reasons, meaning will come.

Swarms of goths descend on the winter pavements of King Street. Outside the 7-Eleven I squeeze my pram past a group of them squatting against the wall in the rain. I focus on one foot after another. Nahema and Chamade are at it again. 'I'm so-o-o tired ... you never let us stay home ... I'm so-o-o tired ...' As if snorting at that, a taxi pulls up to the kerb and sprays stormwater over them. That does it. They sit on the pavement crying. I push on. They have to learn. This morning I told Ari that I definitely want to sell the car. We don't need it. The girls can go to the local primary school where they can bloody well walk like this every day. And do them good too. Buses are better for the environment and all those Big Fresh bags can be home delivered.

I'm so intent that I almost run her over as she falls out of the taxi, all crumpled velvet and bare ring-stabbed stomach. I wouldn't have known her but for the baby in a sarong, because she's gone fluoro-raver since I last saw her, she's changed from gothic monochrome to bohemian colour.

Steadying herself, the Medicare mother walks over to one of the goth men and whines, something about money:

'I gave ya yar fuckin' money.'

'Nah bullshit.'

'Ya callin' me a fuckin' liar?'

'Yeah, I want me fuckin' money.'

'Look up ya fuckin' arm then, ya fat fuckin' bitch.'

He gives her a shove but she's unsteady and playing up the drama as well. She staggers back against a wall. The baby in the sarong squeals with a gummy thrill. The woman's crying and carrying on and two goth girls try to hustle her off across the road to a café but she won't go, she's doing a real Maria Callas.

Luckily two beat cops come out of the King of Yeeros takeaway and instantly the goths melt into the traffic of King Street. I'm transfixed by whether they'll make it to the other side, the two Morticia Adamses pulling the stoned Paula Yates with a baby bouncing around her midriff. But they do. Through the café window, I see them settling at their table, getting out their cigarettes.

I kick the brake off the pram. I wish I had time to sit around with a *caffè latte* yacking to friends all day. Instead I have to backtrack to get Nahema and Chamade.

That's when I notice a white snowflakey thing on the ground. At first I think it's her dope, that the stupid cow has actually dropped a deal of crack or whatever. But when I get closer to it, I see that it's only a breast pad. Just a disposable cotton-wool nursing mother's breast pad like the packets upon packets of them that I have at home.

I pick it up. It gives off the caramel sweet smell of human breastmilk.

We are running down the corridors of the time before, past a crowded McDonald's, a bookstore, past doors and signs in Japanese and English. The children swing on trolleys as big as the horses. High above their heads a woman stamps their passports. The children play hide-and-seek inside a palace of perfumes and liquors – Opium, Joy, Oscar de la Renta, the House of Guerlain.

At the barriers the mothers give out bunches of kisses, and the camera loves this, snapping wildly into each squeeze against cheeks, trying to get close. Finally a woman with golden wings on her sleeves leads the children aboard flight QF 302 to Christchurch, New Zealand.

We sit in silence in the semi-dark of Danielle and Paul's study. I am appalled, eating my tears and freezing my face. Against all advice Danielle walked into Fuji Photography and retrieved the holiday film with its photo slides of her son. We don't think the pain of these images is worth it. But she sits intently at the light box, scanning through image after image. Her reward comes in the last few slides, when Zeke breaks away from the flight attendant's arms and runs back down the terminal.

He runs back down the long tunnel towards us and, turning full-on to the camera, he blows us a raspberry.

The next time I am sitting alone with the baby under the figtree in St Stephen's. I'm in a mood, a kind of dreamy rage. The sun is setting over Memorial Park. The last of the evening's joggers runs out the gates into Church Street, crunching the gravel. Then silence and shadows.

There is a power in this tree's wild spread. I want to lie my head in its lap. Instead I walk further into the cemetery. It's not especially cold here, just a subtropical winter's night. But the wind has a southerly bite and the damp rising through the earth is grim. The baby's eyes are shutting, she's falling asleep without her bath or evening feed. I should strap her in and go home. It's time to go home.

But the damp air is forgetfulness and dusk rubs out the names on the graves so that I can no longer read them. I'm breathing in eucalyptus, or something else, cloves, marijuana maybe. It's a smell that makes me see fields of flowers – lilium, chamomile? No, I can't place it. I haven't slept through the night for a long time and I am tired.

That's why I see only her lily-white face framed with rough curls, a fantasy of a face disembodied against the headstones. It's her, the Medicare mother. Someone I know lying there on the cold ground.

For a minute all I can think is that she's overdosed and I don't even have a mobile phone to ring 000 so they can get some Narcan into her. Because that's all I'm focused on, *Narcan, Narcan, Narcan.*

I kneel down to her to get a pulse and a kid approaches me from behind the bamboo. He's about fourteen years of age, wiry build, black jeans, torn black T-shirt. He snatches at my bag.

But it won't come because it's a shoulder bag which I've wound across the pram handles.

And immediately I know what I would do if I were them. If I were them I'd get out a knife to cut the strap or if not a knife then a dragging through the grass with my arm half wrenched off and never mind the baby hurtling unstrapped in the pram with the result that there's soft cowl on jutting stone and being junkies they'd probably only get a couple of years at the most because you could never prove a murderous intent but my baby's life and my life would be gone without me even knowing her name *without even knowing her name –*

And suddenly I'm flinging off the bag – 'take it, go on, fucking take it, it's all yours . . .'

They grab it and run off into the night.

I go to the Newtown Police in Australia Street to give a statement. It takes ages because the cops are busy with a homicide in Enmore. Ari turns up toward 9.30 p.m. with the girls in their pyjamas. The baby is hysterical with tiredness so they take her home. I'm left with a young cop who must be terrified of some future bloody Royal Commission over this because he constantly leaves the room to ask colleagues about correct forms, procedure, triplicates and duplicates. Why can't he just do it for God's sake? I'm incensed that it takes him over an hour to list the alleged contents of my bag down to the last Tic-Tac and lippie.

It's all a waste of time anyway because, checking out the garbage bins and skips on the way home, I find the bag in an Otto bin in the car park behind VideoEzy. The cash is gone, of course. But my identification stuff is all there, photographs of the girls, driver's licence, MasterCard, Medicare card, the baby's plastic wrist ID from the hospital.

I hold the wristband under the streetlight. It's so small it wouldn't even go around the baby's fingers now. It's been in my bag for so long that the ink has run and there is nothing but a dark blot where *Baby Schilstein* used to be.

I am considering a name on Section 6 of the Medicare form, Adding a Newborn Child. The name becomes a highway, a ribbon, a belt, a rope, an umbilical cord, a contraction, a labour.

The name becomes the violently quick escalation of induced labour. The peaks are high, I can see them rearing up in front of me on the monitor, bloody high. To do it I need to shed burdens. Chuck all the crap about natural birth – I take the proffered drugs and throw out my disappointment. Down into the chasm it rolls, I barely hear it make a sound. I progress as if my womb is on speed. On the plateau of the second stage, there is no pain, just grunting effort and falling asleep, pethidine-stoned, between pushes.

As my girl is born I see snow piled on branches collapsing into a gorge without end.

Toward morning, while Ari sleeps in a chair, a midwife brings me tea. The old stars hang in the window in the dark before dawn. I gulp the hot liquor as the midwife fills in a brand new Blue Book, the Personal Health Record given to parents by the Department of Health. The midwife's writing unravels into the afternoon, toward that winter's sunset on the road from Arthur's Pass where the children in the car sing along to *Bananas In Pyjamas*. The airconditioning hums, Sophie is half-asleep and Tony drives sharp-eyed along the highway.

Across the Tasman waters my empty belly takes me down into a calm sleep.

I am on a rock ledge in the Himalaya. Everything is crisp with those intense almost painful *National Geographic* colours. Here, where there is more sky than rockface, on a ledge hardly thicker than a dinner plate, my family and I are camping. Each of us is clipped into a green nylon tent that balloons off the rock. Puffing out like cocoons in an ocean of distant peaks, we're just sticking on by ropes, anchors, metal handgrips, snaplinks, karabiners, waist harnesses and ingenuity. As I lie down, I feel something squeeze around my belly. I look down to see a rope made of plaited nylon with coloured flecks – a pulsing snake tied in a climber's knot around me.

The mountain peaks spin and I see that all of us are tethered together with this snake-thing so that we're like trinkets hanging off it, Ari, Nahema, Zeke, Chamade, and behind them the seed-pod faces of all my children-to-be. I reach for my mobile phone to tell Danielle not to worry, that we've got Zeke tied to our party, when the snake squeezes and bucks, the balance shifts and I hear the tearing of steel and nylon.

I awake, gasping. I hear feet from the nurses' station marching towards me. Groggy as I am, I smell the breath of the death dogs.

Inside the churchyard gates I push the pram straight ahead along the leafy path. At the steps of the church I stop to cover my sleeping baby with an extra blanket. Then I enter the chapel. I sit down at a pew and search along the shelf to find a hymn book. Turning its dog-eared pages, I find the first white space. There I write out her name in full. In cursive script it looks magnificent. I stare at my sacred graffiti with satisfaction. I think that maybe I've unravelled this sleeve of care to the bone.

But outside in the street, when I say the name softly to myself, I see that there is no end to such unravelling, that the unravelling itself is the meaning.

Sitting under a figtree, wandering through the orchard of the dead, digging for names, stealing the umbilical cord to tie around me so I can keep one foot going after another on the mountain – all of this is the meaning. Going postnatal crazy, hating ministers of religion, crying in supermarkets, fighting angels, menacing stranger babies, hiding names under my pathetic heart – all of this is the meaning. The meaning is on the dotted line where you may as well write in bold letters **okay, all right, Yes** in the spaces after 'Is your family registered for safety net purposes?'

Because we can't avoid this lifetime lifeline, no matter how hard we try to preserve our virginities. If I have to fade, grow old, haggard, bent with osteoporosis, gnarled and die, let it be totally devoured. Let me meet my last step on the bald mountain in complete exhaustion, to be picked over by vultures, air, wind, maggots – never let me be the still unravished bride.

In The Old Fish Café, I order a cappuccino and borrow the waitress's pen. I take out the crumpled Medicare form from my bag and smooth it out on the table. By winter's light, I write the name again and tick the box which says 'If yes, the child will be added to your safety net family.'

The name unravels to become a trust, a risk, a hope, a cutting off and a hanging on. The name unfurls to be a flag, planted not in heroism or defiance or any triumph of the will but because the mountain says 'Yes', because the mountain says 'No'. The true name of my child I can't reveal to you but there is a perfume made of bergamot, jasmine, ylang-ylang, sandalwood and rose: Samsara, from the Sanskrit meaning 'wheel of life, infinite cycle of birth, death, rebirth'. She is like that.

Walking home the long way, I wheel Samsara past *Time Killers, Sick of The City, Hands Held Violently on to Words That Mean Nothing, Play With Time, Monoxide = Your Doom* and *Nameless Dread*. Rain spits into my face and a swirling piece of McDonald's rubbish gets caught under the pram. As I turn into the La Nita supermarket, I pass a green-dreadlocked woman lying stoned on the pavement. Propped by the open guitar case is the Medicare baby, wide-awake and determinedly trying to find its feet.

The baby's sister dances, her dyed-black hair tied in a kerchief. She dances not like a busker or a beggar but like a child who is rightly heedless of others' space, absorbed in a dream of 'look at me: I am!'

Happily sucking on its filthy toes, the baby does a scrunch-faced shit as I throw a dollar into its cradle.

Homeland

I have the keys to my parents' house. Every few days I come here to look after things while my parents are away in Italy, their first trip back in the thirty-six years of voluntary exile in Australia. Thirty-six years ago they bought their tickets, they played them in the factories, hotels and shops, they had children rapidly and confidently, they paid off mortgage after mortgage and won – home, land, life. For thirty-six years, all they have wanted is to sell up everything and go back to Italy. For thirty-six years, it was as if they were renting this country, handing over their weekly payments in blood and sweat, payments that were always going to be the very last before doing a midnight flit back across the ocean. Yet only my grandmother's old age, the call of the death-bed, has finally forced them to leave.

'It's like being in a village in Africa,' writes my mother. 'Only the villagers speak Italian and sometimes they remind me a little bit of the people I used to know.'

They left, telling us – their grown children and grandchildren small and sweet enough to surely anchor them here – that they might not be back. My father's dream was to sit in the sun with the old men of his village and collect his Australian pension cheque every fortnight. My mother saw herself eating plums in the fields, gossiping with her sisters, lighting candles in the wind-swept church on Sundays. I couldn't see it; here in this house their basil was rampant, their plums heavy on the bough. Their littlest grandchild was starting kindy in the new year, they had a freezer filled with cheesecakes, steak and pizza bases, they were booked for Housie at the Abruzzese Club on Wednesday nights. How could they leave to sit in the sun of sepia photographs and light candles in the church of memory?

I tell myself it's the immigrants' midlife crisis, leaving me playing the abandoned partner, sceptical but frightened. It's not that I can't live without my parents tilling the soil here, spoiling my children and giving us eggs and lemons to take home. It's that with their flight into the past, I have been left behind like a servant in the wake of a revolution.

I know I belong to the masses outside, married to a man with no Italian, raising children who will never wear the Communion veil, tread the grapes or sing the old songs. Yet I am loyal to my parents' house. Outside the gates, I stand as the last of my people, something of a pathetic half-caste, with my Italian lessons at TAFE on

Friday nights, my *Women's Weekly* lasagna, my kids called Emily, Lachlan and Damien. If my parents go, the Old Country inside me vanishes with them, leaving me sitting on a suitcase at a petrol station on a highway, looking into the distance, wandering where I am, where I've been, where I'm going.

Letters arrive saying my mother's not well there, maybe a sign that things aren't working out. She's getting headaches, dizzy spells. She wants to avert her eyes from her dying mother-in-law, my grandmother, an earth-hardened tyrant my mother left Italy to escape. Yet respect is respect – every morning she enters the stifling bedroom and murmurs the pious words. In private she gives my father hell. He shrugs his shoulders, knowing that even in this Old Country, the Brigadoon of her hopes, there's no escaping what she's afraid of. I received a letter this morning where she told me she didn't recognise her sisters. The three of them came down south from Milan to see her and she stared at them in bewilderment, winded by the force of time. The modern Italy roaring around outside means nothing to her, 'it's all McDonald's and pigeon shit.'

I'm worried about her but there's nothing I can do. I don't know where her heart's land is, nor mine either. Sometimes at sunset, as I water her tomatoes, I hear an old woman's voice croaking:

'Take me where the lemon grows, oranges in sweet dark groves. You there, weeping endless tears, what have you done with your youthful years?'

All I have are the keys they have left me, the keys that take me through the tomato plants and photographs deep inside this house. My first key was pinned inside my dress at the age of six. It weighed like gold, like a powerful secret, all the way home from the dust and rabble of the schoolyard. I had to avoid bandits, the Housing Commission kids ready to spring their Little Wog Riding Hood. I had to avoid those who would deceive me – unshaved men offering sweets and the chance to pat puppies. Yet after every long day I made it through the forest. The golden key opened the door of my parents' house and I entered it safe, shutting out the jabbering world outside.

Except for the seven years in exile when my name was not spoken by my family in public or in private, I have always carried the keys to the doors of my home's land. I am the daughter gatekeeper, the caretaker; I rush to hold out cloaks and candles, I stand between the coach hurtling out of the iron gates and down to the edge of the world. Deep inside my parents' house the present feeds on the past as if it were blood-and-bone, everything curling upwards and outwards, new marriages, new grandchildren, new arguments. It's strange, my parents' house may be empty but the place is still alive, sprouting, growing, ripening.

It needs only a daughter's hand to turn a tap in the cool of evening and hold out a hose, open the mail, dust some photographs, pick the plums. I stand up and straighten my back. From under the windows, down the stone path, through the buzz of mosquitoes, I hear it again, the old voice singing hoarsely in the dark:

'Take me where the lemon grows, oranges in sweet dark groves. You there, weeping endless tears, what have you done with your youthful years?'

Long after I'm home, when I've put my kids to bed and I'm lying next to my sleeping husband, I go back there. By a red-tinged evening, those sunsets of persistent dreams, I stand at the door of my parents' house, the house that is always there, immovable through every change of suburb, every rusty letterbox, every pair of neighbours' eyes behind the fence.

I have the keys. I turn the golden key, the false key, the key of dust, the key of ghosts and the key I never had. They open everything and, suddenly, everything is open. Curtains billow against glass, marble lions unlock their jaws. Doors fly apart by the force of the wind, fragrant with far-blown seeds. High above on the balconies and balustrades, at sunset, then under the moon, I spray fine water mists down below. The place just keeps seething along like an old jungle, crafty, full of laughing bananas, childhood fevers, snakes.

There were so many naïve, then frantic, turnings of the lock with false keys I've since learnt to recognise and throw away. I spent so many afternoons sitting on the stone step in tears, neither safe in my home's heartland nor out of the foreigners' dark woods.

'La Malley', as I privately called the Sunday School teacher, was reminding us that Confirmation was about saying 'Yes' again to the responsibilities of Baptism. That's why we needed 'sponsors', the adult version of baptismal godparents, to guide, counsel and bless us through this sacrament. We also needed to choose new Confirmation names, to celebrate the birth of our new selves within God.

I peeled the words off me like skin from a sunburnt arm.

I was thirteen years old and being trained for the receiving of my Third Sacrament of Confirmation at St Anthony's Catholic Church in Coburg, a dingy suburb of weatherboard houses clustered near the city's gaol. My family were not religious but traditional. They drew upon forces more potent than mere Roman Catholicism. In their regions of Italy there still lurked ancient beliefs banned by the modern world – witches and 'wise' women, the *fata*, the *strega*, the *befana,* not to mention the statues of village 'saints' disputed by the Vatican. My troubles started from the first Sacrament of Baptism, which had left me forever stuck with visits from my Sicilian godmother, Concetta Giaccone and her fat boy-mad daughters, crazy about Elvis Presley. Mother bitched about the Giaccones but enjoyed looking down on them.

Concetta only ever lost her Sicilian sense of humour when she'd find out she was pregnant again; then she'd ring my mother late at night, crying and threatening to commit suicide.

The Second Sacrament had been of course my First Holy Communion, where for many months the women of my family on two sides of the world spun me a dress of imported Milanese silk and Abruzzese lace more beautiful than that I eventually wore at my wedding.

The poor Irish-Australian girls at St Anthony's were all lined up in the front pews dressed in white acrylic socks and short white Woolworths frocks. Their red sandy hair was scraped behind white plastic clasps. As I walked down the aisle wearing a tiara and a lace mantilla, my gown threw the stars of its silver netting down to the floor. The congregation of working-class Irish Catholics took a breath, amazed, blinded, maybe discomfited at such a display but expecting it – the Italians always went overboard, it happened every year, little girls dressed up like meringues, like imported bride dolls.

I knew I wasn't a meringue or a bride doll, I was a vision of the Magical Child, a sliver from a dark night of snow and candles. In the mirror I had seen that I was beautiful, that I was the Chosen One with the star on my forehead.

Yet to my horror I couldn't take any joy in it. As I stood next to the Ellens and Kathleens, I felt embarrassed for them, sorry for their thin show, the Woolworths dresses, the pulled hair with wet combs in dingy bathrooms. I was infected by their spirit of poverty, the resignation of the faded carpet homes, the Friday rent and fish-and-chips, the discount ballerina jewellery-box fantasies we girls all shared. I didn't know where my sudden riches had come from; my gown was heavy with glory and shame. I was the *fata*'s daughter, dancing on the graves of slaves and convicts and children drowned at sea.

I knew, without looking around as I kneeled to take the body of Christ, that my parents would have tears in their eyes. Not because I was taking the Sacrament – my parents didn't trust priests – but for the beauty and pageantry of the moment. I know they saw a dark snowy night, lit by a procession of Golden Children filing into a Cathedral of a Thousand Candles. I don't know what the others saw, maybe a meringue, maybe a little girl in the Coburg *Casa di Sposa*'s idea of grandeur, but I felt myself tearing apart inside the silk with the pain of being a freak and a vision.

What a fool, what a waste of pity. I should have flaunted myself while I had the chance. I should have run from the church with my skirts flying, glad to get home for our own celebrations, where I was free to be the *fata*'s daughter, dancing and laughing till midnight on the graves of humble priests and poor Irish souls.

Yet by the time of my Confirmation, I was a treacherous teenager and the idea of repeating the spectacle of the Communion gown appalled me. The thought of Concetta Giaccone, shiny, plump, frilled and hatted, standing behind me as my sponsor was repulsive. I went to a lot of trouble to make sure this time that I would be dressed 'simply', as I put it to my mother.

She shrugged; it wasn't the rightness of dress that irked her, it was my aim not to stand out in any way. My mother had nothing but contempt for that. For her, making a show when you had nothing was the whole point of a labouring life.

Miss Irene Malley was new to the Sunday School teaching game, a young woman like a dollop of cream on a bun. Her blonde hair was piled in a beehive and she smelled of 4711 Eau de Cologne. She wore skirts just above her knee at a time when the well-developed Ellens and Kathleens of her Sunday School class were wearing them up their bums. God was a cotton-wool ball soaked in Dettol to Miss Malley's scratched soul. Jesus Christ listened to a lot of tender, puzzled hurts, slights, pangs, pains and sighs from Irene Malley. Her talks on the Beautiful Heart of Jesus were all about a tissue-box love, a gentle Jesus who kept His long hair neat and dried the tears of sweet girls hurt by a boorish world.

It was wet stuff but it made a change for us in the Sunday School class, used to the traditional gorily crucified Christ, strung up, humiliated, tortured and murdered, all unwittingly, incredibly, but undoubtedly, by us.

The weeks went past with no alternative to the Giaccones as my sponsors. After the last Sunday School before the big day, I approached Miss Malley at her desk. She was using 4711 tissues to wipe the chalk dust from her hands.

'Yes, Maria.'

'Angela.'

'Well, Angela, what is it?'

I took a breath. 'I don't have a sponsor, Miss.'

Miss Malley frowned. 'You don't have a relative, a family friend?'

'No Miss,' I lied. 'All our relatives are in Italy.'

'If you pray hard this week and remind your parents, God will send you a sponsor, Maria.'

Miss Malley was popping her silk-covered Catechism into her handbag and snapping it shut. I had to be quick.

'I was wondering if you could be my sponsor, Miss.'

Miss Malley inspected her hands as if she hadn't quite cleaned all the chalk dust off them.

'I find all this hard to believe, Maria. But if your parents really won't find anyone for you, I will of course be your sponsor. Let me know before Mass next week.' Miss Malley disappeared down the corridor, heels clicking hastily to make Father Fitzgerald's eleven o'clock Mass.

I told my mother that, as I had come top of my Sunday School class, Miss Irene Malley was going to be my sponsor and that my name was going to be Angela Philomena Irene Aguccio. My mother was amazed, appalled, excited and mortified.

She had no idea '*l'inglese*', as she called them, expected yet another set of godparents at Confirmation. How many godparents were you supposed to have visiting every Sunday for the rest of your life? She told me to say nothing about this business with *La Malley* to the Giaccones, whom she knew were already ordering a dozen *bomboniere* from the Bell Street *Casa di Sposa* to present to me and the family in honour of my Confirmation. This insult to my godparents would finish us with the Sicilians. Not that my mother cared – she was a northerner – but my father, the card-playing Abruzzese tyrant, would just about get out the rifle if he thought Adolfo Giaccone, his old Queensland sugar-cane cutting paesan, was getting snubbed by his own flesh and blood.

Over the next seven days, my mother was in the daunting position of preparing a great feast, a great Saint's day, in honour of her eldest daughter, in honour of our family, my godparents, our relatives, our *paesani* and *La Malley*, about whom she knew nothing and who terrified her more than all the revenge in Sicily. Naturally, she cooked until midnight and beyond every night, that was expected. But the days were long and feverish with her panic. She booked the photographer Bario's studio, she cleaned and vacuumed the Holden and she sponged the trimmings. She walked down to the Bell Street Cake

Shop, ordered one cheese-and-tomato sandwich and one egg-and-lettuce sandwich, took them home, unwrapped them, worked out how to make them and prepared five dozen of them, wedged in the fridge.

By the Sunday of my Confirmation, our house was thrown open to the Joys of the Feast, with all of my mother's dowry china on tables spread with linen she had woven and embroidered as a girl. In great pots on the stove and benches were our chickens, broths, veal, lasagne and pasta. In the fridge were the sandwiches, packets of sausage rolls and two large tomato sauce bottles. My 'simple' white dress of crimplene, contemptuously sewn by my mother in half a day from a Butterick's pattern, was lying on my bed, with the Woollies stockings and packet of hairclips.

When I walked down the aisle, nothing rustled, there were no gasps. There was no star on my forehead, no Holy Night of candles, no snow softly falling to the murmur of old women's voices. It was all so simple, really. I was not the *strega*'s daughter but Angela Aguccio, the contract cleaner's eldest kid, waiting to kiss the hand of an old Irish priest.

Before Mass, Miss Malley had been busy letting down the hems on the dresses of the shameless Ellens and Kathleens and making sure we knew our lines in confirming God. There seemed no time to remind her of our agreement. I trusted in the superiority of her adult memory. Yet when I stood alone at the altar, she remained

171

in the front row, in a cream wool suit, a pillbox hat and white gloves.

The visiting Bishop looked up, confused, put off his stroke. 'Where is your sponsor?' whispered Father Fitzgerald.

I turned, surprised that Miss Malley hadn't somehow drifted silently behind me. There was a rustle in the pew as Miss Malley excused her way to the front, hastily genuflected and, red-faced, took her place behind me, as I was presented with my Holy medallion confirming me to be Angela Philomena Irene Aguccio.

Outside St Anthony's, my parents and relatives waited for me and my new godmother. Our car, marked with a white satin ribbon, was illegally parked in a zone marked 'Clergy' and my mother was anxious to get to Bario the photographer's in time. Antonetta and Adolfo Giaccone were muttering to themselves, then gathering together their kids and excusing themselves from the party as my mother pleaded and reproached, stringing together nonsense about 'the English' and her confused daughter, too clever for her own good, getting stuck with a prize she didn't want, not being able to say no to *La Malley*, 'you know how it is, her own teacher – the girl was scared she wouldn't pass her, so she couldn't say no.'

When I appeared with Miss Irene Malley, everyone clapped and we were given flowers by the Giaccone girls.

My parents gesticulated toward our car, smiling and bowing. Miss Malley looked at me.

'I think Mum and Dad want you to come back to our place for a party,' I translated.

Miss Malley firmly pulled herself out of our circle. She shook her head. 'I'm sorry, Maria,' she said. 'Please tell your mother I'd love to come to visit her some day. But it's not possible today. My parents expect me home for our own Sunday dinner. Sorry.'

On Bario's photographs, I appear alone, unsponsored and lost in a beehive hairdo and an ugly white shift-dress, smiling foolishly. I wasn't surprised and I didn't care when years later, during my exile, my mother tore them up; I would have gladly helped her rip that self to pieces. Still, at home we dined on the Joys of the Feast inside the pots and on the tables. Later that night even the Giaccones were persuaded to come to have a glass of wine, after my father spoke on the phone to Adolfo.

Much later, when the house was in darkness and everyone was asleep, I wrapped the Confirmation medallion in newspaper, made my way through the night-breathing tomato plants and chucked it deep into the backyard garbage bin. It was the 'Irene' in the engraved Angela Philomena Irene Aguccio that bothered me. *Irene, Irene* – it was scratchy, a bad fit. I didn't see any point in keeping the thing, like a key that doesn't quite turn in the lock and never will.

It is hot inside my parents' house; these low ceilings retain the heat. I switch on the ceiling fan, I flop on to the rococo velvet Franco Cozzo furniture, which somehow is not as overblown as it looks advertised on late-night television. This is not my childhood house but the house they wanted, worked for, built, the palace of their exile of fortune, at the end of a street full of marble balustrades and crouching lions. I hardly know this house, I left it in a hurry, and, it was said at the time, dishonourably, though after many years, a husband and three children, it's been forgotten, no one mentions it any more. That's the Italian way, *vendetta* then *pasta e piselli*. Maybe. I guess each generation, as it gets older, eventually accepts that a house of scandal, argument and flagrant filial disrespect is less tedious than a lifetime of honourable solitude. This attitude in my family is not perfect but it's practical; the year after I left, my face was ripped out of the family photographs. But somebody kept the negatives.

There was a wardrobe deep in my parents' room that opened with a small silver key. Every morning they hid it so we would not be tempted to pry. Every afternoon I stole the key and opened the door. From the darkness, strange stuff flew out as I looked through boxes, letters, bottles of scent, pressed flowers, ties and old skirts. The spirits sang me deeper and deeper into the back of all these things, until one day, short of breath, I shut the door, replaced the key of ghosts and never touched it again.

I was eighteen, at Teachers' College, unmarried and living the dutiful life of a good Italian girl at home, when Zia Pina, my father's eldest sister, came to live with us after her husband, Fortunato, (or 'Frank' as he was known in Australia), died. Her grown-up kids, my elder cousins, lived in Queensland and had good jobs in real estate and computers (except for the eldest girl who'd run away to New Zealand with a rock band and was never mentioned). When my cousins sold up their parents' fruit shop, the sickly Zia Pina, who couldn't stand the humid heat in Brisbane, decided to live in the granny flat at the back of our place. Dad had built the flat years ago for Nonna Aguccio but even he finally realised it was a fantasy to think that at seventy-eight his mother would ever come out to Australia.

Zia Pina was a diabetic, overweight and suffered from arthritis, high blood pressure and angina. She was a complex bio-system of everything that could go wrong with the human body but still survive in the invalid's bunker of drugs, needles and doctor's prescriptions. There was an Indian doctor, a Dr Patel, whom she trusted completely, an unusual faith in someone who wasn't Italian. I guess it was because Dr Patel had a profound belief in Zia Pina's illnesses and that made her feel better. He prescribed whatever drugs she thought she needed; she liked this reflection of her wisdom about her body. I'd just got my driver's licence and had become the family runabout; I found myself taking Zia Pina down to

Dr Patel's clinic at the local shopping centre nearly every day. Sometimes Zia Pina, panicky and wheezing for breath, would beg me to ring him at night, and in the early hours of the morning, I'd often rush Zia Pina to the Casualty and Emergency clinic of the local hospital.

The array of drugs Zia Pina took fed back on her symptoms until no one could see where the snake lay coiled. This was Zia Pina's genius – she was the architect of an intricate scaffolding of illness around her that was nurturing, secretive and perfectly balanced. When she lay in hospital with drips in her arms, she had the constitution of a vampire. Nothing terrible ever happened to her. She was destroying herself a little bit at a time, but all in all, no faster than the pace at which the worm eats away at the rose.

Television was Zia Pina's morphine, taken in a haze of afternoon cooking in the back flat, the programme guide on one side of her lunch tray, her insulin needles on the other. Zia Pina lay on a velveteen couch plumped with sweat-soaked cushions, wiping her face with linen towels, throwing curses in dialect to the characters rushing headlong to their fates in the soap operas, then cackling, shrieking and laughing at the late afternoon game shows. This flickering, curtain-drawn trance would stop with the six o'clock news: Zia Pina had no interest in *that* world.

After Zia Pina's longest bout in hospital, a stay of two weeks when another more neurotic patient controlled the knobs of the ward's television set, she had returned devoted to 'Could It Be You?', a games show hosted by Gerry Johnston, a rotund and cheeky American-accented overgrown boy, the sort of talkative good-fun type matrons wished they'd married or at least given birth to.

Zia Pina was well enough charmed by Gerry Johnston but it was the particular turn of his wheel of fortune that stopped at her heart. Players in his game of wealth were chosen by a studio audition where women brought in strange objects, dressed in costumes and sang songs – always within the realm of kitchen-cupboard innocence – to arouse Gerry Johnston's curiosity or sympathy. I watched it a few times with Zia Pina and had to admit it worked – it brought out the extroverts, the ambitious, the comic; it uncovered the hopes of old tap and singing lessons in the housewives of his audience. Getting hand-picked to the panel by Gerry Johnston was the kiss of fortune; picking the boxes was just the afterglow.

Zia Pina snorted with contempt when she saw the array of clownish costumes the camera panned over every day. She knew exactly what she had to do to get on 'Could It Be You?'. In the evenings, after I collected her dinner tray and left, she'd get busy. From down the garden path, I heard her tapping softly and singing in her croaky voice:

'*Portami dove i limoni fioriscono, arrance nei dolci boschi oscurri. Tu, li piangendo lacrime infinite, che cosa hai fatto degli anni giovanni?*'

My mother was alarmed when, on behalf of Zia Pina, I wrote requesting tickets to be part of the studio audience of 'Could It Be You?'. I asked for two thinking my mother would be thrilled to take a day off work and accompany Zia Pina, but she refused. My mother lost her temper when I agreed to search out the music and all the words of *La Tristezza*, the folk song Zia Pina dimly remembered and intended, when chosen by Gerry Johnston, to sing. Angrily, she told me that not only would it make a complete fool of Zia Pina but it would inflame her mind and land her back in hospital.

I was taken aback by her attitude. It seemed like some weird conspiracy of illness to me and I told her so – Zia Pina was finally taking an interest in something other than pills and doctors, shouldn't we be supporting her? My mother told me not to get embroiled in the fantasies of old women. 'Don't listen to her,' she insisted, 'you'll just make her worse. Believe me. I know. You'll see.'

The weeks went past with no word from the television station. Yet Zia Pina's nightly labours were growing, still hidden from me behind her yellowing linen dowry sheets. Every day she pressed me about the song. She was worried that Gordon, the organist on 'Could It Be You?' and Gerry Johnston's straight-man, would not know how to accompany her, Gordon not being Italian and unfamiliar with the tune.

At first, searching for the origins of the song was a chore but gradually, as I met frustration everywhere, it began to intrigue me. How could something like that – a tune, I assumed, that countless black-veiled crones would have sung over the boiling pasta – just vanish, completely unknown to the libraries, the tape collections, the ethno musicological literature, the notes of Italian academics and the recollections of nurses in old people's homes? Perhaps it had never been written down; certainly it had changed from region to region, some old Abruzzese and Calabrese people, even old-timers from Molise, had some scraps but no one had it all. Those first words haunted me: '*Portami dove i limoni fioriscono*'. I began to dream of endings, tunes, dances, cries in the wind. My mother, the northerner, was no help at all and my father was unco-operative, disinterested.

The studio tickets to 'Could It Be You?' had arrived in the mail. I was desperate. I decided to ring Nonna Aguccio in Italy. It was the only way. She would know all the words, the entire melody, the place where the snake lay coiled. Never in my life had I spoken to my grandmother; I didn't know her rough mountain dialect, I could barely speak Italian. It would take days to set up the call. I would have to ring my cousin in the village, get him to fetch the half-deaf old woman from the hillside by car and have her waiting in his lounge-room for my call. For what? Just to ask her the words to a folksong. It was a big decision, a crazy idea but it also excited me.

Towards midnight, I sat at the telephone with a notepad and pen and a pocket Italian dictionary. I was speaking to the international operator when I heard my mother's dressing-gown rustle behind me. She took the phone from my hand and hung it up. I spun around. She looked at me. 'Sit down,' she said. 'I'll tell you about that song.'

We talked for many hours through the night, the refrigerator whirring, the hall light casting shadows. I heard the story of Pina Loretta Catoldo, nee Aguccio, my father's eldest sister, the first of seven children, only three of whom survived polio and other unnamed fevers, the influenza epidemic and misadventure on the poor strips of land that were the family's living. Pina spent her childhood trying, not always too well, to raise her siblings while her mother worked like a man in the fields, as the patriarch, Nonno Vincenzo Aguccio spent years in America, sending back what he could. My uncle Frank – Fortunato – was not Pina's first husband and my eldest cousin Luisa was not Frank's daughter. Pina first married at seventeen, resigning herself to accept a man who, as courtship, had ripped off her kerchief one day as she walked into the village. This was his first and last romantic gesture. Married and pregnant with Luisa, Pina travelled to Naples to farewell her new husband to America.

In the first year she had five letters from him, the second year, two. After that, she became a white widow, hearing nothing from or about her husband until the news, eight years later, of his death in Brooklyn, New York, USA. At about this time, Pina's younger sister, my Zia Antonella, had married a man, Fortunato, by proxy and come out to live with him in far northern Queensland. Antonella's first pregnancy was complicated, she developed gestational diabetes, the birth ripped out her insides and the doctors said no more. Yet within three months, she was pregnant again. Through the nine months, she prepared for the birth of her child, my cousin, and the strong possibility of her own death. She made Fortunato – distraught and guilty – promise to marry her sister Pina, so the children would be raised by a mother who would care for them like her own blood. It was a way out for Pina, the wife who wasn't a wife, now a widow, unprotected and vulnerable in the village, the object of women's mistrust and men's fantasies. After the funeral, Fortunato sent for Pina. Eventually she agreed to marry him and together they raised the children, later having a boy of their own.

I thought of Zia Pina watching the afternoon soap operas, as simple as nursery rhymes compared to her own life. I had always known the rest, about how Fortunato gambled, never got along with Luisa and threw her out of home. But what about the song?

My mother lowered her voice, as she did when speaking of bad luck and evil eyes. 'That's what she was singing when the first one tore off her kerchief. Because she wasn't minding herself, keeping quiet and modest. She was always singing with her skirt in the wind, without thinking. Nothing mattered but her singing. Always singing like a child, a bit simple. *Una pazza, senza cervello.* Yes she had a lovely voice but then so does the devil, no? Nonna Aguccio beat her afterwards, for letting herself go, for not watching out. So when the young man saw her walking and singing along the path, he couldn't help himself. He had to have her for his wife. That song was the end of her happiness. Because of that, he tore her kerchief and it cost her all the years of her life.'

I took the day off college and accompanied Zia Pina to the Channel 10 studios for 'Could It Be You?'. Through all those nights, Zia Pina had woven two baskets entwined with small straw roses. They were beautiful but cumbersome as we struggled through the crush of the excited audience, costumed like a suburban mardi gras. Zia Pina had dressed in her best black, not a good colour for television. In the off-camera preliminaries, Gerry Johnston had paused briefly to admire the baskets, then moved on to a woman dressed as a Heinz tomato-sauce bottle. I knew all along that Zia Pina's lined peasant face, her gold teeth and her mangled English were not videogenic, not daytime television. Yet I was unprepared for my sadness when she was passed over as the sea by the wind. I would have liked to have seen the cameras closing in on her old cheeks, her trembling fingers clutching the baskets, her voice, cracked with the grit of the mountains, singing harsh above Gordon's Yamaha chords.

I told her I couldn't find the words or music to *La Tristezza*; that I'd tried but I was too busy with studying for my exams at college. Privately, I translated what words I had, wrote down the guitar chords on a scrap of paper, then put them away and searched no more. That way, I found, only rarely would the tune fly out to catch at my throat.

'Take me where the lemon grows, oranges in sweet dark groves. You there, weeping endless tears, what have you done with your youthful years?'

There are rooms in my parents' house that I have barely entered. Strangely, they built them for us, the adolescent children they were afraid of losing. Just as we were tearing ourselves away from them, they went into a frenzy of building, as if they could dam the rush of our separating hormones, stop the drift of us, their flesh and blood. The new rooms were splendid attic and basement additions, equipped with kitchens, showers, Swedish kit furniture, television sets and telephone extensions.

I saw they were offering me a key of dust that would crumble in the lock of comfort. I left, I fled into exile. For seven years my mother would pick up the telephone, hear my long-distance voice and cry, 'Aren't you dead yet?'

Outside my home's land, I ran to share houses, flats, relationships. I lived with boyfriends, I lived without them, I did what I could to survive. My mother said she had finished with me but she couldn't help consulting oracles. From the letters, the phone calls, the words of friends, the news was the same – I was alive, I lived. Enraged, for seven years my mother hid a key, the key a woman fishes from her womb to give a daughter, the key of blood and milk, of watching and divination, the key I never had.

When my first child, Emily, was born, I held her and saw she was perfect. Some don't feel instant love for their children in this way, it takes a little while, but I was lucky – I was overwhelmed every time with my children and especially with my firstborn. The force of this pledge of myself to her was so strong that I never noticed the drop of yellowish liquid in the corner of her left eye. My husband left for work and I fell back into the pillows to sleep.

Hours later, as if in a distant dream, the paediatrician was at my bed, drawing the curtains and sitting down. My daughter was in the intensive care nursery. They were doing tests on the infection in her eye. It might be harmless or it might be something that would leave her brain-damaged or blind. In a dish in a far-off laboratory across town, a culture was growing. Over the next few days, it would become apparent which it was. In the meantime, the doctors would treat the baby for the worst, bombarding her with medication.

Over the next few days, my fear grew faster than the culture in the laboratory. I planned my suicide should my daughter die – God would have to take both of us or none at all. I breastfed my daughter constantly, willing my milk to cure this evil eye. On the third morning at first light I took a coin, walked painfully down the hospital corridor and rang my mother for the first time in years. 'Come and see your grand-daughter, you old hag!' I screamed. 'Make yourself happy. Come and see us both before we die.'

I went downstairs to the nursery to feed my daughter. She suckled happily, her new blue open eyes watching my every move. How could there be anything wrong with her? My heart was calm. I walked her through the corridors then took her up the hospital lift to my ward.

My mother was waiting for me. I hadn't seen her for seven years but it was as if only five minutes had passed. She brought me minestrone, pasta, bread, cheese, peaches, plums and dahlias. She took Emily in her arms, poked her nose into her face. 'You stupid fool,' she said to me. 'There's nothing wrong with her. It's only "sticky eye". You all had it. Just squirt a few drops of your breastmilk into it three times a day.'

Later that morning, the paediatrician and assorted white coats arrived. 'There's nothing wrong with her,' they said. 'It's only conjunctivitis. Give her these antibiotic drops three times a day.'

My mother placed a gold cross around the neck of her first grandchild. The key I wanted, that secret thing that is unlocked from mother to daughter, was never given to me but was passed straight on, hidden in the apple of time from which my children bite out their nourishment.

Over the past week, I have been waiting for them, waiting for a sign. I have been coming here later, when my day with the kids is done and my husband is settled into the earphones of his hi-fi. This evening, I clear the mailbox. As the light falls, I sit by the window of my parents' house.

'Dear children,' writes my mother, 'meet us at the airport on Friday ... Your grandmother is buried, we have finished our business here ... Put snail-poison out after it rains, pick the plums and figs, don't let the birds get them ... Take out the car and switch on the hot water ... All is lost here, the country changed, the water bad, too many strikes, young people no longer want to work and the doctors are fools ... Your grandmother left you each these few trinkets as if they were the jewels of Victor Emmanuel. Take them now because I don't want to load up our suitcases with the spirits of the dead ...'

I close up my parents' house and deadlock the front door. The moon rises over the balconies and night-watered gardens of the street. As I walk to my car, I am laughing.

In my hand is a tiny golden key.

Part Two

Arias

Harbour

On the first night, the old woman forgets to bring matches. Instead she has to set everything up by torchlight. The eerie circles frighten her. Only candlelight gives her the courage to go through with this task – to walk across the park, to sidle down the street and slip the key in the lock. Candlelight is holy; she has always felt protected under the blessed flame.

Still, the old woman doesn't change her mind. When all is in place, she spreads a blanket on the rough concrete of the shed. Winding the rosary beads round her hands, she kneels and prays.

It was in the thirty-sixth week of Rose's pregnancy, just as she was about to tell her husband's family that she wouldn't need Nonna's help this time thanks very much, that Rose's kids all got the chickenpox. It was going around at Rachel's primary school; she got it first, then Daniel and finally the toddler, Marina.

To make things worse, it was frantic in the Dell'angelos' photography studio, which they ran from a front room in their terrace house in Newtown. Rose – the bookkeeper, proof-checker, neg-masker and print order dispatcher – had gone through the stress of working till the last minute while carrying Marina and had vowed this pregnancy to quit at least a month before the birth and prepare the house properly for the arrival of a new soul. But Tony, Rose's photographer husband, was up all night working on his Aboriginal exhibition and Ellie, the assistant, was away with the flu. On top of all this the batches of print orders for their commercial wedding work were mounting up.

Rose's family were all in Canada; she had no one to turn to in this difficult time but Tony's mother, occasionally, and her widowed seventy-five-year-old Sicilian grandmother-in-law, Nonna Giovina, the razor-tongued matriarch of the clan.

Giovina Dell'angelo had been brought out to Australia in the sixties by her eldest son, Gaetano. While she raised her grandchildren, he and her other married children and their spouses all went into business. Loretta, Michele, Gaetano, and the other two brothers in Queensland all spoke shopkeeper's Italo-Australian with lots of *orright, bewdiful, no worris mate* and *okai luv.* Over the years Nonna Giovina had become bored with her easy dominion over the lives of these adult offspring. She now turned her energies to the families of her more intractable grandchildren, of whom Tony, Loretta's youngest, was the baby, 'the luck child', as Nonna Giovina called him. Australian-born, university educated and with the status of a rising Sydney artist, Tony was the family rebel, their eccentric at the dinner table, their embarrassment at weddings and, naturally, Nonna Giovina's precious jewel.

When Rose, a Jewish former hippie and single mother first moved in to live with Tony, Nonna Giovina had called her a *puttana a*nd wept every night on the phone to the parents of Tony's old girlfriend, the daughter of well-known Italian restaurateurs. When Rose and Tony announced their wedding date, Nonna Giovina offered her grandson his own business, camera equipment, an overseas trip and a Pajero if he would change his mind. Finally, defeated, she bought rosary beads for Rachel and Daniel. After the birth at home of Marina a few months later, the old woman, clucky and by now as *dolce* as *tirami su*, had moved in, supposedly to keep Rose company post-partum. Instead she had kidnapped the three-day-old baby, taken her to an Italian priest and had her baptised in the name of Jesus Christ. Rose had awoken from a nap to find her newborn missing from the basinet and her birthright as a Jewish child snatched from her. Rose wasn't religious but she was affronted and angry.

'This is going too far,' she'd said to Tony at the time. 'I want an apology.'

Religion, convention and tradition meant nothing to Tony either. By marrying Rose – an older woman, twice divorced with two kids from her previous marriage and a traitor to her orthodox Judaism, far less a Roman Catholic – he had finally hammered home to his family that their youngest son was an independent man, as a lover, as an artist and as a rebel from the trap of *parenti e paesani.*

'What's the big deal?' Tony had said, unable to stop laughing as he comforted his firstborn, howling from her baptismal adventure. 'A dago took my baby. So what?'

Chickenpox or no chickenpox, business disasters or breakdowns, Rose was determined to keep Nonna Giovina from darkening her door when it came to this pregnancy. Rose appealed instead to Loretta, her mother-in-law, and Serena, Tony's sister, who came to give her a hand with the kids while she did the backlog of print orders. After only a few days however, these Dell'angelo women felt they had done their best; they might have liked to stay longer but their own businesses – a hair salon and a children's clothes boutique – were suffering.

Immediately, Nonna Giovina, who lived with Loretta's family on the other side of the park, got Serena to drop her off at Rose's, 'to give Marina her *Gattopardo*', a forgotten toy: 'No, I can't come in – tell her not to trouble herself Serena – no, really, Rosa *pliss*, who has the time?'

After Serena left and Nonna Giovina was poking around the refrigerator for something to feed Marina, Rose decided it was time to tell the old woman that she would not be needed for the birth.

'*Eh, va bene,*' said the old woman, unperturbed. 'I've seen enough of what happens between a woman's legs.'

Rose was not sure her grandmother-in-law understood.

'I don't mean the labour, Nonna,' she said. 'I mean afterwards. Tony and I have discussed it and we feel we'd like to be left alone with the new baby this time. Just to have some space as a family.'

The old woman looked at her blankly.

'I'm a very independent person,' said Rose, taking deep slow breaths. 'I like my privacy.'

Nonna Giovina was having trouble hauling out a plastic container from the back of the fridge. Finally she extricated it, sniffed it, then headed off to the lounge room, where the scratchy children had dragged their mattresses, blankets and drinks in front of the television. She muttered in dialect that she'd never seen a household in such a state as Rose's.

'Sick or not sick, pregnant or not pregnant, and don't think I don't know what I'm talking about,' growled Nonna Giovina, feeding the container of cold Maggi noodles to Marina. '*Madon', ho passato le guai.* Do you think I led an easy life in Villa Marino? Independent. Independent. What's this stupid thing, independent? Do you think I don't know what it's like to try to push out a baby from between my legs? With nobody to help me but my own still breastfed infant, God save me? With not another soul to even wipe the blood with the sheets? *O Dio – le cose che ho passato – nessun, nessun li ha passato.* I raised five children alone, in wartime, through the influenza and the polio fever – five children and no hospital, no doctor, no clothes drier, no –' Nonna Giovina sneered, 'no *televisione*. And my house was always clean. *Pulita.* I was never ashamed to ask anyone into my home. There was always bread on the table, a glass of wine. No one ever saw my children with so much as a dirty nose . . .' She jabbed at Marina with a handkerchief.

Rose fought down the urge to rise to Nonna's bait, but lately she had begun feeling nauseous again in the afternoons and it was harder to control her body. She waddle-ran to the bathroom, lunged for the toilet, prised off the lid and vomited into it. When she sat up, gasping, Nonna Giovina was standing over her.

'This no good, Rosa. Sick in first months, *sì, okai,* many womans does this. Sick in last months, bad, no good. *Malocchio.* Bad eye.'

Nonna Giovina fished an object from her lumpy breasts. 'I give something you,' she said, handing it to Rose. 'I make – *come si dice, sacrificio* – offer. I come here, I make every night strong food to you. Maybe *tirtin* nights I pray *La Madonna. Sì* – I do for you *e* Antonio.'

Rose turned the thing over. It was a 1930s postcard of

the Virgin of Villa Marino encrusted in jewels, lire and American dollar bills.

'No thanks,' she said, slightly revolted. 'You keep it, Nonna.'

As Rose handed back the grimy card, she was surprised by the pain on the old woman's face.

'Come on,' said Rose firmly, picking up the car keys. 'I'll get Tony to drive you home.'

Predictably, Rose was soon sick herself: a cough, fever, thick sinuses and a heavy body to match her heavy head. During the night, she'd get up groggy to the children, feeling their burning foreheads, dabbing Caladryl to their sores and encouraging sips of water down their throats. Afterwards she'd lumber down to the bathroom for a pee and two Panadol, the only safe drug in her condition.

One night, while waiting half asleep for the tablets to dissolve, looking, maybe dreaming, through the kitchen windowpanes, she saw a light from a far window.

She blinked, it blinked.

Where was it coming from? It seemed to be from a far window, a patch of light swinging like a weathervane in the dark.

Rose and Tony's half-renovated terrace kitchen was a deck built high on sloping land. Wide windows looked out over their unkempt backyard and the railway yards of Newtown-Macdonaldtown. She squinted and peered into the glass. The light seemed to flicker as the wind started to blow up outside. She wondered why, in all her night wakings, she had never seen this light before. There was something about its small intensity that was disembodied, fragile, yet it seemed to have been there forever. In her exhaustion, the light appeared to be signalling at her, waving at her sleepless night. Was there some other woman out there who was also rocking and pacing these hours of the wolf alone? For a minute, maybe two, she fell asleep on her feet, in a kind of swaying trance.

She jerked awake and swallowed her tumbler of Panadol in one go – God, she felt rotten. Crawling upstairs into bed, Rose wondered whether the light would still be there for her when the children were sure to wake her later in the night. As a sign, a kind of wave, she left their Mickey Mouse lamp on, softly grinning.

Under the blankets her thoughts scattered into clouds over the waters of the English Channel where a mere slip of a girl made her way to Sicily by way of a shark cage that swung through the sea like a pendulum, ticking Yes, No, Maybe …

It was just in the moment before she sank into sleep that Rose saw, in her mind's eye, the bricks of their back fence, the old dunny-washhouse, the shut gate, the laneway and railway yards. There were no houses to the north and west of their terrace. There were no buildings facing her kitchen or the children's rooms. There was nothing but railway line, concrete and rust for miles into the horizon.

On the second night, the old woman leaves the house with stolen matches. The wind is fierce, her frail hands shake. She lights and re-lights the candles.

'Oh most beautiful flower of the Mount, fruit vine splendorous of heaven, blessed Mother of the Son of God, immaculate Virgin, assist me in my necessity ...'

'"Ah", you say, "The necessity, eh? Now that you have the necessity, you come." How can I have the face to ask any favours from You when after all those years I never defended You against him? But Holy Mother, you do what you have to do to survive. For the sake of the family, I had to go along with him. For the family, for peace in the home, I bit my lip, I stayed away.

'Queen of Heaven, at least take into account that I was a girl, I was a child with children. At nineteen, I had already a husband and two small boys. I had a baby born in the seventh month, suddenly, in the farmhouse, with no one to help me, as You might well remember. This stillbirth shocked me so much, I got *l'impressione*, childbed nerves, the premonitions of my death. I knew the *Malocchio* had passed over me. Sure enough, the next pregnancy I carried well but too long. He was too big to be born. In the end the midwives had to crush his head to save me.

'Then my husband left for America. In our family all the men emigrated or were taken for the army. They were hard years. I got a few letters from Vincenzo, and a bit of money – I didn't complain for that – but I could feel him slipping away from me. Finally, without telling me, my parents wrote to a cousin there, who visited Vincenzo and pressured him to come home. I don't know with what; I don't know what was said. After five years, a person changes a lot, even the temperament, attitudes. We didn't know each other. The children kept away from him, they didn't call him "Papà". But worse, we didn't sleep together, we weren't really husband and wife. At night, in bed – nothing.'

Despite all Rose's efforts, there was no improvement to the weary chaos of Pinetarsol baths and Caladryl lotion and the wall-to-wall tantrums of her cranky kids. Nonna Giovina was on the phone to Rose three times a day, exhorting her to take the kids to a doctor who would give them more drugs. 'I believe in science – *la penicellina, la scienza* – not quacks, not *le cose cinese*,' she declared. She advised Rose to cook the family meat broth, to keep the windows closed, to swaddle the kids in blankets. Finally Loretta had to take the phone – *basta, Mamma* – to stop Nonna Giovina from rushing over and forcing her own prescribed antibiotics down the kids' throats herself.

Rose swore under her breath. Thirty-seven weeks, only three weeks to term. *Nearly there baby,* she thought as she heaved the itchy kids one by one into the station wagon to take them to the homoeopath. Nearly there, Rose thought, throwing up in the Marketown toilets as Rachel attacked Daniel with her recorder. Nearly there, she thought, as spotty-faced Marina, with a temperature of thirty-eight and Caladryl lotion crusted all over her face, comfort-suckled at Rose's breasts even as she sat on the toilet.

On the morning of the thirty-eighth week, when Rose was up early helping Tony, she felt something change inside her. It was nothing dramatic, just a small jump from the baby. Probably, she thought, the startle of its Moro reflex. Then all was quiet. Rose stopped her work and waited, leaning against the light box with her blue hands: come on, baby, move. Then, at last, it kicked again. Maybe not as vigorous as before, but active, still there. Relieved Rose squatted against the chair. Tony looked down at her. 'What's wrong?'

'I don't know.'

'Is it starting?'

'No. I'm just … it just … I don't know.'

'Does it hurt?'

'No. No, I'm tired. I'm probably just tired.'

'I'm calling Mamma.'

'What for?'

'To get Nonna over to look after you.'

Rose was incredulous. 'I thought we discussed this,' she said, reaching up to her husband.

'She only wants to help.' Tony sat on the floor. 'Come on, babe. We're talking about an old woman here. An old lady who doesn't understand. She's thinking that you hate her or something. She's been driving Loretta mad about how this will be the first baby in the family that she hasn't helped out with.'

'You mean the first she hasn't completely taken over.'

Tony's face tightened. 'Hey,' he said sharply. 'Nonna's done a lot of good things for our family.' He stood up and ran his hands through his hair. He sighed. 'Rosie,' he said. He knelt by his wife and stroked her arm. 'If it makes her happy to come over and cook you some *brodino* and help you with the kids or whatever, what's wrong with that?'

Rose drew herself to her feet, then, once up, she pushed Tony away. 'You're so gutless, Tony.'

Her husband snapped the light off her light box. 'Jesus Rose. Look at this place. We're drowning here.'

'We've got a business and three children under seven, what do you expect?'

'What do I expect?' Tony punched the table, scattering the morning's work. 'I expect that when we're months behind with the orders and my wife's as sick as a dog and the kids are stuffed and she's about to give birth on the fucking studio floor, that she'd be saying, okay Tony, get some help, call in the family, all hands on deck. But, hey, you don't need anybody, right?'

'Yes. That's right. I'll cope.'

'For Christ's sake get over this superwoman bullshit before we all go under.'

Rose grabbed a tray of slides and forced herself back onto the stool, switching on the light box.

'I swear to God, Tony,' she said, sorting furiously, 'no

way is your grandmother setting foot in our house until I say so. Or this will be the first great-grandchild that Nonna and the rest of your family have nothing to do with. Ever.'

On the eighth night, as she crosses Wilson Street, a car full of drunken kids screeches past the old woman, a can clattering at her legs. Still, she slips past, key in the latch, down the hallway and out the back as easily as a cat.

'O Star of the Sea, help me and show me herein that you are my Mother. O Holy Mary Mother of God, Queen of Heaven and Earth, I humbly beseech you from the bottom of my heart to succour me in my necessity ...

'You know, after a while, Holy Mother, people talk. I wasn't happy with Vincenzo, we were fighting and women whispered among themselves: she's not pregnant. In church I was praying to You, why – why this *Malocchio*? First two babies die and now my husband is a stranger who can't stand to be with me.

'Vincenzo wanted to go back to America. He had letters, in English, from New York. I was upset. I thought he had some *puttana* there. One day, looking in his things I found some soap and linen. Why, when I had been waiting months, dreaming of nice words from him, did he never give this present to me?

'Then his parents died. There were fights between the sons about the way the land was to be divided. Vincenzo agreed to take money instead, so he could emigrate again, try again maybe in Australia or Argentina. I cried a lot. I don't say anything about the present. But I know if he left, he would never write for us.'

That night Rose tossed in bed, half-crying. In her dream she was working at a long, feverish labour. She was in some poor room with bare floorboards, oil lamps in the middle of the night, the sound of wind and, far away, the sea. Dark-haired women urged her to push, shouting in foreign tongues. An old crone stroked a leopard by the fire; her eyes were closed and the animal seemed drugged, its head lolling strangely on the hearth. Into the room, bringing with them the smell of salt and fish, came three men in oilskins. Underneath their fishermen's clothes, they were wearing business suits. Their hands on her belly were cold. She could read the digitals on their Rolex watches: 2.46, strong south to southeasterly winds at twenty knots, barometric pressure 2400 millibars and rising, gale warnings to the eastern coastline.

'At the stroke of four,' said one of the men, taking out a pair of scissors from his pocket, 'it will be two minus one precisely.'

Rose woke. Shaky, she clambered downstairs and sat at the kitchen table. She knew what to do – each of her pregnancies had their night crises. She searched for her well-thumbed copy of *The Compleat Midwife* and found the page:

'The ninth month is the time of demons, visions, guilt. With the approaching child come the mother's mother's mothers, the women with their millennia of pain, fear, grief. They stand at the head and the foot of the bed, whispering, advising, insinuating. In the middle of the night they heal, scratch, weave and cut. Around the thirty-sixth week, the mother – round, vulnerable, torpid – clings to the bed sheet and, in sleep, with her legs almost spread apart by the butting child, she rides the Night Mare.'

Rose breathed hard. My baby is dead inside me, I slept with too many men and so it will be born deformed, I have AIDS and my baby has AIDS, I cannot birth this child and we will both die.

The house was quiet. Rose listened for a cry, a call, anything. Just when she would welcome being taken out of herself, the children slept, they didn't need her.

I cannot birth this child and we will both die.

On her way upstairs, she checked the kids. They were sleeping, fairytale children, rosy-cheeked, perfect. For a moment she thought she saw something outside, a light, a shadow reflecting against the partly-closed curtains. But when she looked again there was nothing but wind over the railway yards.

Jodi, the red-haired midwife at the birth centre, pumped up the armband for Rose's blood pressure. The hiss of release and then the verdict: 140 over 90. It was up. The swish-sticks showed there was a trace of protein in her urine. Nothing major, nothing that added up to anything. Tiredness, suggested Jodi, stress, the flu, overdoing it.

'Maybe,' said Rose doubtfully. 'But I think something's wrong. It's like ... I don't know how to explain it.'

'Take your time,' said Jodi.

Rose faced the midwife. 'I'm not getting any bigger am I?'

Jodi was a mother of two as well as a midwife. On her wall were typewritten lines from the *I Ch'ing*.

> *Seeing the small is insight*
> *Yielding to force is strength*
> *Using the outer light, return to insight*
> *And in this way be saved from harm*

'No, you're not huge,' Jodi said, her hands palpating the baby. 'But every pregnancy is different.' She looked at Rose shrewdly. 'What you need is time to centre down. Take a bath, talk to the baby, practise your breathing and say your affirmations.'

'I want to see it,' said Rose suddenly.

'Pardon?'

'I want an ultrasound.'

Jodi was silent. For years her hands had felt in the dark, resting upon the amniotic waters, calling up movements, cords, placentae, heartbeats. Her hands had massaged feet that had never trod on the earth. Her hands had found small, blind faces squashed wet in bones, crevices, muscle. Her hands were as fine as any ultrasound.

'Go home, Rose,' she said. 'Relax. Take an afternoon nap, go to bed early and come back to see me tomorrow. If you're still worried then, I can get you to Dr Fong.' The midwife studied Rose's face carefully as she put on her jacket. 'Have you got anyone who can come in for a few weeks to help you out?'

'Not really,' said Rose.

Jodi saw Rose out the door. 'Now's the time,' she said, firmly tucking the antenatal card into Rose's bag. 'Call in any favours. If I were you I'd lean on my friends and relatives for all they're worth.'

Tony was not so much against the idea of hiring a mother's help as not used to it. For a start, the fees were ridiculous and they couldn't afford it. Besides, it was unheard of in the Dell'angelo family to bring in outsiders when Nonna was so readily available.

'Not this time,' said Rose. Without any further consultation, she cashed her mother's cheque for the newborn – a generous gift in American dollars – and hired Ellie's younger sister, Tessa, to come in casually for the next few weeks.

On the girl's first morning with the kids, Loretta rang to say she was on her way to work. Could she drop by with Nonna for a few minutes? To get the kids' measurements? 'Nonna's gonna make them jumpers.'

'I'll give them to her later,' said Rose.

Loretta sighed. 'Sure, Rose, but Nonna – you know? There's not much time. She say she gotta do it before the baby's born, so they don't get jealous, you know?'

Living so close by, the Dell'angelos all had keys to each other's houses, a practice Rose disliked in theory but found quite practical, even useful at times. This morning Rose was so busy getting ready to go to her birth centre appointment, trying to fill a urine sample jar while putting on her make-up and wiping Marina's nose, that she barely heard the old woman and Loretta letting themselves in the hallway.

Nonna Giovina surprised Rose on the toilet, Marina at her breast, a hair scrunchie in her teeth and a lipstick in her hand.

The old woman started. '*Madonna delle grazie!*' She called out to her daughter. 'Loretta, *vieni, vieni.*'

Loretta scuttled obediently from the bedroom.

'*Gesù Cristo,*' said Nonna opening the bathroom door wider. '*Madon*', Loretta, what is she doing with her?'

Rose felt the baby pushing at her gullet, that feeling of no more room in there, of having to throw up. She swallowed hard and bent her head wearily over Marina, who took one look at her grandmother and turned back to the breast, suckling even harder.

Nonna Giovina stared at them in disgust. 'Rosa,' she said, 'this no good.'

'She's still just a baby, Nonna,' murmured Rose.

Two minutes with Tony's wife and Nonna Giovina lapsed into the street English she used with her grandchildren, doctors and with idiots.

'She baby? *Wit* all the teeth, talk, walk, do pee-pee in pot? No Rosa, *pliss*, don't say me this. She not baby.'

'She needs it, Nonna. She's been sick.'

'Rosa, *Dio Mio, Dio Mio*, Rosa. Listen me. *Pliss*, is for you I say this. Why you sick? Why you weak? Why is go bad for you?' She turned to Loretta. 'Can't she see she's letting this one steal the goodness from the other one?'

'That's not true,' said Rose. 'That's got nothing to do with it. Come on Loretta – tell her that's crap.'

Loretta, whose three children were each carried home from hospital in the arms of Nonna Giovina and stayed there for most of their childhood, stared from one to the other uncomfortably.

'How can she think this is right, Loretta?' said Nonna Giovina. 'Giving a grown child the milk of her unborn child? This is against nature.' She turned to her squatting daughter-in-law. 'Rosa, this no good. No good for you. No good for baby. In my country we no do this. No womans does what you does.'

'Rubbish. Loretta, you know she did it herself –'

'*Ma che dice questa ignorante?* Never, never did I do this dirty thing. Tell her not to insult me with this, Loretta. I brought up five children, alone, through the war, through the tuberculosis fever –'

'Oh, come on, Nonna, you can't tell me that when they cried you didn't –'

'– with nothing to eat but what we could dig out of the ground. But still my children got food in their mouths. My children all learned how to chew. I gave them food to eat –'

'I give my children plenty of food to eat, Nonna.'

'*La Vege-mite,*' said Nonna Giovina. '*La Vege-mite. Sempre la Vege-mite, la Vege-mite.* You think you can live on *la Vege-mite, le chips, la sandawich?*' Nonna Giovina pinched Marina's legs. 'Skinny, *troppo* skinny. *Ma certo,* she's sick, *certo,* living on *solo la Vege-mite e la pinutta butta.* She's hungry.'

Rose clung to the bathroom rail till her nails went white. 'Loretta, explain to Nonna about comfort-suckling.'

'*È per la sicurezza, Mamma,*' Loretta obliged.

'*Certo, certo.* Don't talk to me like an idiot, I breastfed five children, through the war, through the influenza epidemic –'

From the lounge-room, Rachel and Daniel, finished with 'Playschool', began yelling, 'I'm hungry, Mum – Mum can you make us something to eat?'

'See?' said Nonna Giovina. 'They hungry.'

Rose felt the baby heave against her. Again the hopeless movement. Fear shot through her, and anger. She tore Marina off her nipple, roughly opening her jaws to break the suction. The child slithered down the toilet seat, yelling mightily. The doorbell rang. 'Go on, go to Grandma,' said Rose desperately. 'Loretta *please* – can't I have a minute to wipe my fanny in private?'

Brushing past Loretta, Nonna Giovina swept up Marina into her arms. '*Poverina*,' she said, leading her away. '*Poverina mia*. Don't cry, my heart, Mamma's too busy to feed you now, my lovely … sh, sh, sh …'

Loretta let Tessa into the house. The young girl stood awkwardly in the hallway, taking off her jacket and scarf. In the kitchen, the commotion between toddler and wheedling old crone was escalating. Marina was on the edge of being out of control. The sight of the babysitter tipped her right over. She threw herself against the walls and the floor and the fridge. Nonna Giovina called out, trying to avoid wild legs, having to shout over the two year old's screaming. 'Rosa, *pliss*!'

Rose almost smiled. 'What's wrong, Nonna?'

'Come Rosa! Come quick-quick! *Ma Loretta, questa zingara di mamma*, is she completely heartless? Rosa, *pliss*, give breast!'

Rose was rolling down the toilet tissue. She stopped.

'*What*?'

'*Pliss,* Rosa, she cry. Give the breast.'

'Oh no, no, no,' cooed Rose sweetly. 'We can't possibly do that, Nonna. What about the poor little deprived baby inside me?'

'You see?' said Nonna Giovina bitterly to Loretta and the babysitter. 'You see how this *Australiana* talk?'

The old woman shot an aggrieved look at the bathroom door.

'*Eh ma*, excuse me, Rosa,' she countered loudly, 'but if *la poverina* is always hungry, what else can she do but suckle from you?'

On the tenth night, the old woman stands in the hallway, listening. Upstairs a child cries, a light goes on. Closing the door, she slips round the back alley and pushes instead at the rusty gate.

'O flower of Mount Carmel, there are none that can withstand your power. O Star of the Sea, show me here that you are my Mother. O Holy Mary Conceived without Sin, pray for us who have recourse to thee ...'

'In the winter Vincenzo decided to leave for New York, on the *Mare Lucida* from Naples. I had no one to turn to but You. In those days, many women in Villa Marino made sacrifices, dedications, pledges. I needed some *grazia* badly, and I was willing to pin whatever I had to the holy statue of La Madonna Del Mare. I was ready to give as much as any woman for love, for the family, for a child to have together. But he caught me taking money and a gold chain as a dedication to You.

'"*Ignorante*," he swore at me, "I break my back for years *al'estero*, sweating blood for every *dollare* and you give it to priests. *Scimarella*, wake up and look at yourself. It was doctors, *i dottori, la scienza*, not priests you needed when you were screaming in childbirth. *Porca Italia*, do you think *i signori, i baroni* do this?"

'I screamed at him about his *puttana* in America, about the present he never gave me after all the years of raising and bearing his children, suffering, nearly dying for them. We fought bitterly for the first time since his return.

Later, that night, he turned to me.'

On the ultrasound, in the darkened medical centre, Rose saw something heavy in the amniotic waters, a creature of silver and shadows turning and starting as the sonar scanned through the wet jelly on her stomach. In the darkness, the technician pressed her gently, watching the lights of the screen, searching for clues, measurements, depth of limbs, circumference of head, the ventricles of the heart. Rose stared hard into the light, trying to see her baby in the grid of lines and shadows.

'Is it all right?' said Rose.

'Seems fine to me,' said the technician breezily. 'So let's see, what are you now, thirty-five weeks?'

'Thirty-eight.'

The technician's eyebrows rose.

'What's wrong?' said Rose. 'Something's wrong, isn't it?'

'I'm afraid I can't interpret the data for you,' said the technician. 'I'm sorry. You'll have to discuss it with Dr Fong.' He helped her up from the bed and gave her a sheet of absorbent paper. Rose wiped the jelly from her stomach. Tears broke over her face.

'There's something wrong isn't there?'

'Not necessarily.' The technician had his breezy voice back in place. 'Please try not to worry. Dr Fong is the specialist. He is qualified to interpret the data. Dr Fong will give you more details.'

In the car park at the back of the hospital, Rose sat jammed huge behind the wheel of her old Renault, her face puffy. She'd rung Tony from the hospital cafeteria and arranged to pick him up at a client's in town. They'd hear Dr Fong's verdict together. Inside her all was quiet. Whatever small movements occurred were mostly, perhaps, the quickening of her imagination.

The back of the hospital, trolleys, ambulances and scaffolding dissected the horizon. Along the far balconies moved tiny humans in dressing-gowns.

Rose got out her street directory, looking for Tony's pick-up address. She flicked past the central business district. Beside it was the map of her neighbourhood. She studied it for a moment. It was strange to see her street, the railway yards, the park, the school, the baby health centre, the corner where Loretta's house was. In fact, her street and Loretta's were so close, they shared the same grid – C 7. The laneway behind Loretta's house eventually became, after the park, the laneway to the back of her own.

The baby rolled over, its first movement for maybe twenty minutes. Rose stared at the map, trying to pin down what was tugging at her mind. It was something about the arrangement of streets. She decided it was strangely comforting, the intersections, the meshing, the web of lines, water, gardens, paths, like blood vessels through their lives.

Rose and Tony sat in Dr Fong's office, moist-eyed, holding hands. Dr Fong turned on his swivel chair. He had been poring over sheaves of negatives; now he laid them out like a map on the table, looking for directions, clues, how to navigate this problem.

'Your baby,' he explained, 'is small-for-dates.' He looked at the puzzled parents and elaborated as best he could. Rose heard what she already knew. The baby hadn't grown for a while.

'The cause is unknown,' said Dr Fong. 'It is most likely a virus – your flu, probably, gave Baby a dose as well. The cord could be compromised, the placenta not functioning as well as it should. Many things. Anything . . .'

I cannot birth this baby and we will both die. Rose sat very still. Whatever the reason, it was only a matter of time, tomorrow, maybe a few days, before it would plunge into the well-charted syndrome of foetal distress. It would literally shit with fear into the amniotic waters, throwing itself down the cervix, suffocating trying to be born . . .

Dr Fong looked squarely at the parents. 'Go to hospital,' he advised. 'I am recommending an induction of labour in the next few hours.'

Rose lay on her side under the doona. Her emergency labour-ward suitcase, bought at a discount store weeks ago, was still flat-packed in its plastic under the bed. Her eyes were closed, her face turned to the wall. She breathed slowly.

> *Seeing the small is insight*
> *Yielding to force is strength*
> *Using the outer light, return to insight*
> *And in this way be saved from harm*

Downstairs, the house was in uproar. Nonna Giovina had heard the bad news from Serena. She'd turned up on Rose and Tony's doorstep with several bags and her knitting, ready to mind the kids. Rose had stared at her shocked. She'd told the old woman that she had no intention of going to hospital yet.

'Tony, take Nonna home for God's sake.'

And with that Rose had taken herself off to bed and refused to speak to anyone.

Like a great black seabird, swollen with anger now, Nonna Giovina swooped and plunged on her grandson all afternoon, attacking him from room to room, half-crying, half-cursing in the most bitter dialect.

'*Porca miseria*, but if you were a man, you would do something, you would make her go, but no, you follow her – *quella pazza* – like a puppy, following every silly thing in her silly head, *la scimarella* . . . You fool, can't you see what is happening? Do you think a human being comes into the world, plop, just like that? Don't think I don't know what I'm talking about. I did it alone, in the wartime, pushing out a baby from between my legs, with not another soul to even wipe the blood from – *ma basta. Dio Mio, porca miseria,* don't let me have to say any more –'

Tony was trying to keep Marina out of her mother's room. He was trying to keep his step-children from each other's throats and to order a courier to North Sydney before the print lab shut for the night. He turned brusquely to his grandmother.

'Shut up, Nonna. Rose knows what she's doing.'

He wondered whether he should ring Loretta at the salon, to get her to come over and reason with the old woman, who didn't seem to understand that the birth centre midwives fully supported Rose's decision to wait and watch carefully, to see if she went into labour naturally at home. He gave up on his phone call. 'Come on then. Let's go.'

'*Naturale, naturale* – what *naturale*?' sneered Nonna Giovina. She stood under the stairwell, directly below the supposedly sleeping Rose. 'I believe in *la scienza, i dottori, la penicellina,*' she shouted. 'Not *le ignorante,* not *le quacki,* not *le puttane della berta senta* ... *Naturale* – *ma* what *naturale*? Rosa, God forgive me what I tell you now – but if you don't go to *l'ospedale* – if you wait for *naturale* ...'

215

As Tony grabbed Nonna's bag and bundled her into the car, she made the sign of the cross.

On the thirteenth night, the old woman is agitated. When she kneels, she clutches the rosary beads as if they were an anchor, as if trying to stop herself drifting from one world to the next.

'O fruit vine splendorous of the Mount,
Pray for us.
O Holy Mother conceived without sin,
Pray for us.
O Holy Mother of the Son of God,
Pray for us.
O Immaculate Virgin beloved of Heaven and Earth,
Pray for us.

'As soon as Vincenzo left in the middle of winter, I found out what I suspected. I was pregnant. As a last offering, I left the children asleep in their beds and I went to the sea at night, alone, over the rocks, in the wind, without a father or a brother to protect me. For thirteen nights, I said the Rosary by the sea. I prayed for Vincenzo to return and for the baby to be delivered to us from Your infinite grace and over the wide water.

'The next day the fields were under light snow. My back ached from carting wood. I heard nothing. Night came and still nothing. Then, late in the afternoon of the fourteenth day, the *carabinieri* came to the farmhouse. They told me that at Port Said, the *Mare Lucida* collided with another ship coming into harbour. No one was hurt but Vincenzo was shaken by it. He took it as a sign he couldn't go on with that ship. A week later my husband was back in Villa Marino.'

Rose heard a cry. Or maybe she dreamt it because when she got up to tend Marina, or dreamt in her dream of getting up to tend Marina, the impossible window's light was on, as surreal as a harvest moon. The light splashed onto her face and breasts. She heard Tony through the floorboards in the darkroom beneath her, a traveller in his own night. Never her nights. He never saw this love and terror, the pain of swimming up through pins-and-needles to be cut on a child's cry. In the dark, waiting for the milk to flow, she dreamt she was holding a map upside down, scanning the grid of numbers and letters, freeways and churches. Down the leaf-strewn gutters and windy streets, a smiling Mickey Mouse led her deeper and deeper ... on, off, on, off, like a tiny lighthouse beaming above her.

And still the baby moved.

She dreamt of it turning into place, with head over hands, battening down for whatever tempest it was facing in that sea down, down, down there ...

The candles flare in the gusty midnight wind.

'For the birth, Vincenzo took me to my cousin's in Molina, the big town twenty kilometres away inland from Villa Marino. There a young *dottore* pulled out Loretta with instruments. All day and night, I held her and looked at her, my luck child, her body perfect, her lungs strong. Vincenzo, the fool, said to me, "See, no need to mutter your prayers to the Virgin when an educated man rolls up his fine sleeves and does the miracle in a few minutes."

'I said nothing about my sacrifice. I didn't dare. But I never forgot your grace, Queen of Heaven. You gave me Loretta, You gave me my husband and after, You gave me two children normally, without instruments.

'Because of You, we breathed more easily. Again we were a family, all together. When there is bad feeling, love goes, people slip away. Families should stick together. *Ave Maria, piene di grazie*, forgive the past. Holy Mother, I place this cause in your hand. Star of the Sea, intercede for me again. O most beautiful flower of Mount Carmel, thank you for mercy towards me and mine.

'I am relying on You, Holy Mother.'

Awake at one o'clock, a dragging feeling low in her back, Rose thought she heard something. She turned to Tony. He lay asleep beside her. She listened again. It was a scuttling noise, something falling over in the children's room.

She got up, and as she entered the room she was hit with the first strong contraction. Breathing and swaying, she fumbled for the Mickey Mouse lamp and turned it on. The kids were asleep. But each was tightly tucked in by an extra layer of blankets she had never seen before. On a chair in the corner, neatly laid out, were three hand knitted jumpers.

She felt a gust of wind from a door open somewhere downstairs in the house. Running down the back stairs, she found it was so easy to see where she was going. The light cut a path through the woodpile, the rusty trikes, the herb pots, the clothesline and uncut grass. Her breath was sharp. The wind was strong, a sea wind, a wind that came off the great coastline beyond, hidden, half-forgotten. By the back fence, at the old washhouse toilet, she stopped for another contraction. Wind and stars pressed around her, awash with pain. *Come on baby, we're here, here, here, come in, come in to us.*

The washhouse door was open. Inside, two dozen or more candles were burning in rows on the old planks and on the cracked toilet seat. Nonna Giovina had turned the outhouse into a Mediterranean grotto, with a postcard portrait of the Virgin of Villa Marino sitting above the cistern, garlanded with plastic roses. Rose recognised a photo of herself with Tony and the children, a happy snap at Kiama last summer.

The old woman was praying on her knees on a blanket, wrapped in an old car coat and a black shawl, her rosary beads in her hands. She turned around, with difficulty, in the cold.

'Rosa?' she said, blinking, with surprise.

Rose took the old woman by the hand. For almost a full contraction they leaned on each other.

'It's coming, Nonna,' breathed Rose. 'It's coming fast.'

One hour later, toward the end of the first stage of labour, Tony drove the women to the birth centre. It was Rose's idea. She had a skin feeling that she wanted an endless flow of the hottest water possible. Once in hospital, she lowered herself like a sea mammal into the therapeutic pool and refused to leave.

At a quarter past three in the morning, the baby boy was born bigger than expected at seven pounds. He was beautiful and robust, with only his thin legs to show for the last month's ordeal through a bitter amniotic sea. While Tony and the midwives cut Rose's compressed cord, the luck child spent his first moments on earth swimming in Nonna's hands, his new blue eyes wide open, as if astonished to be birthed into such calm and prosperous waters.

The King
of The Accordion

At mid-afternoon, the gardens of the King's Domain are filtered in Debussy blues. On a bench under the oak trees, a middle-aged woman in a crumpled overcoat hears the music of a far string quartet coming from St Kilda Road. She opens an eye. In her mind's ear, sound rolls as far-off as the Cathedral spires.

She sits up with a groan, blinking in the light. Shit, 2.30 p.m. Audition time. The kid, her nephew, will be waiting on the footpath outside the Art Gallery for her. He'll be showered, trying to quell the nerves in the gut, his tie straight, his sheet music packed, his hands curled tight round a music stand. Shit. Her dirty fingernails scrabble in a Coles plastic bag for her Czerny, the *Urtext* of *The Well-tempered Clavier*. With a speedy lightness, her fingers collect everything – bags, erasers, manuscript papers.

Across the road outside the College of Music, three girls carrying violin-cases covered in Aboriginal land rights and Greenpeace stickers are on their way into rehearsal. They're stopped on the stairs by a distracted looking woman struggling to catch her breath.

'Are you on the list?' she says, tugging at a girl on the wrist.

The leader of the trio is a crop-haired platinum blonde with black roots. 'Beg your pardon?' she says. She shivers slightly at the touch of the woman's hot hand.

'Which room did you get?' the woman says.

For a moment, the girl's scared she's missed something. She has a flash of the music students' nightmare of sleeping in on the afternoon of a graduation recital. The blonde frowns. 'S–106. The Gallery,' she says. 'Is there a problem?'

The woman's grip on her wrist tightens. 'Bad,' she hisses. 'Don't go in there.'

The girls look at each other.

'But we booked it with Admin,' says the crop-haired girl.

'It's in the timetable,' says the other.

'We've got it for the semester,' says her colleague.

They try to move past her to the doors. Then they notice something disorderly about the woman, the dirt-smudged clothes, the chipped nail varnish, the hair back-combed over tangled hair, the smell of cigarettes, body odour and cheap scent. The woman reminds them of a cake where the icing still looks good but a trail of ants is coming out of the sides and underneath.

'Hang on,' says the crop-haired girl. She turns, looking for a college security guard or at least the student desk receptionist. 'Who are you after? Hey!'

But the woman has already hurried past them, through the foyer and down the corridor.

ONE

Candidates must demonstrate all scales and arpeggios, similar motion, contrary motion, chromatic, 3rds and 6ths, staccato double octaves, hands separately and hands together, with all similar motion scales to be played legato or staccato, either piano or forte, as requested by the audition panel.

That's the E-flat melodic minor scale the kid is playing now. Fast, huh?

Breathe in, breathe out.

But not his fastest. Molto prestissimo is fast. Molto prestissimo is bat-out-of-hell fast. This is just presto – fast enough. Especially through E-flat minor, six flats, black notes like bombs waiting to go off – fast, fast, fast, fast.

And when you're coming back down you have to do it differently. You have to pick up that D-flat and C-flat on the way. Like scooping up a baby off a minefield. A thing in your line of vision that wasn't there before. Think about it.

Breathe in, breathe out.

You're thinking about it? Wrong. You haven't got time to think about it. If you think about that C-flat, you're blown away. At this speed, at presto, it's got to be the slight adjustment of a hand pattern in your head. It's like a flight path, it's the grid the scale makes through your nerves that gets you through it, not the C-flat. The C-flat is the baby in front of the tripwire. The C-flat matters but it's irrelevant, if you see what I mean.

Breathe in, breathe out.

Listen to them. Up and down the rooms, hammering out all these little rescue missions up and down the Bösendorfer, the Kawai, the Yamaha – fast, fast, fast, fast.

Impressive? Not really. For these kids, fast and loud go together like fireworks and New Year's Eve. No big deal. But ask them to do it soft as well, so soft it's like dreaming you heard a piece of silk rustling up the stairs.

Tough huh?

Breathe in, breathe out.

Don't worry. I used to be the same. You want to do everything you can to raise their chances. You try to plan, to have a strategy. You take them out of the Suzuki method, you say goodbye to the Miss Dixon they've been with for years and you hassle to get them into the studio of the fifty dollar an hour ABC soloist who's just come back from the Moscow Conservatory. You force them into bed before 8 p.m. so you can get them up in the dark to do two hours practice before school. You think that if you drive them everywhere and excuse them from the dishes, they will have the energy to focus. Because that's what the teachers have always said – has talent but needs to focus. Okay, if they take care of the talent, you'll handle the focus. That's supportive, right? That's doing the right thing by the God-given gift that's entrusted to you, eh?

Nah. Bullshit. You can't do anything for them. Can you go and push their fingers down that staccato B-flat minor scale in thirds? Can you beat that Brahms cross-rhythm into their brains? Can you make them understand that when they play the Tchaikovsky they have to have some idea of the big things of life? Like what it is to be destroyed, disappointed, exhausted. Or in love with someone you can't have. You want to scream at them – don't just click your fingers over this like it's fucking Nintendo! Don't be a smart-arse with your Jeez, not this nineteenth century warhorse again. This is big like they don't write big any more. This is the price of love like no one wants to pay any more. If you don't know what I'm talking about, kid, just take it from me. You do the fingers. I'll do the suffering.

But you can't do anything for them. They either make it or they don't. Music is clean and fair that way. Perform or die.

Breathe in, breathe out.

Luckily they're reasonable here. Relaxed. In this place they put the musicality of the child before mindless technical achievement. They don't have to play their scales from memory. The kids can take in their scale books. They don't have to load up their minds with how many naturals become flats on the way down from E-flat melodic minor in octaves. They don't have to do all that harmonic maths crisscrossing and overtoning through twenty-four keys with all the different sets of fingerings. They can just flip the pages, look it up and whack it out.

Though most of them don't bother. When you've been on the keyboard since you were four years old, you know the territory, from down in your hand and overhead in your brain. A scale book just gets in your way.

Breathe in, breathe out.

So.

How long has your kid been learning the piano?

Breathe in, breathe out.

Breathe in, breathe out.

Hear the girl in Room 106?

She's not your daughter is she? Thank God. Because the Bösendorfer in 106 is a bastard. A couple of the Kawais upstairs are a bit off as well. But 106 is the worst. It's down almost a semi-tone so even if you're playing like Rubinstein, you lose brilliance. Last year three sets of parents fought with the auditions clerk to get out of Room 106 because of that Bösendorfer being just slightly out.

Hey. Why is she's playing that supposed-to-be C-sharp diminished seventh like its Debussy? Yeah, but it's not what they want. They say the technical work should be played clean. Legato or staccato and that's it. She should save her expression for the sonatas, the concerti.

Jeez, that piano is so bad. The E-flat major arpeggio is getting stretched like old chewing gum. She sounds like a cassette tape that's been sitting for a day on the dashboard of a parked car in a heatwave.

Breathe in, breathe out.

Yeah, right. I've read the prospectus too. Co-educational. Equal opportunity. Pastoral care. Blah blah. That's what they say. But lady, believe me, it's always a certain kind of girl who ends up in Room 106.

Breathe in, breathe out.

Ventolin, just two puffs. See? One. Two. Breathe in, breathe out. Don't worry, I know how to do it quietly. I'm not like the dickheads who forget to turn off their watches and bleepers and mobile phones. Hey, last year I sat next to this jerk, a professional city type, you know, with the Ermenegildo Zegna suit and the Busoni briefcase. His mobile went off just as the kid was pausing in the most delicate part of the Chopin *Nocturne in E.* The kid was just lifting his hand off the sostenuto and this suit wrecked it with a phone call.

Not fair, huh? I marched up, grabbed it and turned it off. Hey dickhead, New York has just closed for the day, okay? These people are greedy enough to bring their kids to audition here knowing full well they've got bags of it. What do they wanna scholarship for? Like I said to the lady next to me, they've got a bank of fax machines in their lavatories. One for the Dow, one for the Nikkei and one roll just to wipe their arses with.

Excuse the French. But it's stuffed. Don't you think? When there are brilliant kids around who don't even have their own piano. Whose school piano is some beat-up coffee cup-ringed Selmer that's tone-dead from years of Year Seven girls playing *Chopsticks* on it and the leader of the Senior Big Band trying to do some Grade Three Easy Abridged version of *In The Mood*. So what do you do? What do you do when, for instance, a kid has to catch the 202 bus five days a week to practise on a piano? When you send him off to the Bourke Street McDonald's on the weekends so his fingers can stuff Fillet-O-Fish into cartons?

Breathe in, breathe out.

Jeez. Today is a bad day. I'm picking up all the rubbish in the air, the grit in the streets. All the way in the taxi he's saying 'this Ravel is bullshit, this baroque crap sounds like a fucking sewing machine, this is a try-hard nerd school, and anyway I'm not sure I even want to play the piano ...'

Breathe in, breathe out.

Can you believe this? He's not sure he even wants to play the piano. Easy for them to say, hey? Genius is cheap. Today he's 'not even sure' he wants to be a concert pianist, tomorrow he might want to be a brain surgeon. Hey, okay, no problem! Jeez! They don't remember us forking out three thousand dollars a year since they were three years old for pre-instrumental classes, Suzuki lessons, hiring a Yamaha baby grand for eighty bucks a month, theory and composition and violin second-study.

He's not even sure he wants to play the piano. Look, I said, there will always be days when we realise that what we're doing is meaningless in the big scheme of things. So, yes. You're right. How can you be sure you want to play the piano? Is the world going to be a better place because you're learning the *Emperor* to play in the finals of the Concerto Competition in the Melbourne Town Hall? Is it going to make any difference to the starving babies of the Third World that you get through the cadenza of the Beethoven No 3 in one take for some recording with the Melbourne Youth Orchestra? No, of course not. Let's face it, your genius or your failure doesn't make a dent in the world.

He's not even sure he wants to play the piano. So what? Did Beethoven always want to play the piano every day of his life? No way! Some days he also 'wasn't sure he wanted to play the piano'.

But hey. Beethoven's father had to beat the crap out of him to play the piano. And if he had become another drunken tenor in the local church choir like his old man, no one would have noticed. Big deal. The stars turn.

Breathe in, breathe out.

TWO

The girl in Room 106 is playing Pierozutto's *Fantasie Sudamericaine*. You like it? Yeah, but she has the audition syllabus all wrong. Four works required, one from each of lists A, B, C and D, it says here – first movement of a romantic concerto – it's on the list, and she's playing Pierozutto's *Fantasie Sudamericaine*! I'm not saying there's anything wrong with it. It's a B grade piece nice for advanced piano accordion. Authentic? Nah. It's a rip-off. The tune she's doing now in G minor – that's not South American, it's southern Italian.

You know the one? Claudio Villa's big hit in the 1940s?

> '*Marianna, Marianna* ...
> *La musica più bella dei miei sogni*
> *È per mio angioletto* ...'

Nice eh? You think so? Nah. I hate it. Neapolitan sludge. You think it's about his lover or maybe his bride. But it turns out this Marianna is his newborn daughter and he is crooning over her cradle. He's wishing that the most beautiful music of his dreams will be for his little angel. Yeah right. What a load of sentimental shit.

Livio Simioni did a version of it for his dance-band at the Cumparsita Ballroom. You never heard of Livio Simioni? Lady, Simioni was one of the kings of the accordion. One of the big names of the sixties with Sam Delvecchio and Salvatore Giallo. Simioni's band, the Combo Milano, used to play at La Cumparsita, an old church hall the Italian musicians took over on the corner of Kay and Canning Streets in Carlton. Hundreds of young Italians used to turn up on a Sunday night, cut loose from the church and the factories, looking for something to do, somewhere to go and someone to flirt with, because the Australians didn't want to mix with them in those days.

It was Simioni who baptised me Marianna, or so my father said. Yeah right, what a bullshit artist because when I started school I realised every second Italian girl in my class was also called Marianna. And the ones who weren't Marianna were Anita, because of Anita Eckberg in *La Dolce Vita*. Wanna know how this Simioni supposedly baptised me? Sure, I got time to tell you.

It was my mother's twentieth birthday but she didn't want to go out. I had screamed for the twelve weeks solid since I was born and Lina had slept only two hours at a time. She really didn't want to go out. My father tried to persuade her in the worst possible way, by unhooking her bra and stroking her breasts.

'Leave me alone,' she said, pushing him off. 'I want to sleep.'

'Come on. Don't be like that. Be sweet. It's not just for the baby all the time. You're spoiling her.'

'The baby,' she sneered. 'Now you're the expert on babies? You still can't even say her name. Leonora. What kind of *cafone* can't say the name of his child? Le-o-no-ra. Not "the baby".'

She attached me to her breast, lying back on the pillows, confident she had made an important point. He smiled strangely. In those days my mother didn't know her husband well enough to realise that when he looked at her like that she should shut her mouth and get out of the room. Instead she pointed to a pile of soiled nappies on the floor. 'And take those downstairs,' she said. 'Lift a finger now and again.'

My father pulled me off her breast so roughly that she couldn't feed from that side for a week. Not bothering to wrap me up, he carried me clumsily, with my head unsupported, down the stairs and to the uncleared back junk-room behind the kitchen that was supposed to be my nursery. 'Tonight she sleeps here,' he said. 'She can cry all she likes out here.'

My mother flew down the old terrace stairs fast for a lady who had just had a baby. 'Bruno! We'll go! Bruno – see, I'm getting ready.'

He stopped outside the junk-room door. 'So,' he said, 'you want to go dancing now?'

She held out her hands. 'Please. I'll quiet her. I promise.'

'You're feeling better now? Jumping around full of energy? Eh? Well enough to go out with this *cafone*? This *cafone* who's breaking his back so you can stay home in bed all day?'

'I'm sorry,' she whispered, never taking her eyes off me. 'I'm sorry.'

My father handed me back. He ignored her frantic rocking of me, to and fro, to and fro.

'Don't exaggerate everything. She's only wet,' was all he said. 'And for God's sake clean up that shit upstairs.'

The Ballo Milano started at 8 p.m. and we were only half an hour late. The photos show the birthday table was full of cheek-kissing *paesani* – *Auguri Lina! Buon compleanno! Ma com'è bella questa mammina!* Nonna Betta, who had just gone to live with her other daughter in the Fitzroy house, was jiggling me on her knee, a red wine in one hand and a Capstan cigarette in her mouth, with no idea the Box Brownie was flashing at her, allowing this slutty image to lodge in the family photo album. Down the bottom of the table were Angela and Dora, my mother's girlfriends who had also come out with her on the *Neptunia* as proxy brides from Catania. After a year Angela was four months pregnant but Dora had somehow managed to remain flat-stomached. The girls were still getting used to their husbands. They relaxed when the men went off to play cards and fell silent when they came back.

The old man had finally pulled my mother on to the dance floor, when I woke up, squalling. Great. He takes her out, so they can get it together, stop fighting and make some sweet love-talk. But it's wah-wah-wah. So she wants to go back to the table to get her tits out again. She feeds that kid all bloody day and all bloody night. It was enough to make an immature and jealous twenty-three year old lose patience.

Picking up the tension, Angela and Dora quickly waved Lina off – 'go on, *Romeo e Giulietta*, go, go, go' – and made a big deal of rocking and jollying me along – *bella bimba, bella bimba*. As soon as my parents disappeared, Dora, who had been a nursemaid to an upper class family in Catania, slipped me a few drops of sambuca mixed with *aranciata* on a teaspoon.

Dora now puts out a story that the old man had Lina out in a car somewhere that night and that's how my brother got started. I don't believe her. These days she and my mother like to make out what sensitive, refined, trusting people they are, always the blessed victims, the lambs at the slaughter. Still, if he didn't get her knocked up that night, it was within the following month. Gianni was born as close to me as it's possible to be without us being twins.

What upset Dora was that when Lina came back, she asked her if she had an extra pad in her bag. Lina's face was a mess and she hadn't been able to fix all her clothes. 'What a good thing you were asleep with the angels and not old enough to see this *porcheria*.' I don't agree. Sometimes I dream that it's me who gives Dora the sambuca and puts her to sleep. Then I wander, invisible, up to my parents doing the samba at the Ballo Milano, just two people, a girl and a guy who love to dance.

Fat chance. The old man turned up drunk toward midnight but at least he had won a few quid at cards. The police were looking the other way about the liquor laws but everyone had to be out of the Cumparsita Ballroom by midnight. The band played their last song, *Marianna*. People were shaking hands all around: *allora compare, ci vediamo, no?* My mother was half asleep in her chair. He shook her as he put on his jacket. 'Lina! Hey! Time to go,' he mumbled, with a cigarette in his mouth. Lifting up my bassinette, he joked to the table, '*Stasera, la musica più bella dei miei sogni è per mio angioletto! Buona notte a tutti!*' He held me aloft, the proud father. 'And say goodnight to my lovely Marianna!'

My mother jerked awake. 'Marianna? What Marianna?'

'Marianna. Your daughter Marianna.'

My mother was pale and dazed. 'Give me the baby,' she murmured, avoiding the eyes of her friends.

He laughed. '"*The baby*,"' he mocked. 'What are you? A *cafone* with fifteen children that you can't remember her name? It's *Marianna*, not *the baby* . . . Ma-ri-an-na!'

> Tonight I'm not singing to the stars,
> My song is not for the moon or the wind in the
>   trees,

It's not for a blonde or a sweet brunette no –
Tonight my most beautiful serenade is for you –
Marianna, Marianna, the gypsy king rocks you,
Singing in the olive groves, waiting in the trees.
Marianna, Marianna, the gypsy king wants
    you,
Sighing in the olive groves, waiting in the trees.

Breathe in, breathe out. At the back of the Cumparsita Ballroom, I saw the way music hangs in a net of air, how melodies make the lungs fill, how the throat cries out and rhythm rises to the eyes and fizzes through the blood. By five years of age, I knew them all, *Terra Straniera, Buonanotte Tristezza, Carina, Amorevole, Besame Mucho.* Staggering up to the table, knocking over drinks, my old man would cry like a baby. He'd pat my cheeks, kiss my hair; you'd think he'd given birth to me himself. Sometimes the old man would call me over to the card table when he needed some luck. 'Sing "*La Vita è Bella*" *a* Papà – *canti, canti,* and I give you two bob.'

But when the band played *Marianna* no amount of silver, *dolci* and lollies could get me to sing. When the band played *Marianna,* my mouth was shut, my eyes were dry.

Candidates are advised that adequate steps must be taken to ensure continuity of the music in performance …

He's annoyed by the way she never quite makes the page-turn with his students but hovers at their backs, snatching at the page when they have several phrases still to play. He yells at her 'What kind of bloody beat are you keeping? You've got to be like an angel to these people. You're there but you're not there. The turns are supposed to feel like wings beating. You should be their third hand.'

It takes her a while to learn the art of the third hand. In rehearsal it's not so bad. Down in his studio in the Academy, sitting silently behind the best of his students, her role as the angel of the page-turn is no different to booking gigs and picking up penguin suits at the drycleaners. But in concert, standing in a jersey silk gown behind a pianist, she's jolted by how much she is *out there* in the circle of compressed time. It's exciting. She gets a performance lust no angel should have. At every turn of the page, her fingers on the corners steal phrases early, late, unsettling the soloist.

He has to speak to her. 'Listen. It's quite simple,' he says. 'Do it as if it's you.'

'But I'm not them,' she says, offended. 'I don't know what's in their heads.'

'Sing it then,' he insists. 'Follow it along in your head as though you're singing.'

As though singing. He tells her that she can't read fast enough, that there's something wrong with her rhythm. 'For God's sake, study the scores. Get a grip on yourself. There's no need for you to be nervous. It's not as if you're out there playing the stuff yourself.'

In the Conservatorium library, her hands turn page after page of manuscripts and Groves' as she tries to improve, to study her way to helpfulness.

But she gets sidetracked into reading Mozart's collected letters. It's a relief to turn from musicology to his gossip, jokes and stupid poems, especially the twiddle he writes to his cousin Maria Anna. She likes the wily way he always starts off letters to his father with *Monsieur mon très cher père*! and ends with 'I embrace my dear sister – *carissima sorella mia* – with all my heart, kiss your hand a thousand times ...' She reads him like a trashy novel, following his tour through Munich and Augsburg to Mannheim '... Apropos of Stein's little girl. Anyone able to see and hear her play without laughing must be stone like her father ... She sits opposite the treble notes, not in the middle forsooth, for better occasion of throwing herself about and making grimaces. She rolls her eyes and all kinds of nonsense ... She is eight and a half years old and plays everything by heart. Something might be made of her, she has talent, but on these lines she will come to naught. She will never acquire much speed because she is doing her best to become heavy-handed ...'

She stares at de Carmontelle's portrait of the young Mozarts and their father, celebrity kids at their eighteenth century clavier. The wigged and silk-flounced little prodigy looks at the manuscript with delighted confidence (on another page, he sits alone, a sweet blank-faced child with a wide forehead and slim hands slightly exaggerated by the painter's amazed brush). Behind him is his sister, cut off at the waist by the instrument, standing prettily against a painted sky '... M. de Mechel, a copperplate engraver, is working day and night to engrave our portraits ... Wolfgang plays the clavier, I stand behind his stool and play the violin, and Nannerl rests one arm upon the clavecin while she holds music in the other, as though singing.'

Eventually she gets it. As though singing. He's right. The trick of singing in her head stops the rushing, the desire, the beating heart. As though singing. She stands up and sits down, smoothing her long gown.

She becomes a discreet and silent third hand. She gets so good at it that between pages she has time to drift, to meditate. Occasionally she even wonders why it is that in de Carmontelle's picture of the Mozarts playing together, his sister is the only one who is posing. The only one separated from her instrument.

Breathe in, breathe out.

THREE

At night I coughed a chesty bark that drove my brother and sisters mad. So I was moved out of our shared bedroom at the top of the terrace and settled onto the old sofa in the lounge-room. My mother fretted about the cold and cracked cabbage-rose lino over the floors of the draughty place but Nonna Betta and Z'a Mari convinced her that the Briquette heater, smouldering all night, would keep me warm and safe.

If anything it made me worse. I'd wake in the early morning, sweating from all the undershirts, socks, flannels and army blankets Lina had swaddled me in. But the cough was like a fist in my lungs. In the cold just before dawn, I'd awake to find my coughs turning to gasps. Then I was glad to see the old man push through the fly-wire door of the kitchen, home from taxi-driving. He'd switch on the stove light and I would be there, slumped at the formica table, struggling for breath.

He warmed milk and Cadbury's chocolate powder for me, throwing in torn pieces of bread. Then he heated up the coffee Lina left in the percolator, poured his *caffè latte* into a bowl and sprawled his legs on a chair because his back ached from driving. He rested his cigarettes on the table, trying to resist the urge to light up so as not to make me worse. He smelt of beer, sweat, smoke and the city.

Sometimes he was morose, staring at the stove's gas flame as I coughed and coughed. But usually he was garrulous and happy. He had a set of anecdotes that he'd take out like a deck of cards. Ace of the pack was how on the day he met Lina's ship in Port Melbourne, Livio Simioni, the greatest accordionist in Italy, offered to play at their wedding.

'As he made his way down the gangway he stopped in

front of me,' my father started off. 'He shook my hand and said, *Grazie mille, paisà*. I will never forget what you have done for me on my first day in this country. Here is my brother's address. Call me there at your convenience. It will be an honour if I can play at your wedding.'

He told me how there was no *matrimonio*, no *battesimo*, no *festa di società* in Melbourne then without the Simioni brothers. They were the rulers of celebration. They hired out the Cumparsita Ballroom and the Combo Milano orchestra. They did the catering, the photographs, the invitations, the flowers. Livio Simioni would step up to the microphone to be the master of ceremonies. You could even hire limousines from Dante Simioni's driving school, the Prestissimo Scuola Guida in Rathdowne Street.

According to my father, all this would never have happened without him, Bruno Giovanni Vaccari. 'Without my quick thinking,' he said, 'without my *furberia*, they would have lost everything.'

Livio Simioni was only in his twenties when he left Genova on the *Oceania* for Melbourne. He came to join his older brother, Dante, the guitarist, who was the businessman of the family. Livio was already a brilliant accordionist with a good career in Italy but he was one of those too-good-looking continentals that couldn't stay out of trouble with women. He'd just left his first wife and baby daughter from a shotgun wedding in Milan, never to see them again.

He disembarked at Port Melbourne with four suitcases of sheet music, five accordions, amplifiers, microphones – the stuff coming down the gangway on the backs of porters was like a sultan's procession. The immigration and customs officials had never seen an Italian migrant like this.

To make it worse, the Australians had never seen button accordions, the true Continental accordions without keyboards that were the instruments of the European virtuosi and the Slavonic gypsies, 'and there are no better accordionists, believe me,' said the old man. 'They had a sound, my God, a music that made you drunk with life.'

The officials turned them over, shook them, slipped knives through the lining. If they really were squeeze-boxes, where were the bloody keyboards? Was all this stuff really his own? This dago was either a Mafia courier or trying to get this equipment into one of his dago relative's shops without paying import duties.

'You play-a all-a da squeeze boxes mate?'

'*Sì*. Play all. *Certo. Sono musicista.*'

The officials exchanged looks. Yeah. And they were Jackie Kennedy. This guy's wog haircut and his two-toned poofter shoes were getting up their noses. They grabbed his custom-made 120-bass Crosio which had 'Simioni' inlaid in mother-of-pearl on its side. '*Fascisti*,' said my father. 'Why they no look at the passport, eh? You look at the passport, look *alla fisarmonica*, and you see is belong to him. Is his instrument, is make for him. Bloody bastards. Why they no use their brains, eh?'

When Livio saw them confiscating his instruments, he offered them lire and American dollars. He even took off his watch, which set the officers right off. 'Hey! Put that away, mate. We don't do that in Australia.'

My father was a brash fatherless kid from Naples who had been in the country only two years. I could see him as a smart-arse, full of bluster and big words. Lina, from a little village in Catania, was his proxy bride. He'd got her name from an Italian priest relative of her family, and, after hounding her with letters for a year, Bruno was there to sweep her off to their rented rooms in Fitzroy. The disembarkation was taking a long time. He was edgy, hyped up in his best suit. The officials were a welcome distraction.

'Hey Maestro,' he shouted in what I imagined was his usual reckless way. 'Play these *cafoni una bella canzone*. Maybe they have ears, you never know.'

Livio Simioni knew better than anybody that a song is worth a thousand explanations. Wrestling the accordion from the inspection deck, he hauled it to his shoulders. The young Italian men around him wolf-whistled continental style, leaning back in their shirt sleeves with insolent fingers in their mouths.

'*Bravo! Viva l'Italia!*'

'*Maestro, fa* Torna a Surriento!'

'*Ma che* Torna a Surriento? *Fa* Terra Straniera!'

'*Ma che* Terra Straniera? *Fa* Quel Mazzolin di Fiori!'

'*La Donna E Mobile!*'

'*Nessun Dorma!*'

My old man said Simioni chose the fastest of his classical pieces, *Il Volo Del Calabrone*, because he didn't know how long he had before they'd send for the police to arrest him. *Flight of the Bumblebee* by Rimsky Korsakov, usually played to show off the saltando and spiccato bowing of virtuoso violinists. By the end of it, the smiling officials waved him through.

'That's respect,' said my father. 'Even those bloody bullshit bastards had eyes wide like this,' – he made circles of his thumb and forefingers and shook them at my face – 'They can't believe. They never hear nothing like Simioni play *la bella fisarmonica italiana*. Ha! They look him with respect.'

'Dad,' I said. I tried to wake him before his head fell to the table. 'Dad. Did Simioni play for your wedding?'

'What say?' The old man was slipping into that unpredictable stage, maybe one more question, maybe not.

'You know. Like he said he would. Play at your wedding for free.'

But the old man's mood had turned. 'Hey. What you do here?' It always disappointed me how the tale burned out like a struck match. 'Go to sleep and shut your mouth with the talk-talk-talk,' he said. 'Or I give you *una bella botta in faccia. Capito?*'

The old man was a heavy drinker but the only time I ever saw him totally out of his skull Australiano-style was at weddings. My mother got so tense at *matrimoni* that in the end she couldn't go to the reception and kiss the lace-draped *sposa* without a couple of extra 5 mg Valium in her bag. My brother Gianni got so stoned at his own wedding that he spent the whole night out of it on the balcony of the Southern Cross hotel while his wife went out to play pinball at the Tre Venezie with the guests.

The rumour is that she had it off with the best man, Lazic, a fantastic Croatian bass-player who played in Le Stelle for a while. Someone supposedly saw her with him on the floor of the gents toilets, with the hand-drier on as they went for it. Nice story, huh? I like the blow-dryer. Whoever put that in really knew my sister-in-law. Unfortunately it's bullshit. By the time we hit the Tre Venezie she was so drunk she couldn't stand. I carried her out to whatever toilet I could get to first, which happened to be the men's. She spewed her guts out. Can't remember if there was anybody else in there. But there was no time or inclination for bonking on lavatory tiles believe me. I drove her to her mother's that night because I thought she was going to die. So give the girl a break. She only started doing it with Lazic later.

As for me, I am allergic to something in the air at weddings. I have to dose up with Ventolin to cope with the perfume, the flowers, the fur coats. From the moment the Combo Milano started up, my old man started pouring wine after wine into his glass – and anybody else's he could find – until my mother gently took the bottle off him and eyed the waiters away. '*Basta* Bruno,' she'd murmur, avoiding the glances of his *paesani*.

She gave him one of those martyred smiles that looked around before it was allowed to cross her lips, then thinned across her face with implacable force. She had to show *gli altri, i paesani, tutto il mondo, la società* that she came from people who knew when enough of a glass of wine was enough.

So she would pour him a Chinotto and hope he wouldn't notice. He always noticed. He'd grin and shake his head, you know, *Porco Dio, ma non si può bere un bicchiere di vino?*, laughing at the sneaky little bubbly glass, you know, as if to say what a ladies' joke, to substitute sweet Chinotto for Tuscan Chianti. *Le donne sono sempre così.*

At Dora's sister's wedding, he threw it over her face. The claret ran in bloody rivulets over her neck and dress. At first she sat there; she didn't try to clean it up. Then, pushing back her chair, she stood up, patting her cheeks with a paper napkin and shaking her skirt so the wine wouldn't collect at the top of her five-month pregnant stomach. She was making out like it was an annoying accident. She didn't care what she did in front of him but other people, never.

We were seated far away from the bridal party, with the cousins by marriage and the godparents of the bride, strangers who weren't sure how to react. But when the old man grabbed Lina by her wet arms and half pushed her – not hit her, he never dared to do that in public – but sort of slapped her to her feet – '*Ma che dici? Non vuoi ballare?*' – the men who had been eyeing him through their cigarettes, pushed back their chairs. They walked over to him – '*ma che ubriacone* – hey, *paesano* – show some respect *paesano* – *paesano* – don't make us angry or who knows what's gonna happen? *Capito?*'

Pushing them off – '*va bene, va bene*' – he staggered up from the table, following the music to the front of the hall. The band was playing *Carina*. With his tie off and a cigarette hanging out of his mouth, he danced. '... *diventi tutti i giorni più carina, ma in fondo resti sempre una bambina* ...'

My mother ran to the toilet. She was gone a long time. We got bored waiting unsupervised for her return. My brother and I fought and punched each other. We ran through the tables, between waiters' legs, knocking spoons as we dodged. We pulled up short at the front where Simioni was playing. My father was staggering around while the nicotine-stained old men that hang around the edges of every *festa* clapped and whooped and laughed.

If the next number had been *Amorevole* or *La Verità*, he wouldn't have even seen me. He had his eye on Gianni, who was trying to lift the cigarette lighter the old man apparently got from an American G.I. when they liberated Napoli. Gianni had already stolen it twice. The last time he was given a good lashing with the rubber hose but a six year old has a short memory. He should have copped *una bella botta in faccia* for doing it again. Lucky for him the band struck up an old favourite.

> *Marianna*
> *Stasera non canto alle stelle*
> *E non canto alla luna ...*

The old man scooped me up from the dance floor and perched me on top of his shoulders. With my seven year old's wiry legs around his neck, I hung on to his hair as he half-stumbled and spilled wine, lunging down, swooping up, twisting round.

> *'Marianna, Marianna ...*
> *La musica più bella dei miei sogni*
> *È per mio angioletto ...'*

At *'angioletto'* he did what he thought was an impressive Cossack leap but it was really a drunken half-circle twist that almost toppled us. Two old men righted him, grabbing at his elbows and he was off again, round and round as I screamed and screamed, holding tight to tufts of his brilliantined hair.

At first it was a joke. I was probably getting stoned from the permanent Rothmans he had in his mouth in those days. It was fantastic, the hit of tobacco taken in close, his sweat, the factory worker muscles in his back.

Then my coughing started. I looked around. I couldn't see my mother. I looked for Gianni. He had gone too.

Sometimes she took us home early when things went wrong, marching us grim-faced down Faraday Street in our best *vestiti*. I panicked. Mamma! High above the wedding feast, breathing in the old man's fumes, I looked around – the bride and groom eating and kissing far away at the flower-decked table – the waiters backing out of the kitchen with trays of *brodino* and plates of *pollo e insalata* – the band setting up after the first bracket – Johnnie and Miroslav twanging guitars, Livio spitting 'uno, due, tre' into the microphones.

Mamma! This time they were going, I was convinced of it. And I would be left with Papà. I imagined Lina stripping clothes from hangers, I saw armfuls of nappies thrown in any way they landed, a clutch of photographs, a shoebox of jewellery, silver hastily wrapped in linen tea towels, passports, birth certificates, outpatients books from the Children's Hospital. I saw a woman running out on to Hoddle Street, hailing a taxi, bundling a child into the back, whispering a destination. What? Where? Mamma! Smashing at my father's neck was like banging at a locked trunk.

Above my head, the glass drops of the chandeliers seemed so close I could almost reach out to pick them.

Down below people's hands were thrust out to catch me. *'O la bambina! Bruno! Siediti, Bruno!'* I opened and closed my mouth. Only the smallest trickle of air was coming through. I was a rag doll on a sick merry-go-round – the *paesani* receded with the sounds of laughter – only to roll around again screaming *'O! Bruno! Attento alla bambina!'*

Suddenly underneath me was an earthquake. I was thrown and bobbed and jostled. I barely had the air to whisper – *Papà, basta*, I've had enough – I'll be a good girl – please – *Papà*! But the net of hands was gone. I heard the scraping back of chairs, the pushing back of glasses. From everywhere I saw *signore e signori, ragazzi, paesani e stranieri* – everyone was taking to the dance floor.

The band swung into *La Tarantella Capricciosa*.

High on my father's shoulders, I saw what was making the tables shake and the people go mad. Livio Simioni stood in a spotlight in front of the band on stage. His right hand was flying so fast over the keys that it almost seemed to be standing still. He squeezed and pulled, squeezed and pulled. All the time his bass-hand fingers scrambled over the buttons.

Sparks of music hit my ears, my eyes, my scalp. My lungs opened with the bellows. They opened and closed, opened and closed.

Simioni had sequins on the lapels of his jacket and the ruffles that frothed out of the front of his shirt made him look like Elvis Presley. His accordion was knife-fight red, the colour of the stain on my dress. I didn't remember that it was 120-bass or that it was a custom-made Crosio, nothing like that, but I knew the thing in my body, I knew it the way you know the gates of home.

I wanted to haul the accordion to my arms, slide into its leather straps, pull out the bellows of the thing and lie it against my chest, so that we'd be like two animals breathing together. I saw how it needed to gulp air, that it took in so much air you had to work all the time to make it breathe, that pumping it would be like forever rescuing somebody from drowning or collapse.

La Tarantella got more and more prestissimo. Simioni was stretching and squeezing, squeezing and stretching. By the end of the first repeat I could see what he was doing. When he pulled the pleat out, people would stamp their feet and clap to the right. When he pushed it in, they'd twist and clap to the left. The king of the accordion was the puppeteer and everyone in the hall was his puppet.

Then as he modulated into C major, I saw strings all around the room, gathering up from around people's shoulders, from the tops of their heads, their legs, their arms and drawing into a billowing net of dance. I saw the strings. In that moment all his tricks were mine.

If I didn't lie next to that groaning accordion I would die.

In my head I was calling out to him: Hey! Let me do it too, let me go with you! I didn't know if he'd heard me.

But I could see something had rattled him. Something crossed his face, annoyed, perplexed. Here! Here! I'm here! I watched with a beating heart. He looked up. His eyes were searching over people's heads. From down the front of the hall he was listening. He was looking for me, for the one missing thread. 'I'm here,' I shouted. 'I'm over here!' The next thing I remember is the room spinning down.

I was scooped up by my mother from under a table. My head was throbbing. My father had gone. I kicked and hit out at the women's hands, the *nonne* cooing, '*Marianna – Marianna – ma che vuoi? Vuoi un'aranciata? – vuoi un po' di torta? – Lina, dalle un po' di torta –*'

Jeez, I was a touchy kid, first with the colic and then with the asthma. I got so bad that even Betta and her sister, Z'a Mari, who had brought up fourteen children between them, wouldn't touch me. They couldn't wallop me because I'd stop breathing. They couldn't tick me off because I'd throw myself from the stoop onto the concrete in the yard. The panic attacks – the choking and coughing – the being scared to let my breath in – the not being able to unfold my chest – the shutdown of my in-and-out rhythms and of being furious and amazed by it – so much of my time as a kid was spent pulling at myself like a parachute that wouldn't open.

Hey, listen, I've done homoeopaths. I've done gluten-free, dairy-free, Chinese herbalist, acupuncture. Yeah, all that. I heard this guy on television once, an asthma doctor from the United States who wrote a best-seller claiming that, as well as pollens and tomatoes closing our air passages, we should be looking at the stuff in our heads. He was touring the country, signing books in Myers and Mary Martin's. The television ran a number down the bottom of the screen – the first ten people to call could have a free private consultation with this asthma guru. I got through even though it took me a good half hour to get up the nerve to do it. So they must have been screening people, getting the right balance of colourful problems for this guy.

The television channel sent me a card saying congratulations, a voucher for the book and an invitation to be an audience member on the show. I asked my doctor, a greying Scotsman with hair sprouting out of his ears whom I'd been seeing since I needed a prescription for the Pill at sixteen. 'I know I'm affected by things I can't see in the winds and the air and the food. But the things I can't see in my life? It's just hippy stories and Californian lie-on-the-couch hocus-pocus, right?'

He shrugged. 'There is some anecdotal evidence of psychological stressors for certain respiratory illnesses.'

I didn't go on the show. It was too weird. I threw the book voucher into a smokers' ashtray by the medical centre's lifts. But, you know, that American comes into my mind when I remember what I saw under the table that night, peering through people's legs with my slitty eyes.

My old man dragged Gianni behind him across the hall. Gianni cried, he dug in his heels, he lay on the floor. The old man threatened to cuff the kid and, holding him by the scruff of his navy-blue suit, he frog-marched him over to the musicians.

The Combo Milano was taking a well-earned break. Simioni put aside his wine and shook my father's hand. After a few minutes of bantering, he and my father went off into a corner. Gianni sulked by the drumkit, unpicking his shoelaces. The men talked for a long time. As they negotiated and offered each other cigarettes, my father waved for Gianni to come forward. Instead he stayed where he was, kicking at a music stand with his loose-shod feet.

Simioni laughed. The king of the accordion winked and beckoned my brother to stand in front of him. Stubbing out his cigarette, he reached into his case. The huge 120-bass instrument was lying folded shut. Without air it had a clumsy and startled look, like a beached whale. But with a deft, slightly impatient movement, Simioni pulled at the leather strapping.

Unfastened, the bellows slithered open.

I couldn't believe it. I couldn't believe this horror film that was unrolling in front of my eyes. My breath was still in my lungs; all the air inside me condensed, I couldn't push it out.

Blowing out a spray of random notes, the accordion leapt from the king's hands into my brother's arms.

Candidates will demonstrate the achievement of musical maturity and technical mastery appropriate to the works performed.

Shit! He's rushing through the B-flat major arpeggios and diminished and dominant sevenths. Breathe in, breathe out. Can't you hear the way the notes are jamming together too tight and falling just a fraction ahead of the beat? That's called rushing. Rushing!

Jeez they know how to wind you up, these kids. The first time, he's a little boy, no more than five or six, right? He's been with Miss Ashleigh Dixon about a year. She's a young ABC Concerto winner, smart, Polish-Hungarian trained. She's strict but not in the way I was led to expect. She won't allow her infants to perform. No exams, no eisteddfods and no little blue merit certificates. She doesn't even have a Christmas concert for her star pupils. I start to wonder what Miss Ashleigh Dixon is doing with my thirty-dollars per thirty minutes a week. So I make an appointment to tell her I'm having a problem with my nephew and motivation and stuff. She does me a big rave on Kodaly and Montessori and Steiner and what she believes about gifted children, spontaneity and play. I say, yeah, okay, fine, but an exam certificate right now would give the kid a sense of achievement. She ignores me and raves on about the evils of Suzuki and the mechanistic rote-learning of the Japanese.

I don't say anything, I let her wind down like a ballerina in a jewellery box. Finally she shrugs and says if I want to enrol him, I can. It's just that she will not specifically coach him on four pieces for a year at the cost of his overall musical development.

I order his Grade 3 AMEB piano book and a leather slipcase for his music at a discount from Simioni's. The Conservatorium writes back that his exam is in mid-May.

The night before, his mum and dad bring him over to my place with his overnight bag and his teddy bear. I polish his patent leather shoes and lay him out a new pair of Woolworths pyjamas with *Biggles* fighter planes all over them. Early in the morning we catch a taxi from Smith Street to the Conservatorium of Music in Parkville. I'm not allowed in with him. Look, I say to the clerk, he's five years old, he's only just getting used to going to the toilet on his own.

But no, I have to listen outside the door. The corridor has hard wooden benches, scuffed floorboards and portraits of gowned old men on the walls. Kids put French horns together, rub pencil markings out of manuscripts and poke cleaning sticks through clarinets. A lanky girl in a white dress balances along the floorboard cracks. It smells of patchouli oil, rosin, woodwind spittle and Yardley's Lavender.

I walk to the door. I pick my way through the scattered open instrument cases. I walk back.

I can hardly breathe.

He does well though. I can hear he's scared. But his fingers don't give a stuff. They do what they have to do. It makes me laugh out loud. The White Dress Girl's mother purses her lips but I don't care. Jeez that kid can *play*. There's nothing he can do about that. It's in the blood. Perform or die.

As a reward, I take him up to Lygon Street to catch a tram into work with me. Everyone, students, Maria, old Papà Bacini, Dante, they make a big fuss. They get him to play his pieces on the Yamaha organs in the showroom. It's unreal. The kid is five and a half years old and he's got the buttons all worked out. The customers are impressed. They tell me I should get him on 'Showcase' and 'New Faces'. One of the old men, the grandfather of the biggest blockhead Dante's ever taught, gives the kid ten dollars and gets him to stamp out his name on a piece of paper, as an autograph. Even Dante says, 'Bring him back next week, Mari, he's good for business!'

By afternoon the kid is tired and whingy. At first I don't hear him. I'm sorting through the second-hand accordion music, trying to find *Mamma Stanca* for a customer. The kid taps me on the hand.

'What, *caro?*' I've found *I Sing Amore* and *Love In Portofino*. I can't believe the old crap Dante has here, all out of order, unfiled, unpriced.

'I don't want to.'

'*Che dici amore?*'

'I don't want to play the piano any more.'

I sit back on my heels. The old sheet music has stirred up a lot of dust particles that swim in the afternoon light. The kid looks at me, snivelly and snotty. He looks just like his mother does when she gets that princessy I-only-wear-Laura-Ashley look on her face. And sure enough he starts up about too hard this, you never do that, I don't want to do this, you said and you don't and I never and Mamma says I don't have to anyway. Yeah, I think to myself, what would your Mamma know when she's about as musical as a meataxe? I shake my head. All of a sudden I want to give the spoilt little shit something to really cry about. Like a shove against the wall. A body dragged across the floor. A stick or a rubber hose across his legs.

Breathe in, breathe out. I can't touch him. I know if I touch him, I'll never stop. I look around for my bag. I'm scared that I won't make it. Because my hands want to pull out his hair, they want to sting his skin. It's all I can do to find the bloody bag. I pull on the zipper. Breathe in, breathe out. Preventers and relievers – you're supposed to have them both with you at all times. Thank God. Thank God. I shake the Ventolin, the reliever. Breathe in, breathe out. Okay. Okay. Forget it, he's a kid, he's not even six years old. I take four 5 mL puffs. The drug hits like a fist. Thank God. I close my eyes. So good. So good.

I see the kid has backed off into the stringed instruments section of the store. Simioni doesn't have much of a range, a few school orchestra cellos and violins, cheap Korean bows, shoulder rests, Flexicor strings. The kid goofs around with a full-size cello, plucking it like a bass. Tucking one of the violin cases under his arm, he sprays the place with automatic fire: bah-bah-bah-bah-bah-bah!

Relief floods through me. I get it. I see what this is all about. This is all about nothing. Nothing. I put up my hands for a ceasefire. 'Want to have a go?'

The fiddle is shiny and smells of Chinese glue. His arm has to stretch almost flat to get down to the full-size neck, so he rests in third position and centres into the thing so he can bow it with a full tone. He draws it as parallel to the bridge as a Swanston Street tram. There are no fluffs, no wandering down the fingerboard. I swear in two minutes the kid is trying to figure out the harmonics on the open strings, running his hand from first to third position like he's done it in another life. Like up is down and down is up.

'So,' I say. 'You like the violin?'

'What's a violin?'

I laugh. He's a kid. He's not even six years old. 'I tell you what,' I say, ruffling his hair. 'You can learn violin as your second instrument. Then later, you can decide which one you like the best.'

'I don't have to play the piano?'

'No. You could be a violinist. Or a flautist. Or a composer.'

'I don't have to go to Miss Dixon?'

'You could be a musicologist, a harpsichordist, an organist. Or a conductor.'

He thinks about it for a minute. 'What's a flautist?'

It's almost dark when I put the takings in the safe and lock up. We walk up to the bus in Lygon Street. The wind is fierce. I button up his little coat and he holds my hand, which is a surprise because by his age boys don't usually like to hold hands any more. When we get to Borsari's Corner, I let him stop me at Cecchini's to get a gelato – *nocciola* and *fragola* for him and, as a treat, one half serve of *limone* for me.

His pink little fingers curl around the cone but soon it's all over his face and clothes, a real mess, the stuff sliding down in globs and dribbles.

He can't even handle a whole ice-cream yet.

Plenty of time.

FOUR

The old man drove all night for a Bulgarian who owned a couple of cabs in the Mayfair fleet. His shift finished at 7 a.m., when he cruised into the lane behind our house off Smith Street. He cleaned out the cab of bottles, cans, cigarette butts, vomit and stuff. We watched from the step as he washed his torso at the outside tap. As soon as he reached for his towel, we scattered upstairs. His temper in the morning was bad – any crying, any whingeing, any accidents with baby food or milk bottles and we'd cop it.

One morning he left the muddy cab unlocked out in the lane, untouched, not bothering to return it to the

Bulgarian on time. Instead, he came into the kitchen whistling, hauling a brand new radio-stereogram through the door. My mother was cleaning Farex off Sofia's face. Gianni and I were peering through the balustrades of the narrow staircase.

'Where did you get that?' she asked cautiously.

'Chiodi's,' he said. 'Is AWA His Master's Voice. Beautiful, eh?'

'*Sì*.' Though she said it softly you could still hear the anger in her voice. 'And we can afford it?'

The old man smiled a mysterious smile. 'Feed the baby,' he said, 'and don't worry about nothing.'

In the lounge-room he set about connecting plugs and twiddling knobs. Gianni and I played in the boxes and he didn't even stop to cuff us when we fought.

Finally he stepped back. All through the house poured Mario Lanza's *O Sole Mio*.

The story, he told us, was that it had been dead in the Sunday morning streets. He hadn't had a decent fare all night. He was cruising home along Johnson Street, thinking of packing it in, when they'd waved him down. They were a hot young couple practically undressing each other despite the wind on the corner of Hoddle Street, outside the Chinese café. The guy looked familiar but when my old man picked up his accordion case he realised who it was. The girl he didn't recognise, she looked *australiana*. But he was definitely Livio Simioni. He'd been playing at a private function at the

Collingwood Town Hall and now these two were in a big hurry to go to Carlton.

Once in the taxi, the king relaxed. He didn't mind being recognised. He said *come va, paesano*? and the old man, glancing at him in the rear-vision mirror, told him that, well, maestro, you know, it's not so easy for a self-employed man, a taxi driver with four kids, to import a fine instrument. For someone who wasn't in the business it was like sponsoring a relative to this country. There were customs forms to fill in, money orders to apply for, the foreign exchange desk of banks to approach to convert dollars into lire, import duties and sales taxes to work out and to try to avoid. Everybody was advising him to go through Frank Di Biasi at Elite Music. What did he think?

'Don't bother with those *ladroni*. Come and see us.' Simioni gave him a card and stubbed out his cigarette in the ashtray. He opened the door, sliding across with his arm around the glittering-eyed blonde.

'*Grazie*, maestro,' said the old man. He knew full well that the Simionis were opening a showroom close to the Victoria Markets. 'When is a good time for you? Morning? Afternoon?'

'Any time is as good as any other time, *paesano*.'

The old man jumped out of the cab to open the boot before Simioni had even paid the fare. He hauled the accordion out, taking care not to drag the canvas cover over the boot's sharp metal rim. Simioni indicated that he should leave it on the pavement – 'just here, *paesano*. Don't break your back,' – but my father insisted on carrying it through the gate and up the slippery stone steps of the terrace off Rathdowne Street.

My Dad peered eagerly down the shabby hallway. 'I take it through for you maestro, no problem. Where you want?'

'Don't worry about it *paesano*. How much do I owe you?'

'Nothing. Maestro, I take it upstairs. For you, it's no problem –'

'No, no. Listen, *paesano*. Don't worry about it. This is not my house.' The musician nodded toward the girl. The blonde slipped her hand inside Simioni's jacket, pinched his cigarettes and tottered off down the hallway, switching on lights.

Simioni pressed a couple of notes into my father's hand. '*Mille grazie e buona notte, paesano.*' The girl was throwing her coat on the couch. Her fishnet legs were long, her miniskirt short.

'No, no maestro,' said my father, refusing the fare.

'Come on, *paesano*. Just take the money.'

'Hey, you help me out, I help you out. *Siamo paesani*, no?'

Simioni grabbed the old man's arm. 'Take the bloody money.' He stuffed the note into the old man's shirt pocket.

'Okay, okay! If you insist. Wharrever,' said the old man. 'So I give you a ring soon, okay maestro?'

'Yeah.'

'Maybe one night next week.'

'Okay.'

'We look at some instruments together and you tell me what you think.'

'Ciao.'

Simioni's business number turned out to be the upstairs bar of the Italo-Australian club, where a guy called Mario told the old man, *sì certo*, Simioni had just been in, playing pool, downing a sambuca, a caffè macchiato. Would he care to leave Mr Simioni a message? But the old man preferred to speak to the maestro himself. Morning, lunchtime, night, the old man drove by the Italo-Australian club, parking the cab outside with the hire light off.

'If he's such a good *paisà*,' Gianni muttered, 'how come he gives you this bullshit number?'

My father just smiled to himself. 'You don't understand *la gelosia*, *il malocchio*, *l'invidia*. He has to make sure we're *brava gente*, that we're serious.'

Finally, Mario had a message from Simioni. If Mr Vaccari would like to go down to the new warehouse on Saturday, his brothers would take care of him, they would give him a good price. The maestro didn't say anything about lessons. 'Everything in good time,' my father said, winking at us as he shaved under the bald light-bulb of the lean-to bathroom.

Knowing nothing technical about music, my father was put off by the long shelves of piano-accordions in the upstairs sales room at Simioni Brothers. He was pissed off he didn't know the difference in quality of sound between button or keyboard accordions, 100-bass or 120-bass, the new and the reconditioned, the French, the Korean, the Chinese and the Japanese models or whether the cases should be wood or fibreglass or lined with velvet or glued over with felt.

He didn't trust the younger brothers' *furberia*, their way of doing business as if they were still on the streets of Milan or Naples. It stung him that when he told them how much he was prepared to spend, they took him around in five minutes and left to answer a phone call. My father was scared he'd be fooled into ordering a lemon of an accordion that would make him the laughing stock. He left messages for the maestro at the Club, he squinted at brochures from Elite, he talked on the phone to Frank Di Biasi's in-laws, he wrote to relatives in Milan to research the best accordion and see if it tallied with what he was being told by these *zingari musicisti*.

One evening my father finally drew up all his brochures and scribbled notes off the kitchen table. He tied them up with a rubber band and put them aside. All that remained were a series of glossy photographs, spread over our formica table. 'Okay,' he said, pushing the pencil aside. 'Gianni, come here.' My brother was in the lounge-room, flopped on the couch, listening to the hi-fi with his new earphones.

My father shouted: 'I got here Paolo Soprani, Excelsior, Dalape, Dino Baffetti, Baile, Weltmesiter, Lark, Meteor – which you like?' My brother barely moved from the couch. 'Hey Gianni! I said I got here Paolo Soprani, Dalape, Excelsior, Dino Baffetti, Baile, Weltmeister, Lark, Meteor. Which you like? Which colour you like?'

My brother shrugged his shoulders. In a second the old man lunged over to the stereo and punched it off mid-record. That made Gianni sit up quick, putting his hands over his face.

'What's the matter with you?' barked the old man.

'Nothing.'

'Which colour you like?'

'Doesn't matter.'

'What you mean? Why doesn't matter?'

My brother muttered something unintelligible to himself.

'Doesn't matter what?' insisted my father. 'What doesn't matter?'

My brother turned to face him. 'It doesn't matter,' he said, 'because they're all wog colours.'

My father took a breath.

'Say again. Tell me again what you say.'

Gianni looked at him levelly. 'It's a wog instrument. It's got wog colours. It plays wog music. It's fucking wog bullshit.'

My father sat down next to Gianni. He looked tired, a man sick of working. His big hands were blunt, the varicose veins in his legs like whorls in a plank of timber. He laughed softly. 'You one clever bugger, eh?' He shook his head. 'So this is how clever you are? Wog instrument. *Va bene.* So you listen to you friends, you talk to you friends and they say "wog instrument, wog colour, wog music." *La musica bella è* "wog music" *e la tringa-tranga-tringa-tranga delle chitarre elettriche,* you think that's the good music?'

'I didn't say that,' said Gianni, 'I'm not talking about that.'

'You friends – you clever friends *Australiani* – *naturalmente* this friends are so well-educated, are so well-mannered, they already know how to dance, how to play, how to sing, how to dress, how to talk –'

'I didn't say that –'

'You not so clever, Gianni,' said the old man. 'They jealous. They jealous because you father buy a two-thousand dollar *fisarmonica italiana* – and they parents are *morti di fame,* been here fifty years and still pay the rent to the landlord. Own nothing, be nothing, do nothing. What they father buy for them? What they father give to them? Eh?' The old man put his hand on my brother's neck. 'Listen, Gianni. You think I don't understand nothing. But I understand everything. You feel shy because you dunno nothing *della musica.* You feel, hey, I make the fool here with *la fisarmonica –*'

'No,' said my brother. 'You don't listen. You don't get it –'

'You feel shame. You feel shy to be in front of people –'

'I don't care about that.'

'I was the same. The same like you. The war, my father dead *a l'America*, no education, two brothers, five sisters, no land, no money, no respect to my mother, nothing. I didn't know what to say to people –'

'Dad – Dad, listen –'

'...I'm a small boy, no shoes, always hungry. But I go to the wedding, I go to *la festa*, *il battesimo* and I watch. I think, okay, I play *la fisarmonica*. I play *la fisarmonica* and make some money. Make the people laugh, sing, dance. *La gioia della musica*. Everyone love *i musicisti*, they make the money and make everybody happy. So I watch, I try to learn, I –'

'Well why didn't you?' my brother interrupted this favourite fairytale with venom. He shook the old man's hands off his shoulders. 'If you loved *la fisarmonica* so bloody much, then why didn't you bloody well play it?'

My father breathed in and out. 'What you talk about?' he said softly.

'I'm talking about that this thing isn't for us.'

'Why is not for you?'

'Because you don't give a stuff what we want.'

'Don't speak like this, Gianni.'

'This is for you, Dad.'

'No, no, no. This is for you, *bastardo* fucking bastard. Is for you, *capito*?'

When words ran out for my father, he reacted on gut, blood and muscle. I had seen a single blow from his hands send my brother sprawling across the room. Defiant as Gianni was, he prepared himself by turning his head away. I gripped the door, I knew how to get up to the roof of the outside dunny in a few seconds if I had to.

But my father was back at the kitchen table, his face as cool as a southwesterly change. He turned to me and beckoned me over. He ruffled my hair. 'Marianna,' he said gently. 'You want to help your Papà?' I nodded, mesmerised. He pulled out a chair for me next to his. 'Look here. I got Paolo Soprani, Excelsior, Dalape, Dino Baffetti, Baile, Weltmeister, Lark. What colour you like? You tell your Papà. *Ti piace quella rosa o quella nera?*'

I felt a rush of air blowing away my fear. Pleasure spread across me like chocolate over a Mr Whippy cone.

I had to be smart. There was only one true set of colours for a piano-accordion, the shades of velvet chairs in a palazzo, of sun-dried tomatoes, of pancetta hanging in a cellar. But I didn't pick the scarlets. That would have been obvious. Instead I chose a cream marbelled enamel, snowy like the covers of First Holy Communion prayer books, a virginal colour to suit beginners who have many weddings, sweat, cigarette smoke and *Italia Mia* ahead of them.

As for the instrument maker, it had to be Dalape. I could not go past this most famous company in Europe. I could hear the Dalape *fisarmonica* not only had joy but a sadness that reminded me of a flower-girl sitting alone under the bridal table after everyone has gone. I liked how every note took a breath of its own, each slightly different in timbre. Not like the Korean Meteor. Maybe that was okay for the price but to my ears the notes all rolled out the same – greasy sausages on sticks.

The number of bass-buttons was the hardest to decide. The greater the bass notes, the bigger the accordion. I wanted us to have the full range of notes straight away, even though my sisters and I were small children and we would not be able to play them all for years. On the other hand – and here a fear stabbed at me – if I went for *la grande fisarmonica* of 120-bass – maybe … Maybe my father and Gianni, being bigger … Better to choose the 80-bass; it would be years before I outgrew it and by then we could trade it in, get the full range bit by bit.

I made my choices, pretending to hesitate and deliberate so that my father wouldn't think me stupid, that I was making only play-acting baby decisions. I looked up at him a little uncertainly. The old man liked it when I was gentle, when I didn't whinge. '*Brava*,' he said approvingly at each choice. '*Bravissima*.'

Finally he gathered up all the brochures. 'See Gianni?' he said. 'See how clever is you sister?' He winked at me. 'She got more brains than you. Maybe she play *la fisarmonica* better than you, eh? Maybe she take this *fisarmonica*, she go to the teacher, she learn everything and she play better than you?' He turned to my brother. 'How you like if you sister, she one day play better than you?'

Gianni had his earphones over his head. He got up, put another record on the stereo and closed the lounge-room door.

I took my father's words to bed with me as if they were dolls. How clever is you sister. She play *la fisarmonica*. Under the blankets, I turned them over before I fell asleep: see how clever is you sister ... she play *la fisarmonica* ... she take this *fisarmonica*, she go to the teacher, she learn everything ... see how clever is you sister ...

> Marianna, Marianna, the gypsy king rocks you,
> Dancing in the olive groves, singing in the trees.
> Marianna, Marianna, the gyspy king wants you,
> Crying in the olive groves, sighing in the trees.

I'm yanked like a puppet over back lanes, railway lines, washing lines flapping with laundry. I walk till my feet are bloody. I walk into a wedding party under the plum trees. Black-robed grandmothers bring out plates of chicken legs, unshaven old men pour red wine from a cask. The bride's hair falls down as women and girls dance a Middle Eastern dance, swaying with kerchiefs in their hands. They click their heels, clap their hands. Red silk bridesmaids, hairy-legged matrons in blowsy dresses, men in unbuttoned shirts, dirty-faced children, everyone is dancing, and a hoarse voice sings.

> *In the fields at night I dance,*
> *The moon is my nightgown,*
> *The soil is my pillow*
> *The grapes on the vine are heavy and full*
> *So you tell me my troubled friend,*
> *Why should I sleep inside*
> *When I can have the wind for my blanket?*

He's under the plum tree, his foot on a stool. The king of the accordion has his head thrown back, squeezing and laughing, squeezing and laughing.

Suddenly, the wedding is sucked out of the sky. I'm alone with him on a hilltop roaring with wind.

I feel a terrible love squeezing me inside out.

Breathe in, breathe out.

Breathe in, breathe out.

He takes off his accordion and holds it out. 'Take it,' he says. 'I want to go dancing with my arms free.'

I hesitate. The accordion is a big bastard of 120-bass and I'm just a thin little girl.

> *Take it for a minute, take it forever,*
> *Take it for gold, take it for fame,*
> *Take it for a laugh!*

Breathe in, breathe out.

Breathe in, breathe out.

On a windy hill, I stretch out my hands to the air.

The candidate will be required to improvise upon a given theme or bass.

It turns out the kid has a memory for strange chords and progressions: this goes with that goes with this goes with that! For a few weeks even Miss Ashleigh Dixon raises her unplucked eyebrows. Finally, she asks my permission for the kid to play for her old teacher, Bogdan Kozlowski. He's eighty-two and living in a rambling villa in North Balwyn surrounded by signed black and white photographs of him with Ginette Neveu, Otto Klemperer and David Oistrakh. He dozes fitfully through a sonatina or two, says, 'He's a clever boy,' and Mrs Anna Kozlowski gives me a jar of her quince jam to take home.

Miss Dixon then consults with a jazz pianist colleague at the Conservatorium. I notice how she plays new, more complicated games with the kid, using charts and scarves and candles. For months I watch them put 'sad' and 'happy' faces or 'red' and 'green' clothes on the Doh Scale Family. *Daddy Doh, Mummy Re, Sister Mi, Brother Fa.* For a while it's as if he's collecting them like stamps or Derwents or something. He takes chords out of the piano, smudging and washing and overlapping them over those little *Baa Baa Black Sheep* tunes.

But at the bottom of it he's still with the attitude. 'You said and I don't and Mamma says and why do I have to and I'm tired and it's not fair.'

The Lark violin I get him from work falls apart. More fool me. I should know that Simioni is importing more and more junk because I do the orders. Still, I pay one hundred dollars wholesale for this Chinese half-size and within a week the soundpost snaps and the 'ebony' on the fingerboard wears off to show the painted over radiata pine underneath.

A woman in Camberwell advertises a European half-size in the *Trading Post*. It's a foul day and I have to take public transport. I leave Simioni's early to get there before dark.

'Lucinda's teacher thinks she will outgrow it by the end of term,' the woman says, meeting me at the security gate. I follow her down past the glass-roofed inner courtyard and into the house through a wide Persian-carpeted hallway. A skylight pours the last of the winter daylight on her shoulders. She has that thick blonde hair that, when well cut, looks permanently brushed and expensive. 'We've got a Jerzy ordered for her,' she says. 'Hopefully he's getting on with it.' I nod sympathetically. The Simionis sometimes send the hard string repairs to Jerzy Cernak, the Dandenong violin maker. 'I love him, he's wonderful,' she says. 'But he's a manic depressive, a perfectionist. We've been waiting a year for this fiddle. Still, it'll be an investment. It should more than double in price by the year 2000.'

From where I'm standing, half in the vestibule, half in the kitchen, I can see this girl in a Ruyton blazer doodling over her homework on the long old wooden kitchen table. The pottery lamps are lit and something like rice or potatoes is roasting evenly in the oven. Everything glows softly against the grey outside; the grandfather clock ticks on the Italian tiles, the blue and cream china lies indolent on the country dresser.

'My husband was in London last week,' she says, throwing avocado toast scraps and mandarin peel into the bin. She invites me to sit down, moving the art books off the coffee table. I had to fight through the wind to walk from the bus-stop way up the hill to her place. I'm feeling cradled, almost sleepy. I want to take off my parka and lie my head on her lap. 'And he wanted to buy this uncertified Fiorini. Sothebys weren't confident about it so they were only asking for twenty-thousand.'

When you work in retail you learn to hear when a woman has got to the stage of despising her husband's every move. 'I wouldn't touch it,' I say. 'Forget it. Keep the twenty-thousand for a downpayment on a real Fiorini.'

'You'd think so wouldn't you?' she says, indignant. 'But no! He rings me up and says, Nessa –'

I'm inspired and reckless. '– a beautiful sound is a beautiful sound. A label is only a signature on a piece of glued paper.'

She throws me a surprised and grateful look. 'That's right!' she says. We're almost best friends. 'Exactly. Exactly. God, men have absolutely no idea! So I said to him, Andrew, don't you *dare*. It doesn't even have papers.'

The daughter's violin case is stuck between the cushions on the sofa. The mother hands me the fiddle after she's given it a quick tune. She's a player herself; the fifths ring with a fresh sweet beauty and she casually hits the harmonics as well. 'We were thinking of hanging on to it for Oliver,' she says. I turn the pretty little French thing over in my hands. It has a reddish varnish, an ebony fingerboard, a handcarved scroll and real purfling. That the label is missing doesn't worry me. It wouldn't have said Lark, Shanghai.

'There's no label,' I say, frowning.

'It's a Mireau,' she says.

It's all Greek to me but I take a stab at it. 'It doesn't have the colour of a Mireau.'

'Oh no, not Jacques,' she says. 'His son, Marcel. 1920s.'

'Ah.'

'It's just perfect for Oliver now,' she says regretfully. 'But he loathes the violin. Doesn't he, Lucy? He's keen on the bassoon, heaven help us.'

I notice there's no bow in the case, only a Hill rosin, barely used.

'You're not selling the bow?' I ask.

'Oh God. The bow. Lucinda. You haven't left it at school again?'

The girl kicks her brown-stockinged legs under the table and frowns harder over her Derwents and exercise book.

'I'll pick it up tomorrow,' she says. 'Or if you like, I can send it to you by courier. Andrew's secretary can just pop it in the bag.'

'Whenever,' I say. 'How much do you want for it?'

'Oh I don't know,' she says diffidently. 'Four hundred, I suppose.'

She has to be kidding. Four hundred bloody dollars. 'Hmm,' I frown. 'It's more than I had in mind for a kid's violin.'

She's looking at me strangely. I guess I shouldn't have said kid. 'Actually,' she says, 'I was referring to the bow.'

'Ah.'

'It's a Nuremburger.'

'I see.'

'The violin is twelve hundred.'

'Twelve hundred, yes.'

'Which is virtually what we paid for it.' She doesn't like having to justify herself to strangers. Our moment of sisterhood dissolves. She twists her rings and I notice by her fingers that she is much older than me, the tanned skin dry and slightly spotted.

'We've just moved here from Sydney,' I say, closing the case. 'We're still arranging schools, lessons, that sort of thing.'

'I love Sydney. The weather, the water,' she says, taking me back through the vestibule. The skylight is dark and a fine rain hits the glass. 'I suppose I'd better start looking for that wretched bow. I wonder what on earth Lucy's done with it. Stuffed into someone's cello bag, I shouldn't wonder.'

I smile my kids-will-be-kids smile. 'Well thanks so much,' I say. 'I'll discuss it with my husband and I'll let you know.'

Through Dante's contacts, I order the kid a factory-made German fiddle at twenty per cent off the wholesale price.

FIVE

The piano-accordion arrived in Australia. As soon as it was cleared through customs, my father went down to Simioni's to fetch it. I ran home from school to join my mother and sisters in the lounge-room. We crowded around the huge wooden crate covered in *fragile* stickers and importation details written in Italian.

My father looked around. 'Where's Gianni?'

'He's coming,' I said. I breathed in gulps, my heart going fast. It was so painful, having to keep my hands off the crate.

'Why is coming? Why is not here?'

Gianni had been walking a block behind me all the way home. 'He's coming, Dad. He's coming.'

But the old man wouldn't open it without him. We all stared at the crate. It was as if a lottery prize had arrived at our house. I was afraid there would be a knock at the door and some guy with a clipboard and a panel van would come back to repossess it.

Finally, the back gate clicked and a dishevelled Gianni walked into the room. Usually if Gianni wasn't home on the dot of 3.30 p.m. he'd find the Sicilian Snake, a length of rubber hose, waiting for his backside as he came through the door. But today the old man didn't even tell him off. 'Start at the back,' he said, beginning to jemmy the crate with a screwdriver. He threw a claw-hammer at his son. Gianni just managed to catch it. For a moment his hands curled tightly around it as if he was fighting the urge to throw it back. Then he put it carefully to one side. Slowly Gianni took off his schoolbag and peeled off his jumper. Finally father and son set to taking apart the timber packaging.

My mother, sisters and I edged around, prowling from one side to the other as foam, straw, wooden slats and shredded paper emerged from the hammering. It seemed to take forever, with lots of swearing between my brother and father and the rejection of my mother's unasked for advice.

At last the old man wiped his brow and, smiling broadly, he lifted it out for all to see. There was our two-thousand dollar Italian *fisarmonica* in his arms.

The smile on my face broke up.

The Baffetti accordion was as black as hate and its 120-bass were as heavy as my dumb heart. Dumb, dumb, dumb. I had chosen nothing but to make a joke of myself.

'Well,' said my father. 'What you think of this *fisarmonica* Gianni? What do you reckon? Is a good *fisarmonica*, no?'

But my brother had picked up his school-bag and headed upstairs toward our bedroom.

'Hey Marianna, she like *la fisarmonica*,' said my father. 'What do you reckon? Is a good *fisarmonica*, no?' I felt the sting of tears in my eyes. I couldn't look at the accordion.

'*Sì*, is nice, Bruno,' said my mother distractedly, as she pulled Sofia from crawling toward the hammer and stopped Claudia from eating the foam packing.

My father's face darkened. 'What's the matter? Eh? What's the matter with him?'

'*Niente*,' said my mother softly. 'Leave it for a minute. He's tired.'

'*Porco Dio, disgraziato*,' swore my father. 'He come home, he go to his room, he don't help, he don't say nothing. *Due milioni di lire, mannaggia la Madonna, mica uno scherzo! Porco Dio –*'

'Put it away now, Bruno,' said my mother uneasily, moving off to the kitchen with the crying girls. '*Prima mangiamo e dopo vediamo –*'

My father let out a guttural roar. 'Gianni! You come here! Switch off the bloody radio *e* come here!' He slammed the accordion back on to the packing crate. The sight of this wrong instrument wobbling uncertainly on pebbles of foam, about to be scratched – it was a humiliation. I burst into tears.

'It's not fair,' I sobbed. 'You said I could choose. You said.'

'Be quiet, Marianna,' warned my father, darkly.

But I had no feeling for danger. I raced over to the accordion. Falling to my knees, I lined up the straps and somehow – I don't how I found the strength for that 120-bass that was as big as I was – I hauled the poor Baffetti against myself, unclicking the leather strap-button of its squeeze box and stretching my arms wide. The accordion took its first deep dark breath. 'See?' I screamed. 'It's yuk! Yuk! You said I could have a Dalape! And NOW look!' With a tear-stained face, I played the first few notes of *Rosamunde*. 'You see? Rubbish! This thing is just cheap shit.' I played the next few bars with two hands to prove my point, scrambling about in order to find a simple bass in the key of E minor. Not that I knew it was E minor. It was hard and I missed notes. 'It's supposed to sound like wind and stuff but it doesn't.' Saliva and tears were all mixing together on my face. 'It's all the same yucky thing! You said Dalape and it's *not*. Why did you say you were going to do it when you *didn't*? Why did you say you'd get red when you *didn't*? Why did you get this *yucky stupid colour* and it's TOO BIG –'

I felt a stinging blow to my head. Before I could draw breath, another blow fell to my face. I sprawled in the middle of the rubbish from the crate. The accordion was stripped from my body. I staggered up, wheezing for air.

'*Due milioni di lire, disgraziato!*' The old man cuffed Gianni so hard he staggered backwards into the wall. '*Disgraziato maledetto. Due milioni di lire* spent to educate you, to give you some manners, to get something into your stupid head – and you don't even look at it.'

My brother's nose was bleeding. He wiped the blood with the back of his hands. He spoke carefully between clenched teeth. 'I don't want to play the piano-accordion.'

My father grabbed my brother by the hair. With his big hands he beat him over the head, over his legs, over his back, grunting '*Disgraziato, bastardo, maledetto!*' My mother tried to stop him – 'Bruno, *basta* – no!' but my father pushed her off. '*Puttana!* Get away or I kill you too!'

Gianni was holding himself in and it wasn't too bad. He was taking it, curling up, making himself small and nothing: shut up, don't provoke him. The old man laid into him for a few more minutes, kicking him into the packing crate and then it looked like it was over.

But Gianni is a stupid prick sometimes. Just when my father was walking away, he got up. 'Come on! Aren't you going to bash me some more?' he yelled. 'Go on! Lay into me, I don't bloody care! You can kill me but you still can't make me play that bullshit thing!' The old man picked up the hammer and seized my brother by the hair. The metal flashed. My mother hunched over in a corner, my little sisters choked on their mucus and tears.

'So you don't wanna play *la fisarmonica*?'

'Fuck the *fisarmonica*! I'm never gonna play that fucking *fisarmonica*.'

'Okay – no more *fisarmonica*!'

The old man hammered a hole into the wall. Then he grabbed my brother's head and bashed him alongside it four, five, six times.

'Forget *la fisarmonica*!' he shouted. 'Forget it! Forget it! Forget it!'

Finally he threw the dazed kid off to the other side of the room. He leant over the packing crate and grabbed hold of the instrument by its straps. 'No one likes this *fisarmonica*?' He raised the hammer to the keys. 'Okay I don't have no more *la fisarmonica*! No more *fisarmonica* in this house!'

I ran into the hallway. I picked up the phone, fumbling with the receiver. I dialled a number, any number that came to my fingers. 'I'm calling the police!' I screamed. 'I'M CALLING THE POLICE, DAD!'

For a moment, the hammer hovered wildly over my father's shoulders. The number was ringing. We could all hear it burring.

'Please Dad,' I sobbed. '*Please Dad.*'

Gianni was lying in the packing rubbish, arms wrapped around his head. I made sure the hammer was as far away from him and the instrument as possible

283

before I hung up the phone. My face was puffy and my lungs were starting to fold. Yet the ringing of the phone was clearing my way, making me bold.

'I want to learn,' I said. 'I'll play the piano-accordion.'

The old man put the hammer down. I felt like I was bleeding inside. I was cold and dizzy. I wanted to throw up. My father hauled Gianni to his feet. 'You see the trouble you make for me?' he hissed. He shook his head, half-smiling like it was a joke. He was suddenly conspiratorial, soft. He spoke calmly, not to me but to my brother. He didn't even look at me.

'You think I spend *due milioni di lire* for you sisters to learn *la fisarmonica*? You think you sisters can play in clubs, come home late?' The old man threw his hammer alongside the piano-accordion, the wood resting next to the ivory. '*Disgraziato.*'

He looked around at us, as if to make sure we got it clear once and for all. 'This accordion,' he said, 'is for Gianni. Is for Gianni because he is stupid. Because he has to get manners. Because one day he will get married and work for his family. This accordion is for Gianni because he has to be a man.'

I didn't want to understand. I clutched the phone in my hand. 'But Dad,' I whimpered. 'What about me?'

My father turned to me. 'You shut up and help you mother and you sisters,' he said. 'You don't have to learn anything.' He took the phone out of my hands and replaced it with a neat click. 'You don't have to be a man.'

Candidates will be required to transpose, in the listed keys, simple passages at sight.

It's the first musical thing the kid can't do. He sits staring at the excercise, blank and angry. Transposition is a mystery to him. Probably because violinists and pianists are used to a life where what you see is what you get. He likes to look at a straight black and white world where C is C is C and you hit a note and that's what's written and that's that, right?

So I tell him: think of the stave like a shifting sand. What you've got in front of you is a map of sound patterns. X marks the treasure but the spot could be anywhere. We can map this dune like this, that clump of trees like that. But these things might also exist lower down, in a more temperate zone. Or you might find them higher, in the icy wastes. What you're looking for is in both places at once. Transposition is only possible once you understand that every time reality is laid out in front of you, there's another reality hovering over it.

He doesn't really get it but he's curious. He wants to know more. He starts to hang around French horn players, trombonists, clarinettists. These friends slip and slide around between keys, translating. It's second nature for them to read one thing and play another.

Breathe in, breathe out.

SIX

Gianni began to learn with Frank Di Biasi at the Elite Music Academy on Tuesday afternoons after school. It cost ten dollars a half hour for a private lesson every week, plus the cost of the books, *With A Song In Your Heart* (*adapted for Piano Accordion*) by C. John Harrington and *An Album of Melodies Book 1*, plus his Hannon adapted scale book and the tram fares. To afford it all the old man took a second job as a casual maltster at Carlton and United Breweries three long day shifts a week.

Every Tuesday my mother would steady herself with some aspirin and 5 mg of Valium. She'd leave Claudia and Sofia with Nonna Betta and turn up outside the school in her floral dress, black stockings, black cardigan and a plastic basket with her purse and knitting in it. You could smell the wrapped-up *panini e mortadella* she'd make for eating on the tram. Gianni ignored her, kicking a footy in the playground, all long bruised legs, ripped bag, discarded tie and filthy shirt hanging out. Finally my mother would stride across the ground, grab hold of the scowling kid and try to haul him off.

His kicking mates, John McGrath and Bruce Whelan, sniggered. Monkey-like, they staggered about in front of us. 'Oom-pah-pah, oom-pah-pah, wog-woggie-wog!' Dickheads. It amazed me how they never even got this dead simple taunt to go in three-quarter waltz time. My mother abused them in Sicilian and they hived off down the road.

Tuesdays were magic days; my heart flew out into the unrolling sky as I sat in the middle of the tram, its green Tramways Board curtains flapping in the breeze. As the tram clanked down Victoria Parade, I could smell the barley and hops from the breweries. I took charge of the accordion. I clutched its handle tight. That was my job on Tuesday afternoons, looking after the accordion. I always put it under my seat or guarded it from people knocking it.

At Victoria Parade, the gates of Carlton and United were jammed with trucks and security men. The night shift workers on our tram jumped off and streamed across the road. I squinted out the windows. I couldn't see the old man but I imagined him hauling sacks somewhere beside the dark silos.

Gianni sat well away from us at the back of the tram, sprawled out with his pocket radio and ear-plug, his tie off and his surly eyes fringed by long hair. He only moved to open and close the sliding door for schoolgirls who entered or left the carriage, his eyes hanging on them.

At the Elite Music Academy, we registered with Anita of the long pink nails and fluffy jumpers, who, without looking up from her *TV Week*, assigned us to a tiny room off a cluttered corridor downstairs in the bowels of the building. Every week it was the same. Gianni never played a note.

Frank Di Biasi came in, he opened the Hannon book and said 'C major *per favour*, hands separately, then together.' Gianni took five minutes to set up. He'd move his stool, stand up, sit down, take out a handkerchief, wipe his hands, adjust the music and put his hand over the keyboard. We would all wait a long minute and a half as he stared at the C major scale. 'I haven't practised it,' he'd say eventually. Di Biasi would take a deep breath, run his hands through his hair.

'*Scusi*, maestro,' my mother would interject helpfully, '*Gianni non ha fatto pratica sta settimana.*'

'*Non importa, fa niente,*' Frank said and looked at his watch. Taking the piano-accordion from Gianni, he would run up the C major scale himself, hands separately, hands together, and in thirds and octaves for good measure. It impressed my mother, it entertained me but it did nothing for my brother's playing. Yet we couldn't blame Di Biasi. The lesson was so tortuous that the mediocre Frank – who practised fanatically and only taught when he ran out of rent money – ended up giving a weekly mini-recital to his stupid pupil.

Ten minutes of Gianni was like an hour to anyone forced to hear him plodding through *La Paloma Blanca*, of which he played maybe one note every second bar, with assistance. But listening to Frank Di Biasi stuffing up runs in Brahms' *Hungarian Dance No 5* was somehow even more debilitating. Through a basement window, the smell of factories and petrol seemed to drift into the hot, closed little room, making everything sour.

When time was so heavy and the notes so few and far between that we couldn't stand it any more, my mother would say, tentatively, 'Maestro, *scusi*, but ... my daughter ... maybe she can play a little bit something.'

The last twenty minutes of Gianni's lesson flew past as I ran through the Hannon exercises, *La Paloma Blanca*, *Impromptu*, *Silver Night*, *Wedding Song*, *The Theme From Love Story*, *Tarantella*, *Hungarian Dance*, *Gypsy Melody*, *Waltz in E minor*, *The Blue Danube*, *Rosamunde* and *The Sting*.

Gianni stared out the window.

We boarded the tram at peak hour, jostled by workers, office girls in woollen coats and private schoolchildren with berets and violin cases. Mum and I munched on her *panini* and longed for a hot dinner. I looked out at the city lights. The evening sky trundled past the tram window in patches and glimpses. I clutched the piano-accordion case's handle, happy and full.

In the end carriage, my brother sat as far away as he could from the accordion. His head was in his hands, the transistor radio on his knees. The white cord of the ear-phones circled him as he moved silently, rocking his shoulders and shaking his long hair, dancing to his own beat.

Candidates may present a free piece of the candidate's own choosing to replace any one of the four selected lists.

The kid buys an old B-flat clarinet from a hock shop in Smith Street. He keeps it at my place, he doesn't tell his parents. He gets me to go to his gig at a basement coffee shop in a back alley in Fitzroy. It's crowded on Friday nights, I stand at the back with a *caffè latte*, hanging on to my puffer through the smoke and cappuccino machine steam. The way he blows out his cheeks and swings his body makes me sick. Jeez. Fake boogie in a hippie café makes his toes tap and his eyes twinkle while the Lizst, Rachmaninov and Shostakovich concerti get a blank stare.

Walking toward Smith Street, he gives me his case to carry like in the old days, as if he's still a little boy. 'Well Zia?' he says. 'What did you think?'

I take a deep breath. I have to be honest. 'You're wasting your time,' I say. 'You're a pianist. You're not a wind player.' For a moment I think he's going to hit me. But it's only the movement his hand makes as he throws his scarf around his neck.

'Give me that,' he says, ripping the case out of my hands. 'How the hell do you know what I am?'

SEVEN

On the sixth week of lessons, Frank Di Biasi ran his fingers through his hair. He paced the room and looked out at the feet walking past the tiny window. After a moment, he turned to my mother. 'Signora, I don't teach your son no more. Bring me your daughter every week but leave your son at home.'

'But maestro,' said my mother nervously, 'he will do better. I make him to practise more.'

Frank smiled wryly. 'Please. Signora. Haven't you got ears?'

Despite my father's distrust of them, we moved over to the Simioni Brothers' Academy on the far end of Lygon Street in Carlton. Livio, the maestro, did not teach while he had the Combo Milano. He left the instruction part of the business to Dante, who immediately assigned Gianni to old Roberto 'Papà' Bacini, the white-haired Sicilian patriarch of *Italiano e Continentale* dance music in the city, a master accordionist who in those days was already in his seventies, half-deaf and half-paralysed from a stroke.

One afternoon, the three of us arrived for the lesson as usual, to find a new young teacher waiting for Gianni. He introduced himself as Paul Giacomo. He explained that Mr Bacini was in hospital after a small heart attack. Papà Bacini was all right, Giacomo assured us, but it was doubtful that he would ever return to the stresses of teaching.

Paul Giacomo wore jeans and a T-shirt, he had a beard and long hair, and the battered army disposal backpack open at his feet revealed a baton, an electronic metronome, a couple of Deutsche Grammophon recordings and several small yellow Schirmer scores. For the first time I saw the names W.A. Mozart, Frederic Chopin, Dmitri Shostakovich. Paul looked at me, then at my brother. 'So,' he said. 'Who's having the lesson?'

My brother shuffled his feet. 'She is.'

'No, he is,' I said shyly, flushing with pleasure.

My mother frowned. She looked at Paul with dismay. I could see her thinking how to explain to the old man about the sandals, the hair, the Australian accent. 'Is Gianni who learn *la fisarmonica*, Maestro,' she said. 'Marianna is too young.'

'No, she's not too young at all, signora,' said Paul, smiling. Unperturbed, he pulled out a chair for me. He hauled out our piano-accordion from its case and looked it over, ran his fingers gently over the dent in the enamel where my father had attacked it. He beckoned for me to sit down. 'She's the perfect age,' he said, strapping the accordion around my shoulders. 'So you've been mucking around, eh?'

I nodded.

'Play,' he said.

I started wherever my fingers wanted. I let them find the tracks and they knew them just like that, it was no big deal.

In C there were no complications, no black notes, wishes or regrets. Then, deeper, I managed to find A minor and get into *Bella Notte* with its chiaroscuro melody and the rhythm of wind through trees. Soon I swung into D minor with *Gypsy Nights* – I wanted more dark keys because this was my chance to show Giacomo I could make my way around the accordion's moonlit fields, that I could creep into the olive groves, past the *romanze* between peasant girls and wanderers and deep into the camps of the Romanian gipsies.

> *Take it,*
> *Take it for a minute, take it for a lifetime,*
> *Take it for gold, take it for fame,*
> *Take it for a laugh!*

But you know, sometimes the further you get into the remote minor keys, the less you want to return to the major tonality. You don't deliberately set out to stay in the wild. You wander only in order to return to the simple relief of home. But you can go too far. Then the bright triads in the stave recede, they start to belong to another piece. Suddenly you've broken the barlines into some weird new work and you can't go back.

In those few minutes I played for a wide-eyed Paul Giacomo, I knew I was taking him with me, running down the path of amazement. But when I got to the edge of the woods, I saw my talent fall away. I saw my genius was strewn all around me like wrecked cars in a junk yard.

I couldn't turn back from this sight.

The fact is, my friend, that genius is cheap. Hey, child prodigies are everywhere, there are geniuses in every high school, on the train, in the chemist shop, in jails, on the street. It's frightening how much brilliance there is in the world. Only people who want to keep it to themselves insist that gifts are rare. They are not. Genius is nothing special.

That's what the old man could never understand. After a few drinks my father would rave about the kings, about Simioni, Delvecchio, Giallo. The old man couldn't stand to be crossed. He'd smash his fist down on the table. 'What do you mean, genius is nothing special? It's incredible what some people are born able to do! Not everyone is born with everything under his fingers!'

Yes. All right. Not every flower is a rose. But how many roses lie trampled on the ground? How many in rubbish bins, on stony soil, on dry hillsides, in gardens drowning in water or unborn in seed packets at the back of an abandoned shed?

The rose is special and the rose is a weed.

Listen, it wasn't my father who wrenched me away from what I loved. It wasn't my mother sapping the life out of me with 'be quiet, don't annoy him, try to be good, *bella*, don't say anything, don't make trouble now, wait'. It wasn't the lack of courage of teachers, who all had ears, who all knew what was in front of them. I decided. No one else. In that hot and boxy room I saw that all the roses I had gathered up into my hands were weeds.

She's getting through it, the girl in Room 106. She's on an adrenaline high, dizzy with those black wild chords smashing out of her right to the end, the final chords: *Für Elise – Für Elise! – Für ELISE!!*

A thin-lipped man with glasses looks at her intently. He's the only one on the audition panel who asks her any questions. Such as: how long has she been learning? Who is her teacher? No teacher? In that case, does she play these pieces to anyone who could help her? His colleagues, embarrassed, shuffle their papers. One looks sideways at the other. The look says that this man doesn't understand that without strict measures they would have a list of kids to hear that stretches – without toilet break, coffee, cigarettes or ham sandwiches – till at least midnight.

The panel sit stony-faced, enduring the thin-lipped man's eccentricity. My dear, he persists, why do you want to come here, to this institution?

She says she wants to learn how to get to the ends of things.

EIGHT

Paul Giacomo was silent for a minute after I stopped playing. He shook his head.

'Incredible. That's amazing.' He pondered for a while, stroking his beard. He turned to my mother. 'It will be a waste of time for her to learn the accordion,' he said. 'This music, these little tunes – in a few months she'll know them all. She should learn the piano. She should do exams, study music theory, go into competitions.'

My mother flushed, she looked alarmed. 'But Maestro ... my husband ... just now he spend two thousand dollars for ...' She tapered off lamely, unable to meet his eyes.

Paul Giacomo frowned. 'I'm being honest with you, signora. She has a real gift. I'm not trying to get you involved in any new expenses for nothing here. I'm not saying this to make any more money or anything –'

'No, no, Maestro, I don't say that ...' My mother bit her lip.

'My Dad wants me to play the accordion,' said my brother flatly.

'Yeah,' I echoed helpfully. 'He wants my brother to play the accordion.'

'My Dad likes the accordion,' said Gianni.

'Dad bought it for Gianni to be a man,' I said.

'Shut up.' Gianni elbowed me.

I elbowed him back. 'You shut up.'

Paul Giacomo looked from me to my brother to my mother. I could tell he was thinking, what had he struck here? A mother who didn't want her kid to be a musical genius? It didn't make sense. He stared at the three of us, trying to work out his next move. I waited too, I waited with a lurch in my stomach to see what he would do. Giacomo walked over to the music stand and raised it a few inches. He beckoned my brother over. 'Do you play as well as your sister?' he said.

Gianni shrugged his shoulders. Paul turned the pages of *With A Song In Your Heart* to *Santa Lucia*, towards the back of the book where the harder pieces were. It was in B major. With five sharps, I had trouble doing the bass-line myself. Gianni didn't have a hope.

He stared at the music for a minute, his hands poised over the keys. Looking back now, that's what was strange. How did he know to hold his hands over the B major keys? He didn't have a hope of playing *Santa Lucia*, he wasn't playing, he wasn't making a sound. But he knew he didn't want to play *Santa Lucia* in B major. My throat tightened. Suddenly I didn't want to play this game with Gianni any more.

My brother turned away from the music book. 'I don't like this music,' he said. 'I don't want to play this music.'

Paul Giacomo raised his eyebrows. 'Yeah? So what do you want to play?'

I wanted to scream at him, 'My brother doesn't want to play anything! My brother has hated every one of his lessons! He's never played a note, he's put us through hell, he's never, ever wanted to do a thing on the piano-accordion!'

'I want to play some of that.' Gianni inclined his head towards Paul's army backpack on the floor. Paul took out the first thing that came to hand, a score of Mozart's *Eine Kleine Nachtmusik*.

'This? You want to play this?'

'Yeah.'

'But this is a score. This is for a string orchestra.'

'I can still play it on the accordion, though.'

Paul looked doubtful. I could tell he was thinking it would sound like hell but he was prepared to admit that it was technically possible.

'Okay,' he said, putting it on the stand.

'I don't need the music,' said Gianni. 'I know it off the record.'

I felt my lungs folding up inside me.

'You mean you know it by ear?' said Paul intrigued, looking at him intently.

My brother flicked his hair out of his eyes, staring at the teacher. 'Yeah.'

Gianni played the middle movement, the lovely *Romanze*, breathing it out like a song. The big bellows of the accordion melted into wings. When I remember that twenty minutes of winding andante, all I can think of is that Paul was so wrong.

It didn't sound like hell. It sounded like Mozart.

Everyone in the accordion business who has problems with a student tells them a story of the struggling beginner who tries for years to wrestle with the secrets of the accordion with no success. Then, one day in despair, after listening to Pavarotti singing Verdi – or *L'Ave Maria di Schubert* or *O Sole Mio* – the student sees it all in front of him, he understands everything and he becomes a king of the accordion. This visitation of *la musica divina* is a fairy story for hopeless students and parents not yet ready to face reality.

Reality. You have to face reality. You have to put your cheeks under its jaws, you have to let it bite you and feel the blood run down your neck. The reality was that Gianni didn't discover anything in his soul. He didn't click on to *la bella musica* because he was struck by revelations from Verdi or Puccini.

He just started wherever his fingers wanted. He let them find the tracks and they knew them. It was no big deal.

It was just that he just didn't want to play the piano-accordion.

At first, the grandmothers worried. They nagged and whispered to my mother to be careful because the hate of a brother or sister is a kind of *malocchio*. They brought me the stupid little things old women collect: wedges of *panettone*, hairclips, postcards of the Holy Virgin, *bomboniere* from a long passed wedding and cheap dolls from Woolworths.

They could have saved themselves the trouble. There was no jealousy between Gianni and me. What got me more than the sight of the once hopeless Gianni playing harmonies, rhythms and modulations I had never dreamt of – that made me want to cry out with surprise and longing – was the brilliant forgery of his stupidity, the grand architecture of his deceit. He had heard something, he had followed something and I had not.

I had not.

All the time he was listening to his stupid radio and practising in secret I was happy in the cabbage patch, playing with pebbles – *Gypsy Melody, Tarantella, Love Story, Santa Lucia* – when Gianni had found the river – *Symphonie Fantastique, Toccata* and *Fugue in D minor, Eine Kleine Nachtmusik, Gavotte in D, Pavane Pour Une Infante Dèfunte.*

I was a joke. I was a grinning little doll. I was nothing but a puppet beside his dark explorations, his silent refusal, his secret talent. I was only a child but I saw that a person like me could never be like Gianni. When my brother first played the Mozart – in the wrong key, rhythmically inaccurate but unhesitating, beloved – I saw what was needed to be in that world. The developing artist had to be as unbending as an arrow straight into his desires. A merely talented girl like me was like water – we were everywhere, spilling out wherever we were thrown: pliable, adaptable, grateful to soak up whatever was there.

I was ashamed. I was ashamed that I could spend all my life in the cabbage patch and be thankful for it, that I didn't need much, just the dirt in my fingernails, the wind on my back.

The air was trapped in my lungs. I had to cough to let it out bit by bit – cough and cough and cough. I sat sulkily in doctors' surgeries, mistranslating advice for Lina, leaving my Ventolin puffers on trams, throwing Pentavite syrup down the sink. I had nothing but contempt for the slippery part of myself that was just as happy to flow into ponds and puddles – and failing that, to drain off underground – as through the rivers of creation.

I would let the skin grow over my mouth before I touched the accordion again.

The girl in Room 106 is reaching for Mozart. It will be the *Sonata in A minor*. Yes. The opening theme falls out like a butterfly from a rose.

She runs up that sonata like she's seen the glow of some Kryptonite of genius that's never been seen on earth. Somehow the pages turn, her hands flicking aside the sheets, but she doesn't dare to look back at what she's missing from each page. Rushing: the more you miss, the faster you get and in this place, lady, when you're running scared, you actually sound slower. Her hands get hotter and heavier, she plays fistfuls of wrong notes. '... She will never acquire much speed because she is doing her best to become heavy-handed. She will never master the most necessary, the most difficult, the most important thing in music, namely the tempo, because she has been accustomed from infancy to disregard the beat ...'

You think I'm bagging her? That I'm dismissing her out of hand? No. What I'm saying is that the girl in 106 is not in time and no matter how fast she turns the pages she's in a shadowland between the keys, her notes slipping between the cracks of the out-of-tune Bösendorfer. It still hurts her ears, the sound of their flesh on crackling paper, the search for lips and eyes, the looking around on all sides, remembering to put back everything the way it was yesterday in the Academy practice room at sunset. But now there is something about the way her hands are wandering through this place that tells her this is the false sonata.

That girl is lost playing in a place that is horrible and wrong. In this place there is no angel of adequate steps to turn the pages over.

NINE

Paul Giacomo came from a fantastic lineage of Irish entertainers and Italo-Slavic *zingari musicisti*. He was Dante Simioni's nephew, the only son of Dante's wife's sister. Paul's father, Pino, boasted that he had once played saxophone in the Mozambique band led by the great Sam Delvecchio. Paul's mother, Toni, was an Irish-Italo-Australian singer who had sung Latin-American with the club dance bands before having kids. Toni now managed Paul's sisters, who were making the transition from teenage models to becoming sought-after and respected actors in the local film and theatre scene.

But Pino and Toni's blonde green-eyed son was the serious musician. At only nineteen, he was a post-graduate diploma pianist at the Melbourne Conservatorium, multi-faceted, multi-handed, the kind of player who could get a sound out of anything, who could improvise on the phone book, who wrote and conducted avant-garde music and who unknowingly made lifelong enemies by imitating other pianists' technical flaws as party jokes. The range of his abilities was so obviously freakish that it should have put him beyond envy. It didn't. At the Academy the small-time club players had the gall to mutter about nepotism.

Not us. We could see immediately that we were lucky to have caught him. Giacomo had just come home broke from a summer break on the fringe in New York, London and Rome. Having run out of money months before an application for an Arts Council Young Composers' Grant could be assessed, he was working casually in his uncles' Music Academy to get the rent together for his room in a Carlton share-house.

Despite his Anglo looks, he had the blood of kings. The accordion was like speaking Neapolitan to Giacomo. Dante and Pino had started him on *la fisarmonica* as a cute plump little eight year old in a blue velvet suit. At age ten he had appeared on Danny Ryan's 'New Faces' and at sixteen he had gone into partnership with a Greek wedding photographer to provide packages of music and photo albums at extravagant ethnic weddings. They had made a killing, which helped Giacomo to see his performances of *Terra Straniera* and *L'Ave Maria di Schubert* in an appreciative ethnomusicological light. All that stuff made him smile. He was relaxed and comfortable about everything in those days because the lucky bastard had free range over every domain. A real king all right. By day he conducted Michael Tippett and hung out in electronics studios with the bearded musos of the Conservatorium's composition school. By night it was *La Tarantella* with Mario Sciarelli and The Bella Notte Band.

With such a man as maestro, Gianni could at last bear to touch *la fisarmonica*. But by unspoken agreement – and my mother, ignorant of music, had no choice but to go along with it – his accordion lessons were not taken from *An Accordion's First Album of Melodies Book 1* but Bach's *The Anna Magdalena Book*, the chorales, the organ *Preludes and Fugues*, *The Well-tempered Clavier*, the brilliant *études* of Czerny and the scales and arpeggios and five-finger exercises of Hanon.

They got their hands on whatever they could and they did the transcriptions themselves. There was no other teacher for Gianni. He resisted the old man's attempts to swap him back to the care of the accordionists who would bring his son up in the language of *Buonanotte Tristessa* and *Mariù*. Lina was right, the easy native folk-tongue was all the old man wanted and he never trusted the foreigner in Giacomo – '*il Tedesco*' as he called him. Because the old man was already exhausted by the jabbering of *Australiani* in the unlearnable streets and alleyways outside – 'can't understand a thing you're saying mate, hey you giving us the Cook's tour or what, I said fuckin' Derby not fuckin

Kirby, Jesus how d'youse get a fuckin' licence.' He couldn't stand to confront more gibberish – sonata, partita, gavotte, fugue – that made him a foreigner in his own house.

Gianni wasn't worried – he knew his way back underground. He slid back down into his shadowlands of protective stupidity where it was no trouble to take two repertoires running with him side by side – *La Cumparsita* with Buxtehude, *O Sole Mio* with Cesar Franck.

It was even easier when Paul Giacomo was the gypsy-like speaker of God knows how many musical dialects. He had no problem teaching his Academy pupils a stylish 'oom-pah-pah', as he affectionately called it. But Giacomo also knew the accordion's dark side, that it was related to the cathedral organ like the domestic cat is related to the African lion. So what he slipped across to Gianni, folded inside *An Album of Melodies Book 1*, was a classical pianist's training using the repertoire of an organist. For years it was their illicit specialty, the training of a musician who loathed his instrument.

Gianni got drunk on that Dino Baffetti, swigging his music curled up into a corner of himself. Summer and winter I took my asthma medication, I studied *Approach to Economics Book 1*, *Elizabethan England* and Emily Brontë's *Wuthering Heights*, to the sound of Gianni getting through Bach, Buxtehude, Franck, Liszt and Berlioz out on the concrete tiles. He had to wait till my father left for his night shift or when the old man was so dog-tired asleep he didn't hear the '*brutta macchina*' rhythms he loathed. In the fibro shed at the end of the yard, surrounded by rusted prams and old heaters, my brother abused that Baffetti accordion like Punch beat Judy, like Heathcliff tortured Isobel.

The storm of chords and runs came up through the clothesline and into my room. I lay awake listening to the Baffetti heave and gasp for air as he flooded it with Bach's *Toccata and Fugue in D Minor*, dragging it along the three-part lines of organ notes squashed almost impossibly into two hands, flinging it around, ignoring the accordion's need to gulp air, beating its limitations, exhausting its possibilities.

Breathe in, breathe out. Go for it, Gianni. Every modulation, every ornament was like a punch in the face from the wog-boy whose parents had paid good factory-sweated money for him to learn *Rosamunde*, for him to learn *Volare*. Breathe in, breathe out, F minor, diminished seventh, a quasi-improvised run to the tonic. Screw you! Every contrapuntal theme was like an argument against the fact that the nocturnes of Chopin and Lizst were not for a teenage Italian only-son whose parents sent him every Tuesday night to lessons at the AAA Simioni Music Academy, so that he would grow up to be the magical man who would burst out from our family's table at weddings, light-footed, talented, envied – the king of the accordion.

My dreams were full of Mediterranean brides with mascara-smudged eyes dancing into the wind of a tempest, hair streaming, skin drenched.

In the mornings, I dressed myself for school with clear eyes and treacherous lungs. Nothing burned in me, I heard no songs, there was no sensation in my fingers. At nights I heard everything I wanted to know. Reality: I was getting real. A girl who gets real comes out of the wind, she closes all the doors of her house and inside she tears off her own hands. I was getting real. I pushed everything I was hearing into the abyss at the back of my throat. Hey, I shoved it down and I booted the trap-door shut myself. Screw it. I walked to school holding my puffer tight in my blazer pocket, savouring its small rock-like weight against my burnt-out chest. I didn't care how hard it was to breathe. I pledged myself to say nothing, to be nothing, to do nothing.

It wasn't easy. Sometimes my discipline slipped and I headed off with Gianni to hang around the Academy's electronic organs. For this weakness in making a fool of myself, I'd stuff my face with every preserved food I could find – red colouring, annatto, mouldy cheeses, Coca-Cola – every allergen and every trigger known to my medical file. If I mucked around on the electronic organs, I would also dish myself out the meticulous clearing of my room, no phone calls, no excursions, no sitting around sunning my legs at lunchtime with Despina and Gayle and the Form 3A dags from Cromwell Street High. Say nothing, be nothing, do nothing. It was hard but it had to be done.

One hot January afternoon, Gianni had stopped off at the Academy to pick up some gig music and was taking forever upstairs. I was left alone to wait downstairs in Studio 106, perspiring in my Asian cheesecloth skirt and tank top. On the Kawai was an abandoned book of Clementi sonatas. The heat and the smell of soundproofing chipboard overwhelmed me into a kind of sick and greedy fever. I don't know how it happened but I picked through three of the sonatinas, right through, every movement, not stopping for mistakes or refinements. I played like a pig, it was disgusting how crudely and easily I gorged my way through them.

The door opened and Giacomo walked in.

'Not bad,' he said. 'But I've told you before, you should have lessons.'

I shrugged. His concern was stripping me naked. I felt every thread of cheesecloth on my shoulders, every bead of moisture on my cheeks.

'I'm serious. I'll teach you for nothing.'

I couldn't stand to look at him. The way he moved his arms, the way his hair fell over one eye, the blunt rough beauty. Flushed and dizzy, I stood up and stared morosely out the window, as if I was being handed out a punishment.

'I wouldn't practise,' I said sulkily. 'Music's boring.'

As I left, I almost brushed against his cotton shirt. For days the thought of such a near collision left me trembling.

It was getting hard to breathe. There was a swirl of pollens that summer – mites, grass seeds and scrofulous dusts off the dead skins of animals – all invisible, all borne on hot southerly winds – all suddenly descending into my lungs. Whenever the wind changed, I was bundled off to the Children's Hospital and plugged into a nebuliser. High on steroids, I'd spend the hot days clowning around in pyjamas with all the other chronic regulars of the asthma ward whose lungs collected whatever shit it was that no one else could see.

One morning in the early hours, the sheet was pulled back, a Ventolin mask was strapped on to my face and I breathed, unknowing. I was out of it. I was out and floating in it, I was going to *la bella Santa Cecilia in cielo*, I was catching the last tram home.

> *I want to dance,*
> *I want to go dancing with my arms free,*
> *Take it for a minute, take it forever,*
> *Take it for gold, take it for fame,*
> *Take it for a laugh!*

I pulled the nebuliser mask off my face. The medication hissed fruitlessly into the dark room. I breathed in and out, in and out, large gutfuls of air greedily into my lungs as if I was on a windy hill on the edge of the world.

Okay. Okay. I would relent. But only a little.

I would hold the accordion for the King. I would strap it on to my back, if I absolutely had to, while the king of the accordion danced with his arms free.

To him, she seems no different at first to the dozens of fifteen-year-old girl students crowding around the Yamaha organ, listening to him show off with *Für Elise*. But unenrolled and uninvited, she stays back in his downstairs studio, trying to do it herself, wanting to get to the end of the piece, where it gets dark and difficult and at times violent. That was unusual. Most of his teenage girl students only wanted to play the first few bars, the ones that were quoted in the soap ad.

For him these days the grants and commissions are hard to get. Anyway they're not enough when he and Tatiana buy a block of land and she gets pregnant. So it's true that you really can't be a young composer forever, he jokes, after missing out on a particularly perfect university residency. Yeah well, she says. Gotta pay the bills. He understands – they're both musicians, both realistic. There's no blame and no shame and that's life. So he takes on more of the teaching load, especially when Tony Simioni goes overseas on business. For a while he moves back into town, into Tony's flat above the Academy, which smells of old accordion pleats and cheap violin rosin.

The first thing he does when he moves in is to plug the phone into the bedroom socket so he can ring his wife early and late. Their baby son is a lovely, a fantastic, kid. His first assigned students from Tony arrive at 7.30 a.m. so he's agreed with Tatiana, walking the baby up and down a suburban house way out in Keilor, that he has to stay in town here twice a week, at least for the few months that Tony Simioni is away.

He misses the baby. Tatiana too.

In the light, long evenings, through the upstairs window, he hears Gianni Vaccari's sister fighting, fighting to get through that stormy bit, to find out exactly what Ludwig had to say to Elise.

At first he tries to block her out. He's in the bedroom, wrestling with the jammed window while she stumbles and falters. He looks across the city at the summer thunderstorm sky contracting. Sighing, he sets down his screwdriver and goes downstairs. He can't let that experimental fistful of misread chords set hard and crack up an otherwise polished piece. She should have lessons, he's told her before. She has talent, the Vaccari girl, she could make something of herself but if she keeps on like this, she'll come to nothing with all the bad habits she's learning.

They sit at the keyboard, night after night, later and later. They talk and play, play and talk. Lately the silly melodies, the plodding techniques, are sending him into a kind of stupid daze where he forgets who he is and why he's there. One evening he and the girl creep up the stairs to the flat together. They sit in the half-light, kissing.

They kiss for a long time. Finally, in the bedroom he can firmly close the window to those schoolgirl *Für Elise*s going like merry-go-rounds downstairs.

They surface after the Academy closes. Downstairs, at the Kawai piano, his hands next to hers are precise and knowing. She thinks about what sort of hands Elise had, whether she practised by candlelight and what her father thought of her getting this hot romantic piece from a guy. Was it some kind of pact they had, like they were outsiders or something? *Für Elise*: could she get to the end of it without interruptions, without stopping, without trailing off and forgetting where she was?

They meet after the last of his lessons. Sometimes she gets there deliberately early, and, instead of taking the back stairs from the laneway, she walks dangerously through the front of the Academy. She climbs to the third floor, past the storerooms, padding softly down the corridor, the disused toilet, the empty boxes. She slips the key he has cut for her into Tony's place, locking it behind her. The blinds are pulled shut against the afternoon sun. She throws her things on the bed, makes herself an instant coffee. Her heart pounds as she runs a bath. He's told her not to do it in case someone hears them but she does it anyway. The running water roars loudly.

She lies in the dim room, her skin heating up against the cool pillows. Through the floorboards she can hear his teacher's dance of patience and sometimes, small, dawning victories. There's one of Tony's students, Helena, who drives him especially mad with the way she stumbles around those bright cheap chords that you learn from pictures in Hank M. Hettinger's *Easy Play Piano Method Book 1.* Helena spends a lot of time sittting at her keyboard with the reverb turned high and the Violin/Flute button on, trying to figure out the hard bits of *Für Elise.*

After the lesson with Helena, he's drained, he's had it. He comes upstairs, lights a cigarette, stares at the ceiling. They sit without talking as the sun sets over the city. She sneaks a smoke, reaching over for the packet. He tells her she makes him sick, she's just a schoolgirl and look at her, she's addicted, she's got nicotine on her fingers. Desperate. Totally desperate.

They sit in the dark, breathing in, breathing out. Finally she stubs out her cigarette. She goes to the bed and takes off her clothes.

It's after 8 p.m. The neon from the bottle shop across the road flickers into the apartment. Wrapped in a blanket, she sits at the keyboard. Switched on, it hums the faintest of electronic bass-notes, the light panel glowing its reds, blues and greens.

He comes up behind her softly. 'What are you doing?'

She shrugs. 'Nothing.'

He draws her to him but she shakes him off and continues picking out the keys. This melody of hers has been in his head for days, he hums it at home, while he drives, but he can't pick it.

Anna Maria Dell'oso

'What are you playing?'

'Something.'

'It's very nice,' he says. 'You wrote this "something"?'

'Yeah, maybe,' she says. Scornfully she crashes her hands on the keys and turns to face him. 'What's it to you?' she says. 'What are you playing at?'

He shakes his head, running his fingers through his hair. 'Hey, I'm doing the same thing you're doing.'

'I'm not married.'

He smiles wearily. 'So,' he said. 'I'm dragging you in here by your hair, huh?'

She shrugs. 'I don't care anyway.' She turns and, abandoning her tune, she concentrates on the middle section of *Für Elise*.

'Hey.' He takes her right hand off the keyboard. The act is rougher than he intends it to be so he softens it by kissing her fingers. 'Please. Babe. Don't do that. I'm sick of hearing it all day long.'

'I have to.'

'Why?'

'Because I want to hear it properly.'

'But you're getting out of time there.'

'I want to get to the end of the exposition. I want to get through the whole thing for once.'

He laughs. 'Here, move over. I'll show you.' He squeezes himself into her space and starts to play. She turns off the electricity, punching him in the arm. 'Get off. Go on. Off. *Off*!'

'All right, all right!' he says. 'What's the matter with you?'

When she comes in to pick up her clothes, he grabs her hands and they kiss each other like they'll never get enough.

When she's gone, he sits at the piano and rings his wife. He wants to say goodnight to the baby but he's teething and crying too much to play games with Daddy. 'What's that thing you're playing now?' asks Tatiana. 'It's driving me crazy.'

He shrugs. 'I don't know. Something some kid is putting together. Why?'

'It's got a good hook,' she says. 'It's strange the way that melody keeps following me around, you know, like the moon in the mirror of a car.'

TEN

I was handed my Leaving Certificate at morning assembly, along with the few fifth formers at Cromwell Street High who had been successful. I picked up my bag and my hairbrush and walked off from the quadrangle in the middle of the headmaster's congratulatory speech.

No teacher bothered to stop me. Cromwell Street was a feeder school for Collingwood tech, for the shops, factories and hairdressing salons of Smith, Johnson and

Fitzroy Streets, Collingwood, and the old CES. I walked up two flights of Victorian Education Department stairs into the girls' toilets. Twenty minutes later I walked out wearing a white uniform, a gold-rimmed tag saying 'Marianna', lilac nail polish, Mary Quant white lipstick, Korkease platforms and Gingham perfume. Lugging my bulging grey Cromwell Street High schoolbag for the last time, I walked out of the school gate and up towards the Smith Street chemist shop where I'd been helping out Friday nights and Saturday mornings since I was fifteen.

It was a day of honour for everybody. At George Tsoukanis's Late Night Chemist Farmacia, they could finally arrange for *Sì Parla Italiano* to be permanently and professionally sign-written on the window. Because of my asthma, I'd missed a lot of school. But still, with my marks in the low sixties, I was one of Cromwell Street's star pupils – I spoke English, I had the Leaving Certificate and I scored a cream-collar job. In 1973 there was full-employment and Collingwood was my oyster. I got confidence from elbowing away George Tsoukanis's married brother Con when he brushed up against me behind the counter. Selling Revlon and dispensing Valium gave me the independence to buy my mother a clothes-dryer and a bit of money to throw around on a new *giacca*. We certainly needed the financial top-up. My father was off work, fighting in the courts for compensation from a drink-drive accident where some lunatic totalled his cab one rainy night at Kew Junction.

George Tsoukanis's Late Night Chemist gave me the cash to pay Giacomo for Gianni's A.Mus.A. theory and history lessons and the occasional masterclass type of exchange those two still had on the accordion. When Paul found out I was shelling out for them instead of my father, he made sure a lot of wedding and twenty-first birthday gigs came Gianni's way. Gianni became Paul's 'dep' in the Bella Notte Band, taking over *Tango delle Rose* and *La Cumparsita* for Paul when he double-booked himself or had something better to do, like promoting and conducting Lexicon, his contemporary chamber music group.

Gianni envied the freedom of my white uniformed days. He was no scholar either, he hated school as much as I did and wanted to leave. He had a vague idea of playing the ethnic club bands full-time so he could buy a car and maybe travel up to New South Wales. It was his dream to do Sydney, hitchhike up to Byron, score some good dope. Instead he was hassled into studying for the HSC because the old man wanted him to get into Monash engineering. For the old man, it was time for Gianni to get real. After the years of enjoying his son's exploits with *Terra Straniera*, it was time to haul him out of the bordello of *la musica bella* and into an arranged marriage with a rich professional career. The old man never accepted the kinky secret things Gianni and Giacomo were doing with the instrument anyway. Overnight he insisted his son cool off from the accordion and forget standing up to play *Tarantella Capricciosa* in front of his *paesani* at the Italo-Australian Club. 'Why you still learn from Giacomo?' he'd rage. 'You can play all the songs now! Enough! *L'hai imparata abbastanza!*'

Risking his court case to moonlight for a small cab operation in the outer western suburbs, my father hired a chemistry and physics tutor and threatened to smash Gianni and the accordion if he didn't study at nights instead of playing '*la tringa-tranga-tringa-tranga*' of Bach and Vivaldi in the basement. So Gianni plodded through the nights with *MacBeth* and *Approach to Economics Book II*, breaking out on weekends to play with The Bella Notte Band. He practised Saint-Saens' *Rondo Capriccioso* and Wieniawski's *Polonaise Brilliante* to wind down after gigs.

When his HSC results arrived, Gianni was out the back in the shed, fighting tears as he punched old furniture.

'Fuck. Fuck it, man. This is fucked.'

I took the letter out of his hands. Gianni's way with words aside, I had to agree. Fuck the old man, fuck the Examinations Board. If Gianni had been allowed to do three music subjects instead of these sciences he didn't have a clue about, it would have been a different story. If he'd done music practical, music theory and composition and music history, he would have got As, he would have topped the state. It was time for my brother to take matters into his own hands. Next year I'd make sure he did music practical on the piano no matter what my father said.

'Don't worry about it, Gianni,' I said. The rescue plan was already forming in my mind.

'This is totally fucked, man.'

'Listen to me –'

'Like totally, totally fucked.'

'Fucking listen to me.'

Until now the problem had been that my father's hands weren't big enough to throw Gianni around any more. Instead he had cultivated the idea of Gianni's academic stupidity to bash him with, to make his head go in the right direction all of its own accord, without the old man lifting a finger. Well it didn't have to be like that any more. Piano-accordion wasn't yet an examinable subject for the HSC, so Gianni would have to convert to piano, practise at the Academy every night, or hire one, or buy one or get a secret studio somewhere or something. I wasn't sure, we'd work it out.

My brother took the result letter out of my hands, screwed it up and chucked it on the ground. 'This is complete bullshit,' he said. 'Who needs this bullshit?'

I picked up the paper and unscrewed it. Among the cluster of Ds and Es, his Italian got a B and the compulsory English Expression was a C, not too bad; it could be worked up.

'The old man is right,' I said. 'You need this bullshit, Gianni.'

'No way. I'm not doing this crap again.'

This was the thing about my brother. Mentally he could dive from the highest cliff into the deepest ocean, no problem. Big gestures – no problem. But one disappointment, one little thing wrong – one jellyfish, one pebble, one piece of junk in the sea – and he was out, he didn't want to swim any more. I admired it. I really did. I liked that stupid courage, that suicidal plunge into his secret inviolate self, blah blah and all that. But right then it really pissed me off.

I kicked his music stand. It fell in front of him so that the metal hit the concrete of the shed with a jangling sound. The *Bach Preludes and Fugues Book One* slithered to the ground.

'You have to repeat, Gianni.'

'Why?'

'Because you're uneducated. Because you're ignorant. Because you're untrained. Because you're playing the wrong instrument.'

'Get lost. Get out of here.'

He turned away into the darkness. I picked up the *Preludes and Fugues*. It was covered over with fingerings and markings pencilled in by him and Giacomo. I opened it out at the middle where it was stapled together and I began tearing it from the centre staples outwards. One by one I pulled out the sheets of music and threw them wherever they landed. It was hard work, it was a thick book, I had to concentrate.

For a moment he watched me like I was an accident unfolding in front of him. Then he tackled me against the shed door. 'Fucking bitch!' he spat. My back hit the aluminium with a clank. He ripped the book out of my hands. 'You fucking crazy bitch!'

He started picking the loose leaves of the manuscript up off the concrete floor. He had to get under sacks of Briquettes, old tables, busted fans. The coal dust was whirling and getting kicked around. But I was breathing fine. I was breathing just great.

'What's with you?' he yelled. 'What's your problem, what's the fucking problem with you, what is it?'

'Without the HSC no conservatorium, no university, no college – not even Miss Smith A.Mus.A. down the road – is going to want to know anything about you. Because you don't play the piano, you don't play the organ. You play the accordion.'

'So what?'

'The accordion isn't an instrument. Not according to the Conservatorium of Music. Not according to the Music Examinations Board.'

'I don't fucking care.'

'You think because you can play this stuff in a back shed, that's all that matters?'

'Right. That's all that matters.'

'You think it's just the music that matters?'

'That's all that matters to me so fuck you.'

'Get real, Gianni. See what's going on here.'

'It's you who don't see what's going on here.'

'You have to make the changeover, Gianni,' I said. 'How can you go to the Con without a recognised instrument, without academic qualifications? You think they're going to open the doors and say 'Hey Vaccari, we've heard you're a shit-hot accordion genius. What a wonderful addition you'll make to our symphony orchestra! Here, sit down at this piano. Take a year to get used to it, take your time. In fact, have a scholarship, go to Paris, play for Nadia Boulanger. Hey, let's book Carnegie Hall while we're at it.'

My brother was silent. There was only the rustle of manuscript leaves being smoothed and sorted back into their old place.

'If you do it right, with music, it's not the big thing you think it is. We'll buy a piano. Next year you'll change over and you'll do all this HSC bullshit again. So it might take two years, three years. So what? It's an investment, man, an investment in your future.'

Gianni paused, kneeling, with the sheets in his hands. He ran his fingers over his face. 'Go play with your Barbie dolls, Mari.'

A few pages of the *Fugue in C* had landed under an old kitchen dresser. I had to get on to my stomach to prise them out. Finally I stood up, blowing the dirt off the pages. 'Here,' I said, throwing them at my brother. 'Don't staple them up again though, man. Keep them loose.'

I started to walk away out of that stuffy garage, climbing upstairs, getting out of there. 'Because if you don't get what I'm saying, Gianni, you may as well use this stuff to wipe your arse.'

There are nights in the flat when the moon outshines the street signs. They sit at the keyboard, smoking hash, cocooned in a blanket. He plays through her books of Bartok's *Mikrokosmos*, then roams lazily into a Gershwin tune, loading it up with fancy piano-bar chords. She throws in the campy ice-cube flourishes.

He likes to test her, to play games. 'What's this?'

She leans against him and closes her eyes. 'G minor.'

'And this?'

'A minor.'

'And this?'

'B-flat, A, G-sharp.'

'And this?'

He's entranced. 'God if only I had perfect pitch.' He fantasises that he could have cheated through all his harmony and counterpoint exams. It's a sign, a gift.

'No, I don't know when I realised,' she says. 'It was just there, you know, like my hands and eyes. It's still just there whether I like it or not, whether I can use it or not, whether I want it or not, just like your hands and eyes, right?'

Breathe in, breathe out.

But the time comes in the autumn when she hears from him all kinds of small, weird emotional transpositions, constantly up and down in tiny quarter-tones. She hears his voice slipping and sliding in and out of almost inaudible pitches all the time, putting one reality on top of another but playing the same old tune as if nothing's changed.

In the middle of April Tony's flat is cold, the shuttered window firmly closed. The winter days are short and the evenings sudden yet she waits for him for the longest time. From downstairs Helena's *Für Elise* sends her to sleep, her head on the kitchen table. When she awakes it's night. The flat is silent, empty. The lock has not been turned by his key. She puts on her jacket, drains the half-empty coffee cup into the sink. As she leaves, the irritating tinkle follows her and she realises more than a million and maybe a billion schoolgirls can play the first ten bars of *Für Elise*.

'Hey, let me tell you something,' he says to her. Breathe in, breathe out. 'Perfect pitch isn't the big deal everyone makes of it.' Breathe in, breathe out. 'Total morons can have perfect pitch. Completely unmusical people are born with this party trick where you can tell whether you're singing *Love Story* or Verdi's *Requiem* or whatever in G or in B. It's like having a photographic memory, only you've got a sound memory.' Breathe in, breathe out. 'It's like you've got a tuning fork stuck permanently in your head at A equals 440.'

She rings him at home and he tells her it's because Tony's coming back soon, that's all. That's all, babe. Just don't call me here again. On the nights they have to see each other – I don't care, I have to talk to you – their keys clash turning in the lock, metal scraping metal.

At the piano, it doesn't work. 'Big fucking deal,' he says, exasperated. 'So you've got a tuning fork between your ears. But can you play the Chopin *Nocturnes* like this? Can you hold that sostenuto so that the moon shines into people's eyes?' Hey? Like this, like this, *like this*.

Breathe in, breathe out.

Breathe in, breathe out.

ELEVEN

It wasn't just the Italians who asked for *la signorina* at Tsoukanis's pharmacy. The mums of glue-eared toddlers, asthmatics, the Serapax ladies, they all wanted me because I kept the new Medibank Gap books strictly in their favour, making sure they'd get the radical new Labor Government's rebate. I knew how much it cost to nurse a chronic condition and I didn't forget where I'd come from just because I now got cheap Ventolin and Becotide, discount Vicks and steamers, peak flow monitors and pharmaceutical salesmen's samples of eczema creams, antibiotics and benzodiazepines.

Sitting in the dark of the back tea-room, I took my nebuliser whether I needed it or not. It seemed the demonstrative Con, who just couldn't help his extroverted affectionate personality, somehow didn't find me so sexy with a Coke straw up my mouth and a green plastic mask strapped to my face.

Floating away in the mists, I thought hard about the next step. I tallied up the money Gianni needed for another year of studying. Music tuition in three HSC subjects from either Giacomo – or more likely, because of his Lexicon commitments, the best private teachers instead. Tuition in the rest of the HSC from a private college like Westwood's in the city. The cost of a piano and a studio, because there was no way we could let the old man know what Gianni was up to. The usual transport, books, theatre and concert excursions, manuscript paper, lecture workshops, exam fees.

Breathe in, breathe out. This was serious money. A sales assistant and a first-year apprentice panel beater were not going to raise that kind of money.

To go over to Giacomo's every day was impossible. Gianni had tried depending on him before, hanging around Giacomo's grotty kitchen in his Rathdowne Street days, moving pencils and Czerny *études* and cups of coffee off the piano-lid, explaining ourselves to flatmates who meandered in the door shouting 'Hey, Paul!' after a few minutes of hearing Prokofiev's *Visions Fugitives*. Gianni couldn't work in that situation. It made him jumpy, hostile. It embarrassed him to have to explain to some op-shop jumpered Skip flatmate of Paul's what was going on in his life.

Breathe in, breathe out. There was always the Anglo

solution. Gianni could move out. But that would have to be forever and in another state. If my father couldn't drag him home, he'd get him bashed up or, in a drunken rage, he'd even take down the unlicensed rifle that he kept wrapped in an army blanket in the back of his wardrobe. Anyway, if Gianni left I'd be alone with my bastard of an old man, my benzodiazepined mother whispering 'just do as he says, don't annoy him', and nights in front of the television babysitting my little sisters, washing out my chemist's shop uniform and maybe going out with Con Tsoukanis on the sly, fucking in his car on Thursday nights and getting married to someone else in a few years.

I wasn't ready for that kind of reality. Breathe in, breathe out.

But that's where I'm different to Gianni. The pebbles, the sticks, the boulders in the river – even the trickle to nothingness, the dust where the last drop peters out – it doesn't matter to me. I go everywhere, I've got no principles, I've got no standards.

I saw how it could be done.

I didn't push him. I shut my mouth when he went down to Wilson's Prom with his schoolie mates in a hotted up Mazda for New Year's Eve. I said nothing about the stoned weeks going by down there without him touching the accordion. All summer long, in my lunch breaks I disappeared with my takeaway felafel roll behind the nappy boxes in the tea-room, smoking a quick cigarette with my nebuliser at the ready. Over and over in the long afternoon crawl to 5.30 p.m., I imagined sitting Gianni down, I practised explaining it to him.

'For now, you make as much money as you can. For now, you go for all the competitions, you do all the gigs. For now it's all about dollars and keeping the old man off your back. Okay? Just for now.'

'But all the time, you practise, you study, you do the Bach fugues, the Mozart sonatas, the Debussy preludes, everything. Then, next year, we go overseas. We rent a flat in London, we hire a piano and I get a job. For a whole year, you do nothing but practice. For a whole year, you train, you get your repertoire together, you do eight hours a day – just practise, practise, practise, without interruptions, without having to work, without having to cook, without having to clean – because I'll do the work. I'll take care of everything – scholarships, concerts, teachers, gigs – everything.'

'Then after a year of nothing but practice, you do an audition for the Royal College of Music. You get your doctorate in the piano, you get a teaching studio together, you get a concert career together, chamber music, whatever, and I manage you. You play and I'll be your manager and we'll be rich.'

'That's the plan. Okay?'

At the end of summer Gianni started up as an apprentice panel beater at Joe Lachiati's Smash Repairs in Coburg.

The girl in Room 106 tries to transpose up a third note-by-note, getting herself all tangled up between G major and B major. She finds it hard to change one thing into another, to shift from one world into another, while all the time giving the impression that everything's still in its place.

She sits there, holding back tears. Maybe. Or is she just flushed and defiant as the adjudicators fiddle with their papers? One of them has to tell her, with just a bit of impatience, we've clearly stated that transposition is a requirement at this level. It's your responsibility to check the syllabus.

That girl in 106 thinks she can't transpose so sits she like stone, not knowing what to do next, where to go, which key to head for. But the Bösendorfer is out all the way, right through the keyboard. It's only in tune with itself. What you play on that thing is not what you get. If she's been given an out-of-tune piano, she's transposing all the time. Whether she knows it or not, whether she wants to or not.

Every time she touches the keys of that piano, she transposes.

TWELVE

The work at Lachiati's was hard and dirty. The guys that worked there were real Italian stallions. They talked chicks and limited slip differentials, Alfas and babes, cocaine and fucking, shafts and twin overhead cams, and rods and snorts and cones. They were pigs and I liked them – little boys in love with their dicks. Gianni's muscles got thicker, browner. He came home dog-tired, pulled beers out of the fridge and flopped out in front of 'Blind Date' instead of listening to Brahms on his hi-fi. Gianni had always had girlfriends, there was a sensitivity, an angry darkness in him that made Anglo university girls take him up to their share-house bedrooms to talk about how hard it was to grow up an alienated wog in an Anglo culture and all of that. He had never slept with Italian girls, they were too much hassle when Skip girls coolly slid into bed with him without much up-front obligation, already Pill-ed up or IUD-ed and diaphragmed and without brothers and fiancés waiting down the lane outside the Apia Club for him after gigs.

After he started work at Lachiati's though, I took messages from the Michelles and the Carolines and the Amandas. He didn't ring them back. They faded out of his life and the Marias and the Silvanas and the Teresas from the gig scene faded in, with their tight satin dresses, black lace stockings, high heels and zippy yellow Hondas that Gianni was always taking a look at.

People loved Gianni and were willing to pay good money to hire him and Le Stelle, the band that his fixer, Umberto Scacchi, got together. Umberto Scacchi was a drummer of sorts who'd come through Simioni's Academy, a Melbourne High motor-mouth with big ideas who worked in the Taxation Department and spent most of his time there on the phone chasing 'prospects' for an American network marketing business that sold cleaning products and makeup. His big loves were sales motivation seminars in Noosa and playing drums to *You Are So Beautiful* at wedding receptions.

But his real talents were in petty seduction and fixing gigs. In less than a year the guy was king of the B grade gigs and his extension 281 at the Taxation Department was in the diary of every club musician from Fitzroy to Frankston. When Umberto first summoned Gianni to talk business after a gig at the Italo-Australian club, I let him buy me a rum-and-Coke and ask what a gorgeous girl like me was doing on a Friday night hanging out with my brother. I even let him nuzzle into my hair and stroke the back of my neck. 'Umberto,' I whispered, 'I want to go to bed with you, don't get me wrong. But I'm resisting the temptation to sleep my way to the bottom.'

He looked genuinely amazed. 'Yeah?' he said. 'Why's that?'

With Umberto breathing down my neck I seriously worked Gianni's gig diary. Soon I was booking him for at least two weddings a weekend and when he complained and talked about dropping out to chase waves up at Nambucca, Umberto would pick him up in his vintage Jaguar, drive him out to the Top of The Town, ply him with strawberry daiquiris and margaritas and rave on about how some day they'd own their own record label.

At nights, wearing my Le Stelle T-shirt, I made sure everything was set up okay; the lighting, the amplifier, the stands, the food in the break, the cheques. The one night I didn't go out with them to a wedding at Doncaster (because I had the flu, my period and my asthma) the guys let Gianni get drunk and stoned on tequila, sambuca, Ben Ean and some kind of weird Balinese dope Lazic Dranovic brought back from a P&O cruise gig. Gianni was pulled up by the cops at 3 a.m. on Heidelberg Road and lost the last of his licence points.

After that I got my Class D licence, which meant I could drive trucks if I had to, and I babysat the boys, driving them around to gigs all neatly seatbelted, penguin-suited and telling dirty jokes.

They whinged about their girlfriends and wives who were so jealous of them going out nights; about the lousy pay, their boring day jobs and the lack of time to practise with a young family. Umberto and I had deep-and-meaningfuls about relationships and money and sex while he ogled my breasts and tried to sponsor me into his crazy network marketing business. From out of the corner of my eye, I saw the seventeen-year-old Italian princesses hanging out near my brother, touching his accordion, giggling, asking stupid questions.

After gigs we went down to the Tre Venezie in Lygon Street to play pinball. By then the Italian princesses were just phone numbers in Gianni's pocket. Umberto hung around talking dirty in my ear, lacing my Chinotto with

Johnny Walker Black Label and buying me single roses from the girls who hawked them from restaurant to café.

Eventually the others left to get home to their wives. Even Umberto gave up and slunk off to hail a taxi down Lygon Street.

It was just me and Gianni, talking business.

'We're getting close,' I said. I bashed the flippers hard. The ball ricocheted around the Addams Family Haunted House, briefly lit up the windows, then sailed straight down the middle and out.

Gianni pushed me aside. He pulled himself up a new ball, tapping the flippers right at the last second. 'So,' he said. 'How much have we got?' He tilted and bashed the machine. The lights went crazy.

'About half of it. Almost enough for the plane tickets.'

He whistled. 'That much?' The ball jumped out of nowhere and flew off the panel into nothingness. Grinning, I pushed Gianni aside.

'It has to be more. Pull your finger out and enter a few competitions.'

'I'm pulling my fingers out. My fingers are doing overtime.'

'I wasn't talking about chicks. I was talking about entering a few competitions, you lazy shit.'

'Get off my back, Mari.'

I was doing well with the flippers. The panel was buzzing and the score rocketing. My brother was impatient for the next ball. But I was still scoring after two minutes. Then the whoosh of the Tre Venezie cappuccino machine put me off and I lost it.

Gianni hesitated slightly as he pulled up his ball. 'Mari,' he said. 'I need to borrow a couple of hundred from the account till next week.' He sent the ball flying around the panel. 'I'll pay it back after the Schiarella gig.'

'What for?'

'Private stuff.'

I pushed his hands off the flippers. 'No way. Tell Umberto to finance his own bullshit.'

'Hey, Mari,' my brother grabbed me angrily by the elbow. 'Did you play *Mariù* tonight? Did I see you sweating out *Torna a Surriento*? I'm making this fucking money. I can take it out if I want.'

The pinball machine blurted out the theme from 'The Addams Family', then flashed Game Over. I picked up my bag and keys off the floor. In a way the old man was right. Gianni was not too gifted in the thinking department.

'Yeah,' I said. 'It's your money, Gianni. Get it out. Your name is on the account. Get it out anytime you want.' I paid for the bill and left a tip. 'Play *Volare* and *La Cumparsita* at Calabrian weddings for the rest of your life. Just give the bank three months notice in writing and get it out.'

The set piece for candidates in this year's auditions is Schumann's Traumerei *from Opus 15.* Kinderszenen.

Breathe in, breathe out.

The nurse who gently shakes me awake tells me to get a cup of tea at the cafeteria, to stretch my legs, take a break, go for a walk.

On the hospital balconies, cleaners and kitchen-hands gather to smoke furtively. I edge my way past orderlies sunning their legs. I take a puff of Ventolin, then light a cigarette. I don't go far. I want to be there when the kid wakes but I want to be out of here before my brother comes down from the Dandenongs. I hear Gianni won't sign the methadone programme releases. He wants to put the kid into a private psychiatric clinic out in the country somewhere, a place where they do a fancy new Israeli deep sleep de-toxing programme. Yeah right. I can just see it. The minute the kid gets cleaned up, out he goes into a hippy town where cannabis is the local cash crop and lines of cocaine stretch into the night.

I look out over the tangled inner-city. The quick fix. Always the quick fix for Gianni. And his kid's the same. Stupid kid. So easily led, confused, suggestible.

Across the road I can see the grammar school kids running out, all blazers, caps and good shoes, getting picked up by their Country Road mums in their olive Mercedes.

They audition the music scholars toward the end of fourth term. Even a half scholarship here is worth four thousand a year and the word is that their director of strings and orchestra is a genius.

A prefect meets the contenders and their parents or guardians, walking them down a canopy of jacarandas to the music school. The candidates unpack in a velvety vestibule where honour boards roll out the golden names of Academe. They're permitted to warm up in any of the modern soundproofed practice cubicles they choose. He is so awed by the brand new Bösendorfer upright that he allows her to slip a tie on him. But he pushes her hand away when she tries to comb down his hair – the spikes are not negotiable.

Outside in the courtyard, she sits on a bench with her eyes closed. Kinderszenen: *Scenes From Childhood*. Behind every door is the same *Traumerei*, only dreamed differently. All the pedals are held and let go at slightly different intervals; the Schumann chords are shaded different depths of gold, pink, violet and the pigeons at the top of the steeple fly off into the blue in staggered moments.

Why does one hold on, *sostenuto* and the other lets go, *più breve*?

The phones at work drive her mad, with each ring the possibility of the hospital. She escapes into Simioni's storeroom and sorts the sheet music. They're not big sellers, the classical range. They've been sitting there for years with covers curling and prices fading off. Working in the dust late into the afternoon, all those cheap Embassy, Lark and Stendhal covers start to blur until lots of little Mozarts play at the harpsichord in front of her.

The Mozarts look like glossy air-brushed kids that

would do well auditioning for ads, like half the students at Simioni's. The girl, Nannerl, is definitely the big sister. She's got a confident look to her, maybe because she was ripping through her minuets and fugues while he was still in nappies. The bad reproduction makes it hard to be sure but from what she can see of her face, she looks happy playing along beside her brother. It must have been a big shock the first time they left her at home while the old man and the kid did the big gigs around Europe.

'My very Dearest Sister ... I send you herewith a prelude and three-part fugue ... With time and opportunity I hope to compose five more and then present them to Baron van Suiten ... and for that very reason I beg you not to withdraw your promise and to let no one see my piece. Learn it by heart and play it – it is not so easy to pick up a fugue by ear ...'

Why does one hold on and the other let go?

Her mother warns her not to visit the kid. Gianni doesn't want it, Lina says nervously, declining to come in, her eyes darting into the room. Bullshit, Marianna says. He can't do that, the kid's family, he's my nephew for God's sake. Doesn't matter, says her mother. Gianni's told the hospital. He says you're not a relative. Not any more. He says that he's going to get a restraining order out on you. Marianna cries and swears with frustration. But in her head she's stony, rebellious. I was a good sister to Gianni. She wants to be comforted but her mother is panicky around tears. Lina can't take emotional overload.

I was a sister of the minor keys. I had the same ears and my hands could have followed the same track after his if I had let them. Shh, says her mother. Leave it. Don't go there. What can you do that they are not already doing? Why provoke Gianni with that?

At night the Mozarts' wigged heads and powdered faces come floating up to her. *Carissima sorella mia* ... Learn it by heart and play it ...

During the day at Simioni's, the students are all practising the set piece for the Eisteddfod, the HSC, the Conservatorium High School entry. By evening, in the hospital, the staff have changed the kid's ward and she can't find him. So she walks undetected through busy reception desks, through corridors, past nursing stations, group therapy sessions, meal trolleys and laundrymen, not daring to ask or loiter in case she's thrown out.

Finally in the south wing, in one small ward of patients watching televisions, she thinks she hears someone very much like the kid talking to his psychiatrist. But with the curtains drawn and voices low, she can't tell.

Kinderszenen: it's hard to hear who is who in this hallway of *Traumerei*.

THIRTEEN

I was helping Lazic and Umberto bump the stuff out of the Abruzzo Club after a wedding. Gianni had disappeared. Lately he was only turning up to lend a hand when we had nearly finished. We were loading the last amp when he came out of the dark. He had a girl with him, a *Diorissimo*-laced chick with swept-up long black hair, a gold chain with a single diamond around her neck and a John and Merivale dress rustling over her long legs. 'This is Gina,' said Gianni. He stubbed out his cigarette and moved aside as the boys helped me distribute the load in the car. For these small party gigs we had a Holden station wagon where we put all the gear in the back. Except for the accordion. I always put the accordion wedged between the floor and the back seat.

'Hop in the back,' said my brother to Gina, as he caught the keys I threw him. I shut the tailgate with a bang. The girl stood with her arms folded, shivering in her Zampatti jacket. She peeped through the side window. 'I'm not getting in there,' she said. 'There's not enough room.' She tottered over to the front of the car, opened the door and sidled in next to Gianni.

All the way to the Tre Venezie, I sat curled up in the back with the drumkit bumping against my shins.

That night I played pinball till dawn on my own.

Candidates must bring to the examination room two copies of an original composition of no more than seven minutes in length. They will be expected to explain its structure and demonstrate its essential features of style, phrase, character and the realisation of marked detail.

After months of no contact, the kid fronts up at my door with a quartet of black T-shirt boys. He has sleepers curling up his earlobe, nose studs in his nostrils and a dirty torn op-shop seventies jacket on his shoulders. Their band, Desolation Angel, are serious shit. They thrash out electronic music that sounds, I dunno, like a heart-lung machine in a Fitzroy brothel or something. The kid is their new classical jerk, the johnny-come-lately who's in the band because of his access to my electricity and studio space.

But listening to them, I also see he's the only one who can get it down on paper. They're almost illiterate and he's a musical dictaphone. After a while he gets bored with being their keyboards-secretary and he makes the mistake of offering them original ideas with tunes, harmonies, rhythms. The black T-shirt boys fob him off.

Soon it looks like he's back into it. He sleeps in his clothes till noon and wakes looking scabby and strung-out. He tells me one of the others is using but it's recreational, under control. 'The guy's got a kid he doesn't want to lose access to.' He says he's clean. 'I couldn't play at this level if I wasn't.' Everything the kid does with Desolation Angel is so complicated that I believe him.

Gunslinging for a badge of musical cool exhausts him. Kid, they're dumping on you because they don't have your soloist's technique, the freedom of your classical training. Those guys think they're radical because they play John Cage rip-offs and tattoo their noses. But they're not here at an audition like this because they just can't cut it. Hey, you're being led up the garden path by those black T-shirt jerks. Those pin-prick note-rows sound like a useless session on the toilet. Those in-your-face *sforzandi*, big deal. Those autistic Phillip Glass arpeggios going round and round, *tringa, tringa, tringa*. What's the big deal?

The girl in Room 106, I can't hear her playing. No radical, redefining compositions, no *Synapse MK5s* or *Lacunae Lunastika*. It's quiet in there, still and empty.

After threatening to for years, the Simionis sell up and the Academy students leave. I stay put. There's nowhere else to go. After banging on the doors on Sunday mornings, Dante leaves me alone. His mother's sick and dying; the brothers go to Messina to bury her. Then the ex-wife Livio hasn't seen in thirty years has breast cancer and wants him to visit her, the son and grandchildren. Then, the third trouble. Back here, Marcello, the accountant, bursts an aorta and dies. Dante is too busy to think about evicting me. The estate agents knock once or twice but as their prospects don't push it, they move on. I don't get any more notices from Santano Realty. Maybe Dante thinks he owes me something. Well it's not enough, fuck him. The plumbing begins to go and I can't get the leaves out of the roof gutters.

When the kids first come over to record *Lacunae Lunastika*, I say okay. They're bullshit artists but they appeal to me, their ideas, their morose pessimism about what they're doing and how badly they pretend they don't give a stuff about wanting to do it. I get to like passing the Johnny Walker around the kitchen table and saying 'yeah right' to all the pointless coffee-and-cigarettes arguments about why the city music scene is fucked.

Desolation Angel gets on the dole while they work on *Lacunae Lunastika*. The kid calls his cheques creative development grants. It's bullshit but I think hey, why not? I keep the all-night soup, bread and coffee happening as they work on the last movement. By 1 a.m. every morning they're getting pissed off with each other because they've got to the end of what jamming and group work can do.

I look over the kid's shoulder at their sketches. I can see they need to go back to the first subject and deal with the fact that it has nothing to counterpoint it. That the second subject isn't there. That the whole thing is so linear anyway that it doesn't say anything.

'Expand the A minor theme,' I suggest. 'Give it to the sax. Cut back the fugal *ostinato* stuff. Let it breathe a bit emotionally.'

It's so quiet that I think I hear my music playing on the abandoned keyboards.

The boys go back to work. They take the mugs of

soup out of my hands and the coffee off the tray and start up again, jamming, writing and arguing. I watch them as if they're already behind the glass of a recording studio, talking without words, playing without sound.

Desolation Angel. The sheets on my bed are cold. In the mirror I brush my greying hair till it flies with static electricity. When I wake up for my nebuliser at 3 a.m., the place stinks of marijuana and pizza. The fugal ostinato stuff has gone wild. The A minor theme has disappeared. They're ripping the hell out of each other.

When I flush the toilet I notice his gear and syringe has been hastily jammed behind a stack of *ABC Concertgoer* magazines.

FOURTEEN

Gina. Shadow of my evenings, over-perfumed allergen of my lungs. Gi-na. *Gina*. Her name would bang through my head in the darkness at the back of the Italo-Australian Club as she turned up beside me, leather skirt up her thighs, platform heels wedging into the carpet and fingers curled around a gin-and-tonic. Gina. Gina Angela D'Argento.

Gina was a student kindergarten teacher, the only child of Calabrian parents who owned three delicatessens in Brunswick. At eighteen she got a brand new yellow Celica from them just for passing the HSC not all that well and on her second attempt. Gina didn't pay a cent of board and she had a stack of whitegoods, including an imported Miele fridge and a Swedish Jorg dishwasher, in Heywood's Self Storage. She had plans to move out to a harbourside apartment in Neutral Bay in Sydney and take up her cousin's offer to get into public relations. Once in a strained moment of girl-talk between us, she told me she had a Royal Doulton dinner set, Sheridan sheets, silver service cutlery, everything the best from Myers and Georges', nothing from Kmart, nothing cheap.

I was organised, I was smart but she had the immovable, fixed stare of a snake. She went for my brother like he'd been promised to her as a baby. Turning up at every Le Stelle gig, she sat coolly but with glittering eyes at the musicians' table, ready to fend off the Italian princesses that drifted over Gianni's way in the breaks. Wherever Gianni went with the accordion, Gina was there.

It made me laugh actually. I was more worried about Gianni at Lacheti's. He was getting discouraged, frustrated, he was talking cynically, losing energy. I didn't like the hash, the packet and a half a day in cigarettes and the Asian drugs, but I shut up. In fact I rolled the odd joint with him, I even bought a few cones myself. But when Gianni was smoking every day, wrapping himself up in the ritual of bongs and hiding bongs and growing plants and getting together with other paranoid dopeheads to smoke and talk bongs and busts, I knew I had to heavy Umberto to do something. I knew I had to offer him something different.

On my rostered second Monday mornings off, I visited the British Embassy, the Italian Consulate and the United States Information Service. I looked for scholarships, bequests and fellowships. I filled in application forms and sent tapes of Gianni playing both piano-accordion and piano. In the tea-room at Tsoukanis's Night and Day, I wrote away to music schools and colleges overseas, making notes from handbooks and typing up letters on the shop's IBM. I found my books and notes had the same withering effect on Con's physically expressive personality as my nebuliser. His wife had apparently just gone back to university to finish her arts degree and he was sick of all her 'Germaine Greer bullshit', as he put it.

Finally in the summer I got a reply from the Surrey College of Music saying they were happy to offer Gianni a place as a 'mature age undergraduate performance student in our Overseas Student Programme pending satisfactory performance at a live audition on arrival.'

I waited till after the Friday night gig at the Abruzzo Club. As soon as we got home and I hauled the stands and the music out of the van, I grabbed the letter from the glovebox and ran down to the shed. Gianni and Gina were lying wrapped around each other on the busted old sofa, kissing and smoking a huge joint. 'Hey Gianni,' I said, 'I've got something for you.'

I threw him the letter. He sat up, prised himself away from the elastic-mouthed Gina and unfolded it. Gina straightened her halter top, stuffed half a boob back in and fluffed up her hair. She generously offered me the joint.

'No thanks,' I said.

Gina insisted. 'Go on!' she giggled. 'We're celebrating.'

'Yeah? Don't tell me. You're pregnant?'

'Get stuffed.' She scowled, taking a drag on the joint.

I walked over to sit on the arm of the sofa behind Gianni. 'I've rung around,' I said, massaging his shoulders, 'and the best deal is with Singapore Airlines to London via Bangkok. I've booked for September.'

'September? This year?'

'I put down a five hundred dollar deposit yesterday. We pay the rest in six weeks.'

Gianni stared at the letter. 'I don't believe this.' He shook his head, dazed. As Gina leaned over to read it, he took the joint and inhaled two or three long drags. Mentally I vowed that from tomorrow this dope thing was going to stop.

'There's only one problem,' I said. 'We don't have all the money together.'

'I don't believe this,' my brother kept saying over and over, 'I just don't believe this.'

'Hey. It's okay, I've got it figured out,' I said reassuringly, taking out my folder of brochures and application forms. 'There's the Lillian Jones Bach Scholarship. You've got till the end of the month.'

My brother shook his head. 'No. I don't think so.'

'But it's Bach,' I said. 'How can you miss?'

Gianni looked at Gina. She took the joint, dragged on it long and lovingly and stared into space. It was as if everything swayed in her sweet haze for a moment. Except for me. My head was clear. My eyes were dry. Finally Gianni sighed that pink-eyed hey-man sigh I was starting to hate. 'Look Mari,' he said to me. 'Let's talk tomorrow. I'm stuffed.'

'You're stuffed. You're stuffed? Your dreams have just fucking come true and you're stuffed?'

Gina quietly handed back the letter to me. She cuddled into my brother and slid her hand down his shirt. 'Hey babe,' she said softly. 'Let's tell her our news.'

I looked at them with a beating heart. 'What news?'

Gianni had his head thrown back, his eyes closed. His agony and ecstasy were pathetic. A bit of *Diorissima* perfume, firm long fingers down his pants and a babe who could manage these simple pleasures like a small business, and he was gone.

'What fucking news?'

Gina smiled. 'We're getting married.'

Sliding out of the pleasure zone, she carefully hooked the stub of the joint to a hairpin and held out her left hand. On her ring finger was a diamond and sapphire cluster set in a simple twist of gold.

'Gorgeous, huh?'

I saw them watching television together on a leather lounge suite in a new-built brick veneer in Boronia Park

South, surrounded by Gina's Swedish dishwasher and her Mikasa china sitting on the bench of her blackwood island kitchen.

'It must have cost a fortune,' I said. The light from the stones was cutting up my eyes. 'It must have cost you – God, I dunno. What kind of money does a thing like that cost, Gianni?'

'Tomorrow, Mari. Let's talk tomorrow.'

'No, guys. Come on. Tell me. I'm dying to know. How much does a beautiful thing like that go for these days?'

'Three thousand dollars,' said Gina proudly.

'Yeah? That's impressive,' I said. 'Three thousand dollars. Wow. You got a personal loan on that or what?'

Gina wrinkled her nose. 'No way,' she said. 'Gianni just walked in and paid cash for it today.'

Auditioners will give credit for the evidence of the application of the principles of good teaching.

The red-headed nurse sits beside me with a peak flow monitor, instructing me: breathe in, breathe out.

I wanted to send the kid to a good private school where music was a specialty. But even with a half scholarship Gianni refused to put up the money. He said he didn't have the money. Bullshit. It's not like cars have stopped breaking down and people don't crash them any more. They should try squatting in a warehouse, see how easy it is to support their clever kid on that. Didn't have the money. Yeah right. They'd just put in a new in-ground pool in their house in Glen Waverley, the kid's little sisters had their own VCRs in their Laura Ashley bedrooms. No. The mother wants him in the business. Gina wants him to do an MBA and law and accounting and help them become franchise kings. Vaccari Brake and Steering – the McDonald's of engine shops.

I don't know how to keep going. I've had all the burdens, all the worry. Now I'm getting all the blame. 'Why encourage him?' she says to me. 'Who asked you to give my son these so-called opportunities? To stuff around with his head? Mind your own fucking business. Get married and screw up your own children's lives.'

I should have left him to sing in his cradle. I should have turned my face away from his perfect sound, his chubby little hands finding their way up and down the keys.

The old man used to hear my brother's music just as he was getting up to start his night shift. Bach would drive him crazy, all those sewing machine notes stitched on to his flesh on summer nights. He'd run down into the garage in his singlet and throw the book of *Preludes and Fugues* into the garden. 'This is shit,' he'd yell at my brother, 'this is for funerals. You think this makes people happy? You think people will pay to dance to this – this – *tringa-tringa-tringa?*'

The nurse flushes with alarm at what she reads from the peak flow monitor.

FIFTEEN

One Friday evening about a month later, I was washing out my chemist uniform and looking through the handbooks of the Surrey College of Music when the phone rang. Gina's voice was like an ice-pick in my ear. 'You fucking bitch,' she said. 'I hope you're happy now. I hope you're satisfied.'

'Hello Gina,' I said. 'I hope you had a nice day too.'

But she wasn't playing games. She sounded in a bad way, kind of crying but trying not to let me know it. She wanted Gianni. 'Let me speak to him, Mari. I know he's there.'

I closed the hallway door so that no one could hear our conversation. Mum and my sisters were watching television, the old man had long left with the cab. I didn't understand why I was hearing from Gina, because Gianni had changed into his dinner suit and cummerbund over an hour ago. I thought he had left to pick her up before his Apia Club gig, as usual.

'Isn't he with you?' I said. 'What's going on?'

Gina was now crying openly, which freaked me out completely. For the next few minutes I couldn't get anything sensible out of her. 'Didn't we know?' she kept saying. 'Hasn't he told you?'

'Told us what? *What?* Shut up and talk to me!'

It turned out that Gianni had broken up with her that afternoon. For weeks she felt something was coming, then, after work, in the car, he went very quiet. After a lot of prompting – what's wrong, what's the matter? – he came out with it. They were finished. He said he wanted her to keep the ring but the engagement was off. He couldn't marry her because he 'wasn't sure that he really loved me.'

Gina wanted to go to the Apia Club straight away to confront Gianni and the bitch she felt must be responsible for the break-up. But I saw that a showdown in the middle of *What A Wonderful World* was not one of her brightest ideas. I persuaded Gina to drive over to our place, to talk the whole thing over with my mother. Because despite what Gina thought, I had no idea of what was going on in Gianni's head. I really didn't. I was just getting used to the idea that maybe the dickhead really loved her.

It was only when I hung up that I realised it was too early for Gianni to have gone out to a gig on a Friday night. Before I could throw on a scarf and some lipstick, the phone rang again. It was Joe Caputti, the floor manager of the Apia Club. He wanted to know if Gianni had given the accordion part of the Sinatra medley to Frank Magnana, his stand-in for the night.

Maybe it was there. I don't know. I never went into Gianni's room, I didn't know where he kept his band music. But that night I didn't bother with what Caputti wanted. I mumbled something reassuring, just to get him off the phone. When I put my head around the bedroom door, all I wanted was to check that Gianni's music-stand was gone, the accordion was gone and the thick *Urtext* edition of Bach's *Organ Works Volume 1* was gone.

Rugging up in my duffle coat, I grabbed money and cigarettes and quietly shut the back door. I waited for Gina in the alleyway. It was a freezing night with a razorblade wind. Rain blanketed the deserted small factories and industrial carparks of the back end of Collingwood. My cold feet drummed compulsively on the cobblestones. Finally the headlights of the Celica swung into the lane.

As soon as she pulled up, I jumped in next to her and slammed the door. I told the confused Gina to drive down Johnson Street into the city.

The trials had been going for more than an hour when we walked in. We tip-toed past the thin audience of teachers, friends and relatives through the back of the long Melbourne Town Hall. I picked up a programme. It was the preliminary round and there were a lot of people on the list, mostly pianists and violinists. The adjudicators were getting tired, they stopped most players after only halfway through the first movement of their works.

Gina was careful to clap and do what others did, as if she was in church. When I pointed down the programme to Gianni's name, her eyes opened wide in surprise.

He walked on imposing, polished, dark. A bit of laughter broke out at the sight of the accordion. Yet something about his tall striding body and threatening scowl soon shut them up. Finally the hall was silent of coughs and fidgeting and the adjudicators didn't stop him. Gianni didn't waste any time. The first thunderbolt of the *D minor Toccata and Fugue* boomed out of the accordion and round the hall.

Notes were spilling everywhere, as if from huge organ pipes. But the town hall organ behind him was silent. Its stops were in, its pipes were closed. No, the sound was coming from the well-worn 120-bass Dino Bafetti squeeze-box in front of us. The dark man leaning into the accordion pleat – leaning in and heaving it back out – was busy handling the big swells breaking all around, working the D Minor waves and skimming the fugal rain to haul in his catch of notes.

The adjudicators let him play right till the end of the fugue. The final chord swooped low over the hall, hovering for what seemed like a long silvery-lit time.

The audience didn't know how to react. Two or three pairs of hands began to clap, then stopped. Making sure he had finished, the rest of the applause started to come in, getting stronger and a touch reckless, with a whistle or two thrown in like a coloured streamer. Then it died away.

After a long time, an adjudicator rang the bell.

The little silvery bell sounded and the next contestant, a girl pianist, sat at the Steinway to play the *Sinfonia* from the Bach *Partita No 2 in C Minor*.

Gina and I didn't go backstage till the finalists, an oboist, a violinist and a pianist, were announced. Gianni didn't even get a place. To my surprise, this didn't worry him, just as he didn't raise an eyebrow at seeing Gina and me backstage.

It was the adjudicators' report that he was after. Throwing his tie into his case, he picked up the envelope with trembling hands and ripped it open. His face darkened. Throwing out his cigarette with disgust, Gianni scrunched up the report, threw the piano-accordion into its case, grabbed his jacket and walked off out of the hall, with Gina trailing after him.

I picked up the ball of paper. I smoothed it out and read the handwriting.

'We regret that, much as we would like to, we are unable to comment on your playing tonight. We must refer you to the Rules of the Competition, which is open to PIANO AND BAROQUE KEYBOARD, and orchestral wind, string and brass instruments ONLY …'

I drove the Celica home. None of us said anything. Gianni stared out the window, dishevelled, unapproachable. Looking at his strained face I saw what he might be like at a disappointed thirty, at an exhausted forty. Suddenly I was tired. I was almost asleep watching the traffic lights turn red and green: stop, go, stop, go, stop, go as the airconditioning purred. Glancing in the rear-vision mirror, I saw that somewhere along the twisting roads home, Gianni and Gina had begun to hold hands.

All the lights were on at our place. As I pulled up the back, I was scared to see the taxi parked outside and my father running out to us in his work clothes. Gina's parents were standing at the back gate with my mother. As we got out, Concetta D'Argento rushed to her daughter's side, at first crying, then hitting and yelling abuse at her. La D'Argento and my Mum had been crying for a while. The men were looking bloody.

My father's first blow fell on my face, 'for lying' he said, while Alberto D'Argento pulled him away saying 'Calm down, they're home, they're safe.' I nursed my jaw. I wasn't upset, I knew it was a bit of a circus act – the old man's honour had supposedly been compromised by Gianni breaking off with Gina and he was trying to show these jumped up Calabrians, these up-their-arses D'Argentos, that he was still in charge, that he wasn't a piss-weak *padrone*, that he didn't let his daughters go running about in hot pink lipstick and skirts up their bums all over the city at night. Cuffing me also showed that he was going to get serious about the insult that Gianni had paid to the D'Argento family by breaking off the engagement with their daughter. Alberto, meanwhile, had also cuffed Gina, to show that he also didn't go along with slut daughters that put it out for *morti di fame disgraziati* that had no intention of taking them to the altar.

Inside, the accusations and interrogations went into the early hours of the morning. What did they expect to do about the wedding? What about the priest, the church? What about the invitations? The presents? *Had they slept together?* Gianni sat smouldering in a corner, refusing to answer any questions from anybody, even when my father, goaded by Mr D'Argento, threatened to get out the rifle from his cupboard.

Finally, unable to take it any more, Gianni brushed aside both families. He grabbed his cigarettes, pulled a carton of beer from the fridge and stalked off into the laneway. Gina, who was being restrained so hard by her mother that her arms were covered in welts, broke free by biting Concetta's hand, shouting, 'You don't understand anything!'

Fifteen minutes later, they reappeared hand-in-hand. 'Well?' glared Gianni at the old people. 'Go home. There'll be a wedding.'

With a new assertiveness, Gina picked up the D'Argento car keys and brusquely told her parents to get into the car, she'd follow them home. In the hallway, as the D'Argentos left, she hissed at me. 'You just don't understand Gianni. All the stress, all the pushing. Why don't you just leave him alone?'

'Tonight meant nothing,' I said. 'A technical hitch. If he'd played the Bach on an organ he would have won.'

Gina's hands curled tight with anger. 'You just don't get it, do you? Can't you see he's had it up to here with music? Can't you see he just doesn't want to play that stupid piano-accordion any more?'

Candidates may be asked to discuss their performed works from such points of view as form, period, ornamentation and style and to quote other works from the same composers.

Reality. You have to face reality.

All these parents twisting hankies or knitting in the corridors have to face the fact that only a few kids will be able to open the practice rooms upstairs to do what they like. Only one or two get through a year.

Breathe in, breathe out. I'm standing. I'm sitting. I don't know where I want to be. Excuse me, excuse me. It's all right, stay where you are, don't move away. Yes, I blame myself. No. Yes. It's such a big responsibility.

From the nurses' station she can see the kid's parents behind glass. Gina sits beside her son, stroking his hand, her eyes fiercely reading the monitor. Gianni stands by the window, head in hands, exhausted. The red-headed nurse arrives, holding out a Ventolin puffer. 'Here you go.' Marianna stares at the blue casing as if it's Kryptonite from outer space. 'No, come on, darling,' says the nurse. 'Two puffs. One. Two. There's no point punishing yourself. That's not going to help anybody. Believe me. Come on. There's a good girl.'

'He's done okay though, don't you think?' Marianna says, gasping. 'The kid's in there with a chance, don't you reckon?'

She sleeps for a minute, a thick queasy dream shot with pin-pricks of adrenalated fluorescent light. She wakes to a small rush of white coats and senior nursing staff. Grabbing her purse and keys, she runs after them. Someone asks the mother and father for permission to take his kidneys and eyes. The white coats go through the request matter-of-factly but with insistence. They put it as if it's the only way to be sure of salvaging something of him.

She closes her eyes. She prays her brother and sister-in-law will say 'fuck off. Don't touch a hair on his head.'

They take him off the respirator at a few minutes past midnight.

Breathe in, breathe out.

Breathe in, breathe out, breathe in, breathe out.

SIXTEEN

It was 3 a.m. before the house was quiet. I went to bed exhausted, my head screaming to shut down, but I couldn't sleep. If Gianni, a man, had never been able to win over all these years, what chance did I have?

I dropped a couple of the old lady's benzos, washed down with half a tumbler of Marsala and a couple of drags on a cigarette.

Soon I was drenched in a storm, huddled over somewhere in Fitzroy Street as the wind lashed at my face. A busker was raving drunk in the gutter, stinking of metho and urine. He was playing crazy shrill notes, squeezing and laughing, squeezing and laughing. A plump bride, the groom and her bridesmaids didn't seem to notice. They whirled out of the pub, on and on until the bride spun out of the circle, flying like a piece of chiffon in the wind.

I woke up, panting, coughing. I had to grab the nebuliser fast. Breathe in, breathe out, breathe in, breathe out. It was as if hands had tried to rip something out of my throat.

I hauled my cardboard suitcase down from the top of the wardrobe.

In the lounge-room, Gianni's accordion sat squat in the corner where he had left it. Dino Baffetti, 120-bass, enamelled black, with sometimes the echo of a flutey sadness in its middle registers that reminded me of a flower-girl sitting alone. Every breath slightly different in timbre. A fine instrument that would play Enesco's *Romanian Rhapsodies* long after we had all gone.

> *Take it,*
> *Take it for a minute, take it forever,*
> *Take it for gold, take it for fame,*
> *Take it for a laugh!*

Even though the old man was working without a radio
somewhere out in the western suburbs, I was
superstitious, I was careful. It took a good half hour to
drag my stuff out of the house and down a deserted
Smith Street to just outside Chiodo's. There I rested, my
rapid breath making steam puffs in the sharp air. It was
5 a.m. by the Post Office clock. It didn't take long for an
empty-lit taxi to come skimming along the tramlines of
the wet black road. I hailed it, still scared it might be my
father. But it was a nervous Vietnamese who helped me
with my suitcase and thought I wanted the Queen
Victoria Maternity Hospital. When I slid the accordion
into the boot of the taxi, I almost overdid it, it was
so easy.

It felt lighter than it had ever been.

Flight QF 106 to London via Bangkok didn't leave till
8.45 that night. I spent the day taking my money out of
the bank and changing it into traveller's cheques, half US
dollars, half sterling. I picked up my ticket, paid bills and
bought a travel bag, a money belt and a document pouch.
I rode out to Tullamarine early and stored my luggage in
pay-lockers at the International Airport. Toward late
afternoon, after drinking two rum-and-Cokes in the
flight bar to steady myself, I got a bus back to the city
with the accordion.

At a quarter to five in the afternoon, the Academy was in
its usual chaos. The dance teacher hadn't arrived yet,

Dante was out and Paul had been 'uncontactable' since lunch, according to Maria the receptionist, 'because he switch off the phone. *Mamma mia*, every afternoon he switch off the phone –'

I was clutching the piano-accordion. I couldn't believe how my shoulders and wrists ached.

'Signora,' I said, trying to catch her attention, 'Signora, I got an appointment with the boss.' But Maria was back on the phone trying to handle a consignment of Yamaha keyboards into the shop, get an emergency teacher for the dance class upstairs and take a call from some signora in Bulleen who wanted to change over her son from Elite to Simioni's because he'd been learning two years 'and he still can't play *Quel Mazzolin di Fiori* without stopping. I mean, signora, okay – I don't say he completely can't play, I don't say that. But why does he stop, stop, stop all the time, why?'

With her hand over the phone, Maria gestured for me to go upstairs into the studio – '*Aspetti – aspetti là*. He will come, for sure.'

'Maybe I can see Claudio –' I said.

'*È in vacanza*. Wait upstairs, someone will come, I promise you –'

'– or Tony, what about Tony?'

But Maria was back on the phone to La Signora di Bulleen.

'*Va bene – sì, sì*, I can book him in – but signora, you can't expect him ... How can I tell you? No offence signora, but if he is not *simpatico* ... *Sì, certo, sì* – is all hard work, everything is hard work, Signora, you tell him that ...'

Upstairs, the dance students came in from the street with their sports bags. The smell of public transport sweat mingled with spray deodorant over the wooden floorboards. Dante walked in, an hour late. He beckoned me into the almost deserted upper floor where instruments lay dusty on shelves. '*Allora?*' he said, putting on his glasses. 'What you got?' I heaved the accordion on to the counter. It was like putting down an injured animal. For a moment I imagined it crouched against its case, straining at the straps, snuffling, trying to breathe.

Dante Simioni looked it over shrewdly. 'I remember this one,' he said, 'Baffetti, 1965, expensive. It was for your father, eh?'

'My brother,' I said.

'So he wanna trade-in for a better one?'

'No. He wants to sell.'

'It don't play good no more?'

'It plays great. It's just that my brother's got other plans for his life now.'

'Yeah, I know. He don't like the music. *La Tarantella, Volare, Mariù, E Compare.* He wants Rolling Stones, yeah? Suzi Quatro?'

'Look, Mr Simioni, don't give me all the usual I'll give you this and you give me that. You and I know this is a

Dino Baffetti *fisarmonica*, one of the best in the world. You and I know it's worth more than two grand. Give me eleven hundred and we'll shake hands.'

Dante Simioni closed up the till wearily. 'You find me someone who will pay even five hundred dollars for that *fisarmonica* now.'

'I thought that was your business. The accordion business.'

'Ah signorina, signorina. There's no business in the piano-accordions no more. Now is just drums, guitars, Yamaha organ, synthesiser. The young people don't wanna play the old music no more.'

'You're joking,' I said.

'Look around,' he said. 'These accordions are the last. After this – finish. I don't import no more.'

'What?' I was so pissed off. 'What's this "finish"? You think people won't get married any more? You think there's never going to be an Italian *ballo* again? It's Suzie Quatro who's gonna finish. Not *la fisarmonica*. Jeez, if you can't sell a bloody accordion to the Italians mate, I'll go to Elite.'

By the time I got to the stairs, he had caught up with me. 'Listen. I don't want the accordion,' he said. 'But I want a girl here to help Maria at the reception desk. Start Monday. I give you good money.'

'What kind of money?' Not that it mattered but I was curious, I was caught off-guard.

'What money you like?'

Through the open window, I watched the sunset spread an oily citrus over the city. It smelled of feet and dust on the stairwell, of floorboards, petrol, and the threat of rain. I saw myself in a bedsitter in a Brixton street, my suitcases still not unpacked. I would be sitting in the gathering darkness, putting off the moment of switching on the fly-spattered fluorescent light. After all these years, would my hands find their way just like that through the keyboard? Or would they just go off to pull beers in a Brixton Hill pub?

> *Take it,*
> *Take it for a minute, take it forever,*
> *Take it for gold, take it for fame,*
> *Take it for a laugh!*

In the end, you have to face reality. You have to let it bite you and feel the blood run down your cheeks.

Successful candidates will be notified by letter within fourteen days of the audition date.

The doors are opening. Breathe in, breathe out. They come relieved, exhausted, trying not to laugh, trying not to cry. The kid would always come out pissed-off looking, whether he'd done well or not, he had no objectivity, he relied on me for that, he was so –

Yes, you go. Of course, of course. Parking is terrible here. Get away as soon as you can.

Your son is in there? Well, so fucking what? No, it's not a mistake, it's Roberto – Roberto, Roberto – are you deaf or what? Yes, Roberto Vaccari – sure he's on the list … You look again, lady, he's on the list, 'VACCARI Roberto Bruno, fifteen,' …breathe in, breathe out. The kid used to like to get away fast, the parking was always terrible here, he'd usually wait for me at the car. Anyway I've got to go, all right? I've got to meet him at the car, I've got to talk it over, I've got to look at his chances realistically … Hey lady, with people like you trying to get into this school I'm not so fucking sure I want him to come here!

Breathe in, breathe out, breathe in, breathe out. Excuse me, it won't make any noise. Breathe in, breathe out, breathe in, breathe out, breathe in, breathe out …

I'm pushing people out of the way, running through the crush of the corridor: Roberto, Roberto! I can't see him and I'm dropping music, I don't know exactly what music, 'Hey, don't step on that, it cost me a fucking fortune, don't put your filthy shoes on it, pick it up, come on, pick it up right now!' A crop-haired girl gives the music back to me, looking at it strangely, so maybe these sheets and scraps in my hands, what are they? Of course, wrong edition, wrong piece, its the Beethoven *Streichquartette Opus 18 the G*. Henle Verlag edition – no, no, he studied that with friends last year – was it last year or the year before? – God, it's so fucking hard to breathe, let's go, let's go, let's go …

I'm looking for Room 106. I'm running past bows, feet, cases and kids. Breathe in, breathe out. I have to see her face. I have to talk to her, I have to ask her: what are you doing now? I have to find out her name – Elise, Marianne, Clara, Fanny – what? What is it? Where is her name on the list? I'm going to tell that girl in 106 – take it! Take it and do what you have to do with it! Even if you have to eat your own bones for food! Even if you have to live in the streets with nothing but an old St Vincent de Paul blanket to shield you from the wind!

When she gets there, it's shut tight, the blinds are drawn. She rattles the doorknob, she pushes open the jammed door.

The room is empty. The old Bösendorfer is shrouded with a canvas sheet. The window is closed. Beams of sunset stream in around the pulled-down holland blind.

Are you here? The shadows make it hard to know. On the piano, under the sheet, someone has left a copy of the Mozart *divertimenti*. On the cover, little Wolfgang sits at the harpsichord, wide-eyed and calm. Where are you, what's happened to you? Behind him spreads an eighteenth century painted sky, a little Maria Teresa silken sky, unpolluted, simple, beautiful with artifice.

She rolls the ivory keys under her fingertips. They make a glowing ball. It leaps from her hands and she follows it, just like that. It's spinning, spinning down a mountain road. It passes a field, a field, a stream, a stream, a dark, dark wood, and into the camp of bare-assed brigands and surly-faced gypsies. O my love, my love, my love, my love.

> *Marianna, Marianna, the gypsy king rocks you,*
> *Dancing in the olive groves, singing in the trees.*
> *Marianna, Marianna, the gypsy king wants you,*
> *Crying in the olive groves, sighing in the trees.*

She's gone. She's gone into the groves where all she has to do is breathe from a wide and lovely sky.

Night fills the windows that overlook the King's Domain. The piano trio rehearsing Beethoven's 'Ghost' Trio in the Gallery Room at the College of Music is finished for the day. The young women take down their music stands, unwind bows, collect rosin and manuscript. The Gallery Room is one of the most prestigious rehearsal studios of the new wing. Competition for residency in it is fierce. So the young women take their polystyrene coffee cups, their cans of Coke. They make sure every crumb is off the heritage-coloured carpet and the pianist uses a chamois to remove every trace of fingermarks from the gleaming new Yamaha grand.

The crop-haired girl presses her face to a windowpane. A hard bleak rain hits the glass. She looks down at the peak hour traffic on St Kilda Road. Groups of umbrellas charge the trams as they slide to a stop. Groups of them are beaten away.

She dreads having to run the few blocks to Flinders Street Station. The others are the same. Not a car nor an umbrella between them and they have to lug instrument cases, bags full of sheet-music, awkward steel music stands.

They make their way through the almost empty hallways and down the college staircase to the foyer. The staff at the reception desk are gone, so the crop-haired girl leaves the key in an envelope on a desk and rings her boyfriend from the lobby payphone.

When there is a small break in the rain the others make a dash for Flinders Street.

The crop-haired girl waits for her boyfriend to pick her up. There's hardly anyone around. The security guard gives her a nod as he passes by. She decides to take out her score and work out some bowings on the Beethoven. Unlike her grotty flat, it's comfortable in the college, warm and dry. Even after hours the place still vibrates with the day's energy of other minds working, other fingers, lips, lungs and voices striving. She never feels alone here.

No matter how late she stays, there is always the sound of a far piano in one of the practice rooms somewhere in the old school.